WELCOME TO WHEREVER YOU ARE

JOHN MARRS

Praise for Welcome To Wherever You Are

"A fantastic summer read if you enjoy an unpredictable story with twists and turns." ***** *OK! Magazine*

"A thrilling book!" ***** *S Magazine, Sunday Express Newspaper*

"A twisting page-turner which fans of the Beach, or just a great read, will love." ***** *TV Extra Magazine, Daily Star Sunday*

"Sheer brilliance...I couldn't put it down." *Off The Shelf Books*

"A really engaging book." *alwaysreading.net*

"This is a masterpiece of human psychology." *Zyrell's Library*

"This book, quite simply, blew me away." *Reading Room With A View*

Welcome to Wherever You Are.

First published in 2015.
All rights reserved.

No part of this publication may be reproduced, stored in a retrieval system, or transmitted in any form or by any means, electronic, mechanical, photocopying, recording or otherwise, without the prior permission from the author.

Text © John Marrs
Cover design: Spiffing Covers

The characters and events portrayed in this book are fictitious. Any similarity to real persons, living or dead, is coincidental and not intended by the author.

ISBN-13:
978-1516837052

ISBN-10:
1516837053

Author's note: This book has been written using British spellings.

'Our goal is to discover that we have always been where we ought to be. Unhappily we make the task exceedingly difficult for ourselves.' – *Aldous Huxley*

PROLOGUE

VENICE BEACH, LOS ANGELES

'That's her,' the driver yelled to the three men waiting in the rear of the transit van.

He pointed a gloved finger in the direction of a slender woman walking along the sidewalk up ahead.

'Are you sure?' a gruff voice asked. 'It's pretty dark out there.'

The driver was very sure. He'd watched carefully as his target walked confidently and with purpose in her high heels, and recalled how she'd looked an hour earlier climbing up the silver pole before slowly, seductively, descending.

'Yeah man,' the driver replied, 'I'd know that pretty little ass anywhere. You don't forget a body like that in a hurry, even from this distance.'

As the street lamps and shop signs above illuminated the glitter in her hair with neon colours, the driver was confident their mark was completely oblivious as to her impending fate while she struggled to find something wedged in her clutch bag.

The driver lifted his foot slightly from the accelerator and dipped the headlights as he continued to stalk his prey. Meanwhile, his three colleagues slipped black balaclavas over their faces and adjusted their bodies into position – one knelt with his hand gripping the door lever ready to open it on command; another held plastic restraints and the third clasped a hunting knife with a serrated blade.

'Ready?' the driver asked.

The van picked up the pace, but not so quickly as to throw the hunters from the positions they'd rehearsed many times that day. Then, once the side of the van was parallel to the girl, the door flew open and the first of her assailants sprang out.

The man with the restraints was the first to reel backwards into the vehicle when a bullet from the woman's revolver tore its way through his shoulder blade, taking fragments of collarbone with it. For a split second, the flash from the gun's muzzle illuminated the van's interior as she pinpointed two more would-be assailants poised to drag her inside. Twice more she pulled the trigger, twice more she heard the men screaming from inside.

The driver remained rooted to his seat, baffled by how off

kilter their mission had suddenly become. There was no Plan B.

'Go, man . . . go!' yelled a desperate voice as another bullet lodged itself into his flesh.

The van's tyres squealed as the vehicle lurched forward and along the road, before veering across the central reservation, then crisscrossing back towards the sidewalk.

A combination of adrenaline and fury propelled the girl to kick off her heels and run, firing twice more at the van and shattering the rear windscreen. The vehicle clipped an *LA Times* newsstand, hurling newspapers into the air that fell like large chunks of confetti.

She fired one last time, but the van had already corrected itself and sped off out of range. Then she watched in horror as the force of that final bullet sent a stranger ahead sprawling face forward onto the pavement.

Time momentarily froze as the consequences of that last reckless bullet resonated.

She had just killed an innocent person.

PART ONE – THE ARRIVALS

CHAPTER 1

DAY ONE – TWO MONTHS LATER – VENICE BEACH
INTERNATIONAL HOSTEL, LOS ANGELES

Empty cans of Budweiser and paper plates stained by Bolognese sauce and stiff spaghetti strands littered the corridors as Tommy made his way from his dormitory towards the hostel reception desk.

Three young men, wearing only brightly coloured boxer shorts, lay in a crumpled, unconscious heap, unaware their drunken state had been taken advantage of and their faces and chests used as canvases for felt-tip pen graffiti. Tommy chuckled at the crude images of penises, expletives and slurs.

As was the norm for such an ungodly hour, the vast proportion of guests at the Venice Beach International Hostel were fast asleep and scattered throughout the building's twenty-five rooms. Those drowsily slumped across lounge sofas were surrounded by rucksacks and awaited shuttle buses to transport them to LAX airport, Amtrak railway or Greyhound coach stations.

Tommy knew it didn't require a genius to do his job, checking people in and out of the hostel. There wasn't even a computerised system to master – just a tatty, leather-bound ledger, with a date written in biro on each page and the names of who was allocated to which room. But it was a role he enjoyed, despite the long hours.

And secretly he got a kick from being responsible for choosing which rooms the travellers looking for no-frills accommodation were placed in. Those who barely spoke English were squirreled out of the way towards the back of the building, and those who Tommy hoped to build up a rapport with were placed in dormitories that surrounded his. But the bunk adjacent to his own was kept free for when Sean arrived. *If* he ever arrived.

Tommy reached the end of the corridor, walked down a small flight of steps and arrived at the reception desk where he'd spend the next couple of hours of his morning. He turned on a portable television and scanned the ledger to see who'd checked in overnight.

Once up to speed, he gazed around the room as the darkness outside began to lift and the orange morning light crept through the large windows. A yucca plant had outgrown its pot and its roots spilled from cracks in its side; a water cooler missing a plug housed a half-full plastic bottle and a surface enveloped by a delicate skin of green algae. Brown carpet tiles that only covered patches of floor were frayed and mismatched. A rack of pamphlets was mostly empty, with the exception of a few outdated excursion opportunities to Disneyland, Six Flags Magic Mountain and Universal Studios. There was no getting away from the fact the hostel was a dump, but it was a dump Tommy affectionately called home.

He glanced at some of the familiar faces of people he'd met during his last two months in Los Angeles in photographs pinned to the wall. Most of them, like him, were in their early twenties and while he couldn't always recall their names, he never forgot a face and they never failed to conjure up a smile. He examined an image of himself and realised his irregular eating patterns meant he'd lost weight since the picture had been taken some eight weeks earlier. He could feel his ribs under his T-shirt and even his handful of friendship bands hung loosely from his wrist. His dark brown stubble disguised the gauntness in his face and he made a vow to himself to eat at least two proper meals a day.

'Morning, Ron,' Tommy chirped as the hostel's owner appeared from a small office behind the reception desk.

Ron's glasses hung from a silver chain around his neck, broken links held together by sticky tape. His grey comb-over lifted from his thinning scalp with each step he took and his posture reminded Tommy of a question mark.

'Eight beds need filling,' Ron muttered, making his way up the stairs and out of sight.

'I'm fine, thanks for asking,' mumbled Tommy.

'I didn't,' Ron shouted from the distance.

A poster peeling from the wall drew Tommy's attention like it always did. *Welcome to Wherever You Are*, read a large font placed over an image of a white sandy beach and the bluest of blue oceans. When Tommy asked what it meant the night he arrived, all Ron replied was, 'It means it doesn't matter where you are, just as long as you're somewhere.'

The hostel was Tommy's somewhere, and it was a million miles from the nowhere in England he'd run from.

CHAPTER 2

Beads of sweat gathered across Eric's hairline, the breeze wafting through the vehicle's open windows failing to cool him down.

He pinched the corners of his eyes, pushed his Aviator Ray-Bans up to the bridge of his nose and continued to drive slowly up Pacific Avenue. Hunched over the steering wheel he looked through the windscreen searching for numbers attached to buildings. All night spent behind the wheel of their 1970s pick-up truck with no power steering or air conditioning made him grouchy and achy and feeling more than his thirty-two years. The wonky sun visor couldn't keep the rising sun from touching his head and he was glad he'd decided to clipper his thick auburn hair tightly before he left England.

'It feels like we've been driving round in circles for hours,' he moaned.

'I'm looking but most of the buildings aren't numbered,' replied Nicole, his passenger. 'Maybe buildings in LA think they're too cool to be identified quickly.'

Her thighs were stuck to the leather seats and made the sound of breaking wind each time she fidgeted. Eleven hours ago it had amused them both; now it was just another thing that irritated them. Nicole swept her damp cinnamon brown hair behind her ears and brought the map closer to her eyes so she could read the small print. A gust of warm wind rustled the empty potato chip and candy wrappers strewn across the rear seats.

'Remind me again, why did I give up a good job in London to join you on this magical mystery tour?' Eric asked.

'Because you hated your "good job" just as much as I hated mine and once we find what we're looking for, we might not need to work again for a very long time.'

'Providing this thing gets us there.'

'It'd better; I paid enough to ship it over. Besides, it's a classic pick-up.'

'What do you know about trucks, Jeremy Clarkson? It's a classic heap of shit. We could've rented a 4 x 4 over here with that money, or at least something with air con and a satnav.'

Eric reached into the door pocket to find a bottle of water but with no success so he glanced to his side to see where it had rolled to.

'Eric!' Nicole screamed.

Alarmed, he looked up to spot a dishevelled young man in dark skater shorts and a backward facing baseball cap and shirt, shuffling across the road. Eric jammed on his brakes and swerved, the truck's tyres hitting the kerb with a jolt. The man continued ambling in his own little world, oblivious to his close call, and entered a building.

'You bloody idiot!' yelled Eric, craning his neck out of the window while Nicole took deep, calming breaths. He stormed outside to examine the damage, and then kicked the hubcap in frustration.

'Brilliant,' he began, 'I bet it's already started deflating.'

'I know the feeling, but if it helps, I think we're here.' Nicole pointed towards the building ahead of them. Eric tilted his head towards a faded sign reading 'Venice Beach International Hostel'.

The once whitewashed walls of the rectangular building were greying, and plaster had flaked and fallen from the front façade, leaving parts of the brickwork exposed. Trainers and towels had been hung out to air from the open windows on all three floors, and from the side of the flat roof, poles and tatty flags from around the world drooped, including ones from countries that no longer existed.

Nicole offered a half-hearted smile but Eric was too busy rolling his eyes to notice.

CHAPTER 3

'You nearly got yourself killed there, mate!' Tommy warned Joe as he stumbled up the stairs towards his room, only stopping to rotate his baseball cap to the correct position.

Tommy wondered why Joe always waited until he entered the building before sliding his cap around, as if he assumed the hostel had a straight headwear policy. Then he realised trying to second-guess a crystal meth addict was as pointless as giving a dog a Rubik's cube. He hoped that one day, Joe might have a light bulb moment, like those Tommy had read about in self-help books travellers often left in the hostel library. They'd helped get him through many a boring night shift, and Tommy briefly considered anonymously leaving one on Joe's bed. But he knew that unless Joe actually wanted to alter his life, he'd be stuck in his ever-decreasing circle until an inevitably premature end.

Meanwhile outside, Eric and Nicole unstrapped their suitcases from the flatbed truck and faced the hostel's mucky glass doors, propped open by two buckets of sand and littered with cigarette butts from around the world. Eric removed his sunglasses and mumbled something to himself about jumping out of a frying pan and into the flaming bowels of hell.

'If I'm going to have the American experience Mrs Baker wanted me to have, then I'd like to meet people in the same boat as us, not a bunch of cheerleaders on Spring Break,' Nicole began snootily.

'So you were serious when you said we were staying in a hostel and not a hotel, then? I hoped you were kidding.'

'All the travel guides say it's a rite of passage to stay in Venice,' she replied defensively. 'John Steinbeck, Jack Kerouac and Truman Capote were supposed to have spent nights under this roof back in its heyday.'

'Oh, did they? And who are Steinbeck, Kerouac and Capote, just out of interest?'

'Um,' Nicole paused and wracked her brain. 'Blues singers?'

Eric shook his head at her ignorance and let out an exaggerated sigh.

'Besides,' Nicole continued, 'the only difference between a hostel and a hotel is the letter "s".'

'Yeah, and in this case the "s" stands for "smells like a shit hole".'

Nicole was aware she was fighting a losing battle. For the most part, Eric was her kindred spirit – he could make her laugh like nobody else and he'd been there for her in her darkest days when she'd needed him most. He'd given up his career to spend the last six weeks with her in America on the hunt for something that might not even exist, so she was willing to forgive his occasional moodiness.

'Are you looking for a room?' smiled Tommy, ignoring Eric's presence and focusing entirely on Nicole. He was instantly attracted to her warm smile, her fresh face and her casual attire of cut-off shorts and white vest. Such attention didn't go unnoticed by Eric. She, meanwhile, was surprised by Tommy's British accent considering his California tan and surfer-dude look, albeit a slightly skinny surfer dude.

'I emailed a few days ago to book a private room for three nights,' Nicole replied.

'The Internet connection's a bit iffy and nobody checks the emails,' replied Tommy apologetically.

'We don't have any private rooms left, but we've got a couple of free beds in a dorm?'

'We're expected to share with other people?' interrupted Eric.

'That's the hostelling experience,' smiled Tommy.

'No, that's the homeless shelter experience.'

'It's $20 a night each, plus a $5 key deposit. You'll be in room 14; your beds have clean sheets on them already, blankets are an extra $2 a night, as are towels. There's food served every night in the kitchen, although the chef's not Gordon Ramsay, so don't go expecting much. Oh and there's free beer on Wednesday and Saturday nights at the party in the lounge. I'm Tommy – if you need anything, just come and find me.'

Nicole and Tommy shared a smile and, as she paid him in cash, a cockroach scuttled across the counter.

'Are those complimentary?' asked Eric wryly.

'Only if you buy them dinner first,' replied Tommy.

While Nicole grinned at the lame joke, Eric frowned at Tommy and picked up the pair's luggage and headed for the staircase. A thin man in baggy clothes and a patchy beard attempted to slip in behind them.

'Oi, there's no reason for you to be here, Wayne,' said Tommy firmly, and shook his head as the man left without argument.

*

'Don't think I didn't see you giving him a look,' Eric began as he and Nicole made their way along the hostel corridor, examining their new surroundings.

'What "look"?' she replied in mock innocence, and willed herself not to break into a schoolgirl blush.

'A look that'll put you on the sex offenders' register for ten years.'

'He's not that young.'

'You're thirty-two, sweetheart, he's old enough to be your son.'

'Yeah, if I'd had him when I was about twelve,' sighed Nicole, stepping over a discarded trash bag. 'Okay, so the rubbish doesn't make it the Hilton.'

'It does if you mean Perez Hilton. Why don't we just find a couple of cardboard boxes and sleep under a bridge tonight?'

'Anyway, *Grazia* says it's flattering to be thought of as a cougar by a younger man.'

'A cougar? You're more like one of those mangy old alley cats on their last legs and with no teeth and half an ear missing,' Eric offered with a cheeky grin.

Nicole's lips moved, ready to respond, when the door to their room burst open and four young women in swimsuits ran past them, carrying beach towels and chatting in a language neither she nor Eric understood.

'Of course hostelling isn't *all* bad,' conceded Eric, turning his head to watch as they disappeared down the corridor.

CHAPTER 4

The cardboard sign manager Ron had stuck above the six-feet by three-feet cubbyhole with the words 'Internet Suite & Café' was wishful thinking, Tommy decided.

One desk with two green back-to-back iMac G3s and an ancient modem that required six minutes before a connection was made did not constitute a suite. Likewise, a vending machine that reluctantly dispensed lukewarm coffee all year round failed to make it a café. But with a poor cell phone reception in the hostel, it was the quickest and cheapest way to surf the web and catch up on emails.

Tommy inserted his quarter into the vending machine, pressed number nine, counted five seconds like always and kicked the base, before it angrily spat brown powder and water into a plastic cup.

He sat down, logged into his iCloud account and scanned his messages. The only new ones were those offering Nectar points, his online credit card bill – which he deleted without opening – and a weekly mail-out from online clothing retailer Mr Porter.

Tommy scanned his Facebook timeline updates and clicked on an image in his Friends section so a profile slowly loaded. He checked when it had last been updated; some nine weeks earlier when they were still together. Irked, he addressed a new email to SeanR@icloud.com and put three question marks in the subject line. '*Where the hell are you?*' he wrote and then jabbed the send button.

As he leant back in his chair, his wallet fell from the pocket of his shorts.

The corner of a small photograph poked out. Tommy picked it up, opened it and stared at a picture of his parents.

TWO YEARS EARLIER – NORTHAMPTON, ENGLAND

From his seat at the kitchen table, Tommy watched his mother through the window, standing alone on the decking in the rear garden.

She stared blankly across the lawn, through the wire fencing and into the recently ploughed wheat fields; her body only moving to take long drags from a menthol cigarette.

Tommy had observed her rapid decline from a vibrant, enthusiastic mother-of-three to an empty shell in the space of hours. He recalled how, when he was a child, he had nagged her to quit her 'stinky sticks' as he loathed the smell, and for well over a decade, she'd gone without. But since *that* day, everything had changed and her journey had taken her from naught to sixty a day in a less than a week.

She remained with her back to the house Tommy had grown up in; a place he now avoided whenever possible. What was once a home crammed with spirit and comfort was now just a shell inhabited by three vacant bodies.

Tommy turned his eyes towards the goldfish swimming in circles around the glass bowl on the worktop. The bowl contained no ornamental garnishes, only sandy coloured pebbles where one lonely fish swam day in day out, round and round, going nowhere. The symbolism wasn't lost on Tommy. Suddenly the door to the hallway opened and his father entered. Once a tall, imposing figure, he too had noticeably withered, Tommy thought.

Then, on spotting Tommy, he stopped in his tracks. Father and son made eye contact, neither saying a word, before he turned to leave.

'Dad, please,' began Tommy, and he rose from the table and grabbed the crutches propped up against it. His father paused, but without looking back, exited the kitchen and quietly closed the door.

'It wasn't my fault,' Tommy called out, as the fish swam another aimless lap.

CHAPTER 5

TODAY

'Pretty comfy,' nodded Nicole as she tested the bottom mattress of a dormitory bunk bed nearest the window.

'Probably because it has extra layers of skin shed by the last hundred people to have slept on it,' replied Eric, choosing the one above her.

'For God's sake Eric, you've spent all day bitching and moaning. Believe me, I'm as frustrated as you are that we haven't found anything yet but at least I'm trying to make the best of it. Please, can you just stop complaining for five minutes and meet me halfway?'

Eric dropped from the bed to the floor below and looked at his friend sheepishly. 'Sorry Nic, I'm just tired, hot and bothered. And this place isn't exactly what I was expecting.'

'I know. I think the pictures they used online were taken a few years ago, but we're here now, so let's have a look around, take some time out to rethink and make the best of it before we continue, shall we?'

Eric nodded as Nicole looked around the room. Each dormitory had four curtainless double-length windows, and with no air conditioning, they were the only way to let out the stuffy air of eight bunk beds and sixteen sweaty bodies. Above them, damp clothes were pegged to washing lines running the length of the room, and in the corner was a shared bathroom next to a small area housing grey lockers.

But while the rooms were shabby, Nicole liked that the walls were plastered with photographs of past guests framing a map of the world. Coloured cotton threads linked faces to countries and, despite Eric's vocal reservations, there was an aura about the hostel that Nicole admired.

Suddenly, she noticed a woman sitting with her legs outstretched appearing to place newspaper cuttings into a book. Her skin was pale, her frame dumpy and Nicole noted that despite the heat, she wore jogging bottoms and a long-sleeved T-shirt. Nicole smiled at her and the woman smiled shyly back.

'Shall we see if our stowaway has made it intact?' asked Eric, pointing to a cardboard box in the centre of Nicole's suitcase.

But before Nicole could reply, there came a thumping sound and the sudden appearance of a pair of skinny legs through a ceiling tile. The legs were quickly followed by a man falling to the floor in a heap of tangled limbs and dust. An astonished Nicole and Eric hurried towards him, urging him not to move, then to wriggle his hands and feet one at a time. Small fragments of plasterboard were caught in his wiry, Afro-style hair, and under the dust, his face was tanned and freckled. A roll-up cigarette remained between his lips despite his plunge.

'I'm fine guys, I'm fine,' Peyk reassured them in his Anglo-Dutch accent, and smiled as the door burst open and Tommy appeared.

'What the . . .' he began, his eyes darting around the room between Peyk and the hole in the ceiling the hostel's handyman had created.

'It's all good, Tommy-boy, it's all good,' smiled Peyk, before picking up an electrical cable from the floor and leaving. Nicole and Eric looked at each other and then Tommy, awaiting an explanation.

'Probably best not to ask,' said Tommy, knowing that like God, Peyk moved in mysterious ways. 'I was coming to find you guys anyway – I was heading out for my break and wondered if you wanted a quick tour of Venice?'

'We've got some unpacking to do,' Eric replied dismissively, and went back towards his bunk.

'Well, do you mind if I go?' asked Nicole.

'Do what you like,' said Eric, his attitude resembling that of a sulky teenager.

He glanced over his shoulder as Nicole and Tommy made their way out of the door. He vowed to nip their burgeoning friendship in the bud. There was too much at stake for him to stand idly by.

CHAPTER 6

'Your boyfriend doesn't like slumming it, does he?' began Tommy as he walked through the hostel and towards the reception with Nicole.

'Oh, Eric's not my boyfriend,' she replied. 'We're friends, that's all, and ignore him when he moans because if he's not complaining about something, he's not being Eric. Once he gets used to the place, he'll be fine.'

As they made their way out of the building, Tommy smiled when he spotted Savannah coming towards them, slurping a thick milkshake through a straw. She pushed her black Jackie O-style glasses up into her platinum blonde bob and grinned.

'Hey you,' began Tommy.

'Hi, honey, where are you guys off to?'

'Nicole's just checked in so I'm showing her the local sights and sounds.'

'And you've pounced on her already?' teased Savannah. 'You could at least give the girl time to unpack.'

'That's what I thought,' joked Nicole while Tommy's face reddened.

'Nice to meet you,' continued Savannah as the women introduced themselves and shook hands. 'I'm only kidding, Tommy's a sweetheart really.'

'Are you working tonight?' asked Tommy.

'Yeah, I'm picking up a few shifts later but I'm getting some sleep first. Have a good day, guys.'

'That's the first American accent I've heard since we checked in,' Nicole continued as she and Tommy headed for the beach.

'Yeah, we're more geared towards Europeans than Americans. Euros are quite happy to stay in a hovel in a foreign country, and the Yanks are more up for experiencing this type of place when they're abroad rather than on their own doorstep.'

'Does Savannah live at the hostel?'

'Pretty much – she's friends with Peyk, that fella who crashed through your ceiling. She gets a room to herself and I only put people in there if we're busy.'

'And what does Peyk get in return for his generosity?'

'Nah, I don't think it's like that. He's an odd guy but he's harmless, and Savannah doesn't put up with any crap from anyone. She may seem sweet but I reckon she has her secrets.'

'Doesn't everyone?' Nicole smiled wryly.

CHAPTER 7

Savannah closed her bedroom door behind her and locked it, pulling down the handle to reassure herself it was secure.

She slid her imitation Hermès handbag off her shoulder and placed it on the single unoccupied bed opposite her own. She unclasped the hook and removed a tightly wound roll of $20 bills, then moved towards two lockers and pushed one aside to reveal a jagged hole in the brickwork. She placed the money next to seven more bundles of notes before moving the locker back in its place.

Then she put her fingertips under her hairline, removed her blonde wig and dropped it on a stool. She ruffled her mousey brown hair, and then from her bag removed a revolver and placed it under her pillow.

TWO MONTHS EARLIER – VENICE BEACH

Savannah clasped her hand over her mouth and ran towards the motionless body on the sidewalk as fast as her heels would allow, while Ron appeared from the entrance of a building several feet ahead.

'What the hell?' he began, as both reached the body at the same time.

'I didn't see him there, Ron,' she cried. 'They were trying to kidnap me. He knows where I am!'

Ron glanced around the street checking if anyone had witnessed the chaos, before grabbing the body under his arms, struggling to hoist it back to its feet.

'Savannah, help me,' he snapped.

She involuntarily trembled as they dragged the person through an open doorway and into a brightly lit reception area, laying him on the floor. Ron turned the lock on the door and pulled down a roller blind.

The first words to come from the boy's bloodied lips were followed by a desperate intake of breath, taking Ron and Savannah by surprise. 'Am I dead?' he asked.

'No, thank Christ,' whispered Ron as he rolled the boy onto his chest.

He removed the large canvas rucksack strapped to the boy's back, as light from a fluorescent bulb above bounced off an object inside a small hole in the lining.

Ron stood the boy up and steadied him, watching as he struggled to focus his green eyes. The last thing the boy remembered with clarity was listening to a Coldplay track on his iPhone before something propelled him forward. It happened so swiftly that his forehead smashed against the pavement before he had time to stretch his arms out and minimise the impact.

Meanwhile, Ron fished out the contents from the front pouch of the backpack, including a book he'd vaguely heard of from the 1990s called *The Beach*. Wedged into its spine was the bullet Savannah had fired moments earlier. The boy was still too dazed to question why a stranger he couldn't see properly was hoisting his T-shirt up towards his shoulders and rubbing his cold, thin fingers across his back.

'Lucky bastard,' muttered Ron, and sat him down on a plastic chair.

The boy touched his forehead and felt the swelling. There was a graze to his cheek and grit embedded in his bottom lip. He rolled his tongue around his mouth to check his teeth were still in place. He looked at Ron standing before him, but everything was clouded by a shadow, like he'd overused a filter on an Instagram photo. He only realised there was a third person present in the room when the man spoke again.

'Stay in your room while I clean him up, and hide that thing. Peyk didn't give it to you so you could fire at anyone.'

Savannah didn't question Ron's orders and sprinted up the stairs and out of sight before the boy had a chance to remember her. His blurred vision was slowly dissipating and he scanned his new surroundings, unsure if it was the place he was searching for when fate threw him a curveball.

'What's your name, kid?' Ron asked.

'Tommy,' he replied in a British accent, and pointed to a poster, peeling away from the wall opposite him. 'What does "Welcome to Wherever You Are" mean?'

'It means it doesn't matter where you are, just as long as you're somewhere.'

TODAY

Savannah rested her hands on her hips and looked critically at her reflection in a full-length mirror attached to the bathroom wall.

She was disappointed to see the dark circles under her eyes were still showing despite regular applications of foundation, and her cheeks were red and blotchy. She'd felt under the weather for much of the day and hoped the soya milkshake might give her the sugar rush she needed to wake her up. Instead, she yawned and headed back into her bedroom, setting the alarm on her phone for three hours' time when her day would begin again.

Savannah was unaware of the hand behind the two-way mirror that traced the outline of her body, or the narrowed eyes that watched as she fell asleep.

CHAPTER 8

From behind the blue metal fence, Nicole stared at a dozen or so men and women, bulging veins close to bursting point as they went about their daily workout routines on Muscle Beach.

She'd read about the fitness fanatics' mecca in her guidebook, and was a little disappointed to find it was no more than a large concrete cage crammed with human gorillas vying for the attention of strangers to further boost their already swollen egos.

As she and Tommy continued to walk along Venice Beach's boardwalk, Nicole realised the creative and artistic beatnik generation who founded the area back in the 1950s and 1960s had long since departed. They'd been replaced by a hotchpotch of tacky tourist retail units interspersed with independent boutiques running parallel to the sandy beach. The other side contained an assortment of craftsmen and chancers sheltered under a canopy of 40-foot high palm trees. Their wares included toy planes and cars made from empty soda cans; Tarot card readers predicting customers' fates; self-proclaimed experts in Chinese medicine offering acupuncture and neck massages; and fold-up tables stocked with pamphlets promoting everything from political causes to the health benefits of hemp.

Tommy pointed out the handball and paddle tennis courts, the skate dancing plaza, the numerous beach volleyball courts and a bike trail that went past lavish beachfront properties on Ocean Front Walk where the wealthy and a sprinkling of celebrities had made their homes.

To describe Venice Beach as diverse was an understatement, Nicole realised, and she knew one afternoon wouldn't be long enough to explore all the nooks and crannies that piqued her interest. Muscle Beach aside, she felt the area's appeal.

After an hour of sightseeing in the 80-degree heat, Nicole and Tommy took a break and sat on benches under the shady arches of a café, eating over-generous portions of pistachio ice cream from plastic tubs. Not for the first time that afternoon, hostellers waved at Tommy as they passed by.

'You're a popular guy,' began Nicole.

'It's a combination of my movie-star looks and manly physique,' replied Tommy with a smile. 'Or it's that I'm the first face people see when they check in, so they remember me.'

'I'd say it's probably the latter.'

'Yeah, thanks. So is this your first time backpacking?'

'Is it that obvious? I'm more of a book it on lastminute.com, two-star hotel in Ibiza kind of girl. To be honest, I'm not even sure what the life of backpacker entails.'

'The general consensus is you live out of what you can carry, you travel at your own pace and you sleep where you can.'

'Like tortoises.'

'That makes you "Me Shell".'

'Oh, you're funny,' groaned Nicole and rolled her eyes, despite being quietly amused by Tommy's banter. 'And what do people "do" at hostels?'

'Meet other travellers, shag other travellers, smoke a lot of dope, drink a lot of beer, tell strangers their life stories, and then continue travelling knowing they'll probably never see them again.'

'That sounds fun . . . but kind of sad.'

'I'm not going to lie, it can be both. I've been with some of the most incredible people one minute, and the next I've been at my loneliest. But I wouldn't change the last seven months for anything, as it's been the best thing I've ever done. I'm sure I've discovered parts of America most Americans haven't even seen and the hostel, well it's not the Hotel Bel-Air, but it's become a rite of passage for backpackers.'

'That's what I told Eric, but I don't think he believed me.'

'Out of interest, how did you and your non-boyfriend end up on a road trip?'

'That's a conversation for another time,' Nicole replied, looking at her watch. 'I should be heading back.'

Tommy and Nicole took their ice creams with them and retraced their steps along the boardwalk back towards the hostel. She could tell Tommy had tried to mask his nervousness with cockiness, which she found endearing.

'Are you coming to the party?' he asked hopefully.

'Is that tonight?'

'Uh-huh, and the beer's free.'

'You really know the way to a girl's heart, don't you?' Nicole replied, and realised she was actually beginning to sound like a cougar.

CHAPTER 9

Savannah struggled to find herself a comfortable sleeping position so she abandoned her power nap after an hour and relocated to the kitchen to read about Kim Kardashian and Kanye West's latest exploits in an old *In Touch* magazine another hosteller had left on top of a bin bag.

As she turned the page, she spotted a headline about handsome young actor Zak Stanley that should have been followed by a story and pictures. Instead, they'd been ripped out, and she wondered what was so interesting that needed to be kept away from everyone else's eyes. She'd almost finished her take-out bowl of yesterday's vegetable soup when Tommy appeared, grinning from his morning spent in the company of Nicole.

'So, stud, how was your date?' Savannah asked.

'It wasn't a date, we just went out for a walk and some ice cream,' he replied, and poured hot water into the dirty crockery-filled sink.

'How very 1960s – that sounds like a date to me. You like her, don't you?'

'She's cool,' Tommy smiled.

Actually, he did like Nicole and he liked her a lot. Throughout his American adventure, he'd kissed a handful of girls, but had only become intimate with two, which, according to conversations with other backpackers bragging about their globe-trotting antics, was way below the norm.

But Nicole was different from the other girls he'd met, and he enjoyed her company. She gave as good as she got, she had a sense of humour he appreciated and, of course, he was physically attracted to her. He estimated she was at least a decade his senior, and that only added to her appeal. But the main thing he'd learned from sharing space and personal thoughts with total strangers was that he was attracted to personality above all else.

However, Tommy wasn't naive, and identified two issues that could stand in the way of something blossoming between them. The first went by the name of Eric who, even in their brief encounter, made it clear that he was unamused by Tommy's presence. And the second was that Nicole was only planning to stay in LA for a few days.

It dawned on Tommy that Nicole hadn't actually given much away about herself in their afternoon together. He didn't know where she was from, what she did to pay her bills, what she had given up to go travelling, or why.

Peyk came in, wandering around the kitchen and looking up towards the ceiling tiles.

'What are you up to?' Tommy asked.

'Looking for wires,' Peyk replied without making eye contact.

'For fun?'

'For Ron.'

'For what purpose?'

'For it's none of your business.'

Peyk frowned, squinted at something and then nodded. He pulled a joint from behind his ear and lit it on the oven's electric hob. He took a long drag and then offered it to Tommy and Savannah who both shook their heads. So Peyk blew a smoke ring and left with a wide grin spread across his face.

Out of sight, he took out his basic, text-and-call only mobile phone, typed in the words 'we're back in business', and hit send.

CHAPTER 10

As soon as he heard the bedroom door creaking open, Eric closed his eyes and pretended to be asleep.

He'd been lying on his bed, quietly brooding over Nicole's decision to spend time with a boy she didn't know rather than with him, planning the next chapter of their journey. Even though neither was sure where they were supposed to be heading with the vague instructions they'd been left, he was keen to escape the squalor currently suffocating him.

Nicole sat down on her bunk, making the bed frame bend and squeak. Eric opened his eyes and sat up.

'What time is it?' he asked, continuing the charade by rubbing invisible sleep from his eyes.

'It's just gone three. Sorry, have I woken you?'

'Yeah. Where've you been?'

'Tommy was showing me Venice Beach, remember? You'll love it down there, Eric. It's got this fantastic vibe to it, there are so many places we can explore.'

'I'm sure there are, but we're only here for a couple of days, aren't we.' It wasn't a question.

Nicole paused. 'Well there's no reason why we can't stay a bit longer, is there? It's not like we're on a tight schedule or anything, and we've got enough money to tide us over for at least a couple more months. We've been on the road going from one motel to another on a wild goose chase. This is a once in a lifetime opportunity, so let's start enjoying it a bit more.'

Eric bit his tongue but quietly seethed at Tommy for opening Nicole's eyes. He was also sore at himself for not protesting when she'd asked if he minded her going out.

'If that's what you want,' he replied, using a tone that made it clear he was irked but not irked enough to warrant a confrontation. 'But remember why we're here and what we're trying to find. And – any chance you can tidy your stuff away? You're the messiest person I know.'

'Sure,' smiled Nicole and gave Eric a peck on the forehead. 'Oh, and Tommy says there's a party downstairs tonight if you fancy it?'

Eric offered a smile, which Nicole took to mean 'yes', and moved towards the bathroom, only to spot the woman in the jogging bottoms and long-sleeved T-shirt sat in the same place she'd been hours earlier.

'Hello,' began Nicole.

'Hi,' replied Ruth, then closed her scrapbook and clutched it to her chest before Nicole could work out whose face was stuck on the cover.

'My name's Nicole.'

'I'm Ruth,' replied the woman in an Australian accent, before lowering her head, rising to her feet and scuttling from the room. She headed towards the empty kitchen and, once she was confident she was alone, she carefully placed her book on the table and smiled at the magazine cutting of Zak Stanley stuck to the cover.

FIVE WEEKS EARLIER – VICTORIA, AUSTRALIA

'Potato chips for breakfast? For Christ's sake, girl, it's not even 7.30!'

The disgruntled tone of her mother, Denise, failed to move Ruth to push her unconventional breakfast to one side or turn the television off. Instead, she remained sprawled across the white faux-leather sofa, her head propped up by a cushion and a bowl of corn-based snacks balanced on her stomach.

'Hey, bludger, I'm talking to you,' Denise continued to jibe, pointing at her daughter with a French-tipped fingernail. 'Get your fat arse up, turn the television off and go out for a run or something.'

Ruth ignored her mother's obvious frustration and remained transfixed by the figure on the television screen. No matter what insult her mother or younger brother Kevin threw at her – which was usually weight-related – Ruth's indifference to dieting, make-up or fashion persisted.

In Ruth's universe, the only person whose opinion mattered was Zak Stanley. He was a man who had never picked on her, criticised her, mocked her appearance or made her feel any less of a woman in spite of her 5-foot 9-inch, 15-stone frame. Zak made Ruth feel like a real princess, and not Princess Fiona, the ogreous Shrek character Kevin compared her to. And if Zak were ever to leave his Hollywood home and cast aside his A-list movie career for a relationship with a stranger who could offer him more love than all of his thousands of fans put together, Ruth would be waiting for him with open arms.

When Ruth heard Denise's stiletto heels tap their way across the lounge's laminate flooring and into the kitchen, she turned up the television's volume. Although she'd watched the DVD many times over the last two years, Ruth still scowled at the blonde-haired, large-breasted presenter, proudly standing on the red carpet in London's Leicester Square with Zak's arm around her waist. Ruth didn't care for the way she flirted with Zak but conceded that anyone in the presence of such talent and masculine beauty would find it impossible not to try their luck.

'So what made you take the role, Zak? It's quite a departure.' asked the presenter with a name Ruth had no interest in remembering.

'Well,' began Zak, struggling to hear through the screaming teenage girls penned in behind metal barricades. 'I've always been a big supporter of animal rights, and if my movie helps bring the illegal trade in elephant ivory to the forefront of people's minds, well, that makes it all worthwhile.'

'I bet he loves dogs like I do, too,' thought Ruth. Along with pizza, sunsets, *Friends* reruns and cuddles, it was yet another thing she could add to their list of common interests.

'And what about love – have you found a potential Mrs Stanley yet?' continued the interviewer. Ruth swore she saw her hand slip further down Zak's back and towards his buttocks.

He grinned bashfully. 'No, I'm still looking for her.'

'And what qualities does a girl need to have?'

'I'm a simple kinda guy. All I want is an ordinary girl who inspires me to be a better man, and who I can wake up loving a little bit more each day.'

'And you think she's out there somewhere?' The interviewer fluttered her eyelashes and no longer tried to disguise her desire to be auditioned as Mrs Stanley.

'Oh, I'm sure of it,' replied Zak, brushing his hand though his dark, floppy fringe. 'Who knows? She could be right here tonight or she could live on the other side of the world, but I believe in destiny, and I'll know who she is the moment we meet.'

The butterflies that always materialised in Ruth's stomach when she thought of Zak were now fluttering so briskly, they made her feel sick. 'You mean me,' she mouthed silently, and then smiled.

Once the footage ended and Zak moved on to mix with a British singer called Stuart she'd never heard of, Ruth rewound and played the interview twice more before her mother appeared again.

'You're never going to find a boyfriend if you're stuck in this bloody house every day,' she barked. 'The TV won't love you back.'

Denise picked up her jacket, folded it over her arm and swung a Chanel handbag over her shoulder. 'Look at the state of you, it's no wonder your father left,' she sneered as a parting shot.

Ruth swallowed hard, then began to eat a partially melted chocolate bar she'd kept hidden under a cushion and away from her mother's sight.

CHAPTER 11

TODAY

By 8.15 p.m., the first of the week's two hostel parties was in full swing.

Five beer kegs placed on the floor by the window overlooking the street below were quickly being drained as guests queued to fill their red plastic cups and glasses with free booze.

Others took turns in selecting their own carefully composed playlists from MP3 players and smartphones to plug into a speaker dock. All styles of music, from hip hop to bhangra, from reggae to pop, played as residents danced, chatted, flirted and quaffed beer or cheap bottles of wine they'd purchased from the liquor store across the road. Some hostellers played pool on a table with torn felt using cues with worn-down tips. Others regularly left the room to smoke cannabis out of sight on the building's two second-floor balconies.

Tommy scanned the room and spotted Eric and Nicole talking in the corner. He waited for Nicole to approach the kegs and refill their glasses before he approached Eric. If he could get Eric on side, he reasoned, then he might be able to persuade Nicole to stay in LA a little longer.

'How are you settling in?' Tommy began with a rehearsed smile.

'Oh this place is just delightful,' replied Eric, making no attempt to disguise his disdain. 'A bedroom that reeks of stale feet, people falling through ceilings, and German techno music deafening me. What more could I ask for?'

'Well, there's something I wouldn't mind asking you – is Nicole seeing anyone?'

Eric glared at Tommy, making him instantly uncomfortable, before Nicole reappeared.

'Hi, Tommy,' she smiled.

'How are you enjoying the party?'

'Yeah, it's good fun. Oh, and we've decided to stay in Venice a bit longer.'

'Really?' Tommy tried to contain a grin.

'We?' interrupted Eric.

'Okay, *I* have decided we'd like to stay in Venice a bit longer.'

'You don't seem so keen, Eric.'

'Do you blame me?'

'I've stayed in worse places. This hostel is more about the people than the deco. There's a good crowd here if you just give them a chance.'

Just as Eric was formulating a suitably sarcastic response, a plastic tap burst from the side of a keg and a fountain of beer sprayed his face and chest.

'For fuck's sake!' he yelled, wiping alcohol from his stinging eyes and dropping his glass to the floor. 'I'm soaked!'

'Go back to the room and dry yourself off, it's not the end of the world,' Nicole giggled.

'It's the end of this All Saints T-shirt,' Eric shot back, and turned towards the door, mopping his face with a paper napkin. Before he left, he turned to Nicole and whispered in her ear. 'Don't tell him anything.'

With Eric gone, Tommy burst out laughing. 'Did you see his face?'

'Oh, we shouldn't laugh,' Nicole smirked.

'All Saints? You can tell he's a tourist.'

'What do you mean?'

'The difference between backpackers and tourists is that backpackers don't wear £50 T-shirts. In fact £50 is probably the total value of my wardrobe.'

Nicole nodded and fiddled with the Calvin Klein label at the bottom of her vest to make sure it wasn't visible.

'Well it's a shame to let his beer go to waste,' Tommy continued, and bent down to pick up Eric's glass. He didn't notice a hairline crack down the side and, as he reached for the rim, the glass snapped and tore into the palm of his hand.

'Shit,' he yelped, and pulled a shard from his wound. Nicole instinctively reached for Tommy's hand and inspected it, before pressing a handful of napkins to stop the flow of blood.

'Where's the first aid kit?' she asked.

'In the kitchen.'

Tommy clasped his throbbing hand and led Nicole upstairs to the kitchen where she rinsed it under the cold water tap.

'It's not deep enough to need stitches but it might be worth going to A & E.'

'You're assuming I have medical insurance,' replied Tommy, watching Nicole carefully as she cleaned up his wound with iodine. 'And you've done this before.'

She smiled, and wrapped a bandage around his hand, securing it with two safety pins and some gaffer tape.

'I may have, once or twice,' she replied.

TWELVE WEEKS EARLIER – LONDON

'So much for being bloody waterproof,' muttered Nicole to herself as the torrential rain lashed against her Mackintosh and seeped into her collar, dripping down her back.

The rain that began as harmless drizzle was now torrential and soaking her to the skin. Nicole regretted her decision to cycle the six miles to work instead of catching the bus, and reminded herself of her mother's words, 'a bit of rain never hurt anyone'.

Suddenly, with the hospital in sight, the hem of her coat became caught in the back wheel's spokes and yanked her body to the right. After failing to regain her balance, she toppled off the saddle and landed cheek first on the pavement.

'Bollocks,' she yelled, picking herself up, then her bike, before kicking it and walking with it the rest of way.

*

Hospital rules stated that a person could only run through a ward in an emergency.

But having fallen foul of Matron's displeasure over poor time-keeping three times already that fortnight, Nicole decided that to avoid being any later than she was, it was indeed an emergency. Quickly, she squeezed the sanitiser from the wall-mounted dispenser into her palms and rubbed her hands as she dashed past the beds on the geriatric ward, before reaching the room behind the nursing station where Eric sat, reading *Esquire* magazine next to a half-full, tepid pot of coffee.

'How have you got the time to sit down and read?' Nicole asked.

Eric's reply was to act out looking at his watch, tapping it and then raising his eyes towards Nicole.

'Don't start,' she snapped, in no mood for a lecture. She swept her sopping wet hair from her face and glanced into the mirror at a graze on her cheek. 'Do we have any antiseptic?'

'Nic, we're a hospital. We bleed antiseptic.'

Nicole was searching a desk drawer for the first aid kit when a surly matron walked in.

'Late again, Nurse Grainger?' she asked rhetorically, and gripped Nicole's face to examine her injury. 'Get a move on and cover this up. Your patients don't need to see the results of your drunken nights out.'

Before Nicole could protest, Matron had stomped back out of the room to make someone else's life miserable.

'How's Mrs Baker?' Nicole asked, powdering her cheek with foundation.

'She's had a rough night,' Eric replied. 'She's been asking Nurse Ryan if you're on shift today.'

Nicole moved into the nurses' station, shuffled the clipboards around on the desk until she found Mrs Baker's charts, and headed towards a private room.

*

By the time the cancer had reached Grace Baker's bones, she knew it was unlikely she would see her seventieth birthday. In the space of eight months, she had shrunk from a sturdy, strong-willed woman with a love of travel to a thin, frail, grey-skinned old person waiting to take one last journey.

Mrs Baker could have easily afforded to end her days in a private hospital, but she knew from her late husband's experience just how quiet and soulless such places could be. And without a family to visit her, the hustle and bustle of an NHS hospital made her feel less alone.

After a night where sleep was disrupted by pain and her loss of bladder control, Mrs Baker struggled to keep her eyes open and drifted off to sleep moments before Nicole entered her room. She pulled up a seat and sat by her side, holding her hand.

'Bridget?' mumbled Mrs Baker, vaguely aware she had company.

'No, Mrs Baker, it's Nicole. How are you feeling today?'

'I can't really feel much because of the morphine. I've asked, but they won't tell me what will happen next.'

'I don't think they can, I'm afraid. It's now just a case of managing the pain rather than trying to find the cause of it.'

Mrs Baker nodded and slowly opened her bloodshot eyes. 'Do you have time for my usual?' she smiled.

Nicole turned her head towards the door for any sign of Matron, then reached into the bedside table drawer and pulled out a lipstick before applying it to Mrs Baker's lips.

'That's better,' smiled Mrs Baker. 'A girl's got to look her best even when she's feeling her worst. Did Bridget come while I was asleep?'

'Um, I'm not sure; I've just started my shift . . .'

'You can tell me the truth.'

Nicole hesitated before answering. 'No, I don't think she did. But you've told me how busy she is.'

'Yes, it must be hard juggling Pilates classes with nannies for grandchildren I never see. I have a daughter who married for social standing and a son I haven't seen in a decade after his father died and he tried to put me in a home and steal my money. I did well, didn't I?'

Nicole wasn't sure how to respond, but before she had the opportunity to, a stern voice behind her made them both jump.

'Nurse Grainger, may I have a word please?'

Mrs Baker squeezed Nicole's hand in anticipation of what was to come and Nicole followed Matron into an office. The only thing to separate Matron from the nursing characters Hattie Jacques portrayed in the *Carry On* films was her modern-day uniform, thought Nicole. During working hours, Matron discouraged fraternisation between staff and patients. Her old-school approach bore little relationship with modern nursing methods.

'May I remind you – once again – there are more patients in this ward than Mrs bloody Baker,' Matron snapped. 'Just because her husband was on the trust board so she gets her own room does not mean she can expect preferential treatment over everyone else. Do I make myself clear?'

Nicole swallowed hard. 'Yes, Matron.'

'Now start your rounds and visit this woman in your own time or you'll be on report – again.'

Nicole followed her out of the office. And if Matron had turned around a second earlier, she'd have seen Nicole giving her the finger behind her back.

TODAY

'A nurse, eh?' began Tommy, his eyes lighting up. 'Does that mean you get to wear one of those sexy uniforms?'

'Yes, that's right,' sighed Nicole. 'We all skip around in high heels and fishnet tights with our shirts unbuttoned so you can see our bras, and slowly pull stethoscopes from between our boobs.'

Tommy was instantly embarrassed by the immaturity of his question, but amused by her response.

'How long are you in LA for?' Nicole asked, changing the subject.

'As long as it takes to figure out what I want to do with my life.'

'And what do you want to do, Tommy? You know, in an ideal world.'

'Right now? I'll give you three guesses,' he replied with a flirty smile.

'I know what I want, too,' whispered Nicole, and smiled, pulling Tommy's bandaged hand closer to her chest. He felt his heart beat faster and he swallowed hard.

'And what's that?'

'I . . . want . . . another beer. Now be a good boy and go get me one.'

In the ten minutes Nicole and Tommy had spent in the kitchen, they'd failed to realise they were not alone until a gentle snoring caught their attention. They turned together to see Joe, sitting on a stool in the corner of the room and slumped fast asleep across a work surface next to two large steaming pots. Tommy examined the pots' contents – one contained an almost solid, rust-coloured mass of sauce, and the other was crammed with charred spaghetti and no water.

'Joe, wake up!' yelled Tommy.

Joe's eyes shot open and he was clearly unsure of his surroundings.

'Mate, you've cremated the pasta. There's a room full of hungry people waiting for this.'

'Sorry, just . . . busy . . . forgot.'

Tommy helped Joe back to his dormitory, removed his baseball cap and put him to bed. As he left, he was startled by Ruth's presence, sitting on the top of a bunk bed and viewing something on her iPad. One headphone was plugged into her ear and the other dangled by her shoulder.

'Hello,' Tommy began, and Ruth gave an awkward, tight-lipped smile. 'It's Ruth, right? I checked you in. I've not seen you about much.'

Ruth continued smiling but didn't reply.

'Aren't you coming downstairs to the party? There's free beer if you fancy a drink.'

Ruth shook her head.

'Not much of a drinker?'

Ruth shook her head again.

'Or talker?'

By the time Ruth plucked the teeth whitening trays from her mouth, Tommy had given up on the conversation and left her with only the sounds of the party a floor below to keep her company.

CHAPTER 12

'Wanting . . . needing . . . waiting . . . for you, to justify my love . . .' came Madonna's breathy vocals over the trip hop drum loop as the song's heavy bass boomed from the speakers above the stage.

The punters watched in silence as the dancer began her slow, sensual descent down the pole and towards the rubber matted floor. She held on with a baseball-style grip, swung her outside leg into a hook and picked up her inside leg, which followed suit. She threw her head and shoulders back to accentuate her breasts, and pouted. Despite the track being older than her, she knew every word and every beat off by heart as she'd danced to it twice per shift for the last four months.

Before Savannah stumbled into a career as an exotic dancer, she had a preconceived notion strip clubs were sleazy dives patronised by paunchy, middle-aged men, like she'd seen depicted in cable TV shows like *The Sopranos*. But both the décor and the clientele of Santa Monica's Pink Pussycat Club changed her mind.

Open twenty-four hours a day, and a ten-minute cab ride from Venice Beach, the spacious lounge area housed two stages and two poles on either side of the room, with a bar to separate them. Wipe-clean leather armchairs and Chesterfield-style sofas surrounded the stages, and there were lamps with purple shades balanced on dark, wooden tables. Smaller corner booths were roped off and reserved for VIP guests or parties who spent their dollars freely.

Savannah had no desire to work at that strip club, or any strip club for that matter. But compared to the first place she'd danced at days after arriving in the city of angels, this was like a palace and offered her the security she needed. She could also bank up to $500 on a busy night – more than Dunkin' Donuts or Wendy's paid in a week.

But in order to do the job, Savannah had imposed upon herself a moral code. Totally nude dances, private backstage lap dances and dating the clientele were all strict no-nos. They were sure-fire ways of doubling her daily income, and while she didn't judge the other girls who took that route, she feared losing even more of herself than she had already. So no matter how much money was thrown on the table or slipped into her bra, she would not budge. The furthest she would stretch to were topless dances and peep show performances, involving her surrounded by customers in private booths pleasuring themselves behind two-way mirrors.

As 'Justify My Love' gradually faded out, she scooped up her tips and made her way back towards the changing room where she stared into an illuminated mirror. She wiped the perspiration from her forehead and underarms, removed her smoky eye make-up with a damp tissue, then reached into her handbag for her mascara, and found an embossed business card Tommy had given her two days earlier.

'Some bloke came in here looking for you,' he'd informed her. 'He didn't give me a name, but he was an intimidating bastard. Had two big guys with him. He gave me his card but I didn't tell him you lived here.'

Savannah had forced herself to sound calm as she took the card then raced up the stairs and into her room. Inside, she'd shut and locked the door, made for the bathroom and vomited into the toilet bowl.

The card only contained a number that she didn't recognise, but that worried her more. She knew being afraid of the unknown was worse than being afraid of the expected, so she took her phone from her handbag, changed the settings so her number remained anonymous, and nervously dialled.

SEVEN MONTHS EARLIER – MONTGOMERY, ALABAMA

'Be gone devil! With the spirit of Jesus in me, I am ordering you to leave this child's body and make her clean again.'

The audience was transfixed by Reverend Devereaux in anticipation of the miracle they had queued much of the morning to witness. With the exception of scattered 'amens' yelled by pockets of onlookers, the only voices to be heard through the arena speakers were those belonging to the Reverend and his male assistants, muttering their approval at what was to come.

The Reverend allowed the tension to build gradually before he cupped the chin of the child who stood trembling before him. He placed the palm of his other hand on her forehead and clasped it so tightly it left the impression of his gold sovereign ring on her ochre skin.

'Speak child . . . speak!' he yelled. The temperature from the bulbs in the lighting rig above made sweat trickle down his forehead and drip from the microphone fastened from cheek to ear.

'Speak to me! Speak to your people! Speak to us all!'

The girl's head continued to quiver as he gripped her face.

'Tell everyone how Jesus has saved you!' he bellowed.

'Je . . . Je . . . Je . . .' she began. She looked into the Reverend's narrowed eyes, and then finally parted her lips.

'Jesus has saved me,' she blurted out.

'Louder!' he repeated, specks of saliva landing on her cheek. 'Say it louder!'

'Jesus has saved me,' she repeated, her voice rising to a more confident yell, 'Jesus has saved me!'

The audience rose to its feet, applauding and roaring its approval as the fifteen-strong brass band on the lowest tier of the stage launched into 'When the Saints Go Marching In'.

Reverend Devereaux had already left the girl to his assistant's devices. The assistant hurried her from the stage and into the wings and away from the audience before her stammer returned. They'd learned from mistakes made years earlier about how quickly 'miracles' wore off once adrenaline levels subsided.

Reverend Devereaux took to the centre of his stage, outstretched his arms like he was attached to an invisible crucifix and nodded to the audience. Indoor fireworks exploded behind him as the encouraging noises continued, before he waited patiently for the crowd to quieten. The television cameras focused close enough to capture the broken capillary veins scattered across his cheeks and nose, beaming his image across the amphitheatre on a huge screen.

'Today,' he began in hushed tones, 'Jesus made a crippled woman walk again; He aided a boy born without eardrums to hear for the first time in his life and He removed cataracts from the eyes of a blind grandmother. This is what happens when – not if – you allow the power of Jesus into your life. And for the benefit of our friends at home, just think what you could accomplish if you let Him into your life too. You can do that, right now, by picking up your telephone and calling the number at the bottom of your screen. It doesn't matter how much you donate, but the more you can afford, the more people we can help. Galatians 6:10 said, 'Let us do good to everyone, and especially to those who are of the household of Faith.' Thank you, my friends, and may God's love be with you.'

Reverend Devereaux bowed to his audience as they hollered, whistled and applauded. And in return, he clapped them and his stage helpers before leaving the podium.

There was only person in the arena who failed to arise and show her appreciation of the miracles that afternoon had witnessed, and Reverend Devereaux was fully aware of this.

He would have stern words with her later, but Savannah Devereaux had no intention of obeying her father.

TODAY

Savannah's hand trembled as she held the phone to her ear.

After three rings, the call was answered, but nobody spoke. The stalemate lasted for several seconds, before the door behind Savannah opened and Roxy walked in.

'Hey Savannah, I thought you'd gone,' she yelled before Savannah could hang up. She breathed quickly and wondered if her call had just opened Pandora's box.

CHAPTER 13

The pan of water was too large and too heavy for one person to lift alone, especially with a wounded hand, but Tommy attempted it anyway.

When it was clear his bravado was bordering on embarrassing, Nicole stepped in to help before he poured it across the floor.

'Thanks,' Tommy mumbled.

'It's my first night in Los Angeles and you've got me chained to the kitchen sink. This doesn't bode well for our relationship.'

'Well I can make pasta for one, not for sixty, and certainly not on my own.'

'So you think all women automatically know to cook? That's a bit sexist of you.'

'Oh no, I didn't mean it like that.'

'I'm just teasing,' Nicole replied, scraping burned pasta from Joe's pan with a wooden spoon. 'So how did you end up here?'

'You were with me – Joe was ruining the dinner.'

'Oh Lord,' sighed Nicole, 'I meant how did you end up in LA?'

'Oh right, sorry,' Tommy replied. 'Well I could tell you, but it's not exactly a barrel of laughs.'

Nicole held her spoon over her sink. 'Do you want to do this on your own?' she smiled.

TWO YEARS EARLIER – NORTHAMPTON, ENGLAND

'Do you ever turn that damn thing off?'

Lee glared at Tommy's reflection in the rear-view mirror as he drove. Tommy chose to ignore him and continued to pan the lens of his digital camcorder around the Mini.

'What are you even filming?'

'Nothing much, just you two and whatever we go past that looks interesting,' replied Tommy as the trees outside began to thin and make way for a succession of residential houses and shops. 'I need a backdrop for this project I'm working on.'

'Being around you is like living in the Big Brother house,' continued Lee. 'Cameras constantly following you about.'

Daniel interrupted from the passenger seat. 'That new Arctic Monkeys album is out soon, I hope it's better than last one.'

'Do you want to hear it? It leaked early so I downloaded it last night,' said Tommy enthusiastically. He removed his iPhone from the back pocket of his chinos and scrolled through his playlists, while his video camera continued to record. 'You should try surfing the Russian websites like I do, there's so much illegal pre-release stuff online if you know where to look.'

'Yeah, I've heard some of the Russian websites you surf when you think everyone else is asleep,' Lee smirked.

'Oh yes,' teased Daniel, 'Even Mum's said she's heard your bed squeaking to the sounds of online Russian girls groaning in your bedroom for seventy Rubles a minute.'

'You are such a liar!' Tommy snapped as his face reddened. Daniel and Lee enjoyed embarrassing their younger sibling, knowing the fact that anything to do with the opposite sex would have the desired effect. Despite the two-and-a-half year gap separating the twins from Tommy, and that Daniel and Lee were in their final few weeks of university, they had remained a close family.

The car slowed down as it reached traffic lights and Tommy continued to hunt through his extensive collection of downloaded music.

'When you're done at your lectures can you pick me up from Sean's house?' he asked.

'You can catch the bus back – we're going out of our way as it is to give you a lift there,' replied Lee dismissively.

'That's not fair, Mum and Dad bought you a car while I have to cycle everywhere like a paperboy.'

'And they'll buy you one too if you get into uni. But you're the one who took a gap year and then did sod all with it,' continued Lee. 'You need to get your arse into gear, start looking at courses and get your applications in.'

'Well I still need a bit of time to decide what I want to do,' Tommy replied, bored of being lectured by his parents and his brothers.

'Don't tell Dad that or you'll be in Afghanistan before you know it,' added Daniel. 'If it's film school you really want to get into then he'll come round eventually. Just make a decision and go with it. Stop wasting time.'

'Okay, okay, enough of the pep talk!' Tommy knew full well that at nineteen, he needed to get his act together. Sean aside, most of his friends were finishing their first year at university, while he'd floundered, working part time on a checkout in Tesco.

With his brothers' sponsored university places coming to an end, they'd be trainee Marines by Christmas but Tommy had no interest in the family tradition of joining the armed forces. Instead, he preferred to be holed up in his darkened bedroom making mini-movies and editing them on his laptop.

His focus was often on landscapes – inner city, coastal and countryside – and exploring new ways of filming them. But with only a hand-held digital camcorder he'd bought himself with his supermarket earnings, his ability to develop his skill was limited. He barely went anywhere without it, constantly uploading clips to YouTube in the faint hope a famous director would see his potential and invite him to work as a trainee cinematographer on the set of a movie. But Martin Scorsese had yet to spot his potential.

'Plug this in,' Tommy said, handing Lee his iPhone.

As the green traffic light turned red and the Mini accelerated across a junction, Tommy lost his grip of the phone and it bounced off Lee's thigh and into the driver's footwell.

'Tommy, you dick,' barked Lee, unclipping his seat belt to fumble around for the phone.

For a split second, Tommy noticed a dark shadow through the lens of his camcorder but it moved too quickly for his eyes to process what it was.

Suddenly the brothers' world became deafeningly loud and turned to black as the shadow ploughed into the side of their car, forcing it to roll over twice before it settled on its side.

TODAY

'I've been looking for you,' barked Eric, interrupting Tommy's recounting of his past and Nicole's gradual understanding of the vulnerability of the boy standing before her in the kitchen.

'Sorry, it's my fault, I asked for Nicole's help,' replied Tommy.

'Could I have a word, Nic?' Eric glared.
'Um, sure.'
'In private?'

Nicole followed Eric from the kitchen and down the corridor before he came to a halt. The smell of beer remained on his skin.

'I've been standing downstairs like an idiot waiting for you, but surprise, surprise, you're up here with him,' he began heatedly.

'What's your problem with Tommy?' Nicole replied, startled by his outburst.

'I don't have a problem with Tommy,' Eric continued, trying to control his frustration. 'What I do have a problem with is being left alone while you make a fool of yourself.'

'Jesus, Eric. I'm getting sick of your mood swings today.'

'I don't trust him. He's probably tried it on with every girl here.'

'He's not like that, and what business would it be of yours if he had? I can look after myself.'

'Yeah, you did a great job with Pete, didn't you?'

Nicole scowled at Eric, angry that he would bring up such a painful memory to use against her. 'That's not fair,' she replied quietly as Eric instantly regretted his choice of ammunition. He softened his tone accordingly.

'I'm sorry, that wasn't fair. But I'm your best friend, Nic, and if it weren't for me, you wouldn't have even known Pete was screwing around on you. I'm a good judge of character, so trust me on this, Tommy's no good. I'm a bloke, we know this kind of thing.'

Nicole said nothing and her eyes sank to the floor.

'Look, we're here for a reason,' he continued. 'Maybe thousands of pounds worth of reasons. All I'm saying is don't let some kid you hardly know get in the way of that. Now come here.'

Eric put his arms around Nicole and kissed her on the cheek. She always felt safe when she was with Eric even when he was thoughtless, but she was reluctant to believe Tommy had any agenda. He was right when he told her about travellers wanting to share their lives with others in short spaces of time. But it wasn't something she could reciprocate.

'Let me help him out with dinner, and I promise I'll be down in fifteen minutes,' Nicole conceded.

Eric nodded his approval and Nicole headed back into the kitchen.

'Everything okay?' asked Tommy chirpily.

'Yes, it's fine,' replied Nicole, and said very little else during the rest of their fifteen minutes together.

CHAPTER 14

DAY TWO

Matty and Declan left the cooling ocean water in just their underwear and made for the towels they'd left spread across Venice's sandy beach.

'I can see your li'l fella,' began Matty, pointing to Declan's boxers, the water having made them transparent.

'Less of the "li'l",' Declan replied, and rubbed his hair with his towel. 'It was fecking cold in there.'

Their walk from Santa Monica via Venice Beach Boulevard in the blistering heat had been exhausting, especially with two bulging rucksacks strapped to their backs. So their brief respite in the ocean had been a welcome diversion.

Despite not having stepped inside a gym for the best part of a year, Declan was grateful good genetics meant his chest and arms retained their muscular shape. He'd used the last squirt of sun block earlier that morning, and with each passing hour he felt his milky Irish skin reddening further.

'I'll kill you if they're fully booked after days on that stinking fecking thing,' warned Matty, andhe took a swig of water.

'It was your idea to save money and go freight-train hopping.'

'You're supposed to be the sensible one and talk me out of crap like that! Besides, we could've managed a Holiday Inn if you hadn't blown our money in Reno trying to be Billy Big Bollocks in front of the showgirls.'

'Where else am I going to find a bird with firm breasts and feathers stuck to her arse?'

'A henhouse?'

Their arrival in Los Angeles early that morning was the culmination of a five-day expedition riding the railways from Seattle to Idaho, then the length of Nevada, cross-country to Utah before finally reaching LA. Although strictly illegal, freight train hopping was the cheapest way to travel long distances and witness parts of America that couldn't be negotiated by car or bus.

An article in a *Reader's Digest* magazine Matty found in a hospital waiting room in Florida gave him the inspiration to trek by boxcar. The written recollections of former rail-riders got him wondering what it must have been like to travel the country in search of new jobs and new beginnings during America's Great Depression. In reality, it had proved an ordeal, and much more precarious than his naive imagination had anticipated.

The first hurdle was finding freight yards where trains and their boxcars passed through or were parked up. Then once a slowed-down train was in sight, they had to run to keep up with it, promptly pick a carriage with an open door then hurl themselves and their luggage into it. Twice they'd failed and had been forced to wait ten hours for the next train to pass.

Once inside, their final hurdle was to stay alive, because manoeuvering around a fast-moving carriage was awkward and clumsy and would regularly result in them being hurled around like wrestlers in a ring. The sound of the grinding wheels on the steel tracks was often so deafening, they'd insert their in-ear headphones to nullify the noise.

The nights were cold and the carriages stank of the products being transported. For two of their six journeys, they'd picked the wrong boxcars and slept on bags of fertiliser and boxes of bottled bleach. Another was spent in an open carriage, zipped up head to toe in sleeping bags to protect them from the 60 mph winds. Only their last journey was more pleasant, tucked up amongst crate after crate of mattresses, computer games consoles and Blu-ray players.

Matty and Declan learned to avoid other freight train hoppers. Often, they were nomadic souls unwilling to have their space invaded or were suffering addictions to narcotics or alcohol and wanted to rob you at knifepoint. Matty noted the magazine story failed to mention any of those perils.

Only once during a routine check at a station in Utah had an armed security guard discovered them. But experience had taught them they could get away with a lot if they exaggerated their accents and ask Americans if they had any Irish in their heritage. Invariably their interrogator would say yes, and claim to be one tenth Gaelic, to which Matty and Declan would respond that they'd known immediately. Then they'd then be left alone to go about their business by their flattered and gullible distant compatriot. But as uncomfortable and anxious as they'd often felt, it had been the journey of a lifetime, and they'd seen more of America than most of its natives.

Once they finally reached LA, and reeking of train grease and body odour, they made their way to the coast and charged straight into the ocean to clean up.

As they walked along the beachfront, Declan removed his T-shirt, dousing it with water from a bottle and wrapping it around his head. Meanwhile Matty's sweat-sodden shirt clung to his skinny body and he felt one of the blisters on his heels burst and weep inside his dirty white Converse trainers. The straps of his rucksack dug into his bony shoulders and chafed his skin.

'Hold up, this is the place, said Matty suddenly, pointing to the dilapidated building ahead of them.

'Here we go,' Declan replied, staring at the faded sign reading Venice Beach International Hotel. 'Another shithole we can't afford.'

'But we always find a way, don't we?' replied Matty, patting his rucksack and grinning. 'And this time we have a secret weapon.'

CHAPTER 15

In the 217 days since Tommy and Sean's plane taxied towards its stand at New York's JFK airport, much of the £8,000 Tommy had carefully scrimped and saved had been spent on travel, accommodation, food and alcohol.

Now with a depleted bank balance and mounting credit card bill, he was a beggar who couldn't afford not to choose the hostel jobs manager Ron threw at him. So he worked eight-hour days across a variety of tasks from cleaning to cash and carry food shopping to pay for his bed and board.

For the rest of the morning until Sadie took over, Tommy was on rota to cover the reception desk. Bored and with no one to talk to, he fiddled with the aerial on the television set to get a sharper picture then resisted the temptation to peek under his bandage to see how his cut hand was healing.

He grabbed a pile of magazines and stacked them on a shelf, colour-coordinating their spines. He picked out a couple of roll-up cigarette butts from the always-close-to-death-but-never-quite-there Yucca plant and sniffed them. He recognised their familiar cannabis scent before flicking them in the bin; while smoking dope was commonplace in dorms and on the roof, it was an activity he was wary of.

He thought back to the conversation he'd begun the previous night with Nicole, the only person on his travels he'd ever told about the car accident that changed the course of his life. And even then, he hadn't explained to her the complete story because that was a can of worms best left unopened. So in retrospect he was glad Eric had interrupted them even if Nicole's mood had shifted somewhat on her return.

'Tommy!' yelled Sadie's voice from upstairs in the lounge. He recognised her distinctive bossy New York twang immediately and wondered why, even though he was her equal on the reception desk, she appeared to believe he was her employee. 'Get your ass up here.'

'What's up?' he replied, narrowing his eyes.
'Now!'
Tommy took the stairs two at a time, and when he reached the lounge he offered a puzzled frown before launching into peals of laughter.

CHAPTER 16

'I'm not sure I really get it,' began Eric, removing his shades and turning 180 degrees to gain a better view of Venice Beach boardwalk and its colourful residents.

'What's not to get?' asked Nicole.

'I just don't get the appeal or why the guidebooks say it's so special. It reminds me of Blackpool but with a better beach.'

Confused by his indifference, Nicole's patience wore thin and she put her hands on her hips. 'You have got to be kidding me.'

She and Eric followed the route Tommy had taken her a day earlier, before kicking off their flip-flops and making their way across the warm, sparkling sand. The beach was quiet, apart from a few families eating picnics close to the ocean's waves. In the distance they could barely make out Santa Monica pier as the sun hid behind clouds of smog. But a hundred metres out to sea, brightly coloured sails bobbed up and down as windsurfing boards glided across the water's surface.

Eric removed his everyday rucksack, took out two plastic bottles of Sprite and placed them on either end of a weathered road map to stop the light breeze from carrying it away. Nicole flicked through the dog-eared pages of an atlas, skipping past pages of towns leading off Route 66 they'd circled in red.

'So we went where we thought we were supposed to go,' began Nicole, 'and that was following Route 66 from where it starts in Illinois and ends in Santa Monica.'

'I was there, Nic, I can remember this.'

'I know, I'm just saying it out loud to get it clear in my head. And somewhere en route, we missed what we were looking for. So our options are this: reread her letter, take a closer look at each town on the Internet, or completely retrace our steps.'

'Are you kidding me? It's a miracle that truck has made it 3,000 miles – there's no way in hell I'm doing that journey again.'

'I don't think we need to. I have a feeling we are in the right neck of the woods, give or take a few hundred miles.'

'And do you have any thoughts as to what we're going to find when we get there?'

Nicole shook her head. 'Not a bloody clue.'

ELEVEN WEEKS EARLIER – LONDON

Nicole fanned herself with her hand as the digital clock on the TV above Mrs Baker's bed hit 21.00 hours.

'It's a bit hot in here, isn't it?' Nicole asked and went back to painting Mrs Baker's fingernails. Her shift had ended an hour earlier, but Nicole wanted to find a way of cheering up her patient and friend. Mrs Baker's nails were grey like her skin, so Nicole added French tips and painted them a deep red. She smiled at her handiwork and wondered if she should have stuck with her original post-A Levels plan and trained as a beauty therapist instead of a nurse.

Mrs Baker was sitting upright for the first time in days, albeit awkwardly and with pillows supporting her aching back and neck. 'Before Joseph opened the jeweller's we spent the first eighteen months of married life backpacking around the world,' she recalled. 'India, South Africa, Australia and America. It was quite a wild thing to do back then when everyone else our age was settling down and having babies.'

'That sounds incredible,' said Nicole.

'Oh it was, dear. Joseph and I travelled Route 66 in 1971. We bought a brand new pick-up truck in New York and started from the road's origins in Chicago and drove all the way over to California, visiting everywhere from big cities to ghost towns. The happiest night of my life was when we pushed the seats down and slept by the banks of a lake. The wind was cold, we had the heater on full and we just lay there listening to a cassette over and over again.'

Nicole caught herself smiling, trying to imagine being there.

'"A long, long time ago",' Mrs Baker began to sing quietly, '"I can still remember how the music used to make me smile." We stared at the stars shining like diamonds.'

'I've never had the time or the money to travel,' said Nicole.

'I'm sure that will change one day. Do you mind me asking what made you become a nurse?'

'Well, I was thirteen when my mum was diagnosed with breast cancer. For years she was in and out of hospitals having tests and treatments and operations and I'd see how hard the nurses worked to make her feel comfortable. And when she lost her battle four years later, I thought it'd keep a bit of her alive if I could help other people.'

'And now? Because – and tell me if I'm speaking out of place – but you don't seem too happy with your lot.'

Nicole sighed. Eric once nicknamed her 'Cling-film Face' because she was so transparent and, try as she might, she found it near impossible to disguise whatever it was she was feeling at that moment.

'It's harder than I thought,' Nicole admitted. 'I don't get along with Matron, I never have any money and I have more bags than a Prada catalogue under my eyes. It's not the life I thought it'd be.'

Mrs Baker clasped Nicole's hand. 'I hope you don't mind me saying, but I'm sure your mother would've been very proud of you. I know I would be if you were my daughter.'

Nicole blushed. It had been fourteen years since her mother had passed away, and although her father had appeared intermittently throughout her life, it had been a decade since their paths last crossed. She'd grown to understand she didn't need a relationship with a name on a birth certificate.

'Is there a young man in your life?' continued Mrs Baker, 'someone to go home to and who cooks you dinner or massages your feet?'

'No, not since Pete,' Nicole replied, and for the first time that week, his face appeared from the smoke in her memory. When confronted by the photos Eric had taken and WhatsApped her, Pete claimed the drunken girl had thrown herself at him and the picture was taken from a deceptive angle. But she'd believed her best friend when he'd told her he'd seen them together at least twice before in the bar.

Pete begged his childhood sweetheart to stay with him, and for a while, Nicole remained, but try as she might to convince herself it was just a bump in their well-travelled road, she knew she could never trust him again. Each night he spent out with the boys, or working overtime at the estate agent's, or the after-hours texts he received made her doubt him. So, with Eric's help, she packed her clothes and moved out of their terraced house and into a rented one-bedroom flat, leaving behind everything that Pete had tainted with his infidelity.

At first, Nicole missed him terribly. Then gradually, it was their future she missed rather than the man himself. A small piece of her crumbled each time she walked past the hospital maternity unit and saw new parents tenderly cradling their babies, knowing she and Pete would never be like them.

She'd imagined what it could've been like if she and Eric had ever stepped over the line, but try as she might, she couldn't think of Eric in a sexual way. He'd always be like a brother to her. She once broached the subject of co-parenting a child with Eric in a roundabout, joking kind of way, but he seemed dismissive of the idea of being either a hands-on or hands-off father.

And Nicole's only attempt at a date in the last twelve months had ended when she walked out of the cafe after his first words were, 'Now here's a girl who likes her food.' So Nicole vowed if she hadn't found Mr Right by thirty-five, she would go it alone and explore artificial insemination. While Eric wasn't willing to supply his sperm, he did supply her with company, nights out and a shoulder to cry on, and not once had he attempted to take advantage of her vulnerability.

'I thought maybe you were courting that young man outside,' Mrs Baker continued. 'My ears can't hear speaking voices very well from a distance any more, but I often hear you two giggling together.'

'No, he's my best friend but he's not my type.'

'But I bet if I ever met him and asked him the same question, he'd answer differently,' smiled Mrs Baker. 'And who could blame him, you're a pretty, intelligent girl with an enormous heart. Any man would be mad not to snap you up.'

A deliberate cough from the doorway interrupted their heart-to-heart. Both turned their heads to see an immaculately dressed woman with a pashmina draped over the shoulders of a cream Burberry suit.

'Hello, Mother,' said the woman coldly, and entered the room, slipping off her jacket and passing it to Nicole without making eye contact. 'Find somewhere for this, then close the door.'

'Did you take a wrong turn getting here, Bridget?' asked Mrs Barker.

'No, why?'

'Because I've been here almost a fortnight and you've yet to make an appearance. I presumed you'd got lost in the car park.'

Nicole felt uncomfortable as the once pleasant atmosphere iced over and Bridget glared at her. Nicole stood up and moved awkwardly towards the door.

'I'll see you tomorrow, Mrs Baker,' she smiled, then closed the door behind her, dropping Bridget's jacket to the floor on her way out.

CHAPTER 17

TODAY

Tommy couldn't stop laughing at the sight of Peyk's head hanging upside down from a jagged hole in the ceiling tile.

'Right, now's the time to tell me what you're doing or I'm leaving you hanging,' Tommy began.

'I told you before, I'm doing something for Ron.'

'So Ron's asked you to fall through every ceiling in his building, has he?'

'Are you going to help me down or not?' Peyk replied crossly. Two joints fell from his shirt pocket to the floor below.

'Well if you stop smoking that crap, you might keep your balance.'

'And if you start smoking this crap and you might chill out and get laid.'

Tommy smiled, shook his head, waved goodbye to Peyk and Sadie and headed back to reception, with the sound of Peyk's Dutch obscenities following him down the corridor. They could still be heard when he reached the top of the stairs and spotted Joe's unkempt pal Wayne entering the building with a mangy dog wearing a rope for a collar.

'Hey, I've told you before, get out,' ordered Tommy, and without protest, Wayne turned around and shuffled away sheepishly. However, his dog had its own agenda and suddenly bolted past them both and into the hostel.

Tommy chased after him up into the kitchen where he found it hovering by Ruth's feet, its head bowed, eagerly licking her ankles. A delighted Ruth scratched behind his ear, enjoying the attention from the four-legged stranger.

FIVE WEEKS EARLIER – RSPCA DOG SANCTUARY, VICTORIA, AUSTRALIA

'Uh-oh, you-know-who is on his way over here,' warned Colleen, and straightened her back as she swept the floor.

'Who?' asked Ruth, placing her dirty mop in the plastic bucket. She wiped the sweat from her brow with her shirt sleeve.

'As if you have to ask,' chuckled Colleen, 'Your bloody shadow, who else? Whenever you're here, you know he's never going to be that far behind. We work with enough dogs to know when one's on heat.'

Ruth felt her face redden as a smiling Mickey walked towards her. Dogs leapt as high as their hind legs would allow in their gated pounds, and poked their snouts through the metal bars when he passed.

What Mickey lacked in his 5-foot 5-inch stature and unremarkable looks, he made up for with persistence and optimism. The three eager strays on the end of their leads strained as they approached Colleen and Ruth, desperate for their attention.

'And what can we do you for?' began Colleen, knowing full well what, or who, had brought him over.

'I've come to see this beaut,' Mickey began, his big, beaming smile revealing a less than proportionate tooth to gum ratio.

'I thought you might've. Don't distract her for long, we've got another dozen pounds to scrub before it's clocking-off time.'

'So how's about it, then?' Mickey directed at Ruth.

'How's about what?' she replied, shyly.

'The same "it" Mickey asks you every time,' interrupted Colleen.

'Oh, that.'

'Every week I ask you out for some tucker and every week you tell me you're busy. C'mon, Ruthy, does a bloke have to go down on his hands and knees in dog shit and beg?'

At twenty-four, Ruth had yet to accept a date invitation from Mickey – or from any man, for that matter. When she'd relayed to her mother Mickey's interest some months earlier, Denise trawled through his Facebook profile and offhandedly advised her daughter, 'Neither of you are in a position to be picky.'

Ruth was sure Mickey would make some girl very, very happy, at least at the beginning. Because eventually, he would leave that girl and break her heart, as that's what all men were programmed to do to women – her mother had reminded her of that enough times over the years.

Even her brother Kevin took pride in showing Ruth the begging texts he'd received from girls he'd duped, slept with, and then dumped. And she'd watched enough movies and soap operas to know that relationships rarely worked out like they were supposed to. Men would say all the things you wanted to hear, but in the end, they'd replace you with someone else once they grew tired of you.

Ruth wouldn't allow Mickey to do that to her.

There was only one man she was certain would love her as much as she loved him. Zak Stanley's lips would be the first – and only – pair she would ever have pressed against hers.

'Thanks, but I can't,' Ruth told Mickey assertively, then paused. 'I'm seeing someone.'

Mickey and Colleen looked at each, then at Ruth.

'Really?' they replied together.

'You don't know him,' replied Ruth, pre-empting their next question. She picked up her bucket and walked towards a drain to empty the dirty water. 'I'm going to check on Bobby.'

'Maybe if I had four legs and licked my own balls she'd be interested,' mumbled Mickey sulkily before wandering off, while Colleen pondered who on earth Ruth could have fallen for so quietly.

*

The groggy Border Terrier lay on a soft fleece blanket in his cage, slowly regaining consciousness.

His black, dimpled nose twitched when he smelt Ruth's familiar bleachy scent as she entered the recovery room. A gauze bandage was wrapped around his front left leg, and an IV drip stretched to a bag attached to the front of his cage.

Ruth carefully opened the latch on the cage door and put her hand inside to stroke his wiry black head. He nuzzled Ruth's wrist before closing his brown eyes and drifting back to sleep.

Ruth's favourite of all the centre's unwanted dogs had resided there for a month after his neighbours reported him for howling at all hours in his garden. When the RSPCA arrived, officers discovered him sheltering from the rain under a rotting wooden door propped up against a shed. When the officer finally persuaded the shivering creature to trust her and exit his makeshift sanctuary, his matted body was covered in flea bites, stale blood and his sibling's teeth marks. Ruth knew how it felt to be bullied in your own home, so she'd visit him three times a day, every day of the week, just to remind him not every human was cruel.

'Don't get too attached, Ruth,' began Mr Rogers. She jumped at hearing the voice of the dog pound's practice manager. 'If the antibiotics don't start working soon, we'll be wasting our time and money . . . and you know what that means.'

Ruth had watched Colleen wheel enough blanket-covered bodies towards the incinerator to know exactly what Mr Rogers meant.

*

'No, no, no, we are not keeping that thing,' Denise began, folding her arms defiantly.

Ruth stood before her mother, cradling a bewildered Bobby in her arms. One hour and two bus journeys earlier, he'd been enjoying his post-anaesthetic dreams about a nugget of chicken he'd found on a lawn. Now he could sense the animosity coming from the aggressive human in front of him.

'That wretched thing is not coming into this house,' continued Denise.

'Which one?' added Kevin, much to his own and his mother's amusement.

'Please, Mum, they were going to destroy him,' Ruth pleaded. 'You'll be no trouble, will you Bobby? Look, he can't even walk properly.'

To demonstrate Bobby's disability, Ruth placed him gently on the grass, where he sat down and took in his new surroundings.

Then as quick as a flash, he was up on all fours and charged out of the garden. By the time Ruth reached the road, she'd already heard the thud of the car bumper colliding with him.

*

The first shovel of dirt fell into the hole and covered Bobby's body. Ruth continued digging as her family looked on from their seats on the patio.

'That thing's gonna stink in this heat,' murmured Denise as she took a long sip of her Long Island iced tea.

'Which one?' replied Kevin, and he laughed as Ruth continued to dig.

CHAPTER 18

TODAY

On those lazy mornings when his parents were out and Tommy promised them he'd spend his time wisely by job-hunting, he instead spent many an hour lying on the sofa with a TV remote control glued to his fingers flicking through hundreds of Sky channels.

Overtly charming presenters desperately flogging ostentatious must-have watches and clothes that went up to size XXXXL amused him the most, but he'd never lingered on the religious channels until he arrived in LA. Now he'd become fascinated by their broadcasts on the reception desk television. He puzzled at how people could be so daft, and hand their money over so readily to preachers who claimed to be carrying out God's work when they were blatantly serving their own financial agenda.

Today's focus of attention was an evangelist by the name of Reverend Devereaux; a peculiar but amusing-looking man whose bark sounded worse than his bite. Tommy leaned back on his chair, flicking peanut butter M&M sweets into the air and catching them in his mouth. Most bounced off his lips or nose before he finally succeeded.

'You beauty,' he cried proudly.

'Thank you!' replied Savannah, watching him from the doorway. Surprised, Tommy fell from his seat and quickly scrambled back to his feet, to Savannah's amusement.

'Quiet afternoon?' she continued.

'It's dead. How's yours?'

'Dull, apart from a few Bunker Hill financiers putting money in my bra instead of in their kids' college fund. Am I still sleeping alone?'

'Yep, the room's all yours.'

Savannah leaned over the counter and gave him a peck on the cheek. She felt comfortable and unthreatened by Tommy; they'd talk with ease about how they'd just spent their day, but they never went into detail about their past and what brought them to their crossroads. Sometimes when Savannah returned from work in the early hours and Tommy was working a shift, they'd keep each other company watching old black and white films before she'd invariably fall asleep on his shoulder.

Neither enjoyed spending time alone, and neither told the other why.

On several occasions, Savannah considered admitting that on the night of his arrival, she had been the one who came within two book chapters of blowing a hole through Tommy's spine. But then she would have felt obliged to reveal why she had a gun and what she was really hiding from in Los Angeles. And they were secrets she'd only shared with one other person under that roof. So she decided against unburdening herself as it would likely damage their friendship and serve no purpose to either of them.

'It's normally ten bucks for a peck,' she smiled.

'Will you take an IOU?'

'For you, yes, but don't tell your girlfriend.'

'Nicole's not my girlfriend. I've not even seen her today.'

'Not yet,' smiled Savannah.

Her light mood abruptly changed when she recognised a familiar voice preaching about sinners and Satan coming from the television. 'Why are you watching this?' she snapped.

'Rev Dev's a funny guy. Why? Have you seen him before?'

Savannah's eyes narrowed. 'He's not a funny guy, he's a dangerous, sadistic sonofabitch.'

SEVEN MONTHS EARLIER – MONTGOMERY, ALABAMA

'Wipe this black stink off me,' Reverend Devereaux roared at a teenage boy.

The terrified lad grabbed two white cotton face towels from the table in the Reverend's dressing room and began to dab at his employer's clothes. Meanwhile the Reverend took a handful of wet wipes from a packet and rubbed his jowls and hands.

'Why do you allow them on stage if you don't like touching them?' asked Pastor Jackson, flicking the scroll wheel of his Blackberry and checking his employer's emails.

'Because the blacks are where the money's at,' the Reverend replied with disdain. 'All those Ella Mae Joneses sitting in front of their televisions in their ghetto swamps are praying for their drug dealing sons to see the errors of their ways. And they ease their consciences about parental failure by donating money to my ministry – all those dollars add up. So if I have to touch their coalmine faces to convince them their dollars are worth my prayers, then so be it. But I don't have to like it and I ain't gonna have their smell on me a second longer than I need to.'

'I think you're very brave,' the Reverend's wife began, and kissed his forehead. A small black curly Afro hair fell from his shoulder and landed on the hem of her Diane von Fürstenberg skirt. She brushed it to the carpet with the tip of her fingernail, then cleansed her hands using a pocket-sized bottle of antibacterial soap.

Reverend Devereaux took a swig from a bottle of chilled sparkling water, his eyes darting towards Savannah and her younger sister Roseanna, sitting quietly side by side on a plastic-covered sofa.

'And next week may I at least get a smile from my own flesh and blood?' he asked.

'I'm here, aren't I?' Savannah replied, making little effort to disguise that she'd rather be anywhere else.

'When one of the dozen television cameras pans across the audience to focus on my "beloved" family, I expect my viewers to see them caught up in the joy I'm bringing,' he continued, 'and not sitting there turning their spoiled little noses up like skunks have crawled up their asses. Do you understand me?'

Savannah and Roseanna nodded their heads.

'Good. Now bring me joyful news from the world of ticket receipts, Pastor Jackson. Tell me how well have we done this evening.'

His head of finances clicked on the latest email to reach his phone and smiled. 'Preliminary figures suggest around the $75,000 mark so far from the folks at home, and they're still counting donations from the collection plates. But with 12,000 seats sold, the arena was full to capacity, so that's going to be a lot of donations for the church.'

'Good, good,' smiled the Reverend and turned to his wife. 'Looks like we'll get that estate by the lake just in time for summer after all.'

*

'I hate him, I absolutely hate him,' Savannah whispered.

The heat from the Starbucks coffee mug began to burn her hands as she clasped it tightly, but she kept them in place. Physical pain helped to block out the animosity and frustration she felt each time she failed to stand up to her father.

After each Sunday morning and Wednesday evening wasted at his weekly telecasts, Savannah spent the rest of the day nauseated by the genes she shared with a man who so eagerly misled the vulnerable. She felt a permanent unease for the folk who could barely afford to eat regularly, yet saved up their cash and spent $25 a ticket to witness one of his sermons in person.

That afternoon, Savannah kept recalling the shy little black girl with the stammer, and the terror that spread across her face as the fat white man shouted at her and tried to withdraw imaginary demons from her young body. There was nothing demonic inside her; she was made of love and trust and raised by caring parents who believed in their hearts they were doing what was best for her. The Reverend was not God's vessel on Earth like he claimed; he was a charlatan who profited from blind faith.

Savannah wondered if she was the only audience member to have noticed the child peeing herself when Reverend Devereaux gripped her face. She was convinced her father had seen it too and got a kick out of it. Then Savannah remembered later, backstage, passing the crippled woman who'd taken baby steps in front of the audience earlier that day. Moments later and out of view, she was back in her wheelchair, praying for the pain in her knees to subside.

Savannah often chastised herself for remaining under the Reverend's roof and accepting his soiled dollars. As a beneficiary, she felt complicit, and it sickened her.

'Baby, you just have to hold on for another year and then we'll be able to get somewhere of our own,' reassured Michael from his seat opposite her. He placed his hands upon hers. 'Let him pay for your college fees, and once you graduate I'll put in for a transfer and we can move to New York like we planned.'

'It's not my dad who's paying for all this, is it though?' she reasoned. 'It's his congregation, it's the collection plate he robs so we can live in a twenty-room mansion, so I can drive a Mercedes, go to dance classes, buy clothes, shoot guns at the rifle range and have the best education those people's money can buy.'

'But you'll make it up to those folk once you leave college,' Michael continued. 'Do some volunteer work, work full time for a charity . . . whatever you need to do to earn yourself some good karma. And you're doing this for us, not just for yourself.'

Savannah knew what Michael said made sense; if she were to storm out of the family home on principle to go it alone, he too would suffer from the loss of her generous allowance that helped to pay for his college tuition. Michael also abhorred his inability to pay his own way, but he knew he was benefitting for the greater good.

'I can't afford to put myself through med school on my own, or I'd be paying off loans until I retired,' he reminded her.

'But once I'm qualified, I'm going to work in the public sector. I'm going to help you give back what your daddy has taken away.'

All Savannah had to do was offer an occasional half-smile in front of her father, her mother and the cameras for a little while longer, and then she'd be free to start living her life as she should, with Michael. And she couldn't wait. Keeping a boyfriend secret from her family for almost three years was difficult. She'd learned to lie to them about seeing friends, attending non-existent college parties, social mixers and extracurricular college classes, all so she could spend time with him.

'Okay, I know, you're right, it's just tough sometimes,' she admitted.

Michael clasped her hands gently and smiled. 'I know, baby, I know. But you're doing real good. And once you leave that house for ever, think of the look on that racist's face when he realises his daughter's boyfriend is a black man.'

Savannah grinned and leaned over the table to plant a kiss on Michael's lips, unaware Pastor Jackson had stopped in his tracks outside the coffee shop, unsure as to whether his eyes were deceiving him.

CHAPTER 19

TODAY

'Hey, buddy, how's it going?'

Tommy looked up from the TV set to find two men standing before him, one tanned, one the colour of a boiling lobster, and both unshaven and sweating. Tommy wasn't sure if they were drunk or friends of Joe.

'Can I help you?' he replied curtly.

'Actually we're here to help you,' replied Matty, and flashed him a big, crooked smile.

Tommy raised an unconvinced eyebrow. By sight alone, he knew their type, because every hostel he'd stayed in had them: wannabe alpha males in a community made up of omegas. They were the loudest; the most opinionated; the effortlessly confident; the biggest boasters; the ones who were first to laugh at themselves and then at others; who'd travelled the furthest, the longest and through the harshest of terrains. They were everything in a traveller that Tommy disliked because they were everything he didn't have the confidence to be. And he didn't want them under his roof.

'By special delivery from Ireland, we've brought to you the life and soul your hostel needs, in two rather handsome packages, if I might be so bold. I'm Matty, and my friend here is Declan.'

Tommy remained deadpan; already, their presumption that the hostel could not function without their presence made his hackles rise.

'My esteemed pal and I need shelter from the elements,' Declan persevered.

'It's 30 degrees outside,' Tommy replied.

'Precisely,' added Matty. 'We need a roof over our heads to cool down.'

'The trouble is we have a wee cash flow problem,' added Declan. 'We're waiting for some nicker to be transferred from home, but we can settle up with you at the end of the week if you can offer us a couple of beds?'

'Does it say "homeless shelter" outside?' asked Tommy. 'We're not a charity, so you'll have to sleep on the beach till you sort out your "cash flow" problem.'

'Ah, but that's illegal,' replied Declan, still smiling.

'That's not my problem.'

'That's not very Christian of you,' added Declan, tilting his head towards Reverend Devereaux's television broadcast, 'and I can see you're a man of faith.'

'The telly only gets three stations.'

'Okay, what if we made a donation in the form of these?' asked Matty. He and Declan unclipped their backpacks and removed an Xbox One and a Sony Blu-ray player they'd taken as souvenirs from a boxcar. Matty and Declan smiled hopefully at Tommy.

'So, let me get this right. You have no money but want to pay for a bed with stolen electronics? I don't think so.'

'Come on, man, have you got no heart for a neighbouring countryman? We'll kip on the floor, we're not fussy,' pleaded Matty. They were used to talking people around to their way of thinking.

'Nice to meet you, but goodbye,' replied Tommy, smiling to himself. 'Not today,' he thought.

'Oh you fecking bellend,' snapped Declan, banging his fist on the counter just as Ron appeared from his office.

'Is there a problem, Timmy?' he asked gruffly.

'It's Tommy, and no, there's no problem – these gentlemen were just leaving.'

'Didn't room four empty this morning?'

'Well yeah, but they're broke. And they're trying to pay for it with stolen goods.'

'Can you boys cook?'

Matty and Declan looked at each other and smiled, while Tommy looked aghast.

'We certainly can, sir,' replied Matty.

'Organise the evening meals and you can stay,' said Ron before Tommy had a chance to argue, and immediately he'd regretted telling Ron about the previous night's issues with Joe. 'And make sure Peyk installs these kind donations in the lounge, Timmy,' added Ron, pointing to the boxes.

'We'll have two keys, please, Timmy,' added Declan with a victorious grin, 'and bring our bags to our room, there's a good lad.'

CHAPTER 20

34.02419N was the first line of numbers the needle began to etch in black ink.

Once the Hispanic tattoo artist finished, he dabbed blood and excess colour from between the seventh and eighth of Jake's ribs with a tissue. Then he continued with the next row – 118.4814W. Jake had chosen a simple Arial font, the same as the other twenty-four rows of numbers that preceded it and that stretched from just under his armpit and down towards his hip bone.

The tattooist cleaned Jake up and passed him a mirror. Jake smiled as he examined the latest numbers in his collection. Once a thin plastic sheet had been taped to his side to protect his body art, Jake paid his $45 for the work, then swept his long, chestnut brown hair into a ponytail, threw his battered rucksack over his back and continued his journey along the Venice Beach boardwalk.

'Remember who you are, not who you were,' he repeated over and over in his head, and absent-mindedly bit down on the inside of his cheek as he walked.

CHAPTER 21

As the morning progressed, Tommy's light began to dim to a darkness that would often permeate his world without warning.

Matty and Declan's appearance hadn't helped his mood, but they weren't the root cause of it. He didn't know what had encouraged the clouds to blow in late that day, all he knew was that each time they appeared, he'd get the sudden urge to break from the norm of surrounding himself with others and ensconce himself in silent contemplation.

He made no effort to placate a grumpy Sadie when she arrived for her shift and took him to task for not helping to free Peyk from the ceiling. Instead, he made his way towards his empty dormitory, crawled into his sleeping bag and curled himself up as much as the material would allow.

After a few moments, he reached into the rucksack under his bed and removed a small leather pouch, from which he poured four memory cards into his hand.

Three of them he'd sometimes slot into his digital camcorder to watch and remind himself of how far he'd come with his new life as a backpacker.

But the other he could still not bring himself to play. He kept it in the centre of his palm and stared at it, surprised that something so small could frighten him so much.

TWO YEARS EARLIER – NORTHAMPTON, ENGLAND

Tommy was unaware how long he'd remained unconscious in the back of his brothers' car before he came to.

His eyelids flickered as he struggled to acquaint himself with his whereabouts, and he became distracted by a figure skirting around whatever it was he was caught inside. He thought he could see the whites of their eyes glaring at him coldly like the grim reaper. It made him shiver. As his vision slowly returned, Tommy's forehead palpitated like the time Daniel had accidentally smacked him full-force with a cricket ball as a child.

And as he turned his head in the direction of a sudden noise, a shooting pain jumped from his left shoulder and up into his neck.

Tommy knew something in his world was askew. Now, through a cracked window, he could see an unfamiliar woman and a man, and he didn't know why he was watching them from a peculiar angle. He felt strangely calm, as if he were caught in that cosy period just before he fell into sleep but had already begun to dream.

Suddenly a gentle thumping on the window became a louder, more urgent banging and he thought he heard someone say something like: 'One in the back . . . moving.'

Then, like the sudden force of the impact of the shadow that had ripped into their car, Tommy knew exactly where he was. Fear and panic rose in tandem as he twisted his aching head from side to side, absorbing the carnage Lee and Daniel's car had become.

He couldn't understand why he was alone; from where he sat, the driver's seat was empty, with a twisted gear stick protruding at a right angle. The door had been struck so hard that it jutted inwards, towards the passenger seat. Tommy accepted the shadow he'd seen through his camcorder must have been the other vehicle that had collided with them and pushed their car onto its side. And judging by the state of the internal and external fittings, it had been a serious smash. But where were his brothers? Why would they have left him there without trying to help him escape?

'Lee!' he began, 'Dan?'

'Don't move,' came Lee's voice from outside.

Thank God, he was alright, Tommy thought, and for a moment his alarm began to subside. He patted down his arms and legs and only his foot looked wrongly placed, pointing at an awkward angle, yet it didn't ache as much as his neck.

He reached for the seat belt buckle and clicked the release button, and after several attempts it came loose. Grabbing at the other seat belt, he began hauling himself towards the window where faces outside were watching him. However, a bar of metal wedged across that glass prevented his release.

His eyes darted around the car, desperately trying to find another route to freedom. He noticed the windscreen had shattered but the roof had been pushed down, leaving a means of escape only a child could squeeze through.

It was at that moment he caught a glimpse of the front passenger seat. At first, his brain couldn't deconstruct what lay twisted on it – heaps of clothes, stained by a red liquid and what resembled sinew and bones jutting out in strange positions.

Then suddenly, he knew what it was.

His brothers' bodies shared the seat, melded together with torn flesh and metal like Siamese twins. Tommy stared at them in horror, unable to work out who was who. One of their heads was now concave, while the other's was only held in place by a visible sliver of bone. Tommy couldn't make sense of it, he would have sworn on a stack of bibles he'd just heard Lee's voice outside. But here lay Lee with Daniel, tangled together with no pulse between them.

In sheer terror, he had to get out of the car and he had to get out *right now*. He began screaming at the people outside for their help but no sound came from his throat. He kicked and pulled at the back seats to smash the rear window but it just made the bones in his foot audibly crack.

'Help me,' he began quietly, his voice gradually returning. 'Help me, please help me.'

'There's an ambulance and a fire engine on its way, son,' came a voice, and Tommy saw that a small crowd had gathered. He felt like a terrified circus animal surrounded by baying crowds and swore he could see a mobile phone's camera flash.

Tommy gradually felt more and more numb until he curled himself up into a tight ball, where he remained for the longest hour of his life, alone with his brothers for the very last time.

TODAY

Tommy continued fixating on the memory card in his hand; the final footage he'd taken of his brothers. But he was afraid that by watching it, it'd bring back more of the day than the fragments he remembered and had run so many miles to escape.

He was scared to see Lee and Daniel's faces again; to be reminded of that awful sound of pounding metal against metal; metal against tarmac; shattering glass and the helpless feeling of being trapped inside that tomb.

Tommy knew that if he could gather the courage to insert the memory card and press play, then maybe, just maybe, he could come to terms with what happened that day. But the risk that it would make him feel even lousier than he did already was one he wasn't ready to take.

He recalled how the WPC who came to the family house and handed back his camcorder had explained it had stopped filming seconds after the impact and offered investigators about as much as the broken traffic cameras mounted above the junction. They had their suspicions as to the identity of the driver of the stolen car that collided with them, but it was hard to prove.

'I need to do something,' Tommy told himself, urgently craving a purpose. He climbed out of his bed, changed into his shorts and pulled a cash and carry discount card from his toilet bag.

As he approached the reception desk and heard Ron's voice coming loudly from his office, Tommy realised the longest conversation they'd shared was the first night he appeared on Ron's doorstep. His memories were still a little fuzzy, but he recalled hearing a loud crack and then felt something shove him forward before his head smashed against the sidewalk.

Later, Ron had told him he'd been shot, but Tommy felt strangely accepting of the news. He wondered how many more times he'd need to stare death in the face before it took him once and for all.

Ron had offered him a bed and work at the hostel in the hope Tommy wouldn't report the incident to the police and bring unnecessary attention to a hostel that walked a fine legal line when it came to occupancy numbers, building code regulations, under-age drinking, pot smoking and a whole host of other dubious activities.

Tommy agreed, and the only question he'd asked was about the identity of the woman's voice he'd heard as he came to. He couldn't remember anything else about her, like her accent or what she'd said. Ron acknowledged someone had helped to pull him inside, but said it was a passing stranger. But Tommy got the impression Ron wasn't being honest with him.

'If I had it, I'd give it to you!' Tommy heard Ron yell from inside his office, before slamming the phone down.

The longer Tommy spent under that roof, the more suspicious he became about what else Ron wasn't telling him.

CHAPTER 22

Nicole's truck turned left at the traffic lights off Ventura Boulevard before pulling into the car park of a collection of medium-sized retail outlets.

'Thanks for helping me out,' began Tommy as they grabbed a shopping cart and walked through the sliding doors and into the cash and carry. 'Where did you tell Eric you were going?'

'I said we were going to get the tyre checked out as it looked a little flat after we hit the kerb when we arrived.'

Tommy smiled and appreciated that she'd lied for him. 'I don't think he likes me very much, does he?'

'He's just a little over-protective at times. I don't have the greatest record with men and he doesn't want to see me get hurt.'

'And he thinks I'll hurt you?'

'You're presuming I'd allow you close enough for that to happen! But no, he thinks any man will hurt me.'

'Apart from him, right? I think he likes you as more than just a friend.'

Nicole dismissed the idea immediately, like she had when Mrs Baker had suggested the same thing. 'Really, he doesn't.'

However Nicole had secretly begun to wonder if there might be an element of truth in it. Because during their great American adventure, she'd come to notice that Eric had found a way of getting in between her and any fellow traveller who paid her even the slightest bit of attention. Gradually she realised it wasn't inconceivable that their closeness had grown into something more, at least on Eric's part. And that worried her.

When she and Eric had returned to the hostel from the beach with still no idea of where they should travel to next, Nicole bumped into Tommy in the corridor while Eric was showering. He'd asked her to drive him to get hostel food supplies, but as Nicole didn't have a licence, she offered to accompany him if he drove her pick-up truck. Nicole knew from the previous night's warning that Eric wouldn't have approved of them spending time together with her helping Tommy if he wasn't around. But he wouldn't want to have tagged along either and while she hated dishonesty, he'd backed her into a corner.

There was something about Tommy that she was drawn to, even after such a short time. He possessed an innocence and naivety that she appreciated, and the older she became, the less often she found such qualities in men her own age.

On their way to buy supplies, she'd asked Tommy to continue the story he'd begun the night before, and as he quietly recalled the car accident that killed his brothers, she instinctively placed her hand upon his as he drove.

His honesty made her want to reciprocate and explain why she was in America, but she felt by revealing that, she would be going against Eric's will.

CHAPTER 23

Matty and Declan aborted an attempt to chat up two girls they fancied working behind the frozen yoghurt counter.

As visually appealing as they were, the girls were really just a means to an end – they had food at their fingertips and the boys were broke and hungry. But when it became clear the girls couldn't understand their accents, they admitted defeat and continued their walk along the boulevard. They'd already filled themselves up on other hostellers' boxes of cereal in the kitchen, but their hungry bellies were rumbling again.

'How much cash have we got left?' asked Matty.

Declan opened his wallet and pulled out some low-denomination bills and scraps of paper.

'We have the grand total of $11, plus €5, 90c off a Big Mac meal and a free bag of potato chips if we spend more than $10 at Subway.'

'Feck.'

As Matty replaced the money in his wallet, a newspaper cutting fell to the floor. Declan picked it up.

'What are you doing keeping this? You need to throw it away,' snapped Declan.

'Call it a reminder.'

'Call it fifteen years behind bars if anyone reads it and recognises us.'

CHAPTER 24

Tommy parked Nicole's truck in the multi-storey opposite the hostel.

He'd already dropped her and the industrial-sized bags of food in the alley behind the building, away from Eric's beady eye. And as she helped him carry them up the stairs and into the kitchen, she rehearsed a story about why she had been away for so long, blaming rush-hour traffic.

'Thanks again,' said Tommy, unpacking the shopping and placing it onto shelves in cupboards with missing doors and handles.

'You're welcome.'

'So I'll see you later, then, I guess?'

'I guess.'

The two stood face to face like nervous teenagers at a school dance unsure of what to do next. So Tommy took a silent breath, slowly tilted his head and moved his mouth towards Nicole's. But just as she closed her eyes, they were interrupted by a resounding bang from the corridor. They hurried towards the source of the commotion and found a trembling Peyk with an electrical wire in his hand next to a smoking plug socket.

'Come with me,' said Nicole, rolling her eyes, grabbing Peyk's arm and steering him into the kitchen. 'I should get paid for being your care worker.'

Although concerned for his friend, Tommy cursed Peyk's appalling timing.

CHAPTER 25

Ruth removed an orange dress from her suitcase and laid it neatly across her dormitory floor.

With a travel iron in her hand, she began to press out the creases, but with little effect. Frustrated, she pressed harder until the door behind her opened and knocked her off balance.

'Oh crap, sorry,' apologised Nicole, who held out her hand to lift Ruth back up.

'No worries,' replied Ruth.

'Ooh, Zak Stanley, you are gorgeous,' continued Nicole as she picked up a magazine cutting stuck to the hem of the dress.

'You think so?'

'Of course! Did you see him in that film *Baby Baby*?'

'About fifteen times!'

'That bit when he says "I know this is the first time we've met . . . "'

'" . . . but I don't ever want to lose sight of you again!"' interrupted Ruth. 'It makes me cry every time.'

'I know what you mean. And about five minutes before he's run over by that car in *Forever Us*, I always turn the DVD off so that in my head, that's where the film ends and him and Anne Hathaway live happily ever after.'

One minute spent talking to Nicole was the longest conversation Ruth had had with anyone during her six days in America. She opened her mouth to continue, but closed it again when she recalled her mother's reaction to why she was going to LA. Ruth didn't want to hear the same words from somebody else, but Nicole seemed nice, she thought. Maybe she could trust her?

'Are you busy?' Ruth asked with a whisper, even though there was nobody else in the room.

'Not really, what's up?'

'Can you keep a secret?'

I'm becoming an expert in them, thought Nicole. 'Sure.'

Ruth rifled around in her suitcase and found an envelope with a piece of white A4 paper inside, and handed it to Nicole. Nicole unfolded it and began to read. Halfway through she gasped, her eyes opened wide and she glared at Ruth.

'Oh. My. God. Is this for real?'

THREE WEEKS EARLIER – VICTORIA, AUSTRALIA

Bare breasted, rake-thin women with long, blonde hair extensions tumbling down their backs posed in sexy positions on the posters behind Ruth.

Once, she'd avoid going into her brother's bedroom, as it felt like a dozen pairs of beautiful strangers' eyes were laughing at her sturdy frame. But since Zak Stanley came into her life, everything was different. There was only one opinion that mattered, and it belonged to Zak. He could see beyond a plastic façade; he'd told that interviewer on the DVD he was looking for an ordinary girl, and Ruth was nothing if not ordinary, as her mother and brother made a frequent point of reminding her.

She'd waited for Kevin to leave the house for the second of his twice-daily gym pilgrimages before she switched on his computer. Her mother was fiercely protective of her iPad after Ruth had spilled a milkshake over it and Denise was hit with a $400 Apple Store repair bill. But as long as Ruth deleted the browsing history after each session, Kevin had never been any the wiser.

Ruth sifted through her emails. She hadn't been online for almost a week, and four new messages were waiting in her inbox – three more than she usually received. One was from Facebook informing her she had a new friend request. Out of curiosity, she clicked on it and realised it was from someone writing in a foreign language she didn't understand, but she accepted it anyway, taking the total number of friends into double figures. The other emails were newsletters from online forums she'd joined like 'Zak Stanley Web Ring', 'Circle of Zak' and 'Zak's World'. She scanned them, dragged some pictures on to Kevin's desktop and then added them to her Tumblr and Pinterest collections.

Satisfied with her latest harvest, she was about to log off when she noticed a message hidden in the junk folder. She clicked on it to read the subject heading: '*Official Zak Stanley Fan Club – You Are A Winner.*'

Curious, she clicked on a link, and an audio file began to play as a computerised voice spoke: '*Congratulations, Ruth Donovan, you have been chosen by the Official Zak Stanley Fan Club as this month's winner of our Meet Zak competition. On June 4, you will accompany Zak for a private lunch for two in Los Angeles. Please reply to this email to confirm your attendance and we will furnish you with an address and further details.*'

79

Then a flashing image of Zak's smiling face appeared on the screen. Ruth replayed the message five times until the news sank in – she'd won the online competition she'd entered a month earlier.

'Mum!' she screamed. 'Mum! Mum!'

'What?' her mother snapped from another room.

'Come here!'

Denise tutted and reluctantly made her way towards her daughter's excited voice. 'What are you doing in here? Kevin's going to—'

'Read this!'

Denise removed her glasses from her tracksuit pocket and squinted at the computer screen.

'I'm going to meet Zak!' squealed Ruth. 'I'm going to meet him!'

Her mother let out a long breath, removed her glasses and raised her eyebrows.

'I guess you didn't have to send a photo to win,' she mumbled rhetorically, and left her daughter to celebrate alone.

TODAY

'I'm so jealous,' admitted Nicole. 'You're so lucky!'

'I can't believe it,' said Ruth. 'I'm going to take my scrapbooks to show him what a big fan I am.'

'Maybe that's not the best idea,' said Nicole hesitantly. 'You don't want him to think you're a stalker.'

'Oh, right,' replied Ruth, who hadn't considered that. 'How about this then?'

She went back into the suitcase and pulled out a half-complete jumper she'd been knitting, which hung by the needles. 'It's not finished yet, but see? It's Zak's face.'

Nicole was unsure of how to react to the crude effigy – Zak's eyes faced in opposite directions and he had a mouth like Batman's nemesis, The Joker. But she didn't want to hurt Ruth's feelings.

'I'm sure he'll love it,' assured Nicole, and a huge grin spread across Ruth's face.

CHAPTER 26

DAY THREE

Tommy examined the brown crusts framing two slices of white bread, and used his knife to chip away circles of blue mouldy spores.

He reached for a variety pack of store-brand cornflakes, pulled open the plastic packing and poured them between the slices to make a sandwich. It tasted just as he guessed it might, like two things that can sit together comfortably on the same table but shouldn't be combined into one dish.

But one cooked meal a night courtesy of the hostel didn't give him enough fuel to keep going throughout the day. He wondered how supermodels managed it.

'Living the high life eh, Tommy-boy?' began Peyk as he wandered in with Savannah, and slouched across the table. His arm still tingled from his electric shock.

'Prisoners eat better than I do,' Tommy replied, taking another mouthful of his arid snack. 'I'm broke. I need a job as my work here only covers my bed and board and I'm going to be on my way home soon.'

'I can give you some cash if you need it, sweetie?' offered Savannah.

'Thanks, Sav, but I need some regular work.'

'I know someone who might be able to help you,' added Peyk.

Tommy eyed him up suspiciously. 'This isn't going to be something dodgy that'll land me in jail, is it?'

'Trust your Uncle Peyk, Tommy-boy, this job has your name written all over it,' he replied, failing to hide his smirk.

CHAPTER 27

As a rule, Ruth and mirrors were not a compatible match.

It wasn't that she'd deceived herself into believing she was Miranda Kerr and was disillusioned by the reality of her appearance; it was more the empty feeling that grew when she saw the same thing as everyone else.

But that night was an exception.

Instead of throwing on a pair of joggers and a baggy T-shirt like she did most days, Ruth spent the morning rigorously working on her outfit, shaving her legs, straightening her hair, and even slapping on make-up for the first time that year. She was so delighted with the results that she didn't register the sniggers greeting her when she entered the hostel lounge to find Nicole.

Eric was the first to notice her, his eyes working their way up from toes that reminded him of cocktail sausages stuffed into too-small high-heel shoes, her red tights, orange pinafore dress, green shawl and a plastic lily tucked behind her hair.

'What the actual fuck?' he mouthed at Nicole, who was equally as surprised, but pinched his forearm before he vocalised his thoughts.

'Wow, Ruth, look at you!' began Nicole supportively, and glared around the room to stop the handful of other hostellers from laughing.

'It's a designer dress,' Ruth smiled.

'By who, Picasso?' asked Eric.

'No, Topshop,' replied Ruth.

'You look beautiful,' continued Nicole.

'She looks like a traffic light,' whispered Eric, so Nicole pinched him harder.

She stood up to give Ruth a hug. 'Go and have a fantastic time and tell me all about it when you get back.'

Ruth smiled and swung an unsuitably large handbag over her shoulder, clipping Tommy's face as he entered the lounge.

'You're free, Willy!' waved Eric behind Ruth's back.

'Where's she heading?' asked Tommy, cringing.

'For disappointment,' replied Eric, and moved his arm to avoid Nicole's next pinch.

*

It took forty-five minutes for Ruth to traipse from Venice Beach to the Viceroy Hotel in Santa Monica.

At 1.30 p.m. the sun was at its harshest and she struggled with the rising heat as she walked along the boardwalk in heels that were twice as much hard work as her sneakers. Occasionally, she'd stop and rub her ankles where the skin began to chafe.

Ruth took a paper tissue from her handbag and mopped her wet brow, but as she put it back, one of the false fingernails she'd attached with Pritt Stick caught the clasp and fell somewhere in the sand. She hoped Zak wouldn't notice.

With her destination in sight, Ruth made her way up a slope towards Ocean Avenue and spotted the hotel. Once inside, the air conditioning was like manna from heaven. Muffled music came from behind the closed doors of the Cameo bar as a pianist played classical songs she didn't recognise. She turned her head to search for a restaurant called Cast, and smiled as she caught a glimpse of herself in one of the many framed mirrors behind the lobby's marble reception desk. She removed an email printout from her handbag and re-read it.

Sender: Zakstanleyfanclub@hotmail.au

Dear Ruth,

Just to confirm, Zak Stanley will meet you for lunch at 2 p.m. at Cast in the Viceroy Hotel, Santa Monica. A table has been booked in your name and Zak will be there to welcome you. He requests no photographs be taken during your meal. Zak looks forward to meeting you.

Yours,
Paul Mollegh, manager.

Ruth clutched the email to her chest and beamed, unaware the sweat from her dress had absorbed the paper's ink and left a light stain. She steeled herself, took deep, nervous breaths and strode towards the dining room's entrance.

The *maître d'*, accustomed to receiving guests of a certain calibre at Santa Monica's most prestigious of eateries, consulted a list of bookings and was surprised to find Ruth's name.

'You're the first of your party to arrive, Madam,' he began in a hybrid French/American accent.

'Oh, okay,' Ruth replied, checking her watch and realising she was a quarter of an hour early. 'I'm having lunch with Zak Stanley.' Her eyes lit up as she showed him the email.

'How lovely for you,' he replied, wondering if the movie star he'd seated two nights earlier was now involved in charity work.

Once he'd led her to a private dining booth overlooking the ocean, Ruth sat at her table, and when she thought nobody was looking, took an embossed napkin and mopped her armpits. Meanwhile, silent, derisive chuckles came from the waiters, tipped off by the *maître d'*, rubbernecking from the kitchen's porthole window.

A hundred times Ruth had attempted to rehearse what she'd say when Zak arrived, but right then, right there, her mind was a blank. She wanted to tell him she'd seen every one of the ten films he'd made since his transition from teen actor to Hollywood star. She wanted to explain how she'd used his picture from *About the Two of Us* as her phone screensaver before she dropped it in the toilet. She wanted him to know that she loved him for who he was and not because of his fame or his money. And how, if given a chance, she wanted them to be friends. In reality, she wanted far more than that, but that would happen in due time, she told herself.

Ruth practised her smile over and over again, readjusted her top, ordered a Diet Coke, and waited.

CHAPTER 28

'Hotdog and a lemonade, just one dollar,' began Tommy, talking through a white plastic megaphone.

Self-consciously he stood on an upturned plastic box by the boardwalk as passing tourists stared at him and the mobile food trailer behind him. Inside, José, the heavily tattooed and recently paroled chef, yawned and watched a film he'd downloaded on his mobile phone.

'Louder, I need you to be louder,' barked Mr Fiaca in his strong Cypriot accent, waving his short stubby arms from the side of his circular frame.

'Hotdog and a lemonade, just one dollar,' Tommy repeated, more forcefully. Quietly he cursed Peyk for getting him a trial on a fast food stand, even though he was desperate for work.

'No, no, no! Project your voice, and do the English accent more. We're not selling fast food; we're selling a lifestyle.'

'You're selling entrails in a bap,' Tommy muttered to himself and wondered what his brothers would have thought if they could have seen how low he'd stooped to make a living.

'Hotdog and a lemonade, just one dollar!' yelled Tommy, creating loud, grating microphone feedback.

'Yes!' said Mr Fiaca triumphantly. 'Your uniform is round the back.'

Tommy frowned. 'Uniform?'

Any remaining shred of dignity Tommy left had evaporated when, ten minutes later, he mounted his box, enclosed in a man-sized hotdog costume, complete with mustard coloured hat and bap-shaped booties.

'Hotdog and a lemonade, just one dollar,' he muttered, defeated so soon.

'Louder!' bellowed Mr Fiaca's voice from behind the counter.

The only words Tommy heard from Matty and Declan as they passed him were 'fecking' and 'eejit' as they doubled up in laughter.

CHAPTER 29

Ruth waited. And waited. And then waited some more.

When Zak was twenty minutes late, she blamed it on the heavy Friday lunchtime traffic as Santa Monica's natives headed out of town for the weekend. When her watch read 2.45 p.m., she began nibbling at the skin around her thumbs and told herself Zak was probably struggling to find a parking space.

Even after an hour and half, Ruth was still convinced Zak wouldn't let her down. But by 4.20 p.m., even the once-snooty waiters were beginning to gaze at her sympathetically, as she became the last remaining lunchtime customer in the restaurant.

'May I get you anything else, Madam?' the *maître d'* asked as Ruth stood up.

'No, thank you,' she replied, her voice wobbling, and she offered a less than convincing smile. She removed a $20 bill from her purse to pay for her drinks, but the *maître d'* shook his head and gave her her money back, holding her hand for a moment.

Ruth's face began to crumple so she took a deep breath, straightened the hem of her pinafore, and dropped her head to hide the tears rolling down her face.

CHAPTER 30

As night fell, the snoring emanating from the bunk above Tommy's bed went on unabated for what felt like an eternity.

He had no problem falling asleep to the sound of his roommates chatting, opening and closing doors or using the bathroom. But the constant repetition of the same sound, like a ticking alarm clock or a snorer, left him at the end of his tether.

He could have moved into a private room weeks earlier but he chose the company of strangers over complete silence because silent nights were no friend of Tommy's. They gave him time to think about his life, and more specifically, the past. And he'd had enough silence to last him a lifetime.

TWO YEARS EARLIER – NORTHAMPTON, ENGLAND

Tommy's parents sat on opposite sides of the room – his mother in an armchair and his father at the dining room table. Neither of them spoke.

His father scoured the table covered in 'deepest sympathy' cards and vases of flowers. His mother had yet to remove her hat, her greying curls hanging loosely over her ears. She remained transfixed by two Union Jack flags neatly folded on the coffee table, removed earlier that afternoon by crematorium staff after the purple curtains swathed the matching coffins. Her husband hadn't opened a button on his uniform.

Trays of sandwiches, clumps of torn tin foil and partially empty glasses were scattered across occasional tables, the carpet and fireplace. In the hallway, Tommy bade farewell to the wake's last few guests and shut the front door behind them. He rubbed at his eyes, still sore after endless days of tears. He leaned on the wall and readjusted his crutches, took a deep breath, and hobbled slowly back into the lounge.

'Everyone's gone,' he began.

Neither parent acknowledged his presence.

'The crematorium was packed,' Tommy continued. 'The vicar said they were lining up outside because there weren't enough seats.'

His mother and father remained silent, so Tommy made his way towards the fireplace, balanced on one crutch, and stretched his arm to pick up plates and a pint glass.

'I'll make a start on clearing some of this away then,' he mumbled, then grasped his other crutch and began to leave the room.

'Leave them,' said his mother.

'It's okay, I don't mind doing it.'

'You've done enough already,' she replied coldly.

'It's okay, I want to help.'

'That's not what I meant.'

'Fiona, don't,' his father interrupted.

'He knows what he did,' she muttered. 'He knows.'

Tommy felt the anger he'd bottled up for the last ten days since the car accident slowly begin to release.

'I know what? Come on, Mum, this is the most you've said to me all week. What do I know?'

His mother looked him in the eyes with a resentment he'd never seen in her before.

'It's because of *you* they're dead. Don't ever expect me to forget that.'

'It's not my fault!' Tommy pleaded. 'It was an accident. That car drove into us, me dropping my phone had nothing to do with it.'

'They weren't supposed to be at that junction, they were there because you talked them into it because you were too lazy to catch the bus.'

'But they offered to give me a lift—'

'No,' she shouted, and pointed a finger at him. 'You took advantage of the fact they'd do anything for you. You might not have been driving that other car but *you* killed them.'

It was the first time Tommy had heard either parent verbalise what he himself believed. His guilt and shame had been more crippling than his broken ankle and foot. Try as he might to believe otherwise, each time he thought of his brothers, the first picture that sprang to mind was of their bodies entwined in the car's wreckage. He wanted to reason with his mother but he had no words. Instead, he continued towards the kitchen with the dirty dishes in hand. But as his crutch caught the table leg, it knocked him off balance and the dishes landed on the Union Jack flags.

'No!' yelled his mother, leaping towards them to wipe off the spilt lager and sandwich crusts. 'You bloody idiot,' she screamed, her anger taking him by surprise.

As he began a stuttered apology, his mother lunged towards him and slapped him across the face and head with a windmill of flailing arms and hands. Tommy fell to the floor, one of his crutches smashing against his lip and cutting it. He tried to shield his face with his hands as she hit him over and over again before his father dragged her away. His mother collapsed into a sobbing heap on the floor, so his father carefully lifted her up, placed a supporting arm around her waist and helped her out of the room and up the staircase.

Tommy remained on the floor and rolled onto his side, trembling and silently grieving.

TODAY

The corridors were unusually silent as a yawning Tommy abandoned sleep and made his way to the lounge to watch some late-night television. The sudden appearance of Peyk carrying a large, sealed cardboard box startled him.

'Mate, what are you up to at this time of night?'

'Nothing you need to know about, Tommy-boy,' smiled Peyk as he walked towards room 23, hovering outside until Tommy was out of sight.

Behind the reception desk Sadie sat drawing a sugar skull on her forearm with a red felt-tip pen.

'What's in room 23?' Tommy asked. 'There's never a key for it.'

'It's a store room for Ron's stuff.'

'What does he keep hidden in there?'

Sadie started tapping her nose to say it was none of Tommy's business, then turned it around to flip him the finger.

*

The stale smell of beer on the cushions no longer bothered Tommy as he sprawled across the lounge sofa and watched an infomercial for a new juicing machine on the television.

From the corner of his eye he saw a man enter and throw himself into an armchair.

'Can't sleep either?' the man began in a British accent.

'Snorer,' replied Tommy.

'You or someone else?'

'Someone else.'

'Ah, the universal plague of hostels worldwide,' nodded the man, scooping his hair behind his head and tying it into a ponytail.

'Why do they always seem to choose my room?' continued Tommy.

'Have you tried the mattress kick?'

'Yep, didn't work.'

'How about smothering their face with a pillow?'

'Then it'll be just my luck my death row cellmate snores.'

'I'm Jake, by the way,' the man continued, and stretched out a hand. Anyone who first clapped eyes on Jake, male or female, straight or gay, would've been struck by his handsomeness, and Tommy was no exception. Jake's ponytail hung between his shoulder blades; his dark chocolate beard matched the colour of his eyes, which were framed by thick eyelashes.

His perfectly aligned teeth shone thanks to a deep tan that dulled a sleeve of monochrome tattoos poking out from under the cuff of his black jumper.

'I'm Tommy – good to meet you,' he replied, trying not to stare too hard. 'Have you just arrived?'

'I got in yesterday afternoon from New Zealand so my body clock's screwed. Is there anywhere round here I can grab a hot chocolate?'

'There's an all-night café further up Winward, about ten minutes from here.'

'Ah, cool. Do you fancy joining me? I mean, if you're not waiting to see a NASA-designed exercise machine to go with that juicer you seem pretty interested in?'

'Sure, I'll get the order number for that tomorrow.'

CHAPTER 31

There are many physical injuries a pole dancer risks on a day-to-day basis that no paying customer would ever consider or care about.

The most common ailments include pole burn to the performer's inner thighs; the metal pole pinching her skin, calloused hands, bruising from a mis-timed mount and cracked and torn fingernails. And there's also the embarrassing risk of accidentally breaking wind when engaging core muscles too vigorously.

After six and a half months of dancing for a living, Savannah had experienced most of those ailments. After each eight-hour shift at the Pink Pussycat Club, she moaned with relief once she unzipped her white PVC boots, pulled up her jogging bottoms and spread her toes out comfortably inside a pair of sneakers.

'Savvy, you going to join us for a beer?' asked Mindy, waiting alongside two other dancers who'd also finished their shifts.

'Can I take a rain check? I'm tired, so I'm gonna catch a cab home.'

'Jeez, you're no fun anymore,' replied Mindy, 'it's been weeks since we last hit Sunset.'

'I'm sorry, guys, next week maybe?'

'Okay, we'll hold you to that. Sleep well, baby girl.'

Savannah smiled as they made their way out of the changing room and through the club to the entrance, while Savannah opted for the rear exit to avoid any over-enthusiastic punters making clumsy, last-ditch attempts to woo her.

But as she walked towards 3rd Street Promenade's cab rank, she felt a hand press down heavy on her shoulder. She froze.

'My, my, Savannah; you're a hard girl to track down.'

CHAPTER 32

Declan waited by the side of the bath, listening to the pipes gurgle and splutter before lukewarm water finally dribbled from the shower nozzle.

He climbed under it while Matty stood by the sink using the last of his cheap, disposable razors that should've been thrown away weeks ago. Declan couldn't help but notice how thin Matty was beginning to look.

Ingrid and Anna, two Belgian women from the floor above them with whom they'd just spent an intimate evening, had just left their room.

'Where are we meeting the girls for breakfast?' asked Declan, waiting patiently for the water to wash the hand soap he'd used as shampoo from his hair.

'Starbucks at 9 a.m., and they're paying,' Matty replied with a grateful smile.

'Bring it on! Croissants, fresh orange juice, blueberry muffins and actual fruit instead of the usual fast food shite for us, then.'

'Did your bird ask anything about why we're here?'

'Yeah.'

'You didn't tell her, did you?'

Declan glanced at his friend with both eyebrows raised. 'Do you think I'm stupid?'

THIRTEEN MONTHS EARLIER – NAVAN, IRELAND

Since they'd first met at primary school some twenty-five years earlier, Matty and Declan had yet to run out of conversation.

They'd repeatedly bicker in the way best friends do about football, women, music and films or anything else that took their fancy. And because they could often predict what each other was about to argue, the result was always the same – neither would budge an inch or dare offer a potentially incorrect statistic for fear of giving the other the upper hand.

But as they began wandering through Navan's quiet market square, a nervous silence surrounded them.

Both knew what the other was thinking, but neither felt the need to discuss it further than they had already.

It had taken almost an hour and a half to get to the county town on two different buses from their home in Dundalk. But after three reconnaissance trips in the last ten days, they'd grown accustomed to the trek and they'd often ended the day watching international rugby matches on Sky Sports with the locals in the Central Navan bar. Not today, however, because today it was time to get down to business.

'Ready?' asked Declan, looking Matty firmly in the eye.

'Yep,' nodded Matty. 'Let's do it.'

Together, they reached into their jacket pockets, removed black woollen balaclavas and put them on.

Then they pulled pistols out from the dark blue duffel bags slung over their shoulders and opened the door to the post office.

CHAPTER 33

A shiver ran down Savannah's spine when she felt the hand on her shoulder.

She cursed herself for her complacency in leaving her revolver at the hostel; after the incident when she first arrived in the city five months earlier, which rapidly reshaped her plans from thereon in, she should have known better.

Then in the two months since her attempted abduction, Savannah had been on constant alert, scouring both the hostel and the Pink Pussycat's clientele for anyone who appeared to be paying her too much attention. She only ever left the club alone to hail a taxi back to the hostel; she no longer walked anywhere at night, and she dispensed with headphones when in public to help her remain alert.

A dark people carrier vehicle with blacked-out windows pulled up in front of her, and by the sound of multiple footsteps, she worked out there were at least three people standing behind her. She trembled as the hand on her shoulder guided her towards the vehicle and a man in dark glasses with an earpiece opened the door and ushered her inside.

A husky, middle-aged man in a grey, tailored suit followed, then removed his horn-rimmed glasses and pinched the bridge of his nose as the door closed.

Savannah swallowed hard before she spoke. 'How did he find me?'

Quietly she vowed she would scratch, scream, bite and kick until her last breath rather than allow his vehicle to move.

SEVEN MONTHS EARLIER – MONTGOMERY, ALABAMA

She didn't have time to avoid the open hand that slapped her hard across the face.

But its brute force and the element of surprise caused an unguarded Savannah to lose her footing and she fell against the display cabinet by the porch's entrance. She yelped as someone grabbed the back of her long, mousey coloured hair and pulled her to her feet, a handful of extensions falling onto the mahogany floorboards.

Savannah saw the hand rise again and she turned her head to

avoid it, but this time her ear received its force. It instantly rang from the pain and muffled the shouting coming from her attacker's mouth.

'You filthy whore!' screamed Reverend Devereaux, 'You goddam filthy whore.'

The last time she had witnessed her father's violence was when one of his cleaners accidentally dropped a valuable china figurine, shattering it. His immediate reaction was to slap the woman then fire her, knowing her illegal immigrant status meant she wouldn't dare report him to the police. He used his influence with the authorities to have her deported anyway.

The Reverend grabbed his eldest daughter and brought her face so close to his that she struggled to focus on him, but she was still aware of a darkness in his eyes she'd never seen before.

'How long has it been going on for?'

Instinctively Savannah knew he was referring to her relationship with Michael, but the attack and the realisation that somehow he had discovered her secret prevented her from thinking straight and thus talking her way out of the situation.

'What? . . . Daddy . . .' she stuttered.

'Don't even try to deny it! Pastor Jackson witnessed that black boy's hands all over you in a coffee shop. Allowing one of *them* to touch you, to be physical with you . . . how could you?'

'But—'

'Don't "but" me! Tell me how long.'

'Daddy, please . . . let me explain.'

Savannah's heart raced as quickly as the thoughts travelling through her head. She desperately attempted to cobble together a credible explanation for why she would have kissed a black man at all, let alone in public. She struggled to loosen herself from her father's grip but to no avail.

'He's lying,' was all she could think of to say. 'Pastor Jackson is making stuff up.'

'Pastor Jackson does not lie,' her father replied with conviction. 'Besides, he showed me the video recording he made on his phone.'

And with that, Savannah knew the game was up. She wasn't sure whom she loathed more, the snitching Pastor or the man who called himself her father.

'Have you let him screw you?' he raged. 'Has he been inside you?'

'Daddy—'

'Don't daddy me; you forfeited the right to call me your daddy the moment you were soiled by an animal. How long?'

Savannah didn't reply and sobbed instead. Her ear throbbed, her cheek smarted and she wanted to vomit. She shook her head and refused to reply. She was desperate to get in her car and call Michael because when she was in his arms, nothing could hurt her.

'Well if you're not going to tell me, then let's go visit someone who will, shall we?'

CHAPTER 34

TODAY

Ruth was hiding under a bus shelter when she spotted Tommy and Jake leaving the hostel.

While her head was still swimming with the events, or non-events, of the afternoon, she didn't want to even make eye contact with anyone she recognised from the hostel.

Upon leaving the restaurant, Ruth had spent hour upon hour parked on a bench in a small patch of greenery between the beach and the road, overlooking the bright swirling lights of Santa Monica pier. Her mind lurched from disappointment to anger and embarrassment, but none of it was aimed at Zak; all of it was towards herself for being foolish enough to believe she deserved to be happy.

After the sun set and the night crept in, a homeless man with two bin liners of soda cans slung over his shoulder cursed at her for sitting on his bed. So she left the bench and slowly made her way back to the hostel. The beach was too dark and unsafe to navigate by night, so Ruth chose the pavement by the road instead.

There wasn't enough noise from the passing traffic to muffle her despondent sobs, so she bit hard on her index finger to stem the flow of tears. With each step, her heels dug further into her flesh, so she tore them from her feet and threw them into a trashcan, barely feeling the grit of the sidewalk.

Aware her nose was running, Ruth reached inside her handbag for a tissue. Instead, she unwittingly pulled out the $20 bill the *maître d'* had returned to her. It was folded, but inside appeared to be another piece of paper.

'4765 Sunset Plaza Drive, Hollywood Hills – Zak's address', it read.

It took a few moments before Ruth realised the *maître d'*'s action had been the kindest thing anyone had ever done for her.

CHAPTER 35

Nicole was perched on the windowsill, willing a waft of cold air to blow into her musty dormitory room, when she saw Tommy leaving the hostel and crossing the road with someone she didn't recognise with a ponytail.

Her brows knitted as she reached for her mobile phone and turned it to camera mode, zooming in to see if she could get a better view of who was accompanying him.

'Who've you got your beady eye on, Miss Marple?' began Eric, his head peering over his top bunk.

'No one,' she replied defensively. 'Well, I was just trying to see who Tommy was going out with. It's a bit late.'

'I haven't seen him slobbering over you much today. I presume you've had a little tête-à-tête?'

'If you mean have I had a word with him, then yes, I've cooled it,' she lied.

'It's for the best, trust me. Besides, we're leaving in a couple of days; I'm sure that's probably your replacement he has lined up.'

Eric rolled back on his side and smiled, satisfied at having Nicole to himself again. 'And is there any chance you can clear your crap up from around the bed before rats start nesting in it?'

Nicole ignored him, even though she was aware there wasn't enough room by their bunk to swing a cat, let alone to leave all her clothes and belongings scattered.

With Tommy and his companion now out of sight, Nicole closed her eyes and quietly hovered in that space between consciousness and sleep, when the sound of a sleeping bag being unzipped caught her attention. In the gloom, she squinted to catch Ruth slipping her dress off and packing it away in her suitcase.

'Oh, hey Ruth, have you just got back?' Nicole whispered.

'Yeah, just now.'

'So? Don't keep me in suspense . . . How did it go? How was Zak?'

Ruth paused before offering an answer. 'Really, really great. I'm going back tomorrow because Zak's asked me if I wanted to spend the day at his house.'

'Did he?' replied Nicole, a little louder than she'd intended. 'Oh, wow, well, you must have made an impression on him.'

'I reckon so,' smiled Ruth before entering the bathroom with her pyjamas under her arm.

'Do you think it was the hair, the dress or the air of desperation that won him over?' sniped Eric from above.

'You have a streak of bitch in you a mile wide,' Nicole replied, as she considered whether she had got Ruth all wrong, and that maybe once you really got to know her, her personality was a lot more vivacious than on first impression.

Nicole slipped back under her sheet, shuffled around a little longer before leaning over the side of her bed and grasping for her suitcase. She partly pulled it out, unzipped it and removed a brown, oblong, cardboard box.

ELEVEN WEEKS EARLIER – LONDON

'I bought an *OK!* magazine and a *Guardian* to read to Mrs Baker during my lunch break,' smiled Nicole as she rushed past Eric and into the room behind the nurse's station. 'She likes the news but she loves a bit of celebrity gossip too.'

Eric followed her inside, watched as she unbuttoned her coat and waited for an opportunity to speak.

'Last night she said her eyes are still causing her problems so I'm going to ask Doctor Kotnis if he can take a look at them later.'

'Nic—' began Eric, but Nicole interrupted.

'I know what you're going to say, but Matron can't complain if I'm seeing her in my own time.'

'I'm sorry, Nic, Mrs Baker passed away earlier this morning,' Eric began gingerly. 'Doctor Stephens thinks it was probably her heart that gave out.'

Nicole's face dropped and she bit her bottom lip as Eric held her and kissed the top of her head.

'I tried to call you but your mobile was turned off.'

'Was she on her own when she . . .'

'I think so.'

Nicole shook her head. 'She'd have hated that.'

Before Eric could reply, Matron appeared and thrust a small brown Jiffy bag into Nicole's chest. Nicole looked at it – her name was written on the front.

'She left this for you in her drawer,' Matron began gruffly, as Eric eyed it up suspiciously. 'Now spare me the tears, nurse, you've lost patients before.'

'Mrs Baker was special to me,' replied Nicole.

'They all are. Now go and strip her bed, as you have work to do.' Matron grabbed a clipboard and began to walk away, but not before Nicole saw red.

'What is wrong with you?' Nicole asked angrily. 'When did you stop caring for people and become such a bitch?'

'Excuse me,' a surprised Matron replied, and turned slowly on her heels.

'You heard me. Why do you feel the necessity to be such a cow all the damn time?'

'Right, you are on report. In my office – now!'

'No,' Nicole replied firmly, and caught sight of Eric's aghast expression. 'Fuck you and fuck your job. You win, I'm out of here.'

Both Matron and Eric were speechless as Nicole grabbed her coat, stormed out of the room and out of the hospital.

*

Nicole opened the door of her flat and remained in the doorway, surveying her poky home.

She'd bought most of her furnishings on eBay, at IKEA or in end-of-line sales at Next. And with just a lounge/diner and galley kitchen leading towards a bedroom and bathroom, she hadn't spent much filling it up. She'd tried hard to make it feel like home, but it didn't, and it never would. It was a bridge between her past and an undisclosed future, but the thought of spending the rest of her life living alone in that box terrified her.

Matron couldn't understand Nicole's logic, but making time to talk and listen to a patient was equally as important as making sure they were clean and medicated. It was the human touch that attracted Nicole to nursing, and the inability to offer that was the reason she'd just quit. But quietly she worried whether she'd let her mother's memory down by making such an irrational, life-changing decision.

However, Mrs Baker's travel recollections had planted a seed in Nicole's mind that was quietly germinating. She allowed herself to imagine what it must feel like to live for the moment; to wake up and not have your day mapped out in front of you; to go where you pleased; to meet new people from all walks of life and to absorb sights most people only witness in TV documentaries. It was all just a fantasy, of course, because when Nicole thought about it, she knew she had no savings to do any of that.

So she slipped off her coat, closed the door behind her, blew a kiss to a photograph of a bare-chested Zak Stanley stuck to the fridge door and poured herself a glass of wine.

The next two pre-bedtime hours would be filled, as most evenings were, by a mixture of soap operas and reality TV recorded on her digibox.

Little did she know a forgotten Jiffy bag in her coat pocket would soon alter everything.

TODAY

Quietly in the darkness of the room, Nicole pulled back the Sellotape that held the lid of the cardboard box in place, and smiled as the metallic silver urn slipped out. She ran her fingers down its side and checked to make sure the lid was still secure.

'We'll find a home for you somewhere soon,' she whispered.

CHAPTER 36

Four empty mugs sat on the counter of the coffee bar as Tommy and Jake spent their second hour flopped in leather armchairs comparing notes on their travelling experiences.

The walls surrounding them offered a stark warning of what can happen when success and excess collide. They were covered in framed photographs of iconic actors and singers including River Phoenix, Marilyn Monroe, Janis Joplin, John Bonham, Dee Dee Ramone and John Belushi, who'd all descended on LA to find or revel in their fame and fortune but were spat out by the industry – and the world – at too early an age.

'And you've not heard from your mate Sean since then?' Jake asked.

'Nope. His mum says he's met some French girl and they've gone to Mexico, but I've not heard a thing from him. I keep checking my emails and Facebook but he's gone off radar.'

'Do you miss him?'

Tommy thought carefully about the question before he answered. 'I did at first, but you're never really alone when you're backpacking, are you? You're always meeting people in the same boat at you.'

'Yeah, you develop these intense relationships, trade life stories, then within a few days, you've gone off in your own separate directions.'

'Exactly! And then your name joins the list of a hundred others CC'd on a round-robin email, or you're reduced to a photo on Facebook and have to tag your own name because it's already been forgotten. You sound like you're an old hand at this.'

'Well, I've been living out of a rucksack for two years so far.'

'Wow, it's only been just over seven months for me. So what inspired you to start travelling?'

'Oh, you know, the usual,' replied Jake, vaguely. 'What about you?'

'Pretty much the same,' replied Tommy, unwilling to cast a dampener on what had turned out to be a pleasantly spontaneous middle-of-the-night.

EIGHT MONTHS EARLIER – NORTHAMPTON

'What the hell are you doing here?'

Sean stared wide-eyed at Tommy, who stood on his doorstep, dressed in his army green fatigues and with a large green rucksack attached to his back. As far as Sean was aware, his best friend had another fortnight left of his fourteen-week phase-one army training in Winchester before he was allowed to visit home.

'I've quit,' began Tommy, matter-of-factly.

'But you signed a contract – doesn't that mean you've gone AWOL?'

Tommy brushed off Sean's concerns. 'Can I come in?'

Sean ushered Tommy into the hallway, up the stairs and into his flat. Tommy unstrapped his backpack and it dropped to the floor with a heavy thump. He sank just as heavily into an armchair as Sean turned down the volume of a music channel on his satellite box.

'Mate, you're going to be in deep shit if you've run away,' continued Sean, pensively scratching the blonde stubble on his chin.

'I don't care, I had to leave.'

'Why? Were you getting bullied or something?'

'No, they were a really great bunch of lads, surprisingly, and even the officers are pretty cool once they stop shouting at you. But I just woke up this morning knowing I'd made a massive fucking mistake.'

'I told you this would happen,' replied Sean, emphasising the "told you" part of his response.

'Yeah, well, you were right.' Sean took no comfort in Tommy's admission and was more concerned by the ramifications of his friend's desertion.

'I'm supposed to give fourteen days' notice if I want to leave before three months, or my commanding officer can give me permission to leave.'

'And which one did you get?'

Tommy hung his head and glanced at his boots, still shining despite the seven-hour National Express bus journey and two-mile hike to Sean's.

'So you are AWOL, you bloody muppet! They're going to kill you.'

'Well let them try,' said Tommy defiantly. ''Cos I'm not going back. One of the last things Lee said to me was to make a decision and go with it and to stop wasting time. I was wasting time in the army and living in that house with my parents. I need to do something with my life.'

'I told you not to join, mate, I told you. I said you needed to go to counselling after the accident, not go to university and then drop out and then join the armed fucking forces. What you went through . . . . Jesus . . . I don't even know where I'd begin to learn to live with that. But you are not Daniel and you are not Lee, you're Tommy. You can't continue what they started because that's just not you, and running away and going to a place where they do your thinking for you isn't going to help.'

Tommy shrugged; when they'd had this conversation months earlier, he'd known Sean was right. But his desperation to win his parents' approval had blinded him. However, even when he'd left home for basic training, they failed to wave him off or show an ounce of pride like they had for his brothers.

'So what are you going to do now?' asked Sean.

'It's not what am *I* going to do, it's what are *we* going to do,' replied Tommy.

Sean grimaced. 'Am I going to like this?'

'You might. Do you fancy joining me on an adventure?' Tommy smiled and hoped his friend would agree. 'I've been reading this book,' he continued as he pulled out a copy of Alex Garland's *The Beach* from his backpack. 'Have you read it?'

'No, but I saw the film – Leonardo DiCaprio, yeah? Didn't turn out too great for him, did it?'

'Yes but you're missing the point. Whether he found paradise or hell, at least he was out there looking for something. All we're doing is killing time here, so let's go and find our own beach.'

'What, you want to go on a road trip to find a beach?'

'Well no, I don't mean an actual beach, but a metaphorical one. Let's just pack up our stuff and travel the world. I've got some savings and that accident compensation money burning a hole in my bank account, so what could go wrong?'

Plenty, thought Sean. And eventually, he was right.

CHAPTER 37

Savannah dug her false fingernails into the palm of her hand and felt them bend as she waited for the man to reply to her question.

'Is he in LA?' she asked, her voice beginning to crack.

'Who?' replied the man.

'My father. He knows I'm in LA and that's why you're here. To take me home.'

'I'm sorry but I have no idea who your father is or if he knows where you are.'

'Then who sent you?'

'I'm not the kind of man who can be "sent" anywhere, Savannah,' laughed the man. 'My name is Nicholas Van Lien. You may have heard mention of me from some of your work colleagues.'

Savannah nodded, and unclenched her balled fists. Mr Van Lien owned two of the largest gentlemen's clubs in Los Angeles, where only the cream of the stripping crop were invited to work.

'I'm opening a new club at the end of the year, in that building just there,' he continued, pointing towards an empty unit across the road. 'And I'd like you to be one of my hosts. I have seen how you work, how you interact with your customers, and you're the kind of pretty young thing who could do well in my employment. Plus there are . . . extracurricular benefits of working for me, as you may also have heard.'

Savannah was aware of how many young actresses had earned their first big break under his wing. Or just under him, period. His discreet clubs and parties in the Hollywood Hills were a honeypot for Hollywood executives who offered bit parts to aspiring starlets in exchange for their one-on-one company.

'I'm sorry, but no thank you,' replied Savannah.

'Compared to what your current employer offers, you're working for scraps. I can guarantee you a regular salary, plus much, much more.'

'It's not that I don't want to, I just can't.'

'Might I ask why?'

Savannah hesitated and contemplated telling him the truth. Instead, she chose to remain ambiguous. 'I have . . . plans . . . so it's impossible for me to commit to you. Thank you for the offer though, I appreciate it.'

'Take my card, think about it,' added Mr Van Lien. 'Now may I offer you a ride home?'

'I'm good, thank you,' replied Savannah. She accepted his card as the door slid open and she hurried to the sidewalk.

As Mr Van Lien's SUV pulled away, Savannah steadied herself against the wall and waited until her heartbeat slowed down to its regular pace.

TWO YEARS EARLIER – MONTGOMERY ALABAMA

Reverend Devereaux kept his sweating palms on Savannah's shoulders as he frog-marched her through the hallway and into the kitchen, where his astonished staff watched, too afraid to intervene.

Tears burned the raw, slapped skin on Savannah's face as her father pushed her out of the house, across the lawns where the plantations once lay, through the water sprinklers and towards a white-panelled workshop. He yanked opened the door and shoved her inside and, as she grew accustomed the gloom, she gasped when she spotted the whites of Michael's terrified eyes. He sat with his feet and arms bound together with plastic fasteners around a wooden garden chair; a cut above his right eye bled down his face and into his torn white T-shirt.

'Michael!' she whispered, before the Reverend cuffed her around the back of the head. Pastor Jackson and two of her father's burly security man flanked her boyfriend.

'You cry for this thing?' Reverend Devereaux asked her, scarcely believing what he was witnessing. 'You are actually shedding *tears* for this *thing*?'

'I love him!' she pleaded.

'He's nothing – look at him! A hundred years ago and he'd be castrated and hanging from a tree for what he has done to you.'

'But he loves me and he is a good man. Please believe me.'

'He has no prospects, none of his kin do.'

'He's not what you think – he's in medical school, he's going to be a surgeon.'

'I don't care if he's going to be the first black man on the moon, he is a black man, and black men have no place corrupting good Christian families. So let's see how the good doctor is going to put his hands to use after I perform my own procedure.'

In the blink of Michael's blood-soaked eye, the Reverend grabbed a wooden mallet from a workbench and smashed it against the back of Michael's hand. He screamed as the smiling Reverend repeated the action on his other hand, this time catching the base of four fingers too.

'No!' Savannah pleaded to deaf ears.

'Tell me you will never cross paths with this animal again and I will let him go while he still has his eyesight.'

Savannah attempted a reply but her throat was too dry to respond. She stared at her terrified boyfriend who was biting hard into his bottom lip to counteract the pain. Her mind raced – how could she promise never to see Michael again? But what choice did she have? She swallowed hard.

'I won't,' she whispered.

'You won't what?'

'I won't see him again.'

'Good,' replied the Reverend, then swung the mallet and caught Michael clean in the centre of his forehead. Savannah screamed Michael's name as he stared at her, his eyelids fluttering before snapping shut and his head falling forward.

A smile slowly crept across Reverend Devereaux's face as he turned towards his bodyguards.

'Get him out of here,' he barked. 'And lock her in her room.'

CHAPTER 38

TODAY

'My round – do you want another hot chocolate?' asked Jake, slipping his hand into his jeans pocket and pulling out a faded canvas wallet.

Tommy took a last gulp of his drink and shook his head.

'No, mate, I've got to be on the reception desk in about . . .' he looked at his watch, 'two hours. Shit! We've been here all night.'

'I know,' replied Jake, pointing at the window. 'It's getting light out there.'

They stood up and headed for the door, waving the waitress goodbye and leaving a tip on the counter.

'Are you coming back to the hostel?' asked Tommy.

'No, I think I'm going to sit on the beach and watch the sun rise. I've seen it come up from the northern, eastern and southern hemispheres, but never from this far west. There's nothing like a new sun in a new continent to start your day.'

'Next time I'll join you,' replied Tommy.

'I'll hold you to that. And thanks for the company, it was really nice chatting to you.'

Tommy squinted at Jake. 'You kind of remind me of someone, but I can't work out who.'

Jake flinched, but hid it, like he'd done on three previous occasions when people had said the same thing, before he trotted out the same rehearsed response.

'Ah, I've got a very generic face,' he said, smiling, and headed towards the beach.

'If that's generic, then I'm a horror story,' Tommy told himself, quietly flattered someone with such worldly experience and good looks would want to hang around with him.

CHAPTER 39

DAY FOUR

It took an hour and a half before the Metro bus dropped Ruth off on Sunset Boulevard.

From behind the dusty bus window she noticed road signs for places she'd seen on television like Beverly Hills and Hollywood, but while they were in touching distance, Ruth had no interest in seeing any of them first hand. Instead, the base of the Hollywood Hills was where she wanted to be.

Almost 22,000 people lived above her in the seven square miles between the boundaries of Crescent Heights and Griffin Park. But there was only one face Ruth was there to see.

With Elastoplasts attached to the back of her heels where the stilettos had blistered them, she began her steep climb up the sidewalk towards Sunset Plaza Drive. The higher you went, the larger the properties and estates became, as if they were competing to have the most expansive city view. And if you wanted the much sought-after views from downtown to the ocean, you needed deep pockets.

Ruth glanced at her watch; it was 8 a.m., and twenty-four hours ago she'd been preparing herself to meet Zak Stanley for lunch. She couldn't understand why Zak hadn't turned up, and when she checked her emails in the hostel before going to bed, there'd been no communication apologising for, or explaining, his absence. It didn't matter now, she decided, because this was going to be so much better. She was going to his home. *His actual home.* And that was so much more personal than a meal in a public restaurant could ever be.

Ruth could barely contain her excitement as she ascended the hillside, singing along to the soundtrack on her iPod of Zak's first romcom foray, *Getting the Girl*. She was aware of the early hour, but she reasoned there was no point in hanging around the hostel any longer than necessary. She guessed Hollywood stars probably didn't get out of bed until about midday, which would give her plenty of time to compose herself and think about what kind of things they could do together that day.

It took another half an hour and many gulps from her water bottle before she followed the directions the Google Maps app on her phone suggested to find the street containing Zak's Spanish-style property; a two-storey building that stood behind a whitewashed wall and wooden gates. She could clearly see blossoming trees and palm leaves clumped together in landscaped gardens. When the wind blew gently, she caught the waft of chlorine from a pool.

      Ruth placed her hand over her mouth but it was too late to muffle a feverish squeal.

CHAPTER 40

Tommy cursed his iPhone's alarm when it rang just two hours after his head hit the pillow.

He showered, changed into a clean T-shirt, shorts and his favourite Adidas trainers, left the dormitory and headed to the reception desk for the start of a five-hour shift. But he was already pining for the hour-long break between the hostel and his new job inside a hotdog costume directing grazing customers towards Mr Fiaca's fast-food trailer.

He stared enviously from the corridor window as the sun's rays shone upon the sidewalk, and wondered if Jake had enjoyed his first LA sunrise. Tommy caught himself smiling when he reflected on his evening. He'd enjoyed Jake's company very much, and since he and Sean had gone their separate ways, he missed having a male confidant. Although he'd made many acquaintances at the hostel, it was rare for him to come across people he could relax around enough to completely bond with. And then two potential friends came along within days of each other: Jake, who, while convivial and talkative about his travels, appeared reluctant to give much of himself away and Nicole, who was witty and attractive but held her cards just as close to her chest as Jake held his.

Tommy became distracted from his musings when he passed the kitchen and paused to watch Matty and Declan puzzling over what do with a 7-pound bag of pasta and twenty cheap cans of chopped tomatoes.

'Where should I stick this?' Matty asked his friend, pointing to the pasta.

'D'you really want me to answer that?' replied Declan, struggling to hook the can opener over the rim.

'Will you look at her!' whispered Matty, staring at two blonde women with Scandinavian accents rinsing their breakfast dishes in the sink.

'Hey, pretty ladies! Could you spare us a moment of your time?' asked Declan.

'What's up, guys?' asked Freja.

'Now what kind of accent is that? Dutch, Norwegian?' asked Matty.

'Swedish,' replied her friend Nina.

'Well you're a beautiful sight for tired Irish eyes. I'm Matty, and this is Declan.'

Tommy shook his head from outside as they took turns in kissing the girls' hands like they were royalty.

'Are you the new cooks?' asked Freja.

'Officially, yes, but unofficially, we're pretty feckin' useless,' said Declan. 'Do you by any chance know what to do with these?'

'You can't make spaghetti?' asked Nina, looking at Freja in mock disbelief.

'It's a Roman Catholic thing, we're not actually allowed under papal law.'

Nina whispered into Freja's ear. 'Okay, if we help you, what will we get in return?'

Matty and Declan looked at each other, then the girls, shrugged their shoulders and grinned. 'Anything you like.'

Tommy had only been at the reception desk for ten minutes when he learned what the girls had received for their kitchen assistance. Wearing just their trainers and aprons, bare-arsed Matty and Declan boisterously charged through reception whooping and hollering before running across the road and doing star jumps.

As the girls' laughter echoed through the open kitchen window above, Tommy scowled and turned up today's televised lecture from Reverend Devereaux. He considered calling to make a cash pledge if Rev Dev would ask The Man Above to rid the hostel of the Irish plague.

CHAPTER 41

Jake grunted as he completed his fourth set of chin-ups on the free-to-use exercise equipment by the beach, then felt the tape attaching his recent tattoo covering begin to tear.

He hitched up his vest and secured it back in place, before crossing his legs, hoisting himself up on metal parallel bars, and beginning a set of bicep dips.

A film of early morning smog had ruined his first West Coast sunrise, turning the sun's golden rays into a grey and purplish fog. But the pollution meant it wasn't too stifling for him as he worked up an early morning sweat.

He lowered himself back to the ground, tensed his arms and watched as the tattooed images from shoulders to wrists came to life. More than sixty hours in artists' chairs around the world had been worth it, he thought. His long hair, beard, muscular frame and gradual but deliberate loss of his northern accent had all helped to transform him into something unrecognisable from his former self.

Not even his most devoted fans would recognise who he once was.

THREE AND A HALF YEARS EARLIER – SHEPPERTON STUDIOS, LONDON

Stuart Reynolds stared into the mirror framed by white light bulbs as Megan placed short strands of his hair in straightening tongs.

His first coat of make-up had been applied after breakfast, then re-applied for dress rehearsals, followed by three more late-afternoon touch-ups and a final dusting an hour before the live shows were to be televised. Familiarity with the process meant he knew that by the end of the broadcast he would remain perspiration free, but his face would feel heavy, like it had been glued to a brick.

The make-up gave him sharper cheekbones and deeper dimples and his bleached-blonde hair was ruffled to make him look like he'd just got out of bed. The light bulbs reflected in his winter blue contact lenses and enhanced their sparkle. Although they looked prettier than the brown irises God gave him, he felt they were another part of him to add to the ever-growing list of fakery.

'Happy with it?' asked Megan, circumnavigating his head,

proud of her handiwork. Stuart nodded and smiled like he was supposed to, but even if he had disapproved, it would've fallen on deaf ears.

For ten consecutive Friday and Saturday nights, he, Gabriel, Josh, Dylan and Ethan had been performing established musicians' hits with their own R & B twist in front of eight million voting viewers at home. Separately, they were five attractive but unexceptional young men in their early to mid-twenties, but together they were a boy band created by TV show *Star People*, and its architect, Geri Garland.

Their song choices, outfits, choreography, hairstyling, rehearsal times, accommodation, fitness regimes, diets, interview techniques and Twitter accounts had all been decided for them by a panel of production company executives and a PR team, all hand-picked by Geri. Even their name, Lightning Strikes, had been chosen for them.

The rest of the band were scattered around their cramped dressing room, hunched over tablets and mobile phones, scrutinising what social media users were saying about their chances of winning that night's finale. From what Stuart had read on Twitter earlier that day, the consensus was that girl-next-door Rachael Molloy might just pip them to the post.

'Right, you're done,' said Megan, interrupting his thoughts as she doused Stuart's poker straight hair with a final coat of lacquer. 'Your turn, Josh.'

Stuart vacated his seat just as the door flew open and Geri marched in.

'Christ, it's a right bloody sausage fest in here,' she yelled in her south London accent as all eyes focused on her. Her dyed, flame-red, shoulder-length hair was given a side parting, and her plump, cosmetically enhanced breasts spilled from the top of her silver sequined dress. Geri sat firmly in her mid-forties, but the best surgery money could buy had shaved off a decade.

Geri revelled in her role as an intimidating presence. Her young male assistant dutifully followed her with an iPad under his arm and a headphone plugged into one ear. A different young man flanked Geri every time she appeared, noted Stuart, and he wondered if there was a pile of blood-drained bodies stacked up in her cellar.

'Are you boys ready to go out there and win this thing for Mama G?' she continued.

'Yes,' all five replied, too muted for Geri's taste.

'Well I hope you've got more in you than that when you get out on that stage, or you're fucked. Stuart, can I have a word?' It was a rhetorical question, so Stuart followed her into the corridor. She flicked her eyes at her assistant who scampered away like a scolded puppy.

'How are you doing then, handsome?' she asked softly, straightening the lapels of his jacket.

'If I'm honest, I'm shitting bricks, Geri,' Stuart replied.

'Well as long as you don't shit them on stage, you lot have got this wrapped up.'

'I hope so, but what if the other judges prefer Rachael? Won't it look a bit dodgy when you're the only one there bigging us up? And even Twitter says—'

'Oh Twitter, shitter,' Geri interrupted. 'The public don't know what they want till I tell them. And they don't give a damn what the other two judges think – I pay them to be there and make me look good. We've got through every week without a problem or a technical fault; just one more night and we're home free.'

Geri planted a lingering peck on Stuart's lips, and then wiped off the lipstick she'd left with her thumb and smiled. With the amount of fillers she'd had injected into her face, Stuart found it hard to tell if her smile was flirtatious or if she was having a mild stroke.

'Now get out there and make me proud,' she continued, then patted his left buttock and pushed him towards the dressing room. Stuart took a deep breath and rejoined his bandmates. He glanced around the room, hating that his future lay in the hands of a pantomime villain and four virtual strangers.

Through the open door, he spotted one of the show's young technicians walking past with arms full of microphones. Already fed up of his squeaky-clean look, Stuart wondered what it would be like to go back to his natural dark brown, wavy hair, grow a beard and get tattoos like the man in front of him had.

'Hold up a minute, Jake,' came a voice from behind the technician.

'I like that name,' thought Stuart.

CHAPTER 42

TODAY

Ruth removed her camera phone from her pocket, switched it to video mode, and started to closely examine the home of Zak Stanley through a two-inch by two-inch screen.

At the far end of the house, she could only just spot wide open doors with wrought iron railings surrounding a tiled balcony. She wondered if that was Zak's bedroom. And if his doors were open, he was probably awake already, she figured. Her eyes were drawn to an intercom with just one button. So she took a deep breath and lifted a trembling hand before pushing it. It didn't make a sound so she pushed it again until a whirring noise above her caught her attention. It was a video camera attached to a tree trunk and pointing at her. She looked up at it and smiled, before a woman's voice from the intercom made her jump.

'Yes?'

Ruth steadied herself before speaking. 'Hi, I've come to see Zak Stanley.'

The pause felt like a lifetime before the voice spoke again. 'And you are . . .?'

'Um, I won a competition to meet him but I think he must have been busy.' Ruth turned her head and smiled hopefully towards the camera.

'Mr Stanley doesn't see visitors without an appointment or an invitation.'

'Oh, but I had one yesterday. Can I make another one?'

'You will have to go through his publicist. Thank you.'

'Do you have a number?' Ruth asked, scrambling inside her bag for a pen and paper. 'Hello? Hello?'

The voice did not reply, and the camera continued to target her until she shuffled away.

CHAPTER 43

'If looks could kill,' began Nicole.

As the second of the week's hostel parties was in full flow, Nicole caught Tommy casting bitter glances towards Matty and Declan from the doorway.

'What do you mean?' Tommy asked sluggishly.

'Those Irish lads with the gift of the gab,' continued Nicole.

Matty and Declan sat with their arms around Freja and Nina on a sofa. Every so often, the girls threw their heads back and laughed at something amusing the boys whispered into their ears.

'But you've got to admit, their spag bol is pretty tasty,' added Nicole.

'I wouldn't know, I haven't tried it,' Tommy lied, having eaten his helping in his room so as not to give his nemeses any satisfaction. He took another swig from his plastic beer cup.

'Are you a bit drunk, Thomas?' Nicole smiled. Tommy ignored the question, but it was obvious from his squinting eyes and slightly slurred speech that he'd gone over his self-imposed three-pint limit. Every person he'd spoken to at the party had thrust a fresh drink into his hand and it seemed rude to refuse them. He rolled his eyes when Nina removed some dollar bills from inside her cut-off jeans and handed them to Declan.

'Unbelievable,' Tommy muttered.

'What is?'

'Am I the only one who can see through them?' he continued, louder than necessary. 'They're chancers!'

'They seem sweet, and turn your volume down.'

'They've been here all of two days and they think they're the dogs' bollocks.'

'Aw, are they pushing little Tommy's nose out of joint?' Nicole teased.

'No, I just don't like their attitude.'

'Oh, be quiet, grandad. They're having fun – do you remember how to do that?' Tommy stared Nicole in the eye and tried to focus on her.

'Yes, I remember how to have fun, and I remember how to do this as well,' he began, then closed his eyes and leaned in to kiss her. However, Nicole swiftly moved her head and the only thing Tommy's lips collided with was the wall.

From behind the pool table in the corner of the room, Jake winced.

'I think you've had a few too many,' said Nicole. 'Why don't you go and have a lie down for a bit?'

A muddled Tommy nodded and shuffled away, red-faced, and couldn't help but notice Matty and Declan laughing at what they'd just seen.

CHAPTER 44

Savannah focused on her reflection in the bathroom mirror and adjusted her hairpiece so her fringe sat straight.

The figure sitting silently on a stool behind the two-way mirror edged his face towards Savannah's when she moved closer to apply colour to her lips. Inches apart, he mimicked her movements; blinking when Savannah blinked, pouting when she pouted and ruffling his hair when she ruffled hers. It was only when she threw her handbag over her shoulder and walked towards her bedroom door that he pulled his trousers up.

But as Savannah turned the handle, she felt the locking mechanism snap and watched the knob fall to the floor. She tried to re-insert it but to no avail, and then jabbed her fingers in the hole to see if that might unlock the door.

When that attempt also failed, she felt the adrenaline course through her veins as she dropped to her knees.

SIX AND A HALF MONTHS EARLIER – MONTGOMERY, ALABAMA

The fortnight Savannah spent locked in her bedroom felt endless.

The only contact she was allowed with another person was when one of the kitchen staff unlocked her door, passed her a food tray with an apologetic glance, and then closed it again. Three times a day this happened, and not a word was spoken by the prisoner or the prison cook. For the first few days, Savannah refused to touch her meals, hoping that by starving herself, her father would be forced to release her. But when each rejected tray made no difference, she succumbed to hunger and hated herself with each mouthful she took.

With no cell phone or Internet to contact the outside world for help, Savannah passed her days flicking through television channels, watching endless *Kardashians* and *Real Housewives* re-runs, home renovation shows and music videos.

She'd peer through the locked glass balcony doors and down the half-mile driveway that led to a world away from the one she detested. Her sister Roseanna had tried to visit but was ushered out of the corridor by their father's staff. Occasionally Savannah spotted her in the garden playing frisbee with the dogs and chasing them through the lawn sprinklers. She'd look up at Savannah with a shared sadness.

Sometimes Savannah glanced into her en-suite bathroom mirror to reassess the swelling and bruising to her face, and at night when she was enveloped in complete silence, she hoped the ringing in her ear from her father's fist might eventually subside.

The worst aspect of Savannah's incarceration was the time she'd been given to worry about Michael. She was frightened about what had become of him; the most positive aftermath was that following his attack, he'd been dumped outside his college apartment with a threat to keep quiet about his injuries or face further consequences. Few would believe his version of events over those of a respected television evangelist, and the only witness was locked away in her bedroom like a character from a fairy tale.

She was afraid that her first and only love now hated her for what she'd put him through. The swift and cruel end of their relationship meant hands that were supposed to guide his career and heal the helpless were no longer fit for purpose. And the well she siphoned money from to pay for his tuition had also run dry, leaving him with nothing. She'd ruined his life simply by loving him.

The worst-case scenario for Michael's fate . . . well, Savannah couldn't bear to think of that.

By the tenth day of her incarceration, Savannah briefly contemplated suicide as her only means of escape. But the moment she accepted she had nothing to lose by dying, was also the moment she decided she had nothing to lose by doing her damndest to escape.

And by day fifteen, she knew exactly how she was going to do it.

TODAY

'Pull yourself together girl,' Savannah said aloud, and replaced her short, shallow gasps with deep, drawn-out breaths. Eventually she got to her feet and made her way to the bathroom to find a nail file she kept in her make-up bag that she hoped to unpick the lock with.

Suddenly she heard a click at the door and when she returned to it, it was slightly ajar. She opened it fully and scanned the corridor up and down, but it was empty.

CHAPTER 45

DAY FIVE

Four days had passed since Tommy last checked his emails, and again, there was nothing from Sean in his inbox.

Tommy sat back in his chair with his arms folded, hoping the paracetamol he'd taken earlier would soon rid him of his hangover. He remembered bits and pieces from the night before, in particular, crashing and burning in his second stab at kissing Nicole. And he vowed not to make a fool of himself again with an older woman who obviously didn't take him seriously.

Suddenly, a small brown paper bag fell from above and onto his lap.

'That's just to say thanks for the company the other night; I really appreciated it,' Jake's voice began. Tommy opened the bag and found a box of brightly coloured foam earplugs. 'They should put an end to sleepless nights with snorers and coffee with jet-lagged strangers,' Jake continued.

'Thanks, mate, but you didn't need to,' Tommy replied, appreciative of the gesture, 'although they'll come in handy.'

'You got much on today?'

'Nope, I have a day off from both the hostel and the hotdog stand. Why, have you got something in mind?'

*

The bridge of Tommy's nose throbbed where Jake had headbutted him.

But neither could stop themselves from laughing after crashing onto the concrete boardwalk by the beach. They'd hired their inline skates from a store and clumsily rolled their way only a couple of hundred metres along from Venice Beach to Santa Monica before colliding and crumpling into a heap.

'I thought you said you could skate?' began Tommy, rubbing his nose and struggling to get back on his feet without something solid to hold on to.

'Does the blood pouring down my leg look like it belongs to someone who can skate?' replied Jake. 'It's lucky I'm like a cat with eight lives.'

'What happened to the ninth?'

'Oh, I lost that a long time ago. Shall we ditch these things and walk instead?'

'Good idea.'

Jake and Tommy yanked the Velcro straps from their skates, slung them over their shoulders and walked barefoot on the beach by the side of the boardwalk.

'I didn't see you at the party last night,' continued Tommy. 'Didn't you fancy it?'

'I was there, but I didn't want to interrupt you while you were laying your moves on that girl.'

'Ah, so you saw me get blown out then,' replied Tommy, a little surprised that he didn't feel that embarrassed in front of someone who probably had girls falling at his feet.

'It happens to the best of us,' Jake replied, and patted his new friend on the shoulder. 'Onwards and upwards, right?'

'If you tell me there's plenty more fish in the sea, I'm going to kill you.'

'That depends on how big your bait is and where you dangle it.'

CHAPTER 46

'What do you think of this?' asked Eric, and carefully placed a panama hat on his head, careful not to misplace his fussily waxed hair.

Nicole wasn't listening. Instead her eyes were focused on Tommy and a person she vaguely recognised from the hostel, as they fell into each other and then to the ground. It was only when she spotted the ponytail that she realised it was probably the same person Tommy had left the hostel with so late two nights earlier.

'Has your toy boy found a new friend to play with already?' Eric teased, following her line of sight. Nicole elbowed him in the ribs.

'He's prettier than you, I'll give him that,' Eric continued, 'but his beard isn't as long as yours.'

'One hair!' Nicole replied defensively. 'You found one hair on my chin a year ago and you're still taking the piss about it.'

'Ah, but that's how it starts; first it's one innocuous little strand poking out of your chinny chin chin, and the next thing you know, you wake up looking like Dumbledore's brother.'

'You're such an arse.'

'And you love me for it.'

Eric removed the hat and placed it back on the head of the dummy, satisfied that Tommy had found someone else to sniff around. Because he needed Nicole's undivided attention.

ELEVEN WEEKS EARLIER – BELGRAVIA, LONDON

'What do you think is inside it?' began Nicole.

Her voice echoed around an airy room housing hundreds of stainless steel safety deposit boxes of varying sizes, all stored on shiny metal shelves. Security cameras covered every square inch of the room. Eric glanced at the key in Nicole's hand and shrugged.

'So what now?'

'Let's see what's inside the box before I make that decision, shall we?'

The Jiffy bag Mrs Baker had left for her had completely escaped Nicole's mind. She'd been slumped on her sofa deciding that now she was jobless, she'd spend the rest of her life surrounded by cats, streaming classic Brit flick romcoms on Netflix and waiting for her Tommy Castle, William Thacker or Mark Darcy to appear on her doorstep and sweep her off her feet. Instead, she had Eric brandishing a sympathetic ear, a bottle of Prosecco and a slab of something delicious from Hotel Chocolat.

Later that night, he reminded her of Mrs Baker's Jiffy bag, and together, they tore it open and frowned at the contents – an address for Safe Securities, Belgravia, London, and a key with an engraved number. The following morning, the hungover pair caught a tube into central London, pressed a buzzer in a discreet doorway and, after proving her identity with a driver's licence and credit card, Nicole was surprised to learn a safety deposit box had been registered in her name. A staff member in a smart suit ushered Nicole towards box number 23 and pulled out a key of his own.

Together they inserted them in two locks, turning them in unison before the man removed a foot-long container, placed it on a table, and left Eric and Nicole to open it alone.

'Something tells me Mrs Baker's death could mean a new start,' whispered Nicole.

'Not for her it isn't.'

'I meant for me, idiot. I have a gut feeling there's something in this box that's going to change everything.'

Nicole lifted the lid, and once they saw what was inside, they frowned.

CHAPTER 47

TODAY

Once the early morning smog lifted, the horizontal wooden floor planks of Santa Monica pier became red hot to the touch under the midday sun.

So with their skates still hanging from their shoulders, Tommy and Jake tiptoed barefoot down the concrete road ramp and towards the shadows cast by the shops and railings.

Tommy had never ventured onto the pier before, for the same reason he'd yet to catch a bus up to Malibu or hike to the Hollywood sign – there was a fine line between being a tourist and being a traveller.

They glanced up at the arc-shaped entrance sign and wandered slowly past the amusement arcades, aquarium, pub, restaurants and trapeze school. Tommy raised his digital camcorder to record familiar landmarks he'd seen in films like *Hancock*, *Iron Man*, *Not Another Teen Movie* and, embarrassingly, *Hannah Montana: The Movie*.

He pointed it upwards to capture the red and yellow cars moving clockwise on the Ferris wheel as he and Jake continued to absorb the fishy and candyfloss smells until they reached the end of the pier. They found space between a dozen or so fishermen whose rods, perched against the rusty blue railings, dangled into the ocean below. Together they stood in a comfortable silence, staring across the ocean and towards the horizon, each enjoying their day.

Tommy closed his eyes and inhaled the salty scent in the air, while Jake contemplated how many more oceans he might need to cross until he finally found himself a home and complete anonymity.

TWO YEARS EARLIER – LONDON

The frenzied cheering started before Lightning Strikes reached the climax of 'Unchained Melody'.

Geri Garland was the only judge to join the audience on their feet, and applauded with her arms stretched high above her head. Clearly proud of their performance, Stuart and his bandmates hugged and frantically bounced up and down before being joined by *Star People*'s affable presenter, Tracy Fenton.

'Well done, guys,' she enthused. 'Let's go to Rocky Rhodes first – your verdict, please.'

Behind a brightly illuminated TV studio desk, aging record boss Rocky's body language announced his opinion before he spoke. 'Gentlemen, I'll be honest with you,' he began with folded arms, 'I didn't think that was your best performance and I don't know if it's good enough for you to win.'

However, the jeering audience drowned out any of his scripted follow-up comments, good or bad. Geri stood up again, and, ensuring the camera was focused on her, gave him two thumbs down.

'And James Nicholson, you've had number ones around the world with your band Driver,' continued Tracy. 'Do Lightning Strikes have what it takes to do the same?'

James shook his head and ran his fingers through his hair. 'I thought it was very average, Tracy. For the final song of this competition, I expected more. I think Rachael might have nailed it.'

'Finally – Geri Garland.'

'Well,' began Geri, looking from side to side at her fellow panellists. 'I think you two need your bloody ears testing, because that was brilliant!' she began, and paused until the audience's roar of approval began to die down. 'Boys, that's an old classic, but you brought passion to the song, you made it your own and there will be an injustice tonight if you don't win.'

'Twitter, shitter,' thought Stuart, and behind his back crossed his fingers as a floor manager ushered their fellow finalist Rachael into position next to the band.

Then Stuart held his breath and didn't exhale for the next eighteen months.

CHAPTER 48

TODAY

Nicole and Eric tucked into their polystyrene takeaway boxes of burritos and salad that they'd carried back to the hostel kitchen from the beachfront.

The more Nicole considered it, the more envious she felt that Tommy had found someone new to occupy his time. It wasn't that she didn't want to kiss him during his previous evening's failed pass, but she was too old for a first kiss fuelled by alcohol and in the most unromantic of circumstances. Besides, she didn't want any animosity between her and Eric, so she made a decision not to reciprocate Tommy's clumsy advances.

'Hi, Ruth,' Nicole shouted when she saw the hostel's quietest resident pass by in the corridor. 'How was your day at Zak's house?'

'It was fantastic,' replied Ruth without hesitation. 'He has this great big house and a great big garden and we ate caviar and we drank wine – the posh red stuff that costs tons – and we sat by his pool all day.'

Nicole didn't need to see Eric's expression to know that he didn't believe a word of it either. But as Ruth's fantasy caused no harm, Nicole played along with it. Eric had other ideas.

'What did you talk about?' he asked.

'All kinds of things, really. You know.'

'Like?'

'His films,' stuttered Ruth, 'His life. And . . . um . . . stuff.'

'Oh wow, now I'm really jealous!' interrupted Nicole, aware Eric was trying to catch her out.

'I'm going back tomorrow,' continued Ruth. 'Zak said we could watch some of his films and then I could go see him make a movie. Zak said he might get me a part.'

Ruth grinned and then headed back to her room, and Eric stifled a chuckle.

'Go on, get it off your chest. I can almost smell the evil about to come out of your mouth.'

'Exactly what part is Zak Stanley going to get her in a film?' laughed Eric. 'Australian Werewolf in Hollywood?'

'I really don't know why I'm friends with you.'

'Come on, Nic, look at her. One of the most famous guys in the world decides he wants Ugly Betty as his best mate? I don't believe a word of it.'

'Well she seems pretty convinced, so what does it matter? And maybe Zak's fed up of Hollywood bimbos and wants to meet someone normal.'

'I bet you anything she's spent the day sitting in a park talking to herself.'

Nicole shook her head, reluctant to concede Eric was probably right. 'I bet you $20 that she's at his house tomorrow like she says she is.'

'Deal,' replied Eric, and shook Nicole's outstretched hand. 'How are you going to prove it?'

CHAPTER 49

Declan wiped his backside with the last remaining sheets of paper on the roll and flushed the toilet.

Although he'd been in the bathroom for just ten minutes, he'd kept the door slightly ajar so as to keep an eye on Matty in the bedroom. His friend lay on his side on the bed reading a dog-eared European copy of *FHM* that he'd picked up in the dining room, completely aware of his best friend's beady eyes. The furthest they were ever apart was a partially open door – one of several unspoken rules between them.

'Did you call your mammy?' asked Declan, drying his hands on his T-shirt.

'Yeah, she sends her love.'

'Is she okay?'

'The usual, a bit tearful . . . you know what she's like.'

'And you?' Declan replied hesitantly.

'I'm good.'

'You know we can go back if you change your mind, don't you? I'll go with you, you won't be on your own.'

'Yeah, I know, but I also know what'll happen if we do.'

THIRTEEN MONTHS EARLIER – NAVAN, IRELAND

Mr John Wallace was proud to have held the title of Navan's postmaster for the last thirty-six years. To take the pressure off his arthritic ankle, he leaned against the counter as he weighed Mrs Flynn's parcel. He approved of her traditional use of brown wrapping paper and string to hold it together firmly, rather than cramming it into a padded envelope and reinforcing it with sticky tape.

It was the sudden hollering that startled him more than the sight of two figures wearing balaclavas, brandishing handguns and standing by his open door. Mr Wallace had survived six post office robberies to date unscathed, and he was confident number seven wouldn't be any different.

He'd learned from experience that the modus operandi rarely varied: remove all the notes from the safe and the till, place them inside the bags the raiders always brought with them as quickly possible, and once they left, phone the *gardaí*.

Four weeks later he'd be reimbursed by the powers that be.

'This is a stick-up,' shouted Matty, failing to control his trembling voice. 'Do what we say and nobody gets hurt.'

Mr Wallace chuckled to himself, wondering if all armed robbers read from the same handbook.

'This is a stick-up?' Declan asked his friend quietly. 'Who the feck says that these days?'

'Well, in case you've forgotten, this is my first robbery – have you got something better?' whispered Matty through gritted teeth.

Declan shrugged so Matty continued. 'Any of you fucking pricks move, and I'll execute every motherfucking last one of you.'

Declan rolled his eyes. 'Really? You're going to start quoting *Pulp Fiction* now?'

Matty's empty threat was greeted by a collective disapproving sigh from the handful of elderly customers waiting in line to be served. Matty and Declan glanced at each other, puzzled; they'd expected to be feared, not groaned at.

'Is there any need for that kind of language in front of ladies?' asked Mr Wallace, evidently offended.

'Sorry,' replied Matty, before Declan landed a sharp elbow in his ribs.

'What was that for?'

'Why are you apologising?'

''Cos I upset the old fella.'

'Less of the old,' interrupted Mr Wallace.

'Little gobshites,' added Mrs Norton, grasping her walking frame and tartan shopping bag. 'It's bad enough you have to rob a post office but to come in and call us . . . what was it again?'

'Pricks,' replied her friend, shaking her head.

'Pricks? The mouthy bastards! Shame on you both.'

'Ladies and gentlemen, you're missing the point,' began a rapidly exasperated Declan. 'We're here to rob the place, not to make friends.'

'Well that's a blessing, because with that language, you're not going to make any fecking friends in here.'

'Give me your money, everything you've got,' continued Declan, reasserting his authority, until it was Matty's turn to elbow Declan. 'Please,' he added reluctantly.

To a chorus of further disapproval, Declan used his gun to usher the customers towards the wall, while Matty headed towards Mr Wallace. Matty lobbed their two duffel bags over the thick

Perspex counter screens, and Mr Wallace complied, stuffing them with euros before throwing the first bag back towards him. He wondered why the postmaster didn't look more concerned.

'It's a shame you didn't come yesterday,' Mr Wallace casually added, 'Tuesday is pension day, and you'd have got away with a lot more.'

'Dec, d'you hear that? We should have come yesterday,' said Matty, lifting the bag from the floor.

'Don't use my name, you eejit!' snapped Declan.

'Will you be wanting the coins too, Dec?' added an amused Mr Wallace.

'Jaysis! No, just the notes, thank you.'

As Mr Wallace hurled the second bag over his booth, he couldn't help but notice the barrel of Matty's gun was solid. He'd been eye-to-eye with enough barrels to spot the difference between a real gun and a fake.

'Well it was nice to meet you all,' added Matty, as he and Declan slung the bags over their shoulders. 'And sorry about all of this.'

'Ah, don't you worry yourselves, lads,' smiled Mr Wallace, now the holder of the divisional record of most robbed post office in the Republic. His wife was always proud when his picture made the local newspaper.

As Declan opened the post office door, Matty grabbed a handful of euros and dropped them inside Mrs Norton's shopping bag, offering her an apologetic shrug.

'Sorry for the bad language,' he added, before he and Declan bolted out of the door and through the town.

'Ah, what nice lads,' said Mrs Norton, swiftly changing her tune once she calculated how many Lotto scratch cards she could buy with her windfall.

Suddenly her attention was drawn to Mr Wallace's peculiar gasping sounds and she turned her head to watch him fall to the floor, clutching his chest.

CHAPTER 50

TODAY

'Where's this?' asked Tommy, as he swiped his way from right to left on Jake's mobile phone.

'This is a wind farm I worked on in White Hill, New Zealand, set in 24 square kilometres of land at the bottom of a hill.'

Tommy and Jake sat under the shade of a lifeguard tower, drinking bottles of beer – strictly prohibited on the beach – hidden in brown paper bags.

'And this?' Tommy continued.

'That's the Lumbini Buddhist pilgrimage on the India-Nepal border.'

'How did you end up there?'

'I was in New Delhi having a coffee enema . . .'

'. . . as you do . . .'

'. . . as you do, and I got chatting to the woman who was shoving the pipe up my arse. When you're naked, flat on your back, cupping your balls with a stranger holding your legs in the air, polite chit-chat's a good way of stopping yourself from farting five litres of Nescafé in her face. Anyway, she told me about this town supposedly being the birthplace of Buddha, so I ended up there teaching English to the local kids.'

'It looks beautiful.'

'Yeah, it is. But the enema was a waste of time 'cos I got chronic dysentery and had to leave after a month. Then it was over to Thailand, Vietnam, Singapore, Australia and New Zealand.'

'How long do you stay in each place?'

'It depends. I travel by three rules – never outstay your welcome; leave when no one's looking and always leave them wanting more.'

'So I should expect you to disappear when I'm not looking?'

'It depends on whether there's something worth staying here for.'

Tommy glanced up and down Jake's two tattoo sleeves, which appeared to be inspired by religious iconography. The lines of numbers running from just below Jake's armpit and down the side of his ribs caught his attention.

'What are they all about?'

'They're the map of my journey from the start to here,' Jake replied. 'Every time a place makes an impact on me, I get a tattoo of the coordinates.'

'So you're like a six foot tall Ordnance Survey map.'

'I guess you can say that,' Jake chuckled.

'And what about that?' Tommy continued, and pointed to a number 23 etched on the skin between Jake's thumb and forefinger.

'It's my lucky number. Or unlucky, depending on your way of thinking.' Tommy frowned. 'Google it,' added Jake.

Suddenly a blonde-haired girl in a one-piece red swimsuit caught Tommy's eye; her resemblance from afar to Pamela Anderson made him do a double take. He recalled fondly the first porn film his brothers had shown him when he was in his early teens – a sex tape involving Pamela Anderson and an intimidatingly well-endowed ex-husband.

'I met Pam backstage once,' began Jake without thinking, and then immediately shut his eyes and cursed his careless tongue.

'You did what? No way! Did you speak to her?'

'For a bit.'

'And?'

'And what?'

'And what was she like?'

'Yeah, she was . . . nice.'

'Backstage where?'

'Something an old friend was working on.'

Tommy waited for Jake to expand on his answer, or at least offer an anecdote, but neither was forthcoming.

'Don't give much away, do you?' Tommy continued, growing ever more curious and fascinated by his new friend. 'I thought us travellers were supposed to share our life stories?'

Jake smiled. 'Always leave them wanting more, Tommy.'

CHAPTER 51

DAY SIX

Eric prayed their pick-up truck hadn't been towed away or ticketed by a meter maid as he and Nicole returned to the street where they'd parked.

Earlier that morning, they'd decided to delay planning the next stage of their mission which had so far resulted in frustrated dead end after dead end. Instead, they took their minds off their failed journey with a competition to see if Ruth had been telling the truth about her friendship with Zak Stanley. They'd followed a bus from Santa Monica for over an hour and watched from a safe distance as it dropped Ruth off in Melrose, where she then waited for another ride. They followed that bus for a further thirty minutes before she alighted at the foot of the Hollywood Hills. Nicole jumped out of the truck and made a beeline towards the convenience store Ruth entered, crouching out of sight behind a postal van while Eric parked and ran to join her. They couldn't help but laugh at the absurdity of their actions.

When the convenience store door buzzed, Ruth appeared with a bulging plastic bag and began her familiar traipse up the Hollywood Hills. Eric and Nicole waited at a safe distance before they followed. However, twenty minutes into what felt like a vertical walk, they were breathless and their target was nowhere to be seen.

'Bollocks, we've lost her,' said Eric, craning his neck to look around the intersection for signs of Ruth.

'Shhh,' whispered Nicole, 'she can't be that far ahead, and I don't want her to hear us.'

'She'll be too busy listening to the voices in her head to know we're here.'

'Let's just keep going upwards – I read somewhere the higher you go in the hills, the bigger the houses are. And she seemed to know where she was heading so she's clearly been here before.'

Eric felt the sweat beginning to trickle from his neck, down his back and under the waistband of his boxer shorts. What had seemed like a fun wager was fast becoming a chore, and he was prepared to hand over his $20 bet to Nicole even though he knew Ruth stood more of a chance of joining the royal family than becoming Zak Stanley's BFF.

They turned their heads when they heard a vehicle behind them and saw a minibus crammed with tourists driving at a snail's pace up the hill. Through the windows, they could hear a tour guide over a Tannoy.

'And further up this avenue is where we find the three Zee's,' came a chirpy female voice. 'We call it that because this is where Zac Efron, Zach Galifianakis and Zak Stanley live.'

'Bingo,' smiled Nicole, beginning to jog to keep up with the bus. 'We're making a habit of turning up at strangers' houses, aren't we?'

ELEVEN WEEKS EARLIER – HOLLY COTTAGE, GREAT HOUGHTON, NORTHAMPTON, ENGLAND

The ancient white painted walls and thatched roof resembled someone's idea of what a cottage should look like and not something that actually existed, thought Nicole as she and Eric opened the wooden gate and made their way up a crazy-paving pathway towards the front door.

As their taxi pulled away, Nicole recalled it had been a long time since she had taken a day trip out of London. She'd forgotten not everywhere smelled of exhaust fumes and ambition.

Mrs Baker's garden was colourful, pretty and very neatly kept. The flowers and shrubs in the borders were spaced symmetrically, the expansive lawns were the greenest things Nicole had ever seen, and the only thing to look remotely twenty-first century was a set of cubed wooden furniture sheltered under a large cream parasol.

Nicole examined the key in her hand and the address attached to the fob – it hadn't been what either of them had expected to find when they'd lifted the lid of the safety deposit box.

'Do you think your fairy godmother has left you the keys to the castle?' asked Eric.

Nicole shook her head. 'I doubt it, but someone's been here recently because the lawn's been cut.'

Nicole looked at Eric pensively and then knocked on the door.

'What are you going to say if someone answers?' he asked.
'"A dead woman left me a key and your address – do you mind if we have a nose around?"'

When there was no answer, Nicole inserted the key into the

door's lock. But before she could turn it, a surly woman with short, curly hair and a masculine air about her swung open the door and looked them up and down.

'Oh, sorry, we didn't think anyone was in,' Nicole began. The woman didn't reply. 'My name is Nicole Grainger and this is my friend—'

'I know why you're here,' the woman interrupted, and stepped back into the house leaving the door open.

Nicole and Eric glanced at each other, unsure of how to respond. Nicole pulled the key out of the lock and followed her into an immaculately furnished lounge.

'Wait here,' the woman ordered, and left the room.

'I think that's Maria, her housekeeper,' whispered Nicole. 'I saw her visiting Mrs Baker a couple of times.'

They scoured the room. Photographs in ornate frames covered a piano and two occasional tables, and above a large open fire was a shelf tightly packed with books. Nicole noted most were either travel guides or collections of images from around the world. She moved on to the photographs, some black and white, some colour, of Mrs Baker and her husband, and her son and daughter as young children. Recent images included Mrs Baker and three small children.

'Where do you think the housekeeper's gone?' Nicole asked.

'Probably to put the family skeletons back in their closets,' added Eric, before a cough interrupted them.

'You'll find what you're looking for in there,' Maria instructed, pointing to an open door leading off the kitchen.

Nicole and Eric tentatively walked towards it. The room was pitch black and colder than the rest of the house, and Nicole groped around the wall for a light switch. She felt a string and pulled it, and as the fluorescent strip light flickered on, Nicole smiled at what she saw.

CHAPTER 52

TODAY

Savannah . . . could I, like, bum, a few bucks off you?' Joe asked when their paths crossed in the hostel corridor.

Savannah knew exactly what Joe planned to spend the cash on, but it didn't dissuade her, so she reached into her purse and removed a $20 bill. 'Promise me you'll use at least some of it for food?' she asked hopefully.

'Yeah, sure,' Joe replied and smiled gratefully. But the years spent watching her father at work in front of a congregation meant Savannah could spot a lie in the dark.

She reached her room, then paused when she found the door unlocked. Ron had been quick to replace the broken handle when she'd asked him, and her safety obsession meant each time she left for work, she'd take a photo of the key in the lock. So later, when she'd question whether she'd locked the door, she had photographic proof it was secure.

'Hello, I'm Jane,' came a loud, cheery English accent from behind her.

Savannah jumped as a chunky woman with cropped grey hair barged past. She stood in the centre of the room with her hands on her hips and a broad smile emblazoned across a make-up free face. The woman's body shape reminded Savannah of an egg. She put her in her mid to late fifties, and judging by her cargo pants, her checked shirt and walking shoes, she wasn't in Venice for the beach life.

'Is it just us girls?' Jane beamed.

'It *was* just me,' came Savannah's unwelcoming response.

Savannah frowned at Jane's open suitcase lying on the spare bed, with rolled-up clothes scattered across the floor. 'I'm sorry I'm a bit messy,' continued Jane, 'but don't worry, I'll have this place spick and span in a few minutes. What's your name?'

'I prefer to keep the door locked when there's nobody here.'

'Well we're both here now, aren't we?' grinned Jane, as she continued to unpack.

Savannah sulkily threw her work clothes and make-up box into her handbag, checked the combination padlock was still attached to her locker and went to leave.

'See you later then, roomie!' continued Jane, undeterred by Savannah's hostility.

'Yeah, bye,' muttered Savannah, deliberately slamming the door behind her.

CHAPTER 53

Nicole sighed when she spotted Ruth squatting on the kerb outside what she presumed must be Zak Stanley's home.

Ruth's handbag lay by her side, and she seemed engrossed in her scrapbook of stories about Zak. Nicole was now 100 per cent certain that Ruth hadn't spent the previous day with the film star, and wasn't completely convinced she'd even met him for lunch. She preferred to find the good in people, and had hoped that by some strange fluke, Ruth had been telling the truth. But the sight of her, so hopeful and yet so doomed to fail, broke Nicole's heart.

'Should I go over and say something?' Nicole asked Eric. 'I don't want to embarrass her, but this isn't right. She's going to get arrested for loitering or stalking or something.'

'She's not doing any harm,' replied Eric, momentarily sympathetic towards Ruth's pathetic figure. 'I think we should leave her be. It's none of our business what she's doing or why she's doing it.'

'If this is some sort of delusional disorder or if she's having a breakdown, don't we owe it to her to help?'

'She's not Kathy Bates in *Misery* and you're not a nurse any more, Nic. You need to let this go. You can't save everybody.'

The friends remained in silence for another couple of minutes, neither knowing what they were expecting to happen.

'Come on, let's go,' said Nicole eventually, and reluctantly began the journey back down the hill.

'You owe me $20 by the way,' added Eric.

'Technically, I don't. I bet you she'd be *at* his house. You didn't specify she had to be *in* it.'

'Cowbag.'

'Whatever.'

*

Unaware she'd been followed, Ruth carefully placed her scrapbook back inside her handbag and turned around to look at Zak Stanley's home again.

She smiled when she imagined what it was going to be like when Zak left his house and saw her for the first time; how she'd walk up to him and explain how much he meant to her, how grateful

Zak would be and how she might even receive a hug and a peck on the cheek. And if she made a really good impression, he might even invite her inside for refreshments.

So until that happened, Ruth vowed to remain where she was, and removed a club sandwich and a bottle of Sprite she'd bought in the convenience store. After many failed attempts to diet, she no longer cared about what she ate. Zak would love her no matter what size she was.

Ruth had piled on a stone in weight for every year her father had been absent from his family, and there had been seven to date. Many of their family friends thought of Phil as a cliché for leaving his wife for a secretary less than half his age. Denise was humiliated and hadn't seen it coming, and dutifully, their friends promised to shun him. With her reputation meaning more to her than anything else, Denise would've been mortified if they'd ever discovered Phil's secretary was a nineteen-year-old called Robert. She only discovered her husband's double life when, by chance, she stumbled on Robert's Twitter feed. He and Phil were supposed to be on a business trip to Italy, not lying on a beach and holding hands in Thailand.

Once Phil moved into an apartment in the city with his boy toy, Denise banned him from ever entering the family home again. Even years later, Kevin still remembered being coached by Denise to tell the police that his father had placed his hand in places no adult should ever touch a child. Kevin tried to go along with the lie but his mind became muddled, and after gentle interrogation from a sensitive officer, the investigation didn't lead to a charge.

Meanwhile Ruth tried to maintain contact with her dad, but as the years went on, he made it increasingly difficult. She missed his hugs and him calling her sunbeam, and sometimes she only remembered how his voice sounded from the recorded voicemail messages she'd hear when she called him. She wouldn't have recognised his handwriting now even if he had remembered to send her a birthday card.

She took another bite from her sandwich and recalled how in the beginning, she refused to believe her mother when she claimed her husband was abusing Kevin, and later when she said it was Ruth's fault for his departure, that because she was a big girl, he was embarrassed to be seen with her. Then, as the contact between father and daughter shrank to virtually nothing, Ruth came around to thinking her mother must be right – why else would a father wilfully ignore his child?

She suddenly snapped out of her thoughts, removed her phone from her handbag, and took a grinning selfie with Zak's home behind her. She was about to email it to her dad, to give him good reason to be proud of her.

Then she remembered why she could never contact him, or anyone else back home, again.

CHAPTER 54

Tommy returned from his bathroom break and dry-retched when he came across Joe lying face down, sprawled across the landing floor.

The stench of Joe's urine on a hot day was overpowering, but it was another smell that made Tommy nauseous.

'Jesus, Savannah, he's actually shitting himself! Shall we call an ambulance or something?'

'We should probably leave him,' she replied, her arms folded, all too aware that her cash donation had probably contributed to the situation. 'He's too high to control his bodily functions, that's all.'

'How's it going to get any better for him? Get money, buy drugs; get high, shit yourself; get some sleep then get do it all over again?'

'Maybe he hasn't hit rock bottom yet.'

'How far down is there left to go?'

'I don't know, honey, and it breaks my heart, it really does.'

Tommy shook his head, stepped over Joe's body and made his way towards the hostel's courtyard where he'd left Jake. The sun had moved behind two large buildings that overlooked them, leaving the rarely used courtyard in a cool shade. Tommy joined Jake on cushions placed upon empty rusty upturned beer kegs, and hunched over a table to continue their game of chess. The board was frayed but the squares were still visible, and missing pieces had been replaced with random objects like bottle tops, pen lids and coins.

'I've not really met anyone like you before,' said Tommy, moving his rook horizontally.

'Is that a good or a bad thing?'

'It's all good, don't worry. It's just that you've seen it all, you've done it all . . . you seem, you know, pretty sorted. I wish I was like that.'

'Oh, it's all just an act. I'm just as fucked up as everyone else in this building.'

Jake was far from being fucked up, thought Tommy. In fact he was probably the most level-headed, laid-back and engaging person he'd ever met. Their day together had flown by, peppered by laughter, anecdotes and Jake's traveller's tales. And Jake was pleasantly surprised by just how much he enjoyed being revered by his spirited younger sidekick.

'Have you stayed in touch with your family and friends much?' Tommy asked.

'No, not really.'

'Don't you get homesick?'

'Again, no – it's the sacrifice you make for a fresh start. What's that saying? "*In change we find purpose*".'

Like Jake, Tommy didn't feel homesick either. Instead, he felt nostalgic for everything he'd lost the day of the car accident.

'Can I ask you a question?' Tommy asked suddenly.

'Sure.'

'I don't mean to get all heavy and stuff, but do you ever think you might have had the time of your life already and didn't stop to notice?'

'If you think like that, the next forty or fifty years are going to be very dull.'

'I dunno. I can't shake the feeling travelling might be as good as my life gets. This could be my "moment".'

'Don't be daft, there might be hundreds more moments or there might be just one. Or the "moment" might be a person. I see it like this – people are like the tide. Some come into your life and bring things you'll only need for a short time, and others will bring things you'll carry forever. But some are just destined to disappear.'

Tommy wondered which category Sean had fallen into.

SEVEN MONTHS EARLIER – GRAND CENTRAL STATION, NEW YORK

'We're here, mate, we're actually here.'

Neither Tommy nor Sean looked pleased as they nervously glanced around the main concourse of New York's Grand Central Station. They craned their necks towards the enormous stars and stripes flag hanging above them and puzzled over the zodiac constellations painted on the terminal ceiling. As they turned, their faces became bathed in yellow light pouring through six high arched windows.

'Take a picture of me up there.' Sean pointed towards one of the pristine marble staircases and Tommy waited for the rush hour commuters to thin out so he could take his shot. When they just came thicker and faster, Tommy gave up waiting so Sean ended up resembling a 'Where's Wally' drawing.

In the eight hours since their plane had left Heathrow and landed at JFK, they'd negotiated their way to the terminal via the AirTrain and an alien subway system that used colours, letters and numbers and made little sense. Their back muscles already ached under the weight of their over-packed rucksacks, so they found a quiet spot and began unpacking under the four-faced golden clock atop of the information booth.

'We need to streamline,' began Tommy, removing a travel hairdryer, electric razor and smart dress shoes. 'There is so much crap here we don't need. We're going to have to bin it or my spine's going to start slipping out of my arse before the end of the day.'

'I don't think I'll be needing these,' answered Sean, removing three cans of Heinz beans, two toilet rolls and a jar of Marmite.

'Keep the Marmite!' protested Tommy, taking out hair straighteners from a side pocket and pointing to them. 'I don't remember you complaining when I put these in.'

'Those are an essential!'

'Nope, if the Marmite goes, they do too.'

'Fine. But when it gets humid, you're going to be looking like a dick hanging out with the only white boy in America with a blond afro.'

Tommy and Sean put their discarded goods into a plastic bag to dump in a trash can, rolled up their sleeping bags, secured them under the backpack straps and hung their spare trainers by their laces from side pocket zippers.

'Right, where are we going first?' asked Tommy.

As they moved towards the departure boards, their bulky presence became unwelcome with the locals when their rucksacks clipped several shoulders.

'Careful, man!' barked one. 'Asshole, are you blind?' yelled another. Sean tried to apologise but nobody listened. New Yorkers walked with absolute purpose, he noted.

'This is too intense,' said Tommy. 'I think we should get out of New York, start off slowly to get acclimatised to America and then come back when we're a bit more used to it.'

Sean nodded his agreement and studied the departure boards. 'We need a plan. There's a train leaving for Stamford in ten minutes, and another one going to Newark in fifteen.'

'No plans needed, I've got a better idea. We've got no timetable to stick to; we can go anywhere we want, whenever we want. Follow me.'

They walked towards the platforms searching for a rare ticket booth without a closed shutter. Eventually they settled on a machine, and Tommy closed his eyes, pushed a random destination button and inserted a $50 bill.

'Let's see where we'll end up, shall we?'

Sean grinned and gave Tommy a high five.

*

Sean shielded his sombre face from the lashing rain with the hood of his cagoule.

'We should've checked where the train was going before we caught the first one out,' he began. Tommy glanced around the near-empty station platform as Sean's finger traced a train line in a map book. A vending machine lay on its side, its glass door smashed and emptied of its confectioneries. Both signs informing them of where they'd reached were covered in graffiti, rendering them illegible.

'So where are we?' asked Tommy.

'I wasn't really listening to the conductor when he said where the final stop was,' admitted Sean. 'But we're about an hour out of New York so we could be north or south. Or west. Or maybe east.'

'Big help, mate.'

'We could be in Rensselaer. No, it's Denville. Or maybe Fairfield. Like I said before, we need a plan.'

'Well at least we're on the move.'

'I think moving again very soon could be a good idea.'

Tommy looked puzzled until he saw what Sean was staring at. Ahead of them, a bearded man in a tatty army uniform, dirty trainers and pushing a baby buggy loaded with empty soda cans shuffled towards them. It was the breadknife in his hand that caught their attention next. They quickly rose to their feet, threw on their backpacks and frantically searched for an exit sign.

'You lookin' at my blade, muthafucker?' yelled the man, wide-eyed, ''cos it's lookin' at you.'

'Oh, fuck,' muttered Tommy, just as a train appeared from around the corner and stopped at the platform. As soon as the doors opened, they darted inside, scurried through the carriages and threw themselves onto seats. They breathed more easily as they slowly pulled away while the man with the breadknife walked alongside the moving train banging on the windows.

Sean leant towards a woman sitting opposite him. 'Excuse me, where's this train heading, please?'

*

Tommy and Sean walked towards the departure board at Grand Central Station, no longer caring who they bumped into or what insults were hurled in their direction.

'Let me spell this out for you. We. Are. Making. A. Fucking. Plan,' growled Sean, and Tommy nodded obediently.

CHAPTER 55

TODAY

Nicole never commented on it so as not to inflate Eric's ego any further, but she was always impressed by how he seemed to know every lyric to every song he heard on the radio. And he didn't have a bad singing voice either.

As they drove back to the hostel from their reconnaissance mission to learn what Ruth was really up to, Eric sang along to both parts of Beyoncé and Shakira's 'Beautiful Liar' playing on a pop radio station. Nicole struggled to keep a signal on her phone long enough to open up Google and seek inspiration on where to travel to once they left Los Angeles.

'Found anything yet?' Eric asked, flicking on the dipped headlights as dusk fell.

'No,' Nicole replied, and, frustrated, threw her phone into the glove box. 'I remember Mrs Baker saying something about her and her husband sleeping in the back of the car one night by a lake. If I could get a bloody signal I'd look up lakes near Route 66.'

'That sounds pretty vague, Nic.'

'No more so or no less than your suggestion of going to Bakersfield just because it sounds like her surname.'

Eric fiddled with the dial on the radio and picked up a classic Seventies music station as the opening bars of a song played. A small part of him still quietly harboured a desire to sing professionally, but, as it was harshly pointed out by Geri Garland when he auditioned to be part of the group Lightning Strikes three and half years earlier, he was more 'old boy' than 'boy band.' He remained grateful that humiliating clip never aired.

'"A long, long time ago,"' he sang along, '"I can still remember how that music used to make me smile . . ."'

'What's this song?' Nicole asked, noting its familiarity.

'How on earth could you not know? It's Don McLean's "American Pie", but I bet you only remember the Madonna version,' Eric sniffed. 'His was a classic but she ruined—'

'Shut up!' Nicole interrupted, and turned the volume up. Six verses and eight minutes later, she slammed her hand down on the dashboard triumphantly. 'It's in the song!' she yelled. 'Where Mrs Baker wants us to go, it's in the bloody song!'

ELEVEN WEEKS EARLIER – GREAT HOUGHTON, NORTHAMPTON

'We trekked halfway across London, then into the middle of nowhere for that?' asked Eric in disbelief.

Before them was an old, left-hand drive white, pick-up truck. Caked in a film of dust, the two right tyres were flat and gave it an awkward stoop.

'We could have cut out the middleman and bought a car from *Exchange & Mart*,' Eric continued.

'It's more than that,' said Nicole. 'It's the truck Mr and Mrs Baker travelled America in on their honeymoon. She didn't mention they'd brought it home with them.'

Nicole peered through the passenger window and spotted a wooden box on the tan leather seat. The door opened with a creak and she lifted the lid to find a handwritten letter inside.

'What does it say?' asked Eric, still disappointed their quest had resulted in such a rusty old treasure. Nicole began to read out loud.

To whom this may concern. Since my beloved husband died, I have spent years searching for a like-minded soul to appreciate what Joseph and I worked so hard to achieve. Reluctantly, I ruled out my family as they were not there when their father took ill or to support me afterwards when I struggled to pick up the pieces. But if you are reading this, then I have chosen you. Like me, you long for adventure. My body will not allow me to travel any further in this lifetime, but yours will. And only when you allow the warmth of new experiences to fill your heart, will you truly realise how precious a gem your life is. With everlasting gratitude, Grace Baker.

'What is any of that last part supposed to mean?' Eric asked.

As Nicole re-read the letter to herself, Eric put his hand inside the box and took out ten rolls of bank notes. He took the elastic band off one of them and counted the £50 notes.

'Jesus, Nic, there's £10,000 in this! So she has left you money after all.'

'No,' pondered Nicole. 'There's more to it than that. What else is in the box?'

Eric dug out a business card with a British address that appeared to be a company exporting vehicles to the US, and some car registration documents.

'There must be a clue in the letter,' said Nicole, before picking up an atlas from under the box and flicking through it.

'Thanks, Thelma, I'll fire up the Mystery Machine – you go grab Scooby.'

'Look, she's left a bookmark on the page for Chicago and another one for Santa Monica in Los Angeles. It looks like the start and end point of Route 66.'

'It's a bloody long road; where will you begin?'

'Where will *I* begin?' asked Nicole, surprised. 'It's not *I*, it's *us*. We're in this together, my friend.'

Neither noticed Mrs Baker's housekeeper standing behind them, her hands clasped and fingers tightly entwined, silently praying her panicked decision had been the correct one.

CHAPTER 56

TODAY

Tommy carried the chessboard and headed towards the cupboard where the boxes of board games were stored, and became distracted by shrieking sounds behind Matty and Declan's closed bedroom door.

He couldn't resist placing an ear to it to hear what was causing the ruckus. But, without warning the door suddenly opened, causing Tommy to lose his balance and fall into a heap on the floor inside, chess pieces scattering across the threadbare carpet.

'We have a guest, ladies,' began Declan as Tommy looked up to find two Asian girls he didn't recognise lying on beds and Matty and Declan wrapped only in towels. Tommy felt his cheeks blush and his hands sprang into action, scrambling around to grab the pieces to put back in the box.

'Next time you can watch if you like!' added Matty, while Tommy took the board and hurried out of the room.

With another successful humiliation under their belts, Tommy vowed to make it a priority to toss the two cuckoos out of his nest as soon as the opportunity arose.

And he wouldn't have long to wait.

CHAPTER 57

Eric leaned back on his plastic chair by the hostel's two coloured iMacs and blew cinnamon gum bubbles as Nicole scanned the computer screen.

Her eyes moved from the web pages to the notes she was frantically jotting in a book. Eric was bored – he cracked his knuckles, picked at a scab on his ankle, felt for rogue, protruding nostril hairs and glanced at Jake sitting on a sofa reading a book about holistic health and yoga. He puzzled over where he recognised Jake from but couldn't put his finger on it.

Suddenly Nicole slammed her pen down and threw herself back against the chair.

'Buffalo Springs Lake, Texas. That's where we're going,' she began with a satisfied smile.

'And how did you come to that conclusion?' yawned Eric.

'Okay, I'll explain, but you need to concentrate. The clues are all in that song "American Pie". Mrs Baker started singing it the last night I visited her and talking about sleeping in the back of the truck by a lake. She was telling me about her trip around America with her husband in 1971 on Route 66 – well, that was the year the song was released. According to Wikipedia the song is about, well at least in part, the singer Buddy Holly dying in a plane crash. That's why Don Henley sings about "the day the music died".'

'Henley? You mean McLean.'

'Whatever.'

'But didn't Buddy Holly die in the 1950s or something?'

'Yes, but he was born in Lubbock, Texas. And which road goes through Lubbock, Texas? Route 66.'

'That road goes through a lot of states, Nic, as you well know, because I drove through most of them to get to LA and I swear Lubbock was one of towns we passed.'

'Will you just let me finish?' Nicole replied, indignantly. 'Read the lyrics. He talks about a pick-up truck and driving a Chevy to the levee – what are we driving?'

'A Chevy pick-up truck. But what's a levee?'

'It's an embankment or flood bank that regulates water levels. And where would you find one of those?'

'At a lake.'

'Exactly, and where did I tell you Mrs Baker and her husband slept one night?'

'At a lake?'

'And near Lubbock, Texas, you'll find Buffalo Springs Lake. The song also has references to the Father, Son and Holy Ghost and "having faith in God above", and there are at least four churches there. He sings about "dancing in the gym" and there are ten schools in Lubbock by my reckoning. There's a line, "I could make the people dance", and there's half a dozen dance studios. As for "The church bells were all broken", well St Theresa's Church hasn't had working bells since 1971. Plus Lubbock contains everything mentioned in the song – a courtroom, an American football team, they even have the All-Lubbock Marching Band Parade. A reference to The Jester? That's Bob Dylan's nickname, and he's twice played Lubbock. Do you see how this all fits?'

Eric knew Nicole was desperately attempting to find clues in almost everything Don McLean recalled about small town life. But he kept it to himself that there were probably hundreds of other towns that might also fit the bill. And in the absence of any better suggestions, he nodded. But the more time he gave himself to think about it, the more he came round to agreeing Nicole could be on to something.

'It's roughly 1,200 miles from here,' continued Nicole. 'If we set off in the morning, we can be there in about a day.'

'And what are we going to find when we get there?'

'Let's cross that bridge when we come to it. But I have a gut feeling this is going to change everything for us.'

Nicole had no idea how right she was, but not in the way she'd hoped.

CHAPTER 58

DAY SEVEN

Ruth was unaware of the poppy seeds accumulating between her teeth as she tucked into a third cream cheese bagel.

She sat on a fold-up chair purchased from an outward bound store in Santa Monica, finished her breakfast and reached inside her bag for her knitting. No one had bothered to answer Zak's intercom that morning, but Ruth was positive someone was inside the house as the patio doors were now closed and the CCTV camera quietly changed direction soon after she pressed the button. But a single-minded Ruth wasn't easily dissuaded when she was so close to her goal, so she sat contentedly and continued to knit Zak's jumper.

She noticed nobody seemed to walk in the Hollywood Hills, as no matter where she wandered – and it was never far from Zak's house – she had yet to speak to another person. Even the uniformed Hispanic staff entering and leaving Zak's neighbours' homes used cars or vans.

Every couple of hours, Ruth made her way around the corner, squatted in a patch of bushes and relieved herself into an empty McDonald's cup. And when the sun began to heat up the sidewalk, she pulled out a stripy parasol that came with the seat and stuck it into the grass verge.

And as the hours ticked past in her lonely public vigil, Ruth's determination to meet Zak grew ever stronger.

THREE WEEKS EARLIER – VICTORIA, AUSTRALIA

Ruth nervously played with her hair as the glass elevator rose to the twenty-second floor of the plush apartment block.

The doors silently opened and she scanned the corridor for Number 223. She was skittish, yet excited, and knocked on the solid wooden door a little louder than she'd intended, so it echoed through the corridor. Inside, she heard footsteps on a tiled floor before it unlocked and her father answered, casually dressed in sweatpants and a T-shirt that was too tight for a man of his age.

'Hi Dad,' began Ruth with an eager smile. Phil looked at his daughter for the first time in almost three years; she was much heavier than he recalled, and it had aged her. She didn't resemble either him or his bitter ex-wife.

'I didn't know you were coming over,' he replied, flustered. He part closed the door behind him but didn't move towards her.

'I haven't heard from you for a while and I wanted to say hi,' continued Ruth, hopefully.

'You really should've called first.'

'I did, I left messages on your machine and at work and on your mobile phone.'

'Oh, right. Okay, well I've been busy – you know how it is.'

Ruth nodded and smiled. 'Can I come in?'

'Um, it's not really convenient right now, Ruth. Another time, maybe.'

'Well I came to say goodbye. I'm going to America to—'

'Okay, well, enjoy yourself,' her father interrupted, smiling vacantly, and began to turn his back on her. Ruth's heart sank when she realised the father who swept in and out of her life on his terms was terminating their all-too-brief reconciliation. She'd imagined they might spend the afternoon together, catching up on each other's news like old friends. He would ask questions about her job and she would tell him all about Zak and the competition she'd won.

Then anger suddenly displaced the disappointment she felt, so she pushed open the door her father was trying to shut.

'Aren't you going to ask why I'm going to America?' asked Ruth forcefully.

'Ruth, I don't have time for this. I'll see you soon, I promise.'

'Why don't you want anything to do with me, Dad? What have I done wrong? I'm a good person, I really am.'

Phil took a bulging leather wallet from his pocket, removed a handful of dollars and handed them to her. 'There, you don't need anything from me now, right?'

Ruth couldn't disguise how let down she felt. She swallowed hard and willed the tears forming in her eyes to go away.

Suddenly a small, sinewy South-East Asian girl, no more than two or three years of age, appeared by Phil's waist.

'Daddy, who's this man?' smiled the girl, and pressed her hand into his palm. Ruth's mouth slowly fell open as her father struggled to find words.

'It's a girl . . . she's a friend of mine, sunbeam,' he replied.

'Sunbeam,' repeated Ruth, realising she'd been replaced.

'Lucy, leave Daddy alone,' a male voice said from behind the door as it opened further. 'Who are you talking to . . . .? Oh, hi Ruth, how are you?'

Phil's boyfriend Robert offered Ruth a superficial smile but she had no idea how to respond to the sight of her father's replacement family, or the new sunbeam in his life. She stepped backwards towards the lift.

'Ruth—' began her father, but the lift door closed before Ruth heard anything else.

CHAPTER 59

TODAY

Eric parked the truck at the hostel kerb, and Nicole and Tommy lifted suitcases into the flatbed and secured them with ropes.

Eric ignored both Tommy's presence and assistance and remained in the truck fiddling with the radio, leaving Nicole to say goodbye.

'Well,' said Tommy, and smiled at Nicole.

'Well,' she replied and returned his smile.

'Good luck with the rest of your trip.'

'Thanks.'

Nicole wanted to tell Tommy that in different circumstances, she would have returned his kiss and that the burden of a secret she couldn't reveal would always get in their way. But both were aware their moment had passed.

'I've sent you a friend request on Facebook,' Nicole continued, 'so we can stay in touch if you like?'

'That'd be good.'

Tommy stretched his hand out awkwardly to shake Nicole's; instead she hugged him and gave him a peck on the cheek until an impatient Eric honked the horn.

As the truck pulled away, Tommy felt a little envious of Nicole's next adventure, even though she'd been cagey about what it involved or where she was going. But while he'd enjoyed her company, he was also looking forward to spending more time with Jake and learning more of the world by living vicariously through his anecdotes.

Jake had encouraged Tommy to consider whether it was time to throw the security blanket of the Venice Beach International Hostel to one side and experience more of America by himself. However, when he gave it proper thought, he knew he was too scared, and too broke, to do it alone.

And it would take the actions of his past and present colliding before he could ever move forward.

CHAPTER 60

'Over there,' began Nicole, pointing to a greenish verge with a panoramic view further up the highway.

Eric pulled the indicator lever down and the truck ground to a halt by the side of the Arizona road.

'What do you reckon?' he asked, and turned to face Nicole.

'Yes, this looks like a nice place.'

They exited the truck and stretched limbs that felt tight after seven and a half hours of continuous driving. Route 66 both ahead and behind them was silent and should've been straight as a die, had the sun's incalescence not made it wobble like jelly. But the mainly barren landscape was pure picture-book America.

Eric lifted himself into the back of the truck to remove the cardboard box where Mrs Baker's urn was stored. Then he followed Nicole as she walked towards a grassy knoll with a canyon-like drop below.

'Hey, it's Eric and Urn,' Eric joked, and looked to Nicole for approval. She ignored him.

'Didn't Bridget ask why you wanted her mum's ashes?' she asked. 'What kind of woman gives something so precious to a complete stranger?'

'The kind who couldn't care less, I suppose. People can be shits, Nic.'

'I guess so. Okay, let's do this.'

Eric passed Nicole the urn, and she tore off the tape that kept the lid firmly in place. Then she took a deep breath and began to shake the ashes into a light breeze and watched Mrs Baker make her final journey towards the snow-capped Mount Elden, beckoning from the distance.

'Goodbye, Mrs Baker, and thank you for this opportunity,' Nicole whispered, and smiled. Eric placed his arm around her shoulder and felt her head tilt towards him. After a few moments of silence, Nicole wiped away the tears pooling in the corners of her eyes, carefully placed the empty urn on the ground and returned to the truck.

Eric waited a moment longer and absorbed the view of the arid landscape surrounding him.

'Goodbye, Mother,' he muttered, and spat on the ground where a small pile of ashes rested.

PART TWO – THE DEPARTURES

CHAPTER 1

DAY EIGHT

'Come on, man,' snapped an unusually competitive Peyk, 'it's an easy shot.'

'No pressure, then,' Tommy replied, and arched his back over the pool table, stretching his fingers over the black ball to knock the cue ball into the yellow. It glided into the pocket with ease.

'Lucky,' said Peyk dismissively, as the music in the hostel lounge became louder.

A group of Australian girls in their late teens scanned a TV screen, awaiting direction before frantically aping the animated dance steps flashing before them. Tommy resented the popularity of Matty and Declan's stolen Xbox One, and the fact that his adversaries had become the centre of attention because of their gift and vivacious personalities.

When one girl lost her balance and jostled Tommy, he missed his shot. Only her apologetic smile stopped him from snapping at her.

'Which rules are we playing,' Tommy asked, 'American or European?'

'What's the difference?' asked Peyk.

'The biggest difference is that Americans don't play a lot of snooker or three-cushion billiards,' interrupted Jake, potting his first, second, then third red with ease. 'Americans mostly play 8-ball and 9-ball, along with some one-pocket or 14.1 straight pool.'

Tommy and Peyk looked at him and raised their eyebrows.

'What? I'm more than just a pretty face, lads.'

When Jake missed the fourth red, he passed the only cue to Sadie, the receptionist. Tommy leaned against the wall, his eyes darting between Jake and one of the amateur dancers who was offering him kittenish glances.

'If this was snooker, would you be going for the pink or the brown?' whispered Peyk, clearly amused with himself.

'What?' Tommy replied, thrown off guard.

'You know what I mean.'

'If I do, then you are *way* off.'

Peyk shrugged and turned to take his shot.

Suddenly the booming bass of a familiar pop song blasting from the TV interrupted their game.

'Hey!' yelled Tommy. 'Turn that off.'

'Why should I?' the Australian girl yelled indignantly.

'Because I said so,' replied Tommy angrily. 'Now!'

'Don't talk to her like that,' warned Declan, who stood by the window with Matty.

'Mind your own business.'

'What did you say?' Declan continued, walking towards Tommy with shoulders squared.

'Leave it, Dec,' said Matty.

The girl turned the song off and abandoned the game, as the others in the room glared at Tommy, surprised by his uncharacteristic aggression.

He looked at the faces staring at him, then he walked out of the room, unaware Jake had slipped out moments earlier.

THREE AND A HALF YEARS EARLIER, LONDON

The cork from the champagne bottle flew through the air like a bullet and rebounded off a polystyrene ceiling panel in the restaurant at the TV studios.

A DJ in the corner of the room mixed James Brown's 'Get Up (I Feel Like Being A) Sex Machine' into Prince's 'Gett Off' as Stuart left the makeshift dance floor and helped himself to a glass of cheap fizz from a waitress's tray. It wasn't the obvious location for *Star People*'s wrap party, but as the floor manager pointed out, the budget had been blown on the series finale's pyrotechnics, choirs, backdrops and staging. And creator Geri Garland held her purse strings tightly.

All eyes were on each member of winners Lightning Strikes. The others boys were well on their way towards intoxication, but Stuart preferred the control that sobriety brought. He watched, with a touch of envy, as families hugged their winning offspring and clenched their hands with affectionate pride. Competition-winning fans interrupted them for selfies, and celebrity guests vied for their attention.

In need of just a moment's peace, Stuart slipped away from the rowdy room and aimed for the bathroom where he planned to lock himself in a cubicle and process the night's events.

He was about to lock the door when a hand yanked it open and a startled Stuart turned to find Geri squeezing herself inside the cubicle.

'I told you you'd make me proud,' she began, placing her hands around his waist. Her breath smelt of cigarettes and Scotch.

'It's incredible,' began Stuart awkwardly. 'I've been meaning to say thank you for—'

'No need to thank me,' she interrupted, closing his lips with her finger. 'Thank those Indian call centres I paid to push your votes up. And this is just as much for me as it is for you.'

Geri unclasped Stuart's hand and in it placed a black Links of London box with a ribbon around it. Inside was a silver bangle bracelet. Stuart turned it over and read the inscription: 'Never Look Back'.

'Those boys need a front man and you've got the looks to do it.' she continued, 'And I have a feeling you're going to make me a very, very, satisfied woman.'

Geri removed her finger from Stuart's lips and gradually moved it down his shirt and towards his belt, before slipping her hand inside the front of his jeans and cupping his balls.

'Geri, I don't think this is a good idea . . .' Stuart mumbled nervously as her fingers moved their way around his crotch. He could feel his dick hardening and he tried to think of anything that might make it shrink again. Instead, his eyes widened and his buttocks pressed backwards against the cubicle wall as Geri gripped him firmly. Then when he was completely but reluctantly erect, Geri kissed his cheek, released her hand and let herself out of the cubicle with a smile.

It wouldn't be a one-off event, Stuart realised, repulsed by both her intrusive actions and his primal response to it.

CHAPTER 2

Two thumps on the left hand side of the shower pipe and three to the right was what it took for water to pour from Tommy's shower.

Only today, there was a special surprise about to burst from the end of the pipe where a shower nozzle should've been attached. It came in the form of a deep gurgling and an army of cockroaches surfing a tide of water.

'Jesus,' yelled Tommy, and jumping backwards against the cracked wall of tiles, he lifted his foot to squash them before changing his mind.

Tommy was aware of the saying 'you get what you pay for', and he paid for nothing in the hostel. But the right to basic hygiene wasn't too much to expect, so with the roaches negotiating the slippery shower tray and scuttling down the drain, he wrapped his towel around his bare waist, felt his feet squelch on a sopping-wet bathroom mat and stormed out of the room.

He was still angry at Matty and Declan for interfering when he asked – well, ordered – that girl to turn off the computer game. But he was more frustrated at allowing his temper to get the better of him and making a fool of himself in front of the others.

'Is he in?' Tommy growled at Sadie, seated behind the reception desk piercing her eyebrow with a needle and an ice cube. She shrugged, so Tommy knocked on Ron's door and didn't wait to be invited in.

However, instead of finding him behind his desk, Ron was standing with a pile of cash, handing Wayne a brick-sized package wrapped in cellophane. Tommy immediately recognised what was inside – dried, compressed cannabis leaves similar to the ones Peyk was so keen on sprinkling into his Rizlas. Ron and Wayne were startled by Tommy's appearance, and when Wayne scurried out past him, Ron opened his desk drawer and swept the cash inside.

'It's not what it looks like,' he muttered.
'Well it looks like you're selling drugs to Wayne.'
'Then it is what it looks like.'
'How? Why? You told me to keep him out of this place.'
Ron sighed and ran his hand through his comb-over, then appeared to wrestle with indecision.

'Things change, Timmy,' he said finally. 'You need to come with me.'

CHAPTER 3

The first time Zak Stanley's eyes met Ruth's, she was sitting motionless outside his Hollywood Hills home.

Ruth had begun to lose all track of time by her fifth consecutive day spent perched on a fold-up chair. An hour could sail by before she'd realise she'd been staring blankly at a rendered wall. But the long-awaited sound of footsteps and an automatic gate slowly opening snapped her out of her unfulfilled daydreams.

She turned around like a shot and there he was – Zak Stanley, in the flesh, and in the presence of his biggest fan.

Zak frowned at her, wondering whether the plump, dishevelled shape was male or female and a threat to his safety. Meanwhile the shape's eyes worked their way up from Zak's tanned legs to his Abercrombie & Fitch-emblazoned sweat shorts, then his white sleeveless T-shirt and MP3 player strapped to his arm before reaching his face. She ached to touch the dark chocolate fringe tucked behind his ears, but she felt paralysed.

Deciding the shape appeared harmless, Zak turned his music up with a remote control attached to his headphones, and jogged up the hills and out of Ruth's sight.

She didn't move a muscle for another ten minutes.

CHAPTER 4

Jane turned a photograph she was holding face down on the carpet when she heard footsteps approaching the door.

Instinctively she knew something was wrong when Savannah appeared, clutching her cheek and trying to avoid eye contact.

'Oh my God, what happened to you?' began Jane, jumping to her feet.

'I'm fine,' Savannah replied, only then remembering a new roommate had been shoehorned into her life.

'No you're bloody not, let me have a look.'

Jane grabbed Savannah's hand and pulled it away, noting her cut lip and a swelling around her eye. 'What happened to you, darling?'

'Nothing.'

'That's not nothing. At least let me stop the bleeding. I've got some antiseptic wipes somewhere—'

'Please,' begged Savannah, now trying to control her emotions, 'Just leave me alone.'

She dashed into the bathroom and closed the door behind her, locking it. She tore off two sheets of toilet paper, looked into the mirror and began dabbing the drops of blood from her split lip.

In the months Savannah had been dancing at the Pink Pussycat Club, she'd never seen a fight amongst customers, let alone been the cause of one. But that changed when she refused a private lap dance to two drunken rednecks who were in no mood for rejection. When one grabbed her arm, she'd yelled for security men Marlon and Kevin for help, and once the fists began to fly, she got caught in the middle of the fracas.

Now tired, bruised and emotional, Savannah swallowed hard but she couldn't fight the urge to cry any longer. So she sat on the toilet seat, held her hands over her mouth and silently sobbed.

'This is not how your life is supposed to have turned out,' she thought, 'working as a pole dancer, living in a backpacking hostel and sharing a room with a middle-aged Mary Poppins.'

But this is what it had become . . . for now, at least.

SIX AND A HALF MONTHS EARLIER – MONTGOMERY, ALABAMA

Savannah watched from behind the linen curtains in her bedroom as her father's black Chrysler began its slow approach along the driveway and up towards the mansion.

As he parked, she took a deep breath. Then, partly shielding her eyes, she drew her arm back and threw a fist-sized solid metal paperweight through her window.

The glass shattered instantly and the paperweight continued its trajectory, missing the Reverend's head by no more than an inch. The car's windscreen cracked as it rebounded onto the bonnet and then to the ground. Reverend Devereaux's alarm rapidly turned to rage when he raised his eyes to discover his daughter standing defiantly by her window.

The front doors of the house smacked against the rubber stoppers, making the wooden shutters vibrate as he ran up the staircase and towards his daughter's room. For two weeks he had kept her locked away in the vain hope she'd understand that breaking his rules had consequences. But she'd inherited his stubbornness and made no attempt to apologise. And if said apology was not forthcoming by the end of the month, he had reserved her a room in a private hospital in Maine which, he'd been advised, offered a medication and forced re-education therapy to assist Savannah in coming round to his way of thinking. But with this further act of blatant rebellion, he would ensure she was en route within the hour.

The Reverend hurried along the hall and turned a key, flinging Savannah's bedroom doors open. He expected to see her still by the window; only his daughter wasn't there. His eyes narrowed and he looked back and forth, scanning the room for her.

Then he dropped to the carpet like a bag of stones and clutched at his neck.

The Reverend's body convulsed as the electricity travelled through a lamp base Savannah held. It flowed under his skin and through his veins like thick, boiling water. He felt his cold heart beating faster than it had ever done before as it, alongside all his other muscles, tightened. Savannah kept the electrical current moving through him as Reverend Devereaux was completely at her mercy, frozen and unable to protect himself.

Time spent with only the television for company had educated Savannah; one DIY show in particular had taught her how to strip the wires from an unused old lamp and upcycle them for an alternative use. It was only when the presenter advised caution as it could transform it into something potentially lethal, that Savannah knew what she must do.

She wore an old pair of galoshes she found in the back of her wardrobe so the rubber would act as insulation and prevent her from being electrocuted. Finally, when she was sure her father would not be rising to his feet for some time, she dropped the lamp. His body looked sluggish, each breath he took was desperate, his pupils were dilated and his body was virtually motionless.

She swiftly yanked off her boots, slipped on her sneakers and rifled through his pockets, knowing he always carried a large number of bills in his wallet. Then she grabbed a pre-packed overnight bag and escaped the confines of her room.

Savannah's hands and legs shook as her 'fight or flight' adrenaline rush took hold, and she threw herself towards the open front doors. Suddenly a voice behind her stopped her in her tracks.

'How on earth . . .' began her mother, brow furrowed, but clearly wary of the determined expression on Savannah's face. Savannah gave her one last 'don't fuck with me' look, and made for her father's car.

'Please, please, please,' she muttered, hoping that in his confusion over narrowly missing the flying paperweight, he had left his keys in the ignition. And she thanked God when she found them there.

Once the engine turned over and the handbrake was released, she put her foot on the accelerator and sped away, spitting gravel in her wake.

*

The Greyhound coach slowly pulled away from its bay outside Montgomery's station and began its long haul towards California.

The overweight Korean man sitting behind the ticket counter's reinforced plastic screen had advised Savannah the journey would take around forty hours, involve three transfers and twenty-eight stops before she reached her Los Angeles destination. But Savannah didn't care, just as long as the bus took her far away from her life. Every minute she spent on the tired old vehicle with its faded blue and grey seats and empty plastic tables was better than being trapped inside a gilded cage.

Once she'd got behind the wheel of her father's car, her first instinct had been to drive to Michael's campus. She was less than a mile away before she had second thoughts. If she loved Michael as much as she knew she did, she would have to let him go.

So she turned the car around and headed downtown instead. She left it parked two blocks from the Greyhound station with the keys in the ignition in the hope it might be stolen or stripped, rubbing salt into her father's wounds. She charged the bus fare to the Reverend's black Visa card, and then left it by the sink in the public bathroom so others could make use of it before it was cancelled.

Savannah's only possessions in the world were the clothes in her holdall and those on her back. She unzipped her hooded top, placed it against the window and leant her head against it, watching the rain gently trickle down against the backdrop of a blood-red sky.

Intuition warned her that no matter how far forward she went, Savannah would always be looking backwards, just in case.

CHAPTER 5

TODAY

Ron handed Tommy a spare pair of sunglasses from his pocket as they stood in the corridor facing room 23.

'Your storeroom,' said Tommy, suddenly concerned as to why Ron, who behaved oddly at the best of times, was luring him into an unfamiliar room when Tommy was wearing nothing but a towel.

'Put them on,' Ron replied, then knocked three times on the door, paused and knocked twice more. They heard two bolts being pulled to the side and then a key turning, before it opened and Peyk's face appeared.

'I see we have company,' he smiled, and ushered them in, quickly closing and bolting the door behind them. They stood in pitch blackness for several seconds until Peyk opened another door to a brightly lit room.

Tommy gazed around in astonishment, his eyes opening wide.

'What the hell have you two done?'

CHAPTER 6

No one spotted Jake slip quietly away from the hostile atmosphere of the lounge and up a flight of stairs towards the fire exit.

He hated confrontation, and was a little taken aback by Tommy's ire towards the girls dancing, but he'd had to leave when he heard the opening chords of *that* song.

The bar across the door hung to one side from a broken screw, so he pushed it open and made his way onto the roof. He realised it wasn't the secret hideaway he first thought it might be when he spotted two stained mattresses, a long disused satellite dish half-full of cigarette butts and scores of empty beer bottles with sun-bleached labels.

Jake walked closer to the edge and leant against the railings, looking down with a new perspective at the cars parked at 45-degree angles in the street below. Sunlight angled off their windscreens and rear-view mirrors, and on the sidewalk, throngs of people made their way to and from the beach. His eyes followed them into the distance before he scanned the rooftops of neighbouring buildings, beyond the tops of palm trees and finally the ocean.

Jake tried to locate Hollywood, wondering if he could ever muster the courage to take a trip there and gain the closure he felt he needed two years on.

As much as he enjoyed the company of other people, sometimes he preferred them in small doses, and today was one of those days. He'd had his fill of being the centre of attention for a lifetime.

TWENTY-SIX MONTHS EARLIER – LONDON

Lightning had certainly struck, not once, but three times as Stuart's band topped the singles charts with a trio of releases.

Then after a newspaper headline-making chart battle, their debut album outsold Coldplay's latest effort three to one to reach pole position. With manager Geri Garland's public relations company driving the promotional campaign at full throttle, Stuart, Gabriel, Josh, Dylan and Ethan's fixed-smile faces were impossible to avoid. From being gunged on a kids' TV show to paparazzi photographers clamouring to take their pictures as they entered nightclubs with models, there was nothing about their public activities their fans didn't know.

Privately, it was a very different matter.

*

With no children of her own – by choice rather than by circumstance – *Star People* was Geri's baby.

She'd created it, so she decided who'd make the live shows. But when the audition process began for season two, Geri grew concerned. She'd later informed Stuart that after a month of travelling up and down the country listening to woeful hopefuls caterwauling, she'd chosen four male solo singers picked for their voices rather than their looks. And as the competition lacked tween fodder, Geri decided the best way forward was to push them together and create a boy band. However, they lacked one vital ingredient – there was no Gary Barlow, no Justin Timberlake and no Harry Styles, and any boy band worth its salt needed a front man. So when Geri met a handsome young porter working at a Holiday Inn in Bolton, her gut instantly told her she'd unearthed the missing ingredient.

Very little took Geri's breath away, except maybe her first cigarette of the morning, but the porter made her middle-aged heart race as he carried her Louis Vuitton luggage to her room. He felt her eyes bore into him from behind.

It wasn't just Stuart's lean physique, his chin as sharp as a razor or his chiselled cheekbones that made her feel like a teenage girl again, it was the aura of bright colours she swore she spotted floating around him when he spoke. She liked that he was blissfully unaware of his own beauty and had an innocence she rarely came into contact with in her shallow industry. Such innocence was there to be exploited, and Geri was the perfect person for the job.

The next morning, two crisp £50 notes was all it took to get Stuart's home address from one of his colleagues. 'This will be easier than I thought,' she informed her driver as her Jaguar pulled into a shabby council estate.

Talking a shocked Stuart into going along with her plan took little effort, as Geri had made persuasiveness an art form and Stuart had nothing to lose. He surprised himself at how readily he opened up to a woman he barely knew as he recounted his childhood and teenage years spent abandoned in foster care, shuttled between temporary parents and social workers, and how it had forced him to learn self-reliance. He revealed how he'd harboured vague ambitions to find a career in the travel industry, but was willing to put that on hold for what Geri was offering.

Stuart was all too aware there was more to life than minimum-wage employment and living in a house where he shared a basic kitchenette with a seven-strong Somalian family and a friendly Russian couple who appeared to have a never-ending supply of British passports in plastic folders on the communal table. Sometimes, when his hotel shift came to an end, he'd study for his Open University travel and tourism course at a table in the corner of the hotel restaurant while furtively watching families dine together.

So when Geri offered to open up a new world to him, one so far removed from his own it might as well have been located on a different planet, he grabbed it with both hands. Fame was something he neither craved nor needed, but Geri had the measure of him.

'See this as a means to an end,' she explained. 'It won't last forever because boy bands never do. Just ride the wave for long enough and you'll be set for the rest of your life.'

What she didn't inform Stuart was how much she enjoyed having the power to change a person's life on a whim. She cherished it all the more knowing that she could bring it to an end just as sharply.

With Stuart on board, Geri had a complete, marketable, boy band ready to roll off the *Star People* conveyor belt and straight into the television live shows. Four reasonably talented lads whose music teenage girls would download and whose merchandise they'd pay over the odds for, plus a beautiful lead singer with a sob story everyone would lap up.

Geri's puppets did what they were told, obeyed the clauses in their lengthy contract about not bringing their brand into disrepute and discreetly bed-hopped with other girl groups and reality TV stars behind closed doors.

When the cameras were on them, Lightning Strikes were the best of friends, larking about and referring to each other in interviews as brothers. But behind closed doors, Stuart barely spent any time with them when they weren't working. He was quietly envious of their families, their closeness and their freedom to be who they were, while they were green-eyed over him being the focus of fans and journalists alike.

As hard as he'd tried, there was little Stuart could do to fend off Geri's frequent sexual advances. She only ever required one of two things – to either give him oral sex or to masturbate him, and never in the confines of a bedroom. Instead, it would occur when Stuart least expected it, like in the back of a limousine, a TV show dressing room, a hotel restaurant and even once in an empty recording studio sound booth. Stuart never climaxed and Geri didn't seem bothered. She never asked for penetrative sex or for Stuart to pleasure her, a small mercy he was grateful for. It was, he decided, just another way in which Geri let him know who was boss.

'Don't forget, I know your secrets,' she'd warned him when he attempted to refuse a blow job.

'Not all of them,' he thought.

'So don't look a gift horse in the mouth,' she continued, before placing his dick back inside the gift horse's mouth.

CHAPTER 7

TODAY

By the time a bruised Savannah finished her solo pity party in the bathroom, she unlocked the door to find the bedroom empty.

A clear plastic bag containing cotton wool buds, a bottle of witch hazel and a packet of antiseptic wipes had been left on her duvet by Jane. Savannah cautiously checked under her pillow to make sure her gun was still in place, then scooped up the medicines and applied them to her grazes.

The stress of the day made her stomach ache, so she lay on her side and faced Jane's bed. But as she struggled to relax, curiosity got the better of her and she decided to snoop on her new roommate. Savannah approached Jane's side of the room and sniffed a lavender candle in its glass jar on a bedside table. Then when she noticed Jane's suitcase was unlocked, after a cautious glance over her shoulder, she casually opened the lid to find Jane's neatly folded clothes and collection of travel books.

The sound of the door's squeaking hinges startled her.

'I was . . . just putting your stuff back,' Savannah blurted out, looking at Jane and realising she didn't actually have anything in her hands.

'Oh, I don't mind, have a nose around, my dear, I've got nothing to hide,' Jane replied with a warm smile. 'How's the swelling?'

'A little better. Thanks for the antiseptic and stuff . . . and I'm sorry for snapping at you earlier.'

'Don't you worry about it,' assured Jane. 'So what happened to you?'

'Some assholes were pissed because I don't do "extras".'

'I'm guessing you don't work in an office.'

'Hardly. I'm an exotic dancer.'

'Well good on you, but no job is worth being beaten up over.'

'Look, I appreciate your concern, but I can look after myself.'

'Okay, darling, but just in case, I'll keep my medicine box under my bed, so just help yourself if you ever need it again.'

Savannah offered a half-baked smile, and then returned to her bed.

'Have you got anything on tomorrow?' asked Jane. 'I was going to catch the bus up to Santa Monica and have a wander round the farmers' market. I could use some company and you're the only person here I've spoken to so far.'

'I don't think it's really my thing. The farmers' market, I mean, not talking to you.'

'I knew what you meant. Anyway, you can't go back to work till that swelling goes down, so shall we say about nine?'

Savannah didn't have the energy to argue, so she nodded her head and quietly wondered what Jane's ulterior motive was.

CHAPTER 8

The two decommissioned dormitory rooms Tommy found himself in had been amateurishly knocked into one large, open-plan space, leaving jagged plasterboard edges and exposed brickwork.

But it wasn't the rooms or the portable lighting rigs throwing out immense heat from their bulbs that grabbed his attention. That honour went to what lay beneath them.

Inside two dozen garden growbags perched on old mattresses were at least 150 cannabis plants of varying heights. The surrounding walls were chock-full of holes with plastic pipes jammed into them for ventilation. Wires and plugs hung from missing ceiling tiles, and black bin bags had been taped to some windows while blackout blinds hung from others to keep out prying eyes. Windowsills below them pooled with condensation.

Like the plants, Tommy remained rooted to the spot, unable to formulate a sentence. He could already feel the sweat from under his arms starting to trickle down his sides. He turned his head towards Peyk, who was standing in just his brightly coloured underwear.

'I see you've come dressed for the occasion,' said Peyk, pointing towards Tommy's towel.

'I just . . . I just wanted some hot water for my shower,' he whispered, before finding his voice. 'What the fuck? You actually have a cannabis farm in the middle of the hostel?'

'Well, it's nice of you to call it a farm, but we're not there just yet,' Peyk replied proudly. 'Give us a couple of months and we'll reach our goal.'

'It's like *Breaking Bad* in here.'

'Let's not exaggerate, Tommy-boy, we're not cooking crystal meth, it's just a bit of weed.'

'A bit? It's a shitload! Look at how many plants you've got in here.'

'It's a good start.'

'A start? You want to grow even more?'

'Of course. There's no point in half measures, is there?'

'But why?'

'To make money and keep a roof over your head,' began Ron as Peyk returned to work, carefully trimming leaves from one of the taller plants with household scissors.

'The hostel isn't worth going to prison over,' Tommy felt the need to point out.

'I think it is,' replied Ron. 'When I came to Venice Beach and took on this old place, I didn't appreciate how much it'd cost to maintain or to run. And if I can't find a way of covering the bills, I'll have to close the doors.'

'But we're almost always full, so surely you must make some money?'

'Only because we're cheap – anything we earn barely covers the overheads. If I charge more, you guys will stay somewhere better. And I have to make regular payments to a city official who turns a blind eye to this place because it's nowhere near to being up to code.'

'And this is why you keep falling through ceilings,' Tommy said, looking towards Peyk.

'Yep, as we started to make a little money from the pot, I began replacing the old wiring so we could get more lighting rigs in here. It's not just the people staying here who are in a transition – it's the building, too.'

'I approached Joe's friend Wayne to test the market and sell some of our product,' continued Ron, scratching his head, 'and so far he's had a positive response. So we need to up our production, but that takes time. These plants need twelve hours of light a day, and that's a whole heap of electricity.'

'If you don't do this, how much longer does the hostel have left?'

'About two months; three if we're lucky. Wayne's a one-man operation, and he can't sell much weed on his own.'

Tommy took a deep breath and another look at his surroundings. He was all too aware of how illegal the activity in that room was, and in ordinary circumstances, he'd have run a mile.

But this was no ordinary life he was leading, and the thought of the hostel closing panicked him much more than it being raided by the police. He possessed no working visa, so even post-recession, he'd find it hard to pick up cash-in-hand work selling hotdogs for a living wouldn't be enough to support him.

Tommy felt safe there, which he knew was illogical, given the circumstances in which he'd arrived that first night. He'd made friends and created himself a little universe – albeit a temporary one. If the hostel shut, the only viable option would be to arrange a return date for his open plane ticket and head home. And he certainly wasn't ready for that.

Tommy recalled what Richard, the protagonist in *The Beach*, the novel that had inspired his travels, had done in not-that-dissimilar circumstances, and it wasn't a 'happy ever after' ending for him. But that was just a story, thought Tommy, as he stood facing his crossroads.

There were two directions he could take – the first was to fall back on his default setting and walk away when a situation became awkward. The second was to slip out of character and step up to the mark.

'I can help you,' he said finally, and folded his arms defiantly.

CHAPTER 9

Twilight had begun to make its presence felt when Zak Stanley's run slowed to a walk as he approached his home.

The first thing he noticed was 'the shape', now standing by his gate. Despite the failing light he could see its eyes were wide open, its lips were apart and it was motionless, gawping at him.

Having a stranger so close to his house made Zak uncomfortable; he'd been victim to several stalkers before, but legal action from an army of retained lawyers had been the most successful way of combating even the more resolute ones. However this one looked harmless – stupid, even.

'Can I help you?' he asked sternly, pulling his headphones from his ears.

Ruth's mouth was dry but she couldn't swallow. Zak Stanley had just spoken to her. Zak Stanley! If she could have pressed pause on any moment of her life, it would no longer have been when she still had her father at home, it would've been right then.

'Well?' Zak asked again, but when Ruth didn't reply, he decided he was wasting his time. He wanted to cool down in his pool before his party began later that night.

Ruth made imperceptible adjustments to her hair as Zak pushed a button on a thumb-sized remote control for his gates to open. Then she suddenly burst into life.

'I'm a really big fan,' she blurted out loudly, making him jump.

'So?'

Ruth didn't sense the animosity in his abrupt reply.

'I've come from Australia to see you,' she continued.

Zak eyed her up and down again, quietly loathing fans who believed that paying to see one of his films meant they were entitled to a piece of him.

'I won a competition to meet you. I went to the restaurant but you weren't there.'

'Well someone's screwing with you because Zak doesn't do meet and greets.'

'Oh.'

'So why are you still here?'

'Um,' Ruth hesitated, unsure of how to continue before a light bulb flashed in her brain. 'I've made you something!'

Ruth dove into her handbag and fumbled around for the jumper she'd spent a week carefully crafting. But by the time she held it up to show Zak, he'd disappeared behind the closing gate.

CHAPTER 10

DAY NINE

'Hotdogs and a lemonade, just one dollar,' echoed Tommy's voice through the megaphone in his best Queen's English.

An influx of tourists at a music festival further down the promenade made for a busy day on the beach and an improved footfall for Tommy and José's hotdog stand. Word of mouth about Tommy's latest addition to the menu had already begun to spread, and Tommy had socialised with enough people from different walks of life to predict by appearance alone those who might want to sample his smokable wares and those he should hide his product from. He ensured the two middle-aged women behind the shirtless frat boys he was serving weren't watching or listening when he spoke.

'Can I interest you in the chef's special?' he asked in nervous, hushed tones after handing them their hotdogs. Then he slipped his hand inside his uniform and removed a small sachet of pot from his shorts to show them.

'Shit yeah!' they replied.

'Go and see my friend behind the stand and he'll sort you out,' Tommy replied, pointing to José in the mobile food trailer behind them. José was grateful for a cut of both the cash and the product in return.

And Tommy couldn't help but grin at the rush of adrenaline his first foray into illegal activity gave him.

CHAPTER 11

The sand's uneven surface made it impossible to predict which direction the football might travel after being kicked.

But it didn't prevent the dozen under-ten year old boys and girls from trying to gain control of it from Matty and Declan and scoring. Their parents sat nearby under sunshades as Matty and Declan entertained the kids, teaching them how to tackle and allowing them the occasional penalty.

Their beach soccer school wasn't going to make them rich, but it was earning them $15 per head per half day and they enjoyed teaching the eager youngsters the skills they'd need to make an impression on the pitch. And occasionally they'd deliver embellished anecdotes about how they'd been trained by David Beckham and had given up promising apprenticeships at Manchester United to go travelling. Today, Declan was the more enthusiastic of the two, though, and he couldn't help but notice Matty flagging.

'Time out, guys,' he called, scooping the ball up into his arms. 'Go and see your folks and rehydrate.'

'Are you alright, fella?' Declan asked as the children scampered back towards their parents.

'Yeah, yeah, I'm just sweating cobs though. The sun's got to me a bit today.'

'I'll get you a drink. Replace your electrolytes and all that.'

'Don't fuss, I'm okay.'

'Or I'll get you a Coke if you want?'

'Dec, give me a break!' snapped Matty. 'I said I'm okay, right?'

As Matty trudged across the sand towards the boardwalk in search of shade, Declan followed him anyway, just to be sure.

THIRTEEN MONTHS EARLIER – DUNDALK, IRELAND

Dogs' eyes on a dozen painted plates hanging from the walls seemed to watch Declan as intently as Matty did, counting the heap of stolen euros on the kitchen table.

'That's €12,276 in total, pretty good for a first try,' announced Declan proudly.

He leaned back on his chair and stretched his arms above

his head – their haul was greater than either had anticipated.

'First and only try,' added Matty.

'That's what I meant. It's enough to pay for two seats in Upper Economy to Ibiza and two InterRail tickets, plus spending money for everywhere else we want to go.'

'We need to be sensible though, we don't know how long it has to last.'

They were suddenly interrupted by the creaking hinges of a porch door. Declan darted to the other side of the kitchen, grabbed a handful of tea towels and threw them at Matty, who in turn covered the cash as his mother appeared, weighed down by two bags of food shopping.

'Can I give you a hand, Mrs O'Keefe?' began a flustered Declan.

'No, it's fine, lads,' she replied. 'What's going on in here? Why do you two look so guilty?

'What are you on about, Mammy, we're just sitting here talking,' replied Matty in a forced, jovial tone.

Matty and Declan looked at each other behind Mrs O'Keefe's back while she placed her bags on the kitchen work surface.

'You two, just talking? Now I know you're guilty of something. Are you staying for dinner, Declan?'

'If you don't mind.'

'Sure it's no trouble. Just move that pile of money you're hiding under my tea towels and set the table.'

Matty and Declan glared at each other again, neither knowing how to respond. So they scooped the money back into their duffel bags and Matty hurried upstairs with them. Before Declan could follow, Mrs O'Keefe held his arm and looked him straight in the eye.

'Promise me, Declan, you'll look after my boy. Please promise me that.'

Declan nodded. 'You know I will.'

Mrs O'Keefe appeared convinced of Declan's sincerity and removed her hand. 'Good lad, I just needed to hear you say it,' she added, and patted him on the shoulder.

CHAPTER 12

TODAY

'It's taken us almost twenty hours in that shitty old truck with the air vents throwing out hot air for this? FOR THIS!'

Eric's frustration reached boiling point, which felt like the same temperature as the cracked brown mud surrounding Buffalo Springs Lake. 'It's just a lake, like any other bloody lake in the world.'

'What were you expecting?' replied Nicole. 'Narnia?'

'I don't know, but something more definitive than this. Something that made it obvious that what was written in the letter was not just the ramblings of a daft old cow on her deathbed!'

'Don't you dare call her that!' shouted Nicole. 'You don't know anything about her.'

'And you do? You barely knew her, but you were still willing to go off on a wild fucking goose chase around the world on her say so.'

'You didn't have to come with me,' Nicole replied, close to tears.

'No, and I wished I hadn't. I don't know which one of us is the more stupid.'

After a day and night driving 1,223 miles, only interspersed by broken sleep and catnaps, Nicole and Eric had finally arrived in Lubbock. And they'd spent their whole day driving around the town and looking at schools, shops and public amenities to see if anything Mrs Baker had written or spoken about jumped off the page.

They'd downloaded 'American Pie' from iTunes and played it over and over again, trying to find more clues hidden in the lyrics, but if they were there, they'd been very well camouflaged. Buffalo Springs was their final stop, and they were still looking for answers.

'It's Cooler at the Lake!' a colourful banner over the car park entrance promised. But once they passed under it, it turned out to be no more than a body of water surrounded by campsites, stores, fishermen, a nature trail and a small, sandy beach. 'Shit, shit, shit, shit!' continued Eric, walking towards the passenger side of the truck and throwing himself into the seat. Then he lifted his foot and twice kicked the air vent on the dashboard with all his might.

He glared at Nicole, climbed out of the truck again and stormed off up the beach.

It was the angriest Nicole had ever seen her friend. She accepted his occasional moodiness and ever-present sarcasm but she'd never witnessed an out and out temper tantrum before. At first, she saw the humour in it, especially when his arms flailed from side to side and reminded her of how puppeteers made the Muppets run. But as his rant continued and his eyes darkened, she felt something new towards Eric – unease.

As Eric's figure grew ever smaller, Nicole took a deep breath, unaware of the favour he'd unwittingly done her.

CHAPTER 13

It had been a long, cold night sitting outside Zak's home in the Hollywood Hills.

To fend off the chill, Ruth wore the jumper she'd almost completed for Zak. Expensive looking cars and yellow cabs dropped a couple of dozen people off at the gate up until around midnight, and although she strained her eyes to get a better view of them, it was too dark to make out their faces.

Ruth was envious when they were granted immediate access to Zak's estate and could only imagine what celebrities he was playing host to so close but yet so far away. Dance music blasted from his garden until the sun began to rise and she began to resent the laughter coming from behind the gates that separated her from her soulmate.

An exhausted Ruth slept through the guests' departures and only woke at the sound of a van's exhaust pipe backfiring. She stretched, took off Zak's jumper, wiped her armpits and face with a moist tissue from the KFC box she'd bought earlier that night and felt her stomach rumble. She had long run out of food but she risked missing another chance to talk to Zak if she left now.

Ruth's eyes were blurry and too sore to finish knitting the last cuff of the sweater and instead she reflected, admitting to herself that her first meeting with Zak hadn't gone according to plan. She didn't blame Zak for being standoffish with her; it made sense once she'd had time to think about it because she'd sounded like an idiot when she'd spoken.

But as soon as Zak got to know her, his opinion would surely change. She was excited about their next meeting, and it came much sooner than she'd anticipated. Because by mid-morning, his gates opened and his SUV began to pull out of the drive. However, the vehicle braked sharply before it reached the road.

'Jesus H...?' began Zak, opening the driver's door and pulling off his sunglasses. 'Have you been here all night? Are you paparazzi? Because you can't prove shit about anything.'

Confused by what he meant, Ruth thrust the jumper into Zak's chest with a huge, hopeful smile. He held it out to examine it – one arm was longer than the other, the neck hole was huge and the colours garish. And when he realised the crude effigy on the chest was supposed to be his face, he couldn't contain his amusement.

'Are you for real?' Zak continued. 'This is fucking hilarious!'

Ruth's face ached with disappointment, and her hopeful smile faded as she watched Zak throw her jumper onto the grass verge and head back to his car.

'And FYI,' he added, 'synthetics give me hives.'

CHAPTER 14

A day in the blazing sun wearing a hotdog costume gave Tommy's face an oval-shaped redness.

He could smell his own body odour seeping into the costume's fabric and he vowed to ask Mr Fiaca to think again about how to promote the business. But even though his skin and ankles were sore to the touch, he couldn't stop smiling at his productivity.

He headed towards room 23 and knocked three times, then twice. Peyk answered cautiously then ushered him inside, glancing behind Tommy to check for prying eyes. Once inside and with his sunglasses on, Tommy fished out handfuls of notes from his shorts and handed them to Ron.

'Sorry if they smell a bit,' he muttered, embarrassed.

'Tommy-boy!' interrupted Peyk and patted his friend's back, while Ron began to count the cash. 'Who knew?'

'There's $628 here,' said Ron.

'And we only stopped because we ran out of product,' said Tommy proudly.

Peyk nodded his head. 'Good work, Jesse Pinkman.'

The buzz Tommy earned from doing something he shouldn't have been doing satisfied him and he justified his actions by telling himself it was for the future of the hostel. It didn't harm that he'd siphoned off $100 from his earnings as commission, something he wouldn't be mentioning to Peyk or Ron.

'Same again tomorrow?' asked Tommy, and his co-conspirators nodded their heads eagerly.

For the first time in weeks, Tommy hoped he wouldn't be crossing paths with the long-lost Sean soon, as his best friend certainly wouldn't have approved of the direction Tommy's journey was taking him.

CHAPTER 15

It had been a quiet day for Jake in Venice Beach.

Out of choice, he kept himself to himself, preferring to throw himself into a book in the solitude of the hostel courtyard and then spending time on the roof. But try as he might to concentrate on *Shantaram*, he couldn't get past the first few chapters of the 900-page epic and regularly became distracted. Several times Tommy appeared in his thoughts, and Jake wondered what he was up to. He vowed to try and catch up with him later and take him to dinner as he enjoyed Tommy's company.

Jake couldn't put his finger on why, but something had brought certain memories flooding back that he'd spent the last two years trying to bury. Sometimes waves from his past came crashing all around him, threatening to drown him, and the only way he could avoid going under was to take some time out by himself and process where everything had gone wrong, and who had been the architect of his misery.

TWO YEARS EARLIER – LONDON

'So next week is your first Brit Awards, and Lightning Strikes have been nominated in four categories – has your new life sunk in yet?'

Stuart couldn't decide if the blonde presenter was flirting with him or just doing her job. He struggled to hear her from their position on the red carpet in London's Leicester Square.

'Yeah, it has, but slowly,' he replied into the microphone, her eyes darting around his face and struggling to find a fault.

'But what we all want to know is if there's any truth in the newspaper stories that you and soap star Katie Begley are getting married in the autumn?'

'Oh, you know what the papers are like – let's just say Katie and I are very happy the way we are and who knows what will happen in the future?'

'Are tabloid rumours the downside of fame?'

'I guess you get used to it, but the secret is to never give away everything about yourself. Always keep them wanting more.'

Stuart gave the presenter a peck on each cheek before wandering up the red carpet and posing for a picture with actor Zak

Stanley, whose film premiere Lightning Strikes had been invited to. Within earshot of their PRs and the press, they offered each other mutual congratulations on their respective success before Stuart rejoined the rest of his band in the cinema foyer.

Zak's assistant had already slipped Stuart an electronic key card to Zak's hotel room. And Stuart couldn't wait for the premiere to finish before he and Zak could spend their first night alone together in three weeks.

TODAY

'Oh, sorry, I didn't realise anyone was up here,' Tommy began.

'I was just thinking I'd not seen you for a while,' replied Jake. 'How's your day been?'

Tommy considered recounting how many laws he'd been breaking but decided against it; he didn't want to be judged by someone whose opinion he valued.

'I've been working on the beach for most of it,' he said, and surveyed the roof. 'So you've found my secret bolthole, then?'

'Ah, so is that your mattress and empty bottles?'

'Not quite, but it's a cool place to come and get away from everyone else. I love this hostel but sometimes I need a bit of "me" time.'

'Same here,' smiled Jake. 'Do you—'

But before he could finish his sentence, the railing Jake was sitting with his back against began to creak. He tried to move his body forward but he couldn't keep his balance. Instead, he felt his back pushing the railings away from the rusty screws that held them in place.

Jake's arms shot out in front of him and his eyes opened wide in blind panic. Instinctively, Tommy grabbed Jake's wrist and, with all his strength, yanked him forward as the railing fell three storeys to the sidewalk below.

Both their hearts pounded and they stared into each other's eyes as their terror gave way to relief. But Tommy's reactions weren't as fast when Jake pulled him forward and kissed him. Instead, Tommy remained frozen for the three seconds it took for Jake to realise Tommy wasn't kissing him back.

Jake stared at his friend, immediately regretting his spontaneity.

'I'm sorry,' he muttered, and quickly walked away, back down the stairs and towards his room.

Meanwhile Tommy wondered if his day could get any more bizarre.

CHAPTER 16

'Your hooves are disgusting,' began Eric, but Nicole kept her bare feet on the dashboard of the truck regardless.

Her red toenail varnish was chipped, and walking around in bare feet had left her soles dry and in desperate need of a pedicure.

'And while you're at it, maybe you could remind your legs what a razor looks like. You're not German, and you're not a lesbian.'

'Okay, I'll shave my legs when you remove that stick from your arse,' Nicole replied, quietly proud of her comeback. 'My feet are sweating down there so I'm letting them air.'

'I love you, but you are a vile beast,' Eric replied. Nicole took his smile as an apology for his earlier hissy fit, and decided she'd overreacted by fearing his mood swing. Nicole's ponytail flicked from left to right as the warm wind blew through the open windows, but Eric's face took the brunt of the sun.

'Sweet Mary, mother of Jesus, this heat is turning my skin to leather,' he moaned and pointed to the air vents. 'And they are making it worse, because it's like being blasted by a hairdryer.'

'There's a garage up ahead,' said Nicole, 'so I'll fill the truck up with petrol and you stock up on more bottles of water.'

Eric pulled the truck onto the dusty forecourt, grabbed his wallet from the dashboard and headed into the store. Meanwhile Nicole grasped the nozzle of the petrol pump and began to fill the tank. Her eyes took in a station that could have come straight from a book of 1940s American photography. The pumps were decrepit but worked, and tiles were missing from the wooden pitched roof of the store.

She looked around the miles and miles of arid land ahead of them and wondered if she should call time on their adventure. *This* had been Mrs Baker's final gift to her, she reckoned; the financial means and the kick up the backside she'd needed to climb out of her comfort zone and spend six weeks on the road travelling with her best friend. There was no pot of gold to find at the end of the rainbow because it hadn't existed in the first place. Her actual reward was being free to do what she wanted to do, when she wanted to do it. And when all was said and done, she couldn't put a price on that.

As the bell on the petrol pump told her she'd reached $40, the sun caught something in the car that dazzled her eye.

She replaced the nozzle and opened the door to inspect the glimmer further, and squinted at the air vent Eric had kicked and cracked. The closer she got, the more it twinkled.

She poked her fingers inside, but the broken diagonal plastic strips were in her way. So, using both hands, she yanked at the air vent until it came away. Again Nicole wiggled her fingers inside, and this time, she pulled out a small, partially open velvet pouch with a drawstring. Puzzled, she undid the knot and poured the contents into her open palm.

It took a moment for her to understand it wasn't a pouch full of broken glass, but of diamonds.

'Only when you allow the warmth of new experiences to fill your heart, will you truly realise how precious a gem your life is,' she whispered to herself, recalling the words written in Mrs Baker's note. Then she recalled how Mrs Baker had spoken of the night she and her husband spent by a lake while the stars above them 'shone like diamonds.' She turned her head and saw Eric at the cash register, paying for fuel and water.

'Eric!' Nicole shouted, and waved frantically to get his attention.

She poured the diamonds back into the pouch so Eric could experience the same surprise she felt, when she saw a small piece of torn paper crammed in the vent. The beaming smile spread across her face was rapidly replaced with confusion, then alarm, when she read the words.

'Don't let her son find these – they're not for Eric.'

TWELVE WEEKS EARLIER – HOLLY COTTAGE, GREAT HOUGHTON, NORTHAMPTON

They had never met in person, but Mrs Baker's housekeeper Maria recognised Eric from old family photographs now locked in a chest in her deceased employer's attic.

Maria had expected someone to arrive at the cottage after Mrs Baker passed away but she hadn't expected it to be Mrs Baker's son.

'Hello, my name is Nicole Grainger and this is my friend—' the girl began. She was as pretty as Mrs Baker had described her when Maria visited her in hospital. But she clamped her mouth shut and tried to hide her uneasiness at the sight of Eric.

He had not been part of the plan.

'I know why you're here,' Maria interrupted, and went back into the house leaving the front door open. She guessed Nicole and Eric were probably looking at each other, unsure of what to say when they followed her into Mrs Baker's lounge.

'Wait here,' she ordered and left the room.

Maria closed the kitchen door behind her and uncharacteristically began to panic. She'd last seen Mrs Baker a few days before her death, when she'd told Maria of her plan to change a young nurse's life. With Maria well provided for and bequeathed the cottage, Mrs Baker desperately wanted Nicole to experience the world. So she dictated a letter which Maria wrote. The diamonds were already in the truck's air vent as instructed, and on the passenger seat was a box with enough money to get the truck up and running and exported to America. Nicole was then to pick it up at a dock in Chicago, the city that was the starting point of Route 66.

In the event that Nicole failed to discover the diamonds, Mrs Baker told Maria that at least her protégé would have had the trip of a lifetime if she followed a vague map, her cryptic note and could recall their conversations together. But Maria knew the last thing Mrs Baker would have expected, or wanted, was for the boy she once described as 'a wolf in wolf's clothing' to have benefited from them.

So Maria needed a Plan B. She darted around the kitchen, silently opening and closing drawers until she found a notepaper and pen. She hurriedly scribbled the words '*Don't let her son find these – they're not for Eric*', and poked it into the air vent before regaining her poise and showing her visitors the pick-up truck.

Then she clasped her hands, entwined her fingers and hoped for the best.

TODAY

The note tore Nicole apart like a bird hitting a propeller.

She was familiar with the expression 'blood running cold' but had never experienced it until that moment. It didn't make sense, she thought – how on earth could her best friend of two years be the son of Mrs Baker? Why wouldn't he have mentioned such a crucial piece of information while his mother was dying in a room next to him or as he and Nicole planned their trip? Why had he never visited her? He'd had every opportunity to do so, so there could only be one probable reason for his silence – he was using his friendship with

Nicole to find his inheritance.

Nicole's mind continued to race, still trying to find alternative meanings in the scribbled note, but there were none. It was what it was, and gradually memories of the last couple of months began to fit together like pieces in a jigsaw – Eric's recent criticism of a woman he never knew; his eagerness to take two-month, unpaid sabbatical from work and accompany Nicole, and then his fury when they reached Buffalo Springs Lake.

'Eric, you can't be . . .' she said out loud.

'I can't be what?' came a voice in her ear, making her yelp.

'What's with you?' laughed Eric.

'Nothing! Nothing,' Nicole replied.

The rapid speed of her pulse made her body judder. Her fist clenched the velvet pouch, and its contents dug sharply into her hand.

'What happened to the vent?' he asked, noticing the plastic casing lying in the footwell.

'Erm, I was picking at it,' Nicole stumbled, and slowly slid the pouch from her hand and into her pocket. Then she picked up the casing and jammed it back in place. 'Can we go?'

Eric returned to the driver's seat, put his seat belt on and pulled away, ready to return to Venice Beach.

As Nicole tried to regulate her breathing, she was unaware the breeze coming through the windows had blown Maria's note under her seat.

CHAPTER 17

Some 3,000 regulars made their way to downtown Santa Monica's farmers' market each and every Sunday.

Unlike other markets throughout the city, Santa Monica's appealed to more than single shoppers or restaurant staff picking up the freshest local produce for their eateries. It targeted young and old with food stalls, arts and crafts stands, face painting and pony rides.

'This looks just ripe enough,' said Jane, picking up a grapefruit and squeezing it. 'It should have a good week left in it.'

'How do you know this stuff?' asked Savannah, who back in Alabama, never had call to set foot inside a supermarket let alone a street crammed with colourful edibles.

'When you're a mum they give you a manual for this kind of thing.'

When a confused Savannah frowned, Jane added, 'I'm kidding, darling.'

'How many kids do you have?'

'Oh, I have two,' she replied casually. 'Well, I had two, but they passed away. It still never sounds like it's me when I'm saying that.'

'Oh God, I'm sorry,' gasped Savannah.

'That's okay. And speaking of children, when are you due?'

CHAPTER 18

There were almost 130 people from 28 different nationalities sleeping under the roof of the Venice Beach International Hostel.

But Tommy still instantly recognised the figure walking along the corridor ahead of him, even with the back of his head obscured. The olive green frayed backpack was a giveaway, decorated with dozens of airport security tags, flight labels, Greyhound and Amtrak tickets and stickers hung from straps and zips; a tapestry of wanderlust that could only belong to Jake.

Tommy felt a sudden sense of dismay when he realised Jake had packed up to leave. He'd already lost one ally in Nicole that week, but that friendship was only ever going to be temporary, and Tommy felt that he and Jake still had some way to go.

Meanwhile, as Jake made his way towards the hostel's front door, he was still embarrassed and angry with himself for letting his guard down and befriending Tommy. Even though he hadn't revealed anything about his past life as Stuart Reynolds, pop star, he'd allowed Tommy to get closer than most. Jake hadn't planned to kiss him and he knew Tommy was straight, but he'd let his emotions get the better of him and acted on impulse, not forethought.

Jake was attracted to Tommy, he could admit that to himself now, and like any gay man who'd ever had a crush on a straight guy, he knew nothing would come of it. So, to stop himself making more of a fool of himself than he already had, he reasoned it was better to just disappear.

'I thought you only left when people weren't looking?' yelled Tommy.

'Oh hi, yeah,' Jake replied, turning around and clearly flustered.

'So?'

'So . . . what?'

'So you can't leave because I'm looking.'

'I made a bit of a tit of myself so I thought it best I just . . . go.'

'Ah, you mean after you tried to snog my face off?' Tommy teased.

'I was a bit emotional. I was thinking about home and, well, I dealt with it the wrong way. I'm sorry.'

'You said being homesick was the sacrifice you make for a fresh start.'

'Using my own words against me, eh? Maybe I'm not as sorted as you think I am.'

'Maybe you're just more human than you realise.'

'Possibly,' thought Jake, 'or maybe I've just made more fucking stupid decisions than you'll ever know.'

TWO YEARS EARLIER – LONDON

The tinted windows of the limousine couldn't completely hide the camera flashes as Stuart and soap actress Katie Begley pulled away from the red-carpet film premiere and drove towards London's Embankment.

Even though the clock was approaching midnight, the roads were overcrowded and they moved slowly as the audience dispersed towards their vehicles and public transport.

A familiar, frosty silence between Katie and Stuart filled the limo as it often did when they were left alone. Theirs was a relationship of convenience, dreamed up by managers and PR experts eager to promote both their brands. In front of the cameras, they were love's young dream, but away from the flashing lights of the paparazzi, they had little in common and even less of a desire to discover common ground in their manufactured worlds.

Katie tucked her strawberry-blonde hair behind her ear, put her fingers down her blouse and pulled out five finger-sized paper wraps from her bra. She expertly tapped out a powdery substance from one of them onto her clutch bag, placed the wraps on it and carefully shaped four lines with her VIP lanyard.

'Haven't you done enough of that already?' Stuart asked. 'You took enough toilet breaks during the film to snort half of Columbia.'

Katie ignored him, then removed a straw from her purse, placed it at the base of her nostril and snorted two lines in quick succession, finishing with a long, hard blink as the cocaine numbed the back of her throat.

'Do you want some?' she asked Stuart, pointing to the remaining lines.

'No, I'm good,' he replied, eager to leave her side and reach their destination.

Aside from the occasional joint, drugs weren't a high priority for Stuart. His social workers had informed him that his parents' substance addiction was the reason he'd been removed from them as a toddler and placed into care. He'd since learned his mother had died of a heroin overdose some years later, and he couldn't bear to read the self-pitying story his father had sold to the *Sunday Mirror* about how much he missed his only son – a son he hadn't bothered to track down until fame came his way.

Stuart had dabbled with speed and cocaine recreationally with the rest of Lightning Strikes and kept a small stash in his apartment for when Zak was in town. Most of the time Stuart only indulged in stimulants with Zak, and that was only to enhance the sex.

'Fucking on coke is like nothing else,' Zak had told him the first night they spent together, and he wasn't wrong.

'Suit yourself,' said Katie, wiping her top lip with a tissue. 'Not much fun, are you? I don't know why I keep agreeing to this.'

'Because being seen with me makes you front-page news,' Stuart sniped. 'Without me, you're relegated to TV guides.'

'Well Geri had better not screw me over.'

'Neither of us is getting screwed the rate this traffic is moving. Driver, how much longer do you reckon it's going to take?'

As the glass partition descended, Katie passed Stuart her handbag with the two remaining lines of coke scattered across it.

'Hold this for a minute,' she said. Her voice wobbled as she accidentally knocked the other wraps into his lap.

'Be careful!' Stuart snapped, but as he gave Katie an angry stare, her eyes rolled back into her head and her body went into seizure.

'We're just pulling in now, sir,' the driver replied as the car moved towards the hotel entrance.

A panicked Stuart knew by heart the well-rehearsed routine that was supposed to follow, but that night would be different.

Because, before he had time to prevent it from happening, one of the hotel staff opened his limo door and half a dozen cameras snapped the star of Britain's biggest boy band with two lines of cocaine balanced on his lap, three wraps of it in his hand and a convulsing teenage actress by his side.

*

TODAY – HOSTEL

'I'm not gay, just for the record,' Tommy told Jake firmly. 'I mean, it doesn't bother me that you are, but I'm not. I just wanted to clear that up.'

'I know, I know' Jake replied, and hitched his rucksack further up towards his shoulders. 'I've booked into a hostel in West Hollywood, maybe we could catch up in a few days?'

'You don't have to go, nobody needs to know you're gay if you'd prefer to keep it quiet. Not that I think anyone here would give a shit, but you can trust me,' Tommy replied.

'People can't let you down if you don't trust them.'

'Another pearl of wisdom, eh?'

Suddenly Tommy grabbed Jake by the cheeks and kissed him, not just a peck on the lips, but a proper kiss.

'There,' Tommy laughed, a little surprised by his own spontaneity, 'we're equal now, so let's put your rucksack back in your room and go get a Chinese.'

As the two headed back towards Jake's room, neither noticed a camera phone pointing in their direction.

CHAPTER 19

'How do you know I'm pregnant?' a startled Savannah asked Jane.

Jane put down the punnet of strawberries she was holding at the market stall and took both of Savannah's hands.

'Sweetheart, you're in a hurry to make money in a job that doesn't match your education. Your arms aren't marked and your pupils aren't dilated so you're not spending any on drugs. I don't see any Jimmy Choo's under your bed so you're not wasting your money on fashion. So what are you doing with it? Probably saving it. And what for? An endgame, of sorts. Now, it could be to move out of the hostel and to get your own apartment, but something tells me there's more to you than meets the eye and that you're doing this job, working these crazy hours and putting yourself in harm's way because you know you can't do it for much longer. So why could that be? Because you're expecting a baby.'

Savannah was taken aback. 'You got all that from sharing a room with me for a day?'

Jane grinned. 'No, I got all that from the positive pregnancy testing kit you left in the bathroom bin.'

Savannah laughed for the first time that day. 'I do one every two or three weeks just to make sure,' she admitted. 'I know, I know, it's crazy considering I'm almost five months gone.'

'Well you're lucky you're not showing yet. And you're keeping the baby when it arrives?'

'Yes, I'm saving for a deposit on an apartment, and Peyk lets me stay at the hostel for free. I'm sure I'll start getting bigger soon, and there's not much demand for strippers with stretch marks.'

'I don't know, there seems to be a fetish for just about anything these days.'

Jane picked up her strawberries, handed them to the stallholder and removed her purse from her handbag. 'You need to keep up your vitamin C intake. We'll get you some satsumas and iron supplements before we go home.'

Savannah was puzzled by Jane's interest in her. Peyk and Tommy aside, it felt like a very long time since someone had offered her kindness. But she couldn't help but feel suspicious.

'I was about your age when I got pregnant with my first,' Jane continued, 'I spent nine months peeing every half hour or vomiting.'

'I've only had morning sickness a handful of times.'

'You're lucky. Are your parents supporting you?'

'No,' said Savannah quietly. 'We don't really have a relationship.'

'That's a shame, you could really do with their help at a time like this.'

'Do you mind me asking what happened to your kids?' Savannah continued, changing the subject.

'Not at all, my friends get this . . . *awkward* look about them when I bring them up so I don't get to talk about them much.'

Jane paused and chose her words carefully before speaking.

'My husband killed our children.'

CHAPTER 20

DAY TEN

'Can I ask what you're doing here, ma'am?'

Zak aside, the private security staff who pulled up outside his address were the first people to speak to Ruth during her week-long Hollywood Hills sojourn.

'I'm waiting for a friend,' Ruth replied, and gave the officers a courteous smile.

'Who exactly is your friend, ma'am?'

'Zak Stanley. He lives here.'

'We are aware of that. And does Mr Stanley know you're camped outside his home?'

'Oh yeah, we've spoken a bunch of times. And every now and again the camera looks right at me so I can give him a wave.'

The guards looked at each other, thinking the same thing – she was a nutjob, but a harmless one.

'Well, ma'am, although this isn't a private road, we do have the authority to ask you to move on if Mr Stanley makes another complaint.'

'Oh he won't, don't worry,' said Ruth, trying to convince herself that despite their last fractious meeting, there was still hope for a relationship of sorts. 'We're friends.'

Ruth had already made the decision before the guards' arrival that until Zak returned and they'd had the chance to talk properly, she couldn't risk leaving her seat outside his house to go back to the hostel. So she'd spent a second evening catnapping on the sidewalk, waking each time a car drove past or she heard a voice, and vacating her spot to traipse down the hill to stock up on sugary snacks at the convenience store or to wash in its customer restroom. Food was a necessity, but buying deodorant, a toothbrush or even cheap clothing didn't cross Ruth's mind, because the longer she spent away from the house, the more risk there was of missing Zak's return.

And as the security men left and the hours rolled by, Ruth became more and more anxious about why she hadn't seen him in almost twenty-four hours.

204

CHAPTER 21

Nicole took quiet, deep breaths in a desperate attempt to ward off a panic attack.

She'd not suffered one in more than a decade, but she recognised the warning signs of hot flushes, trembling arms and nausea. She knew she must control her body as best she could so as not to give Eric any idea everything between them had changed.

Eric drove without a break for the 300-mile leg of their journey on the 1-10W passing through New Mexico and Arizona, and then crossing into California. And for most of it, Nicole's head was turned towards the window as she stared at the desert landscape illuminated by an almost-full moon.

Her heart hadn't stopped racing since she had discovered Maria's note, and her hand remained inside her pocket containing Mrs Baker's diamonds. There had been casual and polite chit-chat between her and Eric, but during the many silences, her thoughts were dominated by what to do once they returned to the hostel.

And time and time again, she asked herself how she'd failed to realise Eric's real identity. The answer was always the same – there had been no reason to doubt him. Eric once revealed his father had died when he was a child and that his mother had struggled to cope, so she'd packed him off to boarding school. The years had estranged them further and he'd even changed his surname to distance himself from his family.

Nicole believed he'd also failed to mention his presence to his mother at the hospital, even though he'd spent the best part of a week just feet away from her. Several times Nicole had asked if he wanted to meet Mrs Baker, but each time he declined, claiming he was too busy – a perfectly plausible excuse on an understaffed ward.

And just days earlier, Eric had even helped to scatter his mother's ashes without so much as shedding a tear. Their two-year friendship, during which Nicole had bared her soul to him, had become rotten.

What scared her the most was where to go from here. Inside her pocket lay a potential fortune, and sitting next to her was a man who'd lied through his teeth to get hold of it. What else might he be capable of? Nicole desperately needed to talk her options through with someone, and an ocean away from home, there was only one person she trusted enough to turn to for advice – Tommy.

After their latest failed mission in Lubbock, it didn't take much for Nicole to persuade him returning to Venice Beach would be a good thing for the both of them. They could relax in somewhere familiar and plan for their return to London.

'Shall we put some music on?' asked Eric suddenly, stretching out his hand to turn the radio on. He flicked around the dial until he found a station, and chirped along to the chorus of a thirty-year-old Fleetwood Mac song.

'Tell me lies, tell me sweet little lies,' he sang, both of them aware of the irony of the lyrics, but neither mentioning it.

CHAPTER 22

'You'd like me to tell you what happened to my babies, wouldn't you?'

Jane guessed that after dropping the bombshell the previous day about the death of her children at their father's hands, Savannah might be curious as to the circumstances but wasn't sure how to ask.

After their shopping expedition to the farmers' market, they had discussed many topics, but nothing about the events that had altered Jane's life for good. And, as Savannah had revealed very little about her father or why she'd escaped his grip, she knew that disclosure was a two-way street, so she had no right to ask. But if Jane wanted to offer a further explanation, Savannah would be more than happy to listen.

They were at the kitchen sink rinsing punnets of fruit under a tap when Jane stopped and rummaged around her handbag, removing a plastic wallet. She opened it to reveal a portable photo frame with space for two pictures. A pair of smiling young faces with brightly coloured ice cream covering their lips beamed from behind a protective film, frozen in time.

'That's Gregory,' Jane began, pointing to a boy of no more than five, with bright red hair and freckles. 'And that's Ruby. She's seven . . . she was seven . . .' Her voice trailed off.

Ruby shared her brother's features, and her auburn curls cascaded across her shoulders. 'They're beautiful,' Savannah replied, saddened that the two innocent souls she was staring at were no more.

'Peter, my husband, was a very controlling, very violent man,' Jane explained. 'And I reached the point where finally I couldn't take any more. Our relationship, if you could call it that, didn't equip us to raise a family, so when I told him I was planning to leave with the children, it was like I'd pushed a detonator and he exploded. He beat me unconscious and I don't remember much else, only waking up on the lounge floor to find the house on fire. I tried to get upstairs to the kids' bedrooms but the heat was too intense, so I ran to a neighbour's house for help and they called 999. We returned with a ladder, but by then, well, it was too late. All three of them were gone.'

Savannah swallowed hard, understanding all too well the damage a domineering patriarch can cause. 'Oh Jane, that's awful.'

Jane offered a grateful half smile, but she couldn't hold it for long. 'The man I married wasn't always bad,' she continued. 'I know there was some good left in him, somewhere. That's why I stayed for so long, because I wanted him to go back to being the man I fell in love with. At least that's what I tell myself, because I don't think I can bear the alternative . . . that I could have prevented this from happening by leaving years earlier and keeping my babies safe.'

'You can't blame yourself,' said Savannah, and placed her arm around Jane's shoulder. 'Is that why you came to America? To get away from what happened?'

'Yes, and because my life had no purpose any more. I wanted to do the things my kids will never have the chance to do, so I decided to see the world for them. It's a bit silly isn't it, a woman of my age chasing a dream two kids were too young to have.'

'No, it's not. Sometimes we have no choice but to leave our old lives just to keep going.'

'Yes, yes, I get that,' nodded Jane. 'But how long can you run for?'

Savannah had often wondered the same thing.

'What about you, you haven't mentioned anything about your baby's father. Is he still around?'

'Huh,' Savannah replied, 'if I was to believe one of my father's sermons, I'd say it was an immaculate conception. But the truth is, I was raped.'

'Oh darling,' said Jane, a look of sympathy quickly spreading across her face.

'It's okay, well, it's not okay obviously, but it could have been worse because I don't remember anything about it. Someone slipped a roofy in my drink and then five weeks and one missed period later, I find out I'm pregnant.'

Jane shook her head. 'The bastard.'

'I could either let it kill me or it can make me stronger, so I'm settling for the latter option. But sometimes I find myself walking down the boardwalk and I see a cute guy who smiles at me and I wonder, 'Was it you? Were you the one who did that to me?' And I could beat myself up about it, you know, never knowing who it is, or I can focus on trying to make the best life possible for my baby. So that's what I'm going to do.'

From the corridor, Peyk listened to Jane and Savannah's heart to heart and watched as Jane put her arm around Savannah and tilted her head towards her shoulder. And he realised the night he first met Savannah, he'd made a serious error of judgment.

CHAPTER *23*

'What the fuck?'

The image greeting Tommy and Jake as they turned the corner stopped them both in their tracks. It was an A3-sized poster, taped to the landing wall, of Tommy and Jake's kiss. It had been blown up, printed and then mounted for all to see.

Tommy stared at it in dismay before Jake tore it down.

'People are going to think . . .' began Tommy, 'it was only a bit of fun—'

'I know,' Jake interrupted. 'I'm really sorry, but look, it's gone now, let's throw it away and forget about it.'

As they walked towards the kitchen bin, both were aghast to see every wall plastered in more posters of their kiss. Jake frantically began to rip them down by the handful – the low profile he'd worked so hard to keep was unravelling.

TWO YEARS EARLIER – LONDON

Stuart paced around his apartment for much of the night, working out his options and devising explanations and excuses for being caught with a convulsing teen soap star and lines of cocaine on his lap.

As soon as the limousine's door had opened and the cameras started snapping, in a blind panic, he'd shoved the unopened wraps of cocaine into his pocket and pushed Katie's clutch-bag to the footwell, showering them both in a cloud of white powder.

Stuart had left Katie to face the consequences of her actions alone while he fought his way through the paparazzi, elbowing one in the nose and knocking another to the pavement as he darted towards the hotel lobby. Once inside the fancy Cardinian building, guests and staff turned their heads to stare at the commotion outside, and all eyes fell on a clearly agitated Stuart as he hurried towards the elevators. He pressed the button for the 23rd floor where Zak always camped out when in town and glanced at his reflection in the copper-coloured metal doors. He could feel himself sweating as he tried not to dwell on how social media and the press were about to have a field day with what their lenses had just captured.

Stuart was desperate to see Zak because Zak would know what to do. As a child star, he'd grown up in the public eye and could count on the best Hollywood PR machine money could buy to cover any indiscretions. Stuart thought back to how he and Zak had first met a year earlier in the green room of a Dutch TV chat show, Zak promoting his latest movie and Stuart and the band performing their new single in an attempt to crack the European music market. They'd chatted politely, but the unspoken spark between them was impossible to ignore. And when they met up again later that night in the bar of their shared hotel, their dangerous liaison began.

Geography and gruelling work schedules meant their time together was often brief and always kept under the radar, away from prying eyes. And the covert nature of their relationship suited them just fine because, as their working lives were spent as public property, both appreciated having something that was theirs alone.

As the lift approached the ground floor, a thought suddenly struck Stuart – with a new type of press attention suddenly thrust upon him, would it be such a wise move for him to see Zak that night? When Stuart lived just a few miles away in Canary Wharf, why would he be staying in a hotel? He'd abandoned Katie in the car, having convinced himself her seizure had been a brief but minor incident, and that if she'd had any sense – which was debatable – she'd have come round and told the driver to get the hell out of there. If reporters did a little digging, it would only take a small amount of financial encouragement for an indiscreet member of staff to reveal Zak Stanley was also a hotel guest, thus allowing them to put two and two together. Granted, it was a long shot, but it wasn't a risk worth taking. So Stuart made a snap decision to leave the hotel and hurried towards a rear fire exit he'd snuck out of after a past tryst with Zak.

With no battery power left in his mobile phone, he was forced to wait until the taxi dropped him off at his apartment block before he could call Zak from his landline, but it went straight to voicemail. Stuart paced around his flat, took a deep breath and logged on to the *Daily Mail*'s website from his iPad. Ninety minutes after being caught white-handed, there at the top of the page and also in the infamous sidebar of shame, was his photograph in all its glory: a wide-eyed Stuart Reynolds with two lines of cocaine on his teenage actress girlfriend's handbag.

There was also a link to a video of the incident, but as soon as Stuart saw the headline, he knew things were worse than he'd feared. It read: '*Soap actress critically ill after drugs binge with pop star boyfriend – she has seizure while he runs.*'

'Shit,' thought Stuart, realising that in a no-win situation, he'd only made matters worse by leaving a poorly Katie alone. The media and fans wouldn't care if they were her drugs and that she'd done this to herself; he would be the scapegoat.

Stuart knew he shouldn't, but he switched to his Twitter app and keyed in his name, but he couldn't keep up with the number of threads that mentioned him, many reposting the *Mail*'s pictures. The UK was alight with a new celebrity scandal, and Stuart was in the eye of the storm. He was relieved Lightning Strikes had yet to conquer America, and immediately decided that's where he would set up camp until the furore blew over.

Stuart's charging phone suddenly burst to life and vibrated the first of dozens of missed telephone call alerts. They were mainly from numbers he didn't recognise, but he speculated they belonged to reporters looking for exclusives. He'd also received voicemail messages from other members of the band. Tentatively he listened to them and grimaced as the words 'fucking idiot' and 'ruined it for us all' were thrown about.

With Zak still on his mind, Stuart called him again, but this time a woman answered.

'I'm sorry, but he's still at the premiere party,' began Mimi, Zak's sister and personal assistant. But Stuart knew she was lying because Zak loathed those parties and only ever stayed for ten minutes to network with the big players in the industry before slipping out. 'I'll tell him you called,' she added and hung up. 'He knows what's happened,' thought Stuart. 'He knows.'

There was only one person who could sort this mess out – his manager, Geri Garland. So Stuart braced himself, flicked through his contacts and dialled.

'Ahh, if it isn't the Wolf of Wall Street,' she began.

'Geri, please let me explain.'

'No need, sweetheart, let Mama G get you out of this one. It looks bad at the moment but I promise you I'll have it sorted by the morning. We'll talk tomorrow.'

'Really?' asked Stuart, surprised by her relaxed tone.

'Really. Trust me. Now go and get some sleep.'

Stuart hung up, turned his phone off and slumped into a large leather armchair.

While grateful to her for whatever she had planned, Stuart wondered what Geri would expect as payback for digging him out of his hole.

CHAPTER 24

DAY ELEVEN

TODAY

Nicole had, at best, just a twenty-minute window of opportunity to find Tommy.

Hours earlier, and with Eric filling the truck with petrol, she'd called ahead to the Venice Beach International Hostel and booked two beds in a dormitory room as she didn't want to be alone in a private room with him.

On their return to Venice, she and a reluctant Eric checked in, and on seeing Sadie covering the reception desk, Nicole momentarily feared that in her four-day absence Tommy too had ventured forth on the next leg of his travels.

More than seven continuous weeks together meant Nicole knew Eric's habits and routines, and she counted on him taking his regimented twenty-five minutes to shower, groom and freshen up. Once he'd announced he was getting out of his sweaty clothes and the shower began running, Nicole flew out of the starting blocks.

She sprinted to Tommy's room and found it empty, but was relieved when a quick scan revealed his sleeping bag and backpack were still by his bed. She considered writing him a note, then decided it'd be easier explaining to him in person what she'd learned about Eric.

She checked her watch, then ran to the lounge and half-heartedly smiled at a few familiar faces as she scanned the room for Tommy. The kitchen and courtyard were also Tommy-less, and, out of frustration, she smacked the wall with the palm of her hand.

Now she had ten minutes to run to the hotdog stand, tell Tommy she needed to urgently speak to him, and get back to her room before Eric was any the wiser.

En route, she asked herself whether telling Tommy about Maria's note was the wisest thing to do. Eric was correct when he'd suggested she wasn't the best judge of character, and it annoyed her now to think he was probably enjoying a smug laugh at her expense when he'd said it.

But she was honest enough to admit to herself her track record was poor.

So could she really trust a boy she'd known for a handful of days, or was she setting herself up for more trouble? Unfortunately she was running out of options.

Nicole's run slowed to a walk when she arrived at the hotdog stand to find the help she urgently needed wasn't working there that day. 'Fuck it, where are you Tommy?' she thought, and reluctantly retraced her steps back to the hostel and back to her room.

'Why are you panting?' asked Eric when he stepped out of the bathroom less than a minute after Nicole returned.

'I was doing a bit of exercise,' she lied, and flashed him graphics on her phone from a fitness app.

'Too little, too late,' Eric replied, rolling his eyes. 'I think the horse has well and truly bolted through that stable door.'

CHAPTER 25

For three days, Ruth survived on chocolate bars, potato chips, 7 Up and very little sleep.

But it was hope and conviction that spurred her on in her vigil outside Zak Stanley's home even if, to date, it had only resulted in two meetings with him, neither of which had gone as she'd envisaged.

Ruth anxiously looked at her watch and realised it had been thirty-seven hours and twenty minutes since Zak had left his home, and she was desperate to know where he was.

There was no battery power left in her phone, so she was unable to go online to see if his whereabouts had been reported on social media. She'd bought a *USA Today* on her last journey to the store at the foot of the hills, but nothing had been reported about Zak either in the news section or its 'Life' supplement.

She paced in a circular motion like a caged bear in a zoo. She nibbled the skin around her dirty fingernails and fretted about his safety. What if he'd been involved in a car accident or if he'd taken ill and was poorly in hospital? How would his friends and family know how to get in touch with his biggest fan to tell her what had happened? Every hour she pressed the intercom buzzer or waved her arms at the security camera to get attention from Zak's staff, but no one responded.

The more Ruth tried to reassure herself that Zak was okay, the more dominant the irrational side of her brain became, warning her something terrible must have happened to him.

And as sleep deprivation and hunger took its toll, Ruth's emotions switched from anger to frustration, concern and then distress, and she promised herself she would remain exactly where she was, no matter how long it took.

CHAPTER 26

The stains on the threadbare lounge carpet were the only things holding it together, thought Tommy as he vacuumed the remnants of the previous night's party.

The vacuum cleaner dated back at least two decades, and was so noisy and vibrated so intensely, he wondered if he should be wearing earmuffs like a pneumatic drill operator.

Sprawled across a sofa, Jake kept him company, skimming through a book on Eastern philosophy he'd plucked from the hostel's library shelf. But he was finding it hard to focus on its teachings in the presence of a shirtless Tommy, stretching backwards and forwards, cleaning the carpets.

Jake already knew how Tommy's mouth tasted, but now he wondered what his body would feel like wrapped against his own, or how his warm breath might feel on his neck . . .

'*Stop it!*' Jake suddenly interrupted his daydreams and moved his head from side to side as if to dislodge the inappropriate thoughts. He told himself he'd only been thinking about his friend in that way because he hadn't been intimate with another person in almost a year. 'It's lust you're feeling – nothing more, nothing less,' he told himself, and placed the book on his lap to disguise his growing arousal.

He noticed Tommy scowl as Matty and Declan walked past the lounge carrying footballs under their arms.

'Ladies,' nodded Declan, slowing his pace. 'You know, it really warms our hearts to see a bit of man on man romance. That touching photo of you guys is the talk of the building.'

'Oh fuck off,' replied Tommy, and took a swig from a bottle of Pepsi.

Matty turned to Declan. 'I'd have expected a bit more gratitude for capturing such a tender moment on camera.'

'I should have known it was you idiots,' said Tommy, to which Matty and Declan grinned and waved before continuing their journey. Tommy opened his mouth to shout to them but Jake spoke first.

'Don't bother replying, they're not worth it,' he said.
'They're going to regret it.'
'Why? What's the point? They've had their fun, just let it lie.'

'They've humiliated me!'

'So you're saying people thinking you're gay is humiliating?'

'No, that's not . . . . no, I meant—'

'Then leave it.'

With the carpets as clean as Tommy could manage without the aid of paraffin and a match, he took a dustpan and brush and began working his way through the first of six sofas, removing the cushion seats and scooping out stray nickels and dimes that had fallen from pockets into the creases. Tommy was fumbling around to pull out confectionery wrappers when his fingertips touched something leathery.

He removed a brown tan wallet and looked inside; there were only a few dollar bills, free McDonald's vouchers and an old debit card with the name Matthew O'Keefe embossed on the front next to a driver's licence.

He briefly considered doing the right thing, but his dislike for Matty and Declan was so intense that he changed his mind and walked towards the plastic bag of rubbish Peyk had cleared earlier. He was ready to take the cash and toss the wallet away when he noticed a newspaper cutting protruding from the bills. Curious, he took it out, and raised his eyebrows when he read it.

'Nail, meet coffin,' he said out loud, and punched the air.

CHAPTER 27

'Jim Morrison was my first crush when I was a girl,' smiled Jane, pointing towards artist Rip Cronk's 20-foot-high mural of a shirtless Doors front man emblazoned upon a wall.

'I must only have been six or seven when I saw him in one of my sister's music magazines, and he made me weak at the knees,' Jane continued.

Savannah lifted her head to look at the painting and, although she couldn't name even one of The Doors' songs, she recognised the band's name from what her father called The Forbidden List – a four-page document of musicians and groups that if listened to, would be tantamount to allowing Satan directly into your heart.

'One of the reasons I came to Venice Beach was to see this mural and where Jim moved to when he and Ray finished university and formed the group.'

Savannah struggled to match Jane's enthusiasm on the subject, but she was coming to enjoy the company of her new roommate. Jane took a photograph of the mural on an archaic pre-Internet mobile phone, before they made their way a couple of blocks back towards the boardwalk. Savannah linked arms with Jane; it had been a long time since she'd felt so comfortable with a virtual stranger. And the more time they spent together, the more she felt her guard slipping.

Frequently they paused to watch the street performers, and now a peculiar duo caught their attention; they consisted of an elderly, wrinkled, white woman in a pink spiky wig, yellow plastic sunglasses and a bikini, and a very tall black man wearing just leopard-skin swimming trunks and a sombrero.

He tunelessly plucked at three strings on a banjo while she banged a tambourine and hopped on one foot.

'Do you think they're a couple?' asked Savannah.

'I'm not even sure they're human,' joked Jane, 'but I love that they've found each other. Like-minded souls can find each other in the most unusual of circumstances.'

Neither Savannah nor Jane recognised the song the clueless entertainers were attempting to play or understood the point of their act, but they admired their tenacity and dropped some loose change in their collection box.

'You mentioned your sister last night – Roseanna, was it?' Jane asked.

Savannah nodded. 'I miss her, we were pretty close. It's funny you bring her up because she turns sixteen today.'

'You could always call her, you know. Just to wish her a happy birthday and let her know you're okay.'

'I've thought about it, but I'm scared of what my dad would do to her if he found out.'

'He can't be that bad, can he?'

'You have no idea what he's capable of, Jane,' Savannah replied, and a flashback of a mallet striking Michael's hands and forehead made her shiver.

'Six months is a long time. You don't know if the situation at home has changed since you left.'

Savannah was convinced it hadn't, and the tremendous guilt she'd felt for leaving her sister behind to fend for herself suddenly returned.

CHAPTER 28

'I can't find it,' said Matty anxiously, the contents of his backpack strewn across the floor of their room.

'It's got to be somewhere,' replied Declan, stripping both beds of sheets and pillowcases and looking under mattresses.

'Yeah, big help, everything is somewhere.'

'Calm your jets, man, it's only got the money we made from pawning your necklace.'

'It's got the newspaper story inside as well.'

Declan stopped what he was doing and turned to face Matty. 'What?' he said slowly. 'That's why you're so jittery?'

'I thought you knew?'

'No, I didn't fecking know! You idiot!'

'I know, I know, you don't have to say it.'

'But I'm going to, because I told you to get rid – if anyone here reads that, we're shafted!'

ONE YEAR EARLIER – DUBLIN AIRPORT

Matty and Declan's box-fresh rucksacks disappeared along the conveyor belt as they left the Lufthansa check-in desk and walked back towards Matty's parents.

'You've got everything: your passports, boarding cards, wallets?' fussed Matty's mother. 'You have that bag, don't you? Make sure you have that bag.'

'Yes, I have it. Now don't worry, I've been abroad before,' Matty reassured his mother. But it failed to placate her, and she promptly burst into tears. Matty's father offered her a hug.

'Don't worry, Mammy, you've known all along I have to leave on my own terms.'

'I know,' said Mrs O'Keefe, 'but you're still our little boy and we're going to miss you so much.'

'Let him be, Deirdre,' interrupted her husband. 'He knows what he's doing. Take care of yourself, son.'

His teary-eyed parents hugged Matty, then Declan, and the boys began to walk towards the departure lounge. Suddenly Matty turned towards them.

'You did a good job, you know. With me. You did a good job. Thank you.'

Matty didn't wait for their reaction or a reply as his own tears began to roll down his cheeks and land on the lapels of his jacket. Instead he turned around and continued to walk as Declan placed a supporting arm around his friend's shoulder.

'It's not too late to change your mind,' he said.

Matty shook his head.

'Not a chance.'

*

The air conditioning blew cold and noisily above the drone of the engines as the plane taxied down the runaway towards its take-off slot.

Declan stared through his window at the country he was consigning to his past, at least for the foreseeable future. There was little about it he would miss; certainly not the parents who'd brought him into that world.

His mother had moved to Shannon three years earlier and Declan had lost count of the number of times she'd texted him her new pay-as-you-go phone numbers. She had stuck to her word and attempted to stay in touch with her sons, but Declan wasn't prepared to listen to her apologies for putting alcohol above her family's needs. Then when he'd finally decided to grasp her olive branch, her number no longer existed.

Declan and his father navigated their home in different directions and at different times of the day. His dad was a nocturnal man, preferring to drink by night and sleep by day. So Declan accepted the mantle of role model to Finn and Michael, his two younger brothers, and in doing so, often became the barrier between them and their father's drunken fists.

Hours after saying goodbye to them, he was already feeling immense guilt for leaving them behind. But he took comfort that they were now both working at the warehouse depot, and from his ill-gotten post office gains, he'd paid the deposit and three months' rent money for their new flat over the curry house and away from their father.

The rest of their booty he and Matty planned to use for their own hedonistic gratification. By the end of that day, there'd be sand between their toes as they watched the sun set at Ibiza's legendary Café Del Mar before hitting the clubs. Then Spain, Italy, France,

Germany, Sweden, Thailand, South America and North America would follow, God willing. After that, well, who knew, as they would most likely be living on borrowed time.

Yes, Declan thought, there was much to be excited about once their plane rose above the asphalt, but there was an equal amount to feel uneasy over too. Sometimes he wondered if uneasy was a feeling he would ever shake off.

'Oh, fuck.' Matty interrupted Declan's thoughts. 'Oh, fuck,' he repeated.

'What's wrong?'

'Look.'

Matty passed him a copy of the *Irish Times* he'd picked up at W.H. Smith's in the airport. Declan recognised a familiar face in a picture the size of a postage stamp.

'*Postmaster dies after bungled armed robbery*,' read the headline.

'What the . . .' gasped Declan, and continued to read.

'A man died yesterday following an armed robbery at his post office a week ago. John Wallace, 68, who ran Navan's only post office for 36 years, collapsed with a suspected heart attack as two robbers attacked his premises. A garda spokesman said: "We believe they might have been captured on CCTV outside a nearby newsagents. If that is the case, we hope to quickly identify them before they strike again".'

'Dec, we killed him,' said Matty quietly, and Declan closed the newspaper. 'We killed someone.'

Declan remained silent, stared at the seat in front of him and gripped the arm rest. After a minute or so, he spoke. 'It was an accident, Matty. He had a weak ticker, it could have happened at any time to anyone. We have to forget about him.'

Matty stared at Declan and didn't reply.

'Matty, I said we need to forget about him, okay?'

Matty nodded reluctantly and Declan put his headphones on, chose a Ministry of Sound playlist and pumped up the volume to drown out his own uneasiness.

He didn't hear Matty tear the story out of the paper, fold it neatly and place it in his wallet.

*

TODAY

By the time their room had been searched from top to bottom, it resembled a Midwestern state trailer park after a tornado.

Declan stood in the centre of the room, rubbing his eyes and pinching the bridge of his nose in disbelief.

'I cannot believe you'd be that stupid. When did you have your wallet last?'

Matty closed his eyes and retraced his steps from the night before. 'The lounge!' he suddenly blurted out. 'When we got back from the beach, I stopped off to buy some gum and came straight back in here for the party.'

'Then let's go find it.'

But as they opened their bedroom door, Tommy was standing on the other side with the missing article in his hand.

'Looking for this?' he smiled.

CHAPTER 29

Despite Ruth's promise to herself that she wouldn't fall asleep again until she was sure Zak was safe and sound, it took the horn of his SUV to wake her up from an unplanned siesta.

Zak glared at her from behind the wheel of his vehicle as the gates to his property opened and he screeched to a halt. Ruth's initial relief that he was still alive gave way to fear when Zak leapt from the vehicle and charged towards her, chest puffed out and nostrils flared.

'Why are you still here, bitch?' he yelled, not giving her a chance to respond. 'This is your last chance to get the fuck off my street!'

Ruth swallowed hard, terrified of Zak's aggression. And when she was too scared and confused to reply, he pulled out his phone and began to dial a number before walking back towards his house. Suddenly she burst into life.

'No, please don't go, Zak, I just want to talk to you,' Ruth pleaded. 'I've seen all your films and interviews and you seem like such a good guy.'

'I'm an actor; I get paid to be nice, and you ain't paid me shit . . . Hi, I'd like to report an intruder who's harassing me . . . yeah, it's Zak Stanley and I'm on Sunset Plaza Drive . . . yeah, as soon as possible, thank you.'

'But I know you love animals and so do I. I nursed a sick dog but he . . . um . . . died,' Ruth added, desperately.

'What are you talking about?' replied Zak, genuinely baffled.

'We could be friends, I know we could.'

'Us? You and me? Ha! You turn up at my house uninvited, and you think we're gonna be buddies? Life doesn't work like that.'

'But it can! Look, that film you were in, *Baby Baby*, the bit where you say, "I know this is the first time we've met, but I don't ever want to lose sight of you again . . ." – that's how I feel about you.'

'It's just a fucking film! And that's the trouble with people like you – you can't see the difference between what's on a screen and what's real life. So you come to my home and harass me and think we'll be besties? Fool!'

'Please, Zak, please, I know you'll like me if you give me a chance, I'm a good person, I really am.'

'Look at you – you're . . . shit, I don't even know what you are. What's with your clothes? You stink of BO, I can smell your breath from here. And that hair! Have you ever washed it? I've dated Miley, Ariana, Iggy . . . Tell me, how would I explain you to my friends?'

Ruth paused for a moment. 'We don't have to tell anyone! We could be secret friends.'

Zak paused to take stock of the latest in a long line of obsessive fans, but none had been as pitiable as Ruth. In his mind, he'd tried diplomacy, he'd attempted to be polite, and he'd used the cruel-to-be kind approach, but nothing had worked. So when Ruth grabbed his arm, there was only one option left open to him. He swung around sharply and grabbed Ruth by the throat, pushing his face into hers.

'Listen, bitch, for the last time, I ain't interested in you or being your pal,' he hissed. 'Now get your stupid fat ass out of here before I do something you're gonna regret.'

Then he shoved Ruth to the pavement and removed his wallet from his pocket. 'If I was poor you wouldn't want me, would you? For people like you it's all about getting a piece of my fame and my money.'

He threw a handful of $50 and $100 bills at Ruth and she wept as the money and her dreams landed in the gutter.

'There, you don't need anything from me now, right?'

The last time Ruth had heard those words, they had come from her father's lips. She promised herself she would never hear them again from someone she loved, and that included Zak.

Zak turned his head when he noticed Ruth's shadow against his gatepost, but before he could react, she plunged her knitting needles deep into his throat.

CHAPTER 30

'It's not what you think,' began Matty, and he and Declan froze, staring wide-eyed at Tommy and the wallet.

'What I think,' began Tommy, 'is that you two robbed a post office, literally scared an elderly man to death and now you're on the run.'

'Prove it,' added Declan.

'I don't have to,' continued Tommy. 'The story might not name you, but I bet the police back home would be interested in knowing your whereabouts.'

Matty and Declan looked at other, then at Tommy, and said nothing.

'Lost for words, boys? You usually have so much to say.'

Declan cleared his throat. 'Cut to the chase, what are you gonna do?'

Tommy grinned. 'What am I going to do, or what have I already done?'

'Tell me you haven't,' said Matty.

'Hmm, I could, but I wouldn't want to lie to you.'

Tommy instinctively turned his head and lifted his arm up to protect his face when Declan lurched towards him, pinning his arm under Tommy's neck.

'You bastard, you've got no idea, have you?'

'I know that you think you can get away with anything if you turn on the Irish charm,' said Tommy, his windpipe throbbing under Declan's chunky forearm. 'Well, you can't anymore.'

'Leave him, Dec, it's not worth it,' interrupted Matty, 'Let's just get our stuff and go, eh?'

'I'd hurry if I were you,' added Tommy, 'it won't take long for that nice officer I spoke to at Dundalk *garda* station to call his colleagues in the LAPD.'

Declan punched Tommy in the stomach, causing him to fold in half and gasp for air. Then he grabbed Tommy's T-shirt and reached his arm back, ready to whack him again, but Matty yanked him backwards to stop him.

'Dec, please, don't.'

Declan hesitated and dropped Tommy back on the floor.

'You might not like the way we carry ourselves, but I'll tell you this for nothing. We'd rather be who we are than you – a petty, spiteful little shite who's terrified of losing his place as King Dick in a poorhouse.'

'You have no clue what I went through before I made this trip,' gasped Tommy. 'And do you think I like dressing up as a fucking hotdog just so I can afford to be here? I didn't just take a short cut and steal.'

'Did it ever cross your stupid little mind why we did it?' spat Declan.

'No, please tell me, I can't wait to hear your excuse for this one.'

'Because Matty's . . . Matty's . . .' Declan's voice trailed off into silence.

'Because I'm dying, Tommy.'

Tommy paused and looked at them both. His initial reaction was to assume they were lying, until Declan punched a hole in the plasterboard wall.

CHAPTER 31

Savannah made the most of the quietness of the near-empty beach.

Instead of sprawling across the sand, today's tourists were distracted by the sights and sounds of an Indian music and food festival spread across the boardwalk. Savannah had already been caught up amongst the throng of performers, and smiled at their brightly coloured saris and dark hats decorated with white flowers. She'd gasped as acrobats hurled themselves up in the air from stilts others held shoulder high, twisting in the sky and landing with precision back on the inch-wide footholds. And she'd gratefully accepted a paper plate crammed with food samples that she ate as she walked across the beach towards the shore. Even from a distance she could hear the singing of traditional Indian folk tunes.

Savannah sat on a blanket with her arms wrapped around her legs and her chin resting on her knees, watching as the tide brought the same piece of sea kelp in and out, over and over again.

Having been raised so far away from the coast, only now could she appreciate how freeing it was to be near to what felt like an infinite body of water that could sweep a person in any direction for as long as it desired. For months, Savannah had lived from day to day, keeping one eye on the present and one eye over her shoulder, waiting for the past to catch up with her. But that afternoon, she allowed herself to consider a future that didn't involve raising a child on a bedrock of fear.

It had been more than two months since someone had tried to bundle her into a van and since she'd accidentally shot Tommy. There had been no further threatening incidents.

Starting there and then, she decided to make a conscious effort to change. While caution would always prevail, she knew she must learn how to trust people again and not assume any new faces automatically had a hidden agenda.

From behind, she felt the vibrations of feet softly plodding through the sand towards her. Her gut reaction was to still scramble to her feet defensively, but this time she didn't act on it and instead, she remained in place.

'I hope you don't mind, but I saw this little romper suit in K-Mart I had to buy for the baby,' came Jane's enthusiastic voice. She sat beside Savannah and removed a variety of baby clothes from a bag. 'Well maybe that was a white lie,' she continued, 'I might've accidentally bought all these things as well.'

'Thanks Jane, but you shouldn't have,' smiled Savannah.

'Well, you don't have anyone else to spoil you.'

'Why are you so nice to me? You hardly know me.' Savannah said, not out of suspicion, but genuine interest.

Jane paused and gazed out towards the horizon. 'For selfish reasons, I suppose. I spent seven years as a mum and now nobody needs me. I feel kind of, well, surplus to requirements, I suppose. I'm sorry if you think I'm interfering.'

'No, you're not. It's . . . nice that somebody cares.'

Savannah closed her eyes, tilted her head towards the sun, and took a deep breath.

'What's wrong, love? Are you feeling a little lost today?'

Savannah paused and put her hand on Jane's. 'You know what? I don't think I am anymore.'

Neither Savannah nor Jane was aware of the figure standing way behind them under the shadow of the lifeguard station. Nor did they know they'd been followed for much of the last two days.

CHAPTER 32

'Sit down,' said Matty, pointing to a chair in the corner of the room. 'Please.'

Tommy obliged, but kept his hand pressed on his aching ribs, still unable to breathe normally following Declan's swift blow. He watched cautiously as Matty removed a washbag from under his bed, unzipped it, and poured out a dozen blister packs and plastic tubs of tablets. Then he took another and did the same.

Matty sat down and leaned his back against the wall. 'I've got problems with my heart, Tommy,' he explained quietly. 'I was born with a congenital heart defect, or to give it its proper name, a complete atrioventricular canal defect. I had a transplant three years back, but this new one's not keen on its new home.'

Matty lifted his shirt to reveal a long, raised vertical scar on his chest.

'He was waiting for another donor before we left Ireland,' muttered Declan.

'But the chances of getting a second match are pretty slim,' Matty continued. 'I've been in and out of hospital my whole life, and I've had enough. I told Declan that I wanted to see the world before it was time to leave, but the only way I could afford it was if we robbed a bank. It was supposed to be a joke until, well, we robbed the next best thing.'

'No one was supposed to get hurt, that wasn't the intention,' added Declan. 'We only found out about yer man's death when we read it in the paper. And we only stole what we needed, we didn't take the piss.'

'We were pretty mortified,' continued Matty. 'Declan's brother reckons the *gardai* couldn't identify us from the CCTV pictures, so for the time being we're safe. But all it would take is a tip-off and who knows what might happen.'

'Wouldn't another transplant work?' asked Tommy, eyeing Matty as he placed his tablets back inside the washbags.

'I'm sick of waiting and I'm sick of these drugs, Tommy. They stop me dying, but they also stop me living. So when my body gives up on me, I want to go out with a smile on my face and my best mate close by. Then I'll know I lived a life.'

The room fell silent for a moment before Tommy spoke again.

'I didn't call them . . . the police. I mean, I wanted to, and I even Googled their number in Dundalk and I was *this* close to doing it, but I bottled it at the last minute. I just wanted to scare you into leaving.'

Matty and Declan let out long, relieved breaths.

'Why do you want us out of here so badly?' asked Matty.

'Why do you reckon?'

'Because we tease you?'

'You do more than that and you know it.'

'But only because you treated us like scum the day we arrived.'

'Yeah, but you were trying your luck to stay here for free. But yes, I know, I was patronising and I'm sorry for that. People like you just . . . "fit in" without having to do anything. It took me weeks to get to know everyone, and that's only because I work here so they're forced to get on with me. And I got . . . well, jealous.'

'Tommy, everyone here loves you, man,' Declan replied. 'You just need to lighten up a bit.' Tommy offered an embarrassed smile.

'So what do you say, shall we call a truce?' Declan continued. 'I mean, I can't guarantee we're not going to rib you now and again, but just give as good as you get, man.'

Tommy nodded and shook hands with Matty and Declan, then passed Matty's wallet back to its rightful owner.

Matty took the newspaper cutting out and ripped it to shreds, letting the pieces float into the bin. And he hoped now that someone else was in on their secret, Declan would have someone to talk to when the inevitable happened.

Because Matty's body was quietly telling him the inevitable wasn't far away.

CHAPTER 33

Zak Stanley knew something peculiar had just happened to him, but he couldn't process what it was.

He turned around slowly to face Ruth and felt a foreign body protruding from his neck. As his fingers fumbled around for the source of his discomfort, he felt little pain until he made contact with her knitting needles.

Then he understood what the crazy bitch who was gawping at him in terror had just done and his eyes opened wider than they ever had before.

Instinctively Zak panicked and yanked the needles out, but that caused air to rush in and blood to pour violently from the small but deep puncture wounds. His legs began to buckle beneath him as he placed the palm of his hand on his neck to stem the flow, but it was coming too thick and fast from his jugular, pouring down his T-shirt and soaking his chest and underwear.

Zak looked around desperately for help and tried to scream but no sound came. He stared at Ruth, his eyes frantically searching hers for mercy. But Ruth remained transfixed by Zak and his urgent need for her; she was the only person Zak Stanley was turning to in his moment of need. Her eyes began to well up and she smiled.

Zak became rapidly weaker and struggled for breath until his legs finally gave way and he hit the sidewalk, knees first. Ruth knelt down by his side and stroked his hair.

'I told you we could be friends,' she said gently, pulling away the hand he held to his wound. Fearing she might hurt him again, Zak made an attempt to crawl away from her, until she overpowered him by pushing him onto his back then straddling him, holding his arms by his side. Zak was too sluggish to fight her off.

'It's okay, you'll be okay,' Ruth continued, then she lay by his side, placing her head on his damp chest. She could hear his heartbeat growing fainter and fainter until, after a couple of minutes, it finally rested in silence.

She lifted her head and then slowly placed her lips upon his; Zak's final, bloody kiss would be Ruth's first.

'I'm a good person, Zak, I really am,' she whispered, and hoped Zak understood that now.

THREE WEEKS EARLIER – VICTORIA, AUSTRALIA

Ruth picked out a pair of snow-wash jeans, folded them neatly and placed them inside her half-full suitcase.

Next came her supermarket-brand underwear, which she rolled up and placed inside the inner lining of the case, followed by two pairs of sneakers and some high heels. Finally when everything was inside, she took the washbag from her chest of drawers and unzipped it.

'Make-up!' she said out loud, realising that if she wanted Zak Stanley to see her at her best at their first lunch together, she'd need to add some colour to her face. But with only a paltry selection of her own, she decided to borrow from her mother's drawer of lipsticks and blushers.

She grabbed a handful of brightly coloured cosmetics and glanced at her mother's body lying under a duvet on her bed. The blood that had flowed from the gash in her head had pooled on the pillow, and over the last half-day had gradually turned brown. She presumed her brother Kevin's pillow would look the same. Ruth tilted her head to one side and reminded herself it was their own fault it had come to this.

The previous night's taunting from Kevin had felt relentless, mocking her decision to travel to LA, laughing about how Zak would react if he ever met her and how she would be scampering back home with her tail between her legs by the end of the week.

'What do you mean *if* Zak ever met me?' Ruth asked Kevin, suddenly. 'I told you I won the competition. I'm having dinner with him. I *am* meeting him.'

'Yeah, about that,' Kevin giggled. 'You didn't win shit. I was messing around with you – didn't you notice the name I gave his manager? Paul Mollegh? Say it out loud Ruthy and it sounds like "pull my leg". I told you to leave my computer alone and you didn't so you needed to be taught a lesson.'

Without premeditation, Ruth lifted the dog-shaped stone doorstop and crashed it against Kevin's head with such force that he was dead before he even hit the floor. When their mother appeared from the bathroom to see what the loud thud was, it took three blows before her face finally stopped twitching.

That night, Ruth enjoyed the best sleep of her life.

Two days later, she padlocked her suitcase, put her plane ticket and passport in her jacket pocket and locked the front door, making her way to the waiting taxi and imagining her new life with Zak Stanley.

CHAPTER 34

TODAY

Guests at the hostel had wandered en masse up to Santa Monica to spend a late afternoon at Ye Olde King's Head.

The British-themed pub was a favourite of ex-pats and tourists who'd make the pilgrimage to the tavern's two bars and attached shop to drink or stock up on British biscuits, sweets, Heinz beans and Marmite – the latter being a commodity Americans had yet to embrace.

Photographs of celebrity visitors like David Beckham, Sienna Miller, Liam Gallagher and Kelly Osbourne adorned the walls surrounding a karaoke machine, a DJ booth and television screen with scrolling lyrics. Tables contained pitchers of Boddington's Ale and Fuller's London Pride, drained pints of Guinness, pencils and notepaper to nominate potential singers and their chosen tracks.

Tommy thought Matty and Declan's tuneless rendition of U2's 'Where the Streets Have No Name' was a clichéd Irish choice, but in the spirit of their truce, he kept his opinion to himself.

'Go on there, Tommy,' yelled a sweating Declan. 'Get off your arse and give us a song.'

Tommy shook his head. 'I can't sing to save my life.'

'Who cares, we're more Shane McGowan than Bono.'

'Ah come on, you big bollocks,' chipped in Matty, and pointed to Jake. 'Drag yer man up there with you.'

Tommy paused for a moment and turned to his friend. 'Do you fancy it? I will if you will.'

'No mate, my singing days are long gone.'

'You used to sing? Full of surprises, aren't you?'

Jake's heart began to beat a little faster at his error. 'No, no, I meant I'm terrible.'

'Then you'll make me look good!' Tommy replied, and grabbed Jake's arm to lead him to the song choice book. But Jake yanked it back.

'I said no, alright?' he snarled. 'You can make a fool of yourself, but leave me out of it.'

Jake slammed his half-empty glass back on the table, threw open the door and stormed out, leaving behind a confused Matty, Declan and Tommy. Jake barged past Nicole coming in through the door, and she made immediate eye contact with a surprised Tommy, who could tell immediately by her anxious glance that something was wrong.

'What are you doing back here?' he began.

'I need your help,' Nicole replied. 'Can we go somewhere quieter?'

CHAPTER 35

Even as the red mist was descending upon him, Jake was aware he was overreacting, but he couldn't batten down the hatches on his temper in time.

Anger gave way to panic, and the need to leave the pub became of the utmost importance. He walked briskly back to the hostel; everyone he knew was in the bar he'd left behind, so maybe he could gain some peace and quiet and hopefully some perspective.

TWO YEARS EARLIER – LONDON

Stuart awoke, slumped in the armchair in his apartment where he'd fallen asleep.

The previous night had been the worst of his life, and his brain had reacted to such high levels of stress by shutting itself down. He'd fallen asleep in his clothes and hadn't woken once in almost nine hours. It was now 10.30 a.m.

Zak was the first person who crossed his mind as he wiped the sleep from his eyes. Over the next few minutes, Stuart called him several times to no avail, then remembered Zak would probably be airborne and en route to his next European premiere. In his heart of hearts, he'd resigned himself to their covert relationship having ended – the team Zak employed to advise and protect their Hollywood golden goose would've seen to that.

Stuart picked up the television remote control and hesitantly turned on Sky News. The news ticker scrolling across the bottom of the screen contained nothing about him being caught with drugs, and for a moment he wondered if manager Geri Garland had unleashed her infamous damage-control monkeys and they'd worked through the night to quash the story.

He popped an extra-strong Nespresso capsule into the machine and poured himself a black coffee. But as the noise of the machine faded and the final drips fell from the nozzle, the newscaster's words chilled him.

'Now, following the death of actress Katie Begley earlier this morning after an apparent accidental drugs overdose, we head over to a live press conference which is just about to begin in north London with TV's Geri Garland.'

Stuart froze at both the news of Katie's death and the appearance of Geri as she confidently stepped towards a podium in what looked like her record company headquarters. His eyes widened further when he saw the rest of Lightning Strikes accompanying her.

'I have a statement to make on behalf of Lightning Strikes, *Star People* and IMG Records,' Geri began gravely. 'Firstly, we would like to extend our deepest sympathies to Katie's family and friends . . . we're all thinking of you. Now, I was as shocked as anyone last night by the photographs and video footage of Stuart Reynolds, apparently caught with drugs and leaving a clearly poorly Katie when she needed him most. I have since discovered from Stuart's bandmates that his drug use was not a one-off incident, but an ongoing problem he has had for some months.'

Stuart's coffee mug fell to the floor and shattered.

'Despite many attempts and several interventions, Stuart has refused to tackle his issues which culminated in last night's events,' Geri continued. 'I would also like to take this opportunity to point out that I personally was unaware of Stuart's substance abuse. Lightning Strikes are a band with many, many, young fans. And while we all love Stuart dearly, this is something we all feel we cannot just gloss over. So it is with regret that Stuart's position in Lightning Strikes has been terminated with immediate effect. We wish him all the best in recovering from his addiction and we will provide him with the help he needs if he asks for it. That's all we have to say.'

Geri nodded her appreciation to the scrum of reporters who attempted to ask extra questions as she left the stage.

Stuart remained rooted to his kitchen floor, unsure of where to turn.

CHAPTER 36

TODAY

The beach was quiet, with the exception of construction workers in the distance building temporary bleachers for the following day's volleyball tournament.

The lifeguard had long since boarded up the windows to his station and headed home, so Nicole and Tommy sat on the wooden ramp, their legs dangling below them, casting shadows onto the sand. Four crushed Nytol mixed with parmesan cheese and sprinkled on Eric's pasta had given Nicole at least a few hours of respite from his all-seeing eyes before they opened again.

'I knew there was more to your trip than you were letting on,' began Tommy when Nicole finished filling him in on the events of the last few days.

'I'm sorry,' replied Nicole, shaking her head, 'Eric didn't want me to tell anyone, and now I know why, considering what was at stake.'

'Why did he never let on Mrs Baker was his mother?'

'She mentioned they'd had some falling out over money and she'd cut him out of her life, but she didn't really go into detail and it didn't feel right to ask. Now I wish I had – maybe I could've put a few pieces together earlier.'

'Didn't she recognise him when he was working in the hospital?'

'Her brain tumour meant she couldn't see or hear properly, and she wasn't his patient, so their paths never had a reason to cross.'

Nicole rooted around her jeans pocket and passed Tommy the small velvet pouch of diamonds. 'Shit!' he blurted out when he looked inside.

'I know. I've been carrying them around all day, as I don't know what to do with them. Eric's dad was a jeweller so I'm guessing they're real.'

'First things first, you need to get them valued.'

'How? It'll look suspicious if I disappear for a couple of hours, and I can't keep drugging him, can I? The money Mrs Baker left me in the truck isn't going to last forever, so we'll have to go home soon, and how am I going to get these things through customs without shipping the truck back? I can hardly keep them on me or post them. And I'm scared to death to be alone with him.'

'Why, has he threatened you?'

'No, not yet. But I've seen his temper when he can't get what he wants and there's a dark side to him I don't want to see again. And if he can keep all this from me, what else is he capable of?'

'I think we need to tackle this one problem at a time. Do you trust me?'

Nicole paused and wondered if she could trust anyone ever again, then nodded her head. She had no choice, she thought.

Tommy smiled and held her hand. 'Then let me help you.'

CHAPTER 37

HOLLYWOOD HILLS

'The home to your right used to belong to Gwyneth Paltrow and Chris Martin back in the mid-2000s,' continued Jenny. 'Although the marriage didn't last, Gwyneth remained here until quite recently.'

She switched the microphone to silent mode and yawned, willing her last tour of the day to finish. She drank from a bottle of carbonated water as the mainly European sightseers inside the air-conditioned minibus took photographs of the Spanish-style villa roof behind tall, red brick walls.

It was Jenny's fourth guided tour of the day, and her voice was gradually turning into a rasp. 'Just one more trip and I can get some rest,' she thought to herself as the bus slowly wound its way up the road. She turned the microphone back on and prepared to fake more enthusiasm.

'And this is for the ladies, because just around the corner is the home of actor Zak Stanley!' she continued, as the female tourists and two gay men chatted excitedly and got their cameras ready. 'Zak has lived here for a year,' Jenny continued, 'And oh, look, his gates are open . . . and that looks like his car . . .'

Her voice trailed off as the minibus driver suddenly hit the brakes, trying to make sense of what he saw. The excited chatter soon fell quiet as their eyes stared at Zak, lying face up on the sidewalk by his open car door, covered in blood and with a woman pressing her head upon his chest.

'Oh my Lord,' gasped Jenny, as the first of the tourists screamed. Suddenly mobile phones were set to video mode and cameras flashed at the dead celebrity and his killer.

'Call 911,' she whispered to the driver.

CHAPTER 38

DAY TWELVE

With her facial swelling and bruising from the fracas at the club beginning to fade, Savannah disguised her injuries with make-up and returned to work for a six-hour afternoon shift at the Pink Pussycat club.

It had been an unusually quiet day, and Savannah's takings were meagre, but she had spent much of her time distracted by a conversation she'd had with Jane. In their six days together as roommates, she'd found herself growing closer to Jane, and because her friend had experienced so many tragic personal events in her life, Savannah appreciated her counsel.

The second payphone booth Savannah tried on Fourth Street had a working receiver so she removed sex workers' flyers from the dial and typed in an out-of-state number she knew by heart. She clenched her fist in her hoodie pocket until the number rang and was answered.

'Hey,' a female voice answered.

Suddenly doubting her decision, Savannah pulled the phone from her ear and was about to hang up, then paused, and changed her mind.

'Hello?' the voice said again. 'Who's this?'

'Hey Roseanna, it's your sister.'

CHAPTER 39

Ron didn't dwell on it when Tommy quizzed him on whether he knew of a jeweller who could offer an honest price for something without asking any awkward questions.

Instead, he flipped through his Rolodex and pulled out a card with an embossed name and telephone number printed on it. 'Tell him you work for me,' muttered Ron, then ushered Tommy out of his office. One phone call and ninety minutes later, Tommy was standing in a brightly lit office above a dry cleaner's in Marina Del Ray.

The deeply wrinkled man with the waxy pallor sitting behind the large mahogany desk had yet to identify himself, either on the phone or in person, while two stocky South East Asian men stood guard at either side of the steel door. If the diamonds were real, there was little Tommy could do if anyone in that room decided he wasn't going to leave with the merchandise he'd arrived holding. He could just disappear and no one would be any the wiser.

The man squinted at Tommy through his thick-framed glasses and rubbed his tongue across his dentures before he asked to see the jewels. He poured them from the pouch into a gloved hand, counted them out with tweezers and carefully examined them one by one though his loupe. Then he weighed them on digital scales and measured them with the tiniest of steel rulers.

Tommy was glancing nervously around the room when a framed photograph on a filing cabinet caught his attention. 'Is that the Hostel in the Woods?' he asked suddenly.

The man pulled his glasses down to the tip of his nose. 'You know it?' he asked.

'Yes, my mate Sean and I stayed there a few months back.'

The man nodded. 'Then you're a man of good taste, because I paid for the fucking place. My son built it and runs it.'

'Adam, the manager? He's your son?' asked Tommy, surprised, as there was little family resemblance.

'Yeah, he's a good kid. I never really went in for all that hippy-dippy bullshit, but I gotta say, he's done a beautiful job with it.'

'Small world,' replied Tommy, and for the first time, the man smiled.

THREE MONTHS EARLIER – MISSOURI

The left hand side of Sean's face was planted firmly on a Travel America guidebook lying on the seatback table.

He quietly snored as the Greyhound bus left the highway and made its way slowly towards the tiny village of Adrian, Missouri. Tommy popped his headphones into his ears, pushed a memory card into his digital camcorder and began to watch video footage he'd taken of their first two months in America.

There was a Fourth of July fireworks display at Cape Cod; Sean being engulfed by a huge wave at Daytona Beach; Tommy snorkelling in Key West; drinking warm hot chocolates in Starbucks as the rain poured down outside in Atlanta; Sean clapping along to a gospel choir in a downtown Chicago church; and the both of them covered in blue waterproofs as the *Maid of the Mist* sailed close to Niagara Falls' cascading wall of water.

In a short space of time, they'd amassed some incredible memories, and as Tommy looked at his sleeping friend, he knew that he wouldn't have had the guts to travel America without him. Only once had Tommy experienced homesickness, but he soon came to his senses when Sean reminded him the home he craved had crumbled the day his brothers died. Tommy felt confident being around Sean, but at the same time he knew the part of him that remained broken meant he was using Sean as a crutch.

In the two dozen hostels they'd passed through in a few short weeks, they'd been in each other's pockets almost twenty-four hours a day. They'd met people along the way, but neither had committed to building fresh relationships with new faces while they had each other for support. There was going to come a time when they'd want to take separate paths, and Tommy hoped that once that happened, they'd still find their way back to each other.

He removed the memory card from his camcorder, placed it back in its plastic case and then glanced at a second one, paused and shook his head.

*

For almost a decade, the Hostel in the Woods had led a quiet existence, hidden in a forest about thirty minutes from Missouri's Greyhound terminal.

From the moment the battered orange VW camper van decorated with Grateful Dead stickers picked Tommy and Sean up from the station, they understood it was not the traditional hostel they'd come to expect. The van came to a halt under palms, cedars, myrtles and moss-covered great oaks, and from the vehicle's window, they noticed dormitories housed in hexagonal, two-tier wooden houses, with some perched high in the treeline above the eighty-acre site.

Sean stepped out of the vehicle and grinned as ahead of them, a man swung from a rope attached to a tree branch and plunged into a pool below, where two friends rested their arms on the wooden edges and cheered him on. Behind them, other hostellers busied themselves picking vegetables from small, irrigated plantation areas and swept wooden verandas. According to Sean's guidebook, which awarded the hostel a rave review, accommodation was inexpensive but guests were expected to help with chores like cleaning, washing up, digging over vegetable patches and cooking.

However, Tommy was too overcome by an instant dislike of their temporary new home to notice Sean nodding his appreciation as he took in nature's sights and smells.

'This is it, the Hostel in the Woods,' began Sean.

'Probably more like *The Cabin in the Woods*,' Tommy replied, recalling how the film of the same name had scared him to death.

'No gas or electricity – you cook your own food over open fires, sleep under the stars and boil your water from a well. It's back to basics for us, Tommy.'

'What part of any of that description do you think appeals to me?' Tommy replied, already pining for the bustle of a big city.

*

Sean was already awake and outside the next morning, acclimatising himself with his new neighbours by the time Tommy woke up and unzipped his sleeping bag.

Tommy's lumbar area ached from the firm mattress he'd slept on, so he stretched and ventured towards the porch, rubbing his pollen-affected eyes. His head itched, and he felt small clusters of raised lumps where mosquitoes had dined on him throughout the night. It didn't help to lighten his dark mood, the same one he'd fallen asleep in.

Outside, many of the hostel's guests were already up and eating a communal breakfast around wooden picnic tables. Tommy was looking at his watch, which read 5.50 a.m, and scowling at the ungodly hour when he felt two sharp jabs in his ankle.

'What the—?' he began and glanced down to find an angry cockerel with a razor-sharp beak pecking him. He tried to kick it away, but the bird stubbornly refused, so he broke into a jog as the flapping creature chased him. He could hear people chuckling at his predicament until the bird finally lost interest and returned to wherever it'd been hiding.

'Always a hit with the birds,' laughed Sean, sitting barechested with two women in oversized checked sleeping shirts. 'Charlotte and Rochelle, this is Tommy.'

As Tommy went for a handshake and Charlotte opted for a peck on each cheek, he became flustered and his hand bounced off her breasts instead.

'We're going for a swim if you fancy it?' continued Sean. 'There's a pool over there made from a natural spring – how cool is that?'

'I'm going to pass, I need some breakfast,' Tommy replied, unable to fake any enthusiasm.

'Oh, breakfast was at 5, sorry, but there's a Twix in my bag if you're hungry?'

Before Tommy could formulate a suitably sarcastic reply, Sean and his new friends began to peel off their clothes and walk naked to the pool. Although Tommy was used to seeing his best friend without a stitch on, he'd had never seen him be so public about it.

'When in Rome!' Sean declared, sensing his friend's surprise.

'Remember what happened to Caesar,' muttered Tommy as he walked towards the toilet block. Behind the cubicle door was a hole in the ground and a bottle of disinfectant.

He opened his mouth to vent in frustration, but closed it quickly when the stench made him gag.

CHAPTER 40

TODAY

'Oh my God, Savvy, where are you?'

Savannah's sister Roseanna tried to contain the volume and excitement in her voice when she realised who was on the other end of the telephone line.

'It's best you don't know, honey,' Savannah replied, comforted by her little sister's voice, 'but I wanted you to know that I'm safe. How are you doing?'

'It's like living in jail here since you left. I hate it,' Roseanna whispered. 'I can't go anywhere or see anyone without one of Daddy's men following me.'

Savannah closed her eyes, wracked with guilt. 'I'm so sorry. And I'm sorry that I left you, but please know that I had no choice. When I'm settled I'll call and maybe we can find a way for you to come and join me?'

'I'd love that,' Roseanna replied, before the tone in her voice altered. 'You need to listen to me, Savvy. Be careful, because I heard Daddy talking and you can't trust—'

Suddenly the line went quiet.

'Can't trust who, Rosie?' Savannah asked, but there was no reply. 'I can't trust who? Rosie? Hello?'

When Savannah heard a deep, throaty cough coming through the receiver, a chill ran down her spine. She slammed the phone back onto its cradle and ran to hail a cab.

CHAPTER 41

Matty lay in his bed until late morning, exhausted after a dreadful night of broken sleep.

His dreams alternated between watching the postmaster falling to the floor over and over again, and seeing himself struggling to fight off a pack of snarling wolves taking it in turns to sit on his chest.

The sound of a shrill car alarm below his bedroom window made him give up any hope of further sleep, so he opened his eyes and felt his head pulsating. Quietly, he took a couple of painkillers from his bedside table and swallowed them with a mouthful of flat Pepsi.

'You okay there?' muttered Declan from his side of the room, his eyes half closed.

'I don't want to be a killjoy, but do you mind if I give the beach a miss later?'

'Of course I mind,' yawned Declan, perching up on his elbows. 'How often do they have *Playboy* beach volleyball tournaments on your doorstep?'

'I know, I just don't feel so great.'

'What's wrong? Have you taken your meds?' Declan asked, suddenly concerned.

'Yeah, I'm just hanging. Too many Jägermeisters at last night's karaoke. I'll sleep it off and maybe see you there later.'

'Do you need anything? Do you want me to find you a doctor?'

'No, it's cool.'

'Okay, look, I'll hang here with you. We'll have a day of chilling instead.'

'Don't been an eejit, go hunt me some rabbits.'

'Alright, if you're sure.'

Declan rolled on to his side to grab another thirty minutes of sleep while Matty lay on his back, staring at the ceiling and trying to regulate his shallow breaths.

CHAPTER 42

Tommy waited the best part of an hour in the office of an unspecified individual in a dubious line of work before the man sitting before him finally offered a verdict on Nicole's jewels.

'What you have here, kid, are sixty-six emerald-cut diamonds,' he began. 'They're very well cut, actually; the clarity is excellent, although to the naked eye there's slight colour weakness.'

Tommy nodded like he knew what the man meant, and cleared his throat. 'How much do you reckon they're worth?'

'Hmm . . .' the man replied thoughtfully, tapping his chin with his index finger. 'I'm prepared to offer you $8,000 for each of them. You'd probably get a lot more if you went elsewhere and went by the book. But it depends on how quickly you need the money, and if you're happy for their origins to be scrutinised. You've heard of blood diamonds, yeah?'

Again, Tommy nodded, aware of the reference to the murky ways war-zone diamonds were sold to finance insurgencies. It was highly probable Mrs Baker's gifts were legitimate, but Nicole had said she trusted him to do what he thought best if an offer was made.

The man removed a calculator from his desk and keyed in some numbers with a stubby finger. 'It's your call, kid. Sell them to another dealer for bigger bucks or walk out of here with $528,000 in cash.'

CHAPTER 43

Eric made his way towards the pick-up truck in the near-empty multi-storey car park, tossed a plastic bin bag into the footwell of the rear passenger seat and began clearing the rubbish Nicole had carelessly thrown around the vehicle throughout their travels.

Amongst the trash were local newspapers, fast food wrappers, empty cans and bottles of soda, and photocopies of maps and highways that marked their journey together. One of the things he'd learned about her over the weeks was that she could still make a mess in a rubbish tip. It was one of the – many – things about her that had begun to grate on him.

As he cleaned, Eric mulled over how Nicole's behaviour towards him had visibly shifted since his outburst in Lubbock. Maintaining his façade day-in, day-out, had been more exhausting than he'd expected, and after one major slip, he was convinced Nicole now looked at him differently.

For the rest of their journey back to Santa Monica, he'd tried to lighten the mood by engaging her in conversation or singing along with songs on the radio, but it had little effect. And by the time their truck rolled into the car park opposite the hostel, he was ready to slap the sulking out of her.

Since their return, Nicole had kept her distance from him, and it had come as a welcome relief. Back in the real world, there was no doubt he enjoyed her company, even if she was a little whiney at times. But he could dip in and out of her worries and woes if and when he liked. On the road, there was no escaping each other.

He recalled the day he realised his estranged mother Mrs Baker had been admitted to his hospital ward and, upon checking her charts, discovered she had little time left. It saddened him that her pain couldn't be prolonged as it was no less than she deserved, not that Nicole would understand why. Eric believed coincidence or fate had reunited them, and it was pure luck and good fortune that she'd built up a rapport with Nicole. But when Mrs Baker had left vague directions of *his* inheritance to *her*, everything changed. Nicole was no longer a friend, she was a means to an end.

However, with no way of knowing what his mother had planned, Eric was ready to throw in the towel and head home. Once he'd finished cleaning out the truck, he planned to go online and price up a flight back to London.

Nicole could do whatever the hell she liked: his adventure was over.

Eric worked his way towards the driver's side pockets, throwing away receipts and chewed gum wrapped in tight little newspaper balls, before digging out rubbish from the passenger's side. When he lost his grip of a stray Tic Tac, it fell under the seat so he fumbled around trying to find it. Instead, he grasped a small piece of paper. He was ready to chuck it away, but its red handwriting caught his attention.

'*Don't let her son find these – they're not for Eric,*' he read out loud.

It took a moment before the significance of the words sank in, and suddenly Eric understood he wasn't the only one who was playing a game.

But he knew Nicole had no idea what she was about to let herself in for.

CHAPTER 44

Jake and Nicole acknowledged each other with polite but wary smiles when he entered the hostel lounge and sank into the sofa opposite her.

Peyk messily slurped miso soup from a bowl balanced on his lap and turned the television on, flicking around the stations for a news channel.

Nicole and Jake had seen each other around the hostel, but had yet to talk. Both were aware Tommy played a part in the other person's life, but not to what extent. Nicole recalled that when she'd rebuffed Tommy's advances, he appeared to devote his attention towards Jake, and now she couldn't help but feel envy at their closeness.

Meanwhile Jake recognised Nicole as the girl from the hostel party Tommy had tried – and failed – to kiss, and was slightly resentful of Tommy's attraction to her.

And while Nicole anxiously awaited Tommy's return from his meeting with Ron's contact and news of her diamonds, Jake also waited for his friend to reappear so he could apologise for storming out of the King's Head pub the previous afternoon. He wanted to offer Tommy an explanation for his sudden tantrum, but the jury was still out as to whether he could trust him enough to tell him the truth about his past life and his subsequent actions.

Because Jake knew what could happen when you mistakenly trusted someone.

TWO YEARS EARLIER – LONDON

Stuart Reynolds was no stranger to loneliness.

Lasting friendships were hard to make in foster homes, and even when he joined Lightning Strikes, his feelings of isolation continued. A part-time, behind-closed-doors relationship with Zak Stanley didn't help him to find the meaning of belonging either.

But as Stuart sat on a wall opposite Geri Garland's four-storey mansion on the wealthy side of Notting Hill, waiting for her to return, he'd never felt more alone in his life. He pulled his hood over his head to shield his hair from the drizzling rain.

He looked from side to side to make sure he wasn't being

watched by a rogue paparazzi and removed two wraps of cocaine he'd kept at his apartment for Zak's visits, dabbed his finger inside and rubbed the powder into his gums.

Eventually he recognised Geri's Range Rover pulling up outside her town house. Her driver opened her door and she exited, putting on her sunglasses for the five-metre walk between the vehicle and her front door. Stuart hurried towards her, the drugs already making him alert and filling him with bravado.

'What have you done to me?' he yelled, and Geri turned around sharply. Another man appeared from the passenger side of her car and pushed Stuart backwards as he approached her.

Geri glanced over the top of her sunglasses and offered an insincere smile. 'It's alright, lads, he's harmless. Come in, Stuart, let's get this over with.'

TODAY

'Fuck, man!' yelled Peyk suddenly, and spat his soup across his bare legs.

He turned up the volume of the television, as a 'breaking news' graphic filled the television screen, along with a photograph of Zak Stanley and the word 'MURDERED!' emblazoned across it.

'This just in,' began the female newscaster, 'Police sources have confirmed that actor Zak Stanley has been found dead outside his Hollywood home after an apparent attack.'

'Oh my God,' began Nicole, watching as cameras broadcast live from the street she and Jake had followed Ruth to days earlier. Black and yellow police tape had been attached to trees on opposite sides of the road to cordon off the area, while forensic investigators wrapped in blue plastic suits placed numbered markers on the road.

Neither Jake's body nor his face moved as he processed what he was watching.

'According to sources, it appears Mr Stanley was stabbed to death by a stalker,' continued the newscaster. 'His body was taken to UCLA Medical Center where he was pronounced dead on arrival.'

A small crowd of hostellers began to gather in the room, all stunned and some sobbing at what was being shown. Nicole suddenly lifted her hands to cover her mouth at the next image to flash across the screen.

'And we have just received this footage taken by a passenger on a Hollywood Hills tour bus. It has yet to be confirmed, but it appears to be an ailing Mr Stanley with his attacker.'

As the HD footage focused in on the figure with her head on Zak's chest, Nicole instantly recognised Ruth.

'No,' she gasped, 'Oh no, no, no.'

Instinctively she wanted to find Eric to tell him the news until she remembered why that part of their relationship was as dead and buried as Mrs Baker.

She turned her head to look at Jake, but he had already disappeared.

CHAPTER 45

The sweat trickled down Eric's face as he furiously rummaged around the truck searching every nook and cranny of the vehicle. He didn't know what he was looking for but he knew from the note it was important enough for him not to be made aware of it.

He hunted under the floor mats, down the back of the seats, inside the boot, under the bonnet and even rattled empty soda cans until he suddenly thought of the one obvious place he'd yet to examine. Remembering the air vent he'd kicked at Buffalo Springs Lake and Nicole had later fiddled with, he yanked out the plastic covering, put his fingers inside and rummaged around, until he found what felt like a small, sharp stone.

He pulled it out and dropped it in the palm of his hand. Instantly he knew it was part of his mother's legacy – a modest but perfectly formed, polished diamond.

'Gotcha,' he muttered, then sat back in the seat and began to consider where Nicole might have hidden the rest.

He promised himself only one thing – this would not end well for Nicole.

CHAPTER 46

'I'm trying, but I'm just not getting it.'

'No, darling, neither do I. Give me Constable or Renoir over this experimental twaddle any day of the week.'

Jane and Savannah's heads tilted at right angles as they stood staring at a 15 foot by 15 foot painting in a plush art gallery on Abbot Kinney Boulevard. Dubbed the 'coolest block in America' by *GQ* magazine, everywhere – from the boutiques to the salons, restaurants and bars – was beyond Savannah and Jane's budgets, but at least the galleries were free to browse. Although quite what they were peering at, neither could be sure.

'It looks like a dwarf playing tennis with an ostrich in a bonnet,' continued Jane.

'It says on the plaque that it's a portrait of a post-apocalyptic snowman.'

'Well, who am I to argue with art? I can barely draw a stick man. What do you say to admitting defeat and grabbing an iced-tea in the café upstairs?'

Savannah followed Jane up two flights of clear Perspex stairs, where they sat on stools sculptured to resemble open-palmed hands. Roseanna's warning that there was someone in Savannah's life she shouldn't trust weighed heavily on her mind. Despite trying to be more trustful of people, several times she'd caught herself questioning Jane about her life back in England to see if her story altered, but there were no discrepancies.

A day earlier Savannah had allowed herself to feel safe and now, so soon, she worried she was heading back to square one. She didn't want to doubt Jane's motives in befriending her or begin pushing her away, but it would be foolish to ignore the obvious.

'I might not understand art, or even the people in Venice some of the time, but I am drawn to Los Angeles,' continued Jane. 'Not all that showbusiness gubbins of course, but areas like Venice, Santa Monica and West Hollywood. How about you? Can you see yourself raising your baby here?'

'I guess so. I don't think I really have much of a choice for now. Once I save up some more money, I'll rent a little apartment and, when he's born, I'll get a part-time job that doesn't involve taking my clothes off or sliding down a pole.'

'So you know it's a boy, then?'

'Oh, no, I haven't asked about the sex. I just have a feeling.'
'Will you miss the hostel when you leave?'
'Yeah, I've made some good friends here and I have someone who's been there for me when I needed him the most.'

FIVE MONTHS EARLIER – SUNSET BOULEVARD

A blown socket in the air conditioning unit meant the humidity in the Flesh For Fantasy strip bar in downtown LA were unbearable.

Savannah put the handful of $5 and $10 bills she'd scooped from the stage into her bag, then grabbed a towel from her locker and patted herself down. She drank two thirds of a bottle of sparkling water she'd left by her mirror, and once she'd showered, she finished off her drink and put on her civilian wardrobe.

On her arrival in LA a month earlier, work had been much harder to find than Savannah expected. The cash she'd taken from her father's wallet and the money she'd withdrawn using his ATM card in Alabama would, she calculated, last her ten days at most once she found herself a cheap motel to book into. And then she would need to find a job. But her only experience in the working world had been to volunteer at a charity for the elderly with friends from the Zeta Phi Beta Sorority House. And without any experience, restaurants and shops weren't willing to take a punt on an inexperienced girl from the south-west.

'You should use that body to make yourself some money,' one waitress at a diner Savannah frequented had suggested.

'I'm not a hooker,' Savannah replied, indignantly.

'That's not what I meant,' laughed the waitress. 'If you can shake your ass and don't mind being leered at by horny guys, you could make a bunch of Benjamins dancing at one of the clubs on Sunset. Just an idea.'

It was an idea that didn't appeal to Savannah, but beggars couldn't be choosers, and right now she was a beggar. She was also a beggar who'd spent her youth participating in beauty and teen pageants thanks to a pushy mother with more interest in showing her off than asking if that's what she wanted to do. Now all those years of modern dance classes and cheerleading might have been worth it.

Two days and one audition later, and Savannah had a trial at Flesh For Fantasy, not the classiest of joints, but by no means the worst of the clubs in LA.

And although the cheap motel she had made home was a dive, she couldn't wait to get back there as the humidity in the club was making her tired and dizzy.

*

The driver slammed on his brakes when the girl stumbled across the sidewalk and fell into the road.

He leapt out of his car ready to yell at her for being drunk, but once he reached for her limp body, he knew alcohol was not the cause of her intoxication.

'Help me, please,' she mumbled, her eyes darting across his face, looking for kindness. 'Drugged . . . been drugged . . . my water . . .' Savannah's head lolled to one side, so the man picked her up and carried her to his car, laying her across the rear seats.

'I'll take you to the hospital,' he said, closing the door.

'No . . .' she continued, 'he'll find me . . .'

The driver was at a loss as to what to do, so he rummaged through her handbag to find an address or a cell phone with a name he could call. He found it peculiar that for a girl her age, she had no phone but around $400 in cash.

Thirty-five minutes after finding a key for the Marigold Motel, Savannah was safely lying on her bed in her room and fast asleep as Peyk made himself at home in an armchair.

CHAPTER 47

TODAY

Eric rushed back to the hostel from the multi-storey car park and managed to slip past the lounge while Nicole and a group of others were preoccupied by something on the television screen.

He didn't have the time or the inclination to discover what had them so silently engrossed. Instead, he bolted up the stairs and along the corridor into their dormitory where he began to rummage through Nicole's suitcase. But as each pocket only yielded socks, underwear, fridge magnets and postcards Nicole had purchased on their travels, Eric became more and more frustrated.

'Looking for something?' came Nicole's voice from the doorway.

Eric stopped his search, switched on a smile and turned around. 'Oh hi, Nicole,' he replied chirpily. 'Where've you hidden the paracetamol?'

'Unzip the top of the backpack and they're in there with the plasters.'

'Cool.'

By the time Eric found them and turned around to thank her, Nicole had disappeared as quietly as she'd arrived.

CHAPTER 48

Peyk didn't question Tommy when a taxi pulled up outside the hostel and he darted out, grabbing Peyk's arm and leading him up the stairs and into room 23.

'How safe is this room?' Tommy asked breathlessly.

'Three deadbolt locks and a reinforced steel door, I fitted them myself.'

'Well your DIY skills don't inspire me with confidence, what with the number of times you've fallen through the ceiling or electrocuted yourself.'

'Do you see anyone else creating a cannabis farm under the noses of 150 unsuspecting people?'

Peyk glanced down and noticed two large, bulging holdalls with the name and logo of a dry cleaners emblazoned across their sides. 'Don't ask,' Tommy muttered, his eyes darting around the room.

Peyk's ability to keep secrets was something Tommy appreciated, and even though he'd yet to discover what made Peyk tick, his gut instinct was that the wiry-haired clown had a serious side and could be trusted.

'The room at the back, under the ceiling tiles, store them there,' Peyk replied.

Tommy made his way towards the storeroom and used a stool to reach and remove one of the polystyrene tiles, where he placed the bags containing Nicole's cash out of view. As he stepped down, his eyes were drawn to a bathroom beyond the storeroom, separated only by a pane of clear glass. He walked towards it, then took a startled step backwards when he saw Savannah enter. She pulled down her shorts and underwear and sat on the toilet. Tommy remained perfectly still so he wouldn't be spotted, before realising he was on the other side of a two-way mirror.

'You okay in there, Tommy-boy?' yelled Peyk, and Tommy joined him back inside the room.

'I'll keep your business private if you do the same with mine,' Peyk added, and Tommy nodded his agreement.

CHAPTER 49

'He called me Nicole. In three years he has never called me by my full name, so don't ask me how, but I'm sure Eric's found out I know who he is.'

Nicole waited nervously for Tommy to finish serving a customer at the hotdog stand.

'You could always admit to what Mrs Baker left you?' Tommy asked. 'You'd get him off your back by splitting the cash.' Nicole pondered his suggestion for a moment before politely dismissing it.

'I'm not being greedy, but clearly his mum didn't want him to have it. And if he's gone to all this trouble to hide who he is, what else is he capable of doing?'

'Well that might be a good enough reason to pay him off, if he frightens you. Keep yourself safe.'

Nicole had left Eric in their dormitory searching for headache tablets and gone straight to meet Tommy at their prearranged destination. He'd explained that while he could have likely got more money if he'd sold the diamonds legitimately, he'd done what she'd asked and made a decision he thought was right.

'This has been a messed up few days,' Nicole continued. 'First I discover my best friend has been lying to me about who he is, then I find his secret mum has left me half a million dollars worth of diamonds and, to top it all, the naive girl I shared a room with goes and murders Hollywood's biggest star.'

'You haven't heard the update, then?' asked Tommy tentatively, unsure whether Nicole was ready to hear more bad news. 'According to the radio in the taxi, police in Australia reckon she killed her mum and little brother before she came over here.'

'You're not serious! Am I just the worst judge of character in the world?'

'It's looking that way,' Tommy joked, but Nicole didn't laugh. 'No,' he added, 'you've just been bang out of luck.'

Nicole let out a long breath and brushed her fingers through her hair. 'What the hell is going on, Tommy? I thought this trip was going to be a new start for me, and it's turned out to be worst thing I've ever done.'

Tommy didn't know how to respond, so he placed his hand on Nicole's to comfort her as two middle-aged women approached him.

'Three hotdogs, no mustard, just salad,' smiled one and winked. Nicole was too preoccupied to notice Tommy twice flash three fingers to José behind him in the trailer or to see José putting three sausages in buns, and then three small bags of pot in each of them. The customer smiled and handed Tommy $50 in return. Moments later, two police officers cycled past and waved at a smiling Tommy.

'So how far are you willing to go to take Eric out of the picture?'

'What do you mean?'

'I mean you can't spend much longer living under the same roof as him and avoiding being alone with each other. You need to make a pre-emptive strike, because if he's cottoned on that you've found what Mrs Baker's left you and haven't told him, he's going to be mightily pissed off.'

'I'm worried about him, Tommy,' Nicole admitted, and shuffled awkwardly on the spot. 'Actually, I'm terrified to be around him. But you know what? Above all else, I hate him. I absolutely hate him. And the more I think about his lies, the angrier I get. So over my dead body is he getting any of that money.'

'If you need a head start to get away from here, there is a way,' Tommy replied, his brain slowly formulating a plan. 'But it's pretty fucking harsh and it'll cost you about $20,000.'

CHAPTER 50

'How about you?' Savannah asked Jane as they placed their bags of shopping on their beds. 'Do you like being in Los Angeles?'

'I'm falling in love with it, actually,' Jane replied. 'I've often toyed with the idea of trying my hand at writing . . . I even took a course a couple of years ago, and I think I have a few stories inside me. Not *about* me, of course, there's enough of those "woe is me, isn't life crap?" memoirs without my contribution. But this city inspires me.'

'So what's stopping you?'

'I think I need a permanent base and to set down some roots. And I can't really do that in a hostel. It's just a thought, and promise me you'll tell me if I'm being silly here, but what would you think about us finding a place to share together?'

'Oh, I don't know,' Savannah replied, feeling herself flinch. She wasn't at ease being put on the spot, even by a friend, and instantly she questioned if this was part of some plan to get her away from the hostel and on her own. Why else would Jane offer a home to a pregnant pole dancer? But it was almost too tempting.

'My baby will be here in a few months,' Savannah continued carefully. 'Do you really want to live with me and a screaming kid?'

'You have no idea how much I'd like to hear that sound again,' Jane replied wistfully.

Savannah felt ashamed of her insensitivity and watched Jane look away and absent-mindedly fumble with a gold crucifix she wore on a chain around her wrist.

'Sorry, I shouldn't have said that,' replied Savannah.

'No, no, you didn't say anything wrong. And you're right, darling, it's a daft idea. A young girl like you wouldn't want to live with an old codger like me.'

'On no, that's not what I meant. It's just that I can only afford somewhere low budget, like above a store or something.'

'Well if money is the only thing holding you back, my husband's life insurance means we could afford a little place in West Hollywood. Nothing big, mind, but I can cover the rent for at least eight or nine months. Maybe he can finally do something good in death that he couldn't do while he was alive.'

Savannah was unsure of what to say to Jane. While the offer was undoubtedly kind, relying on someone else for help hadn't been part of her plan. But she was desperate for Jane to be real.

'Well, if you're sure, we could give it a go, I guess?' she replied, and Jane held her hand out to shake Savannah's.

'Well it's a deal then,' beamed Jane, and Savannah began to tell herself that maybe her fairy godmother had been sent to her for a reason.

CHAPTER 51

'Hey, lazy bollocks, you missed a hell of a day – wall-to-wall *Playboy* bunnies, volleyball, silicone and swimsuits . . . even if you'd dreamed it, it couldn't have been better,' Declan began as he walked into their room.

Matty didn't respond, and lay on his side facing the wall while Declan covered his burned red face and shoulders with aftersun and continued to boast.

'And – get this – I've lined us up a couple of bunnies for tonight. You've got to see them – they're beautiful, Matty. Matty?'

Declan held his breath when he realised Matty's body had remained motionless. He had spent many, many hours watching his best friend sleeping and studying his breathing patterns, and this wasn't normal. Slowly, Declan moved towards him and steeled himself. He put his hand on Matty's shoulder and pulled him over onto his back where Matty remained still, his eyes firmly closed.

'No, Matty, no . . .' whispered Declan, placing his panicked fingers on Matty's neck, desperately searching for a pulse.

Suddenly Matty's eyes opened and he burst into laughter, while Declan reeled backwards in shock.

'You fecking idiot!' yelled Declan. 'What did you do that for? I thought you were . . . you were—'

'Dead? You can say the word, you know!' laughed Matty. 'Just think of this as a dry run.'

'That's not funny.'

Tears streamed down Matty's face as his laughter became uncontrollable, but Declan didn't share his friend's amusement.

'Go fuck yourself,' he growled, and stormed out of their room.

CHAPTER 52

The news of Zak Stanley's death hit Jake with the force of a juggernaut.

Feeling suffocated in a lounge crammed full of strangers mourning the image of a man they never knew, he headed towards the open space of Venice Beach and the calming sounds of the waves washing in and out. He slipped out of his flip-flops and waded into the water until he was waist deep, allowing his breathing pattern to mimic the tide. In and out, in and out, slowly in time with the rhythm of the water, until Jake began to feel calmness return.

Zak had been the person who'd known Stuart best, and even though they'd not seen each other since before the night cameras had caught him with cocaine on his lap and a convulsing girl by his side, his death made Jake feel a little more alone. He'd held on to the hope that one day their paths might cross again, and he imagined engineering a reunion by finding out where Zak lived in Los Angeles and turning up on his doorstep so they could close the chapter they'd left unfinished.

But it was only ever a daydream, and now Jake would never really know if Zak had tried to find him, because three days after making headline news, Stuart's phone and wallet had been discovered lying on the grass by the 500-foot chalk cliffs of Beachy Head.

As far as the world was aware, somewhere in the depths of the English Channel, currents were carrying Stuart's body away, never to be found.

Meanwhile a newly born Jake was on the deck of a ferry sailing from Hull to Zeebrugge, Belgium, using a forged passport purchased from his Russian ex-housemates in Bolton.

TWO YEARS EARLIER – NOTTING HILL, LONDON

Geri Garland held a key card to a metal panel on her glossy black front door, which opened automatically.

She slipped off her cropped leather bomber jacket and tossed it across a Chesterfield sofa in a large, airy hallway.

Stuart and her bodyguards followed her into a drawing room and watched as she poured herself a Scotch from a decanter into a chunky glass tumbler, then dismissed them.

'Mmm, that's good,' she purred, taking a long sip. 'It's been a hell of a morning, hasn't it Stu? You know, they say alcoholic drinks taste better in a heavier glass because the weight of the tumbler can trick the brain in the way it processes taste. But you'd know a lot about tricking people, wouldn't you?'

'Why did you sell me out?' Stuart blurted out.

'Why not?' Geri replied, matter-of-factly. 'Why should I sacrifice a whole herd of cash cows when I only need to send one to be slaughtered?'

'But it wasn't my cocaine! You could have helped me convince the papers of that, or come up with an explanation.'

'An explanation? Like what? That you'd had an accident with a bag of flour? Don't be so naive. If it were just photos then maybe there'd have been a way out, but you were stupid enough to be videoed with it on your lap. On your bloody lap! They had you bang to rights.'

'But you're not listening to me – it was Katie's coke, not mine.'

'It doesn't matter if it was the Queen of bloody England's coke, it was all over you and a teenage soap star. As far as everyone's concerned you're the one who killed her.'

'You didn't have to sack me, you could have said you were sending me to rehab. Loads of stars end up at the Priory, and I'd have been out within a month and everyone would've forgiven me.'

'Not Katie's parents. Because for the rest of your public life they'd have hounded you in the press; look what happened when that lad drowned in Michael Barrymore's swimming pool. He was never allowed to forget that and it destroyed his career and you'd never be allowed to forget running away when that poor girl was dying next to you.'

'I'm the front man of that group, you told me that yourself. That's why you put me in it. The band can't survive without me.'

'Band? You mean brand, because that's all you are. And don't fool yourself into thinking they're going to split up just because of your stupidity. You gave those boys some competition, something to aim for, someone to beat. They've all developed a bit of charisma now, and without you I'm confident they'll step up to the mark.'

Stuart swallowed hard – he would not cry in front of her. 'Bullshit, I've read the Twitter and Facebook messages,' he argued. 'I know it's me they pay money to hear sing.'

Geri gave a deep, throaty laugh and lit up a menthol

cigarette. 'Are you now so deluded that you've told yourself you have a voice?' she asked. 'You can't even carry a bloody note! We all know that, that's why we hired a session singer behind the scenes to do all your vocals for you, even the pre-records for the live shows. I'll give you credit though, you're the best bloody mime act I've ever worked with. But you're just a pretty face with no talent. Face facts, Stu, you were an experiment to see if the public would buy a silk purse made from a sow's ear, and they did. And you knew that from the word go.'

'What about you and me?' he continued, desperately trying a different tack. 'I thought we ... had something.'

Again Geri laughed. 'Let's not go there, shall we son?'

'I don't deserve for it to end like this,' Stuart pleaded.

'You didn't deserve a £1 million recording contract either, or a Canary Wharf penthouse or a Mercedes. But I didn't hear you complaining when you saw the money stack up.'

Geri took a deep drag from her cigarette and inhaled the smoke coming from her mouth with her nose.

'You're not getting it, are you kid?' she continued. 'You're a liability. Nobody will touch you with a bargepole in this business again. You had some laughs, you saw the world, you lived like a star, now move on.'

'But—'

'But nothing. Sooner or later you'd have fucked it up for yourself anyway. Katie and I did you a favour.'

Stuart frowned and chewed the inside of his cheek. 'What do you mean you and Katie did me a favour?'

CHAPTER 53

DAY THIRTEEN

Eric finished flossing his teeth and lifted up his vest, studying his reflection in the bathroom mirror as he rubbed the hairs on his stomach backwards and forwards.

He hadn't found the time to manscape in weeks and was annoyed at himself for allowing things to become so untidy downstairs. He turned to his side and pushed out his stomach as far as it would stretch, then inhaled deeply. He could just about make out his six-pack under a fatty layer of convenience food, sugary soda drinks and a recently acquired penchant for blueberry muffins. He vowed he'd have all the time in the world to get back into shape once his mission was complete, and he predicted this would be very soon once he worked out what Nicole was up to.

Now she was aware of who he was and had greedily unearthed his mother's legacy without telling him, the playing field was level and the game could begin in earnest. It was a game he'd win, of that Eric was sure. And he knew the chickens were coming home to roost a decade after they they'd been thrown from the family nest.

For someone who had little regard for the well-being of people in general, even Eric was aware of the irony of choosing a nursing career. After a handful of expulsions from the country's top private schools, he'd scraped his way through five GCSEs and scratched a living from part-time jobs as a casino croupier and call-centre worker before joining the health care industry.

It was a career he planned would take him around the world once he branched out into the private sector, as that's where the real money lay. Palliative one-to-one care for the wealthy and terminally ill meant he could earn more in the space of a month than in a year within the NHS. But with two more years of experience still required and his current earnings basic, Eric found a lucrative sideline through a single and needy hospital pharmacist who fell easily for his flattery.

Soon after their first tryst, he'd had her keys copied and replaced inside her handbag without her being any the wiser. And not long after she'd turned on the 'closed' sign and gone home for the night, Eric was like a child with free night pass to Toys 'R' Us.

He'd had contacts willing to pay handsomely for past-their-sell-by-date drugs before the pharmacist denatured them or sent them off to an incinerator. He'd also pocket empty order chits while his patsy was otherwise engaged.

Frequently, Eric slipped Alzheimer's, dementia and comatose patients vitamin tablets or placebos instead of their regular medication, believing it made no difference to their well-being what tablets they took: they were doomed anyway. Those pills also sold well on the black market. But while his extra earnings gave him a higher standard of living, it wasn't enough for Eric. Now Nicole held the key to how he should be spending the rest of his life.

Eric exhaled and let his belly expand, pulled his vest down, and steeled himself for his next performance with Nicole. As he opened the bathroom door he saw her hovering around her bed looking nervous, before she turned in his direction.

'I'm heading out for a bit,' Nicole said.

'Where are you going?' Eric asked with a painted smile.

'To the chemist's,' Nicole replied, and smiled back at him. 'You used the last of the Paracetamol. I won't be long.'

As she left the room, Eric knew he'd been lied to, as he hadn't taken any medication. He glanced suspiciously at their bunk beds and, at first, couldn't put his finger on why they looked different. Then he noticed Nicole had uncharacteristically tidied up around her bed; her clothes and empty bags were no longer scattered across the floor; her sheets and pillow were in place, but her sleeping bag was nowhere to be seen. Neither was her suitcase, he thought. He checked under her bed to see if she'd stored them there but the space was empty. He went towards the locker area where Nicole sometimes kept her belongings, but there was no trace of her.

'She's running away,' he realised, feeling his rage rise. Immediately he located his toilet bag and rifled through it, shoving something into the pocket of his jeans. Then he ran down the corridor after her.

CHAPTER 54

Tommy anxiously drummed his fingers on the reception desk, turning his head to check the clock above Ron's office for the second time in a minute.

A full day had passed since he'd last seen or spoken to Jake, but Nicole's troubles gave him more cause for concern than Jake's unexpected outburst at the karaoke bar. And while Tommy didn't hold grudges, he'd quietly hoped Jake would've sought him out to apologise by now.

Meanwhile Savannah perched on a stool behind Tommy and placed spacers between her toes, painting her nails in a deep red. He looked jittery, she thought, but she didn't ask why.

Every so often she felt twinges in her stomach, so she'd gently rub her belly in a clockwise motion, as if to reassure her baby all was well in the outside world that awaited him. She hoped it wasn't a surge of hormones heightening her emotions or preventing her from thinking rationally, but she had a hunch that moving in with Jane was the right thing for all concerned. No matter how much she mulled it over, she just couldn't find fault with Jane. And it was too difficult to resist the offer to live under a proper roof with someone experienced in motherhood to help guide her in those first few difficult weeks. She knew she must put her child's welfare above her own pride.

'Yes,' she told herself, 'I've made the right decision.' Because sometimes trusting a stranger could be the right thing to do.

FOUR MONTHS EARLIER – CAFÉ, LOS ANGELES

Peyk made the most of the all-you-can-eat waffle bar and brought a third full plate back to the table he shared with Savannah.

She wore dark sunglasses to shield her eyes from the bright light that added to the haziness of her memory. She poured several spoonfuls of sugar from the dispenser into her second mug of black coffee and gingerly sipped it.

'Do you know what happened last night?' asked Peyk.

Savannah shook her head. 'I remember feeling dizzy when I was getting changed and I blacked out, but I don't know how long for.

'And now something doesn't feel right, you know, down there. What if he did something to me?'

'I can take you to the police if you like? You know, get you examined.'

'What's the point? I don't know what it feels like to be assaulted in that way, but I'm sure I'd be in a lot more pain if I had been. And I've showered, so there wouldn't be any evidence left.'

'What if he knows where you live?'

'You're not helping me feel better about this.'

'I'm serious. I know somewhere in Venice you can stay that won't cost you anything, you'll be surrounded by people so you'll be safe. And I know a guy who works on the door at the Pink Pussycat in Santa Monica who could get you work so you wouldn't have far to travel.'

Savannah looked at Peyk and realised that under the strangest of circumstances, and despite not knowing a thing about him, this was the first friend she'd made since she'd arrived in the city.

Two hours later she found herself standing in the doorway of a room at the Venice Beach International Hostel. Inside were two single beds, two lockers and a bathroom with a sink, toilet, shower and a large mirror on the wall.

'It's the best room we have,' began Peyk apologetically, sensing Savannah's disappointment. 'But you'll have it to yourself most of the time. I'll make sure Ron only puts people in here if we're busy.'

'It'll be fine. Thanks again, Peyk.'

'Oh, and take this,' he added, and passed her something from his jacket pocket.

'A gun?' Savannah replied, taken aback.

'It's for your protection.'

'Well I didn't think you wanted me to rob a bank with it.'

'Do you know how to use it?'

'Of course. It doesn't mean I feel comfortable with it though.'

Peyk closed the door behind him and left Savannah to acclimatise to her new surroundings. While her motel room was basic, it was still expensive and Peyk offered this accommodation for free. If she worked hard at the new club that Peyk suggested, it would enable her to save up and afford something better.

Savannah looked at the gun and went to put it in the locker, but hesitated and placed it inside her handbag instead. She began to unpack her clothes and hang them up on the rails, and placed her many cosmetics on a shelf in the bathroom.

And she was unaware she was already being watched from a room behind the bathroom mirror.

*

TODAY

Tommy and Savannah's silence was broken by Nicole, who rushed past them out the front door, glancing over her shoulder towards Tommy, who responded with a nod.

Thirty seconds later, Eric walked briskly past him in the same direction as Nicole, and Tommy sprang into action.

'Sav, can you hold the fort here for a few minutes? I won't be long.'

'Sure, honey, is everything okay . . .?'

But before she got her answer, Tommy was out of the door and running towards the beach.

CHAPTER 55

Nicole picked up her pace as she made her way towards the second floor of the car park where their pick-up truck was.

She was not alone, and it took all her strength not to just turn around and stand her ground and confront the urgent footsteps making their way up the concrete ramp behind her. But that wasn't part of the plan, yet.

Finally the Chevy was in view. She reached into her pocket and removed a bunch of keys, looking down to find the one that opened the door.

But before she could find it, she was pushed hard from the side and fell to the floor. Her cheek and wrist took the brunt of the impact, but she was too distracted by the snarling face looking down at her to feel pain.

'Clumsy,' Eric smiled.

CHAPTER 56

Tommy's eyes darted in all directions until he caught sight of the two people he'd left the hostel to find.

He half-walked, half-jogged until they were a few metres away from him, but just as he prepared to approach them with his rehearsed spiel, Jake blindsided him.

'Hey stranger, I've been looking for you. Where are you heading in such a hurry?'

'Oh hi,' began Tommy, his eyes flitting between Jake and his targets. As much as he wanted to talk to Jake and discover what had made him lose his temper at the King's Head pub, now was not the time.

'So what have you been up to?'

'Oh just been busy in the hostel, you know.'

'Okay,' replied Jake, unsure of Tommy's reticence to converse. 'Everything alright? You seem a bit distracted.'

'Look, Jake,' continued Tommy, 'I'm really sorry but I'm kind of in the middle of something right now, can we catch up later?'

'Yeah, sure—' Jake replied, but Tommy had hurried away before he finished his sentence.

CHAPTER 57

Nicole lifted her head from the car park's concrete floor and struggled to focus her eyes on Eric.

'You pushed me,' she muttered, taken aback by his sudden violence.

'You've been pushing me for days, Nicole,' Eric replied. His imposing figure stood over her, arms folded in defiance. 'Now let's cut to the chase, shall we? Where are they?'

'Where are what?'

'Don't play stupid. Where are my mother's diamonds?'

'I don't know anything about any diamonds . . .' Nicole replied, and clambered to her feet. But she wasn't fast enough to shield her nose from the brunt of Eric's headbutt, and she dropped back to the floor, clutching her face and howling.

Eric let out an exaggerated sigh, then kicked her in the stomach. Nicole's eyes opened wide as she fought to breathe. She'd expected their confrontation to be verbally unpleasant and threatening, but she had never seen this Eric before.

'Nicole, you were stupid enough to leave a diamond in the car, along with Maria's note.'

Now it made sense to her how Eric knew about her discovery. She thought she'd covered her tracks, and her mind raced as she tried to settle on a reply, but as she struggled to get to her feet, Eric kicked her again.

'Okay, so we'll do this the hard way,' he continued, and as Nicole fell to her side, he climbed on top of her, rolled her onto her back and pinned her arms and legs down with his own.

Then from the back pocket of his jeans, he pulled out a small bottle with a clear liquid inside and a syringe. He jabbed the bottle's membrane and drew the liquid up the barrel.

'What are you doing?' gasped Nicole.

'I'll give her credit, my mother put up a good fight for a weak woman. Are you going to do the same?'

ELEVEN WEEKS EARLIER – LONDON

The digital display on the medical monitor next to Mrs Baker's bed read 4.45 a.m. when she woke to find someone replacing a syringe driver into her chest.

'Is that you, Nicole?' she asked groggily, and struggled to recognise the figure hovering over her. She felt cold breath against her ear when he spoke.

'Hello, Mum,' whispered Eric, to Mrs Baker's horror. He held his face inches away from hers. 'What have you done with my inheritance?'

Mrs Baker felt her heart racing and her eyes began to water, but she would tell her estranged offspring nothing.

'You know my sister doesn't need it," he continued, his voice growing louder, 'and after what you put me through, it's rightfully mine. So tell me what I'm getting and where to find it.'

Mrs Baker trembled, but again, refused to talk.

Suddenly Eric had a thought.

'She knows, doesn't she? You've told Nicole.'

When Mrs Baker's mouth twitched and her pupils dilated, Eric knew he was correct.

'Once again you choose a stranger over your own flesh and blood. Well you won't make that mistake again.'

When she turned her head to look away from him, Eric clamped his hand over her mouth. He felt the loose skin on his mother's arms brushing against his own as she attempted to bat his hand away, but she was too weak to hurt him or to shout for help. Eric shook his head.

'You are, and always have been, a stupid, stupid woman.'

Eric manoeuvred his other hand towards the syringe driver and plunged the needle into it. In less than a minute, a massive overdose of morphine left Mrs Baker dead.

Eric took in a deep breath, exhaled and smiled, then stretched his arms above his head and yawned.

'Looks like we'll need Nicole after all,' he said.

He turned to face his sister Bridget, who sat in the corner of the room and nodded.

'You didn't give her much of a chance to reply.'

'She was never going to tell me,' Eric added, 'so it was quicker to cut out the middle man.'

Bridget picked up her coat from the arm of her chair and walked towards the door.

'And remember,' added Eric, 'cremation, not burial.'

TODAY

It was one thing for Nicole to learn that her best friend was a liar, and then to be a victim of his vicious nature once he was provoked. But to hear Eric admit he murdered his own mother because she wouldn't tell him what he wanted to know horrified her. She kept a hold on her nerves to keep him talking and to play for time.

'Why?' asked Nicole. 'She was going to die soon anyway.'

'Why not?' shrugged Eric. 'She gave me life and then destroyed it, so I took hers away from her. It's only fair.'

'Of course it's not fair! You could have just gone to her house while she was in hospital and searched for the diamonds yourself.'

'I didn't know if her housekeeper would recognise me from any old photographs knocking around the place, and if she had, it would've got a lot messier. Are you starting to understand the lengths I'll go to get what I'm owed?'

'But you aren't owed anything!'

'And Saint Nicole is? Just because you befriended a terminally ill, vulnerable old widow? You're the same manipulative bastard I am.'

'You killed your own mother for nothing! You're evil.'

'For nothing? Is that what you really think?' Eric threw his head back and laughed, but his smile quickly faded. 'Let me tell you something about your wonderful friend Grace Baker, Nicole. When you're a nine-year-old boy who's being repeatedly raped by your house master at one of the top boarding schools in the country; when you turn to the *one person* for help who should believe you, your mother; when that *one person* says it's in your imagination and you're lying because you're homesick; when you beg and plead and then beg and plead some more and you even try to hang yourself with a bed sheet from the wooden beams of the school refectory because you can't take it anymore; when that *one person's* response is to remove you from that school and shove you into another one without even allowing you a visit home . . . When you kill that person, it is *not* for nothing. It's called karma, and as you're about to discover, what they say is true – karma is, indeed, a bitch.'

The manner in which Eric's story tripped off his tongue without pause or hesitation gave Nicole no doubt he was telling the truth. She didn't want to believe that Mrs Baker could have been so dismissive of her son's plight – and it certainly didn't excuse Eric's subsequent actions – but the part she had played in creating the monster currently pinning her to the floor could not be denied.

Eric hadn't planned to tell her anything about his past, but when he witnessed a slight softening in Nicole's eyes, it only angered him more. 'Do *not* feel sorry for me,' he ordered, 'when it's your own safety you need to be worried about.'

He jabbed the needle into Nicole's arm as she twisted her body from side to side in an attempt to throw Eric off her.

'Just a little more pressure, and the morphine will reunite you with both of our mothers very soon. Now, for the last time, where are my diamonds?'

Nicole's breathing became sharp and desperate. She had completely underestimated his determination and how much he hated her, and glanced around the empty car park, willing someone to disturb them.

'In the air vent!' she finally declared, 'I found them in the air vent in the truck.'

'I've already looked in there.'

'I know, that's why I put them back there an hour ago, I thought it'd be the last place you'd look again.'

Eric stared into each of Nicole's eyes, searching for a tell-tale sign she was lying. 'Huh, clever,' he conceded, then removed the needle, yanked her to her feet and shoved her towards the vehicle.

'Open it,' he barked, pointing to the door. 'Try to run and I will kill you.'

Nicole unlocked the truck, opened the passenger door and leaned inside to pull the air vent out, but it was jammed. She jabbed her fingers between the plastic strips and yanked hard, but nothing moved. Impatiently, Eric pushed her to one side and with two big tugs, pulled the unit from its casing. Nicole made a couple of tentative steps backwards, but when Eric spotted her, she stopped.

He shoved his hand inside the vent, felt around with his fingertips and pulled out a small velvet pouch.

He turned to look at Nicole and grinned.

CHAPTER 58

'You're a bloody idiot, Stuart,' Jake told himself as he watched Tommy run off up the boardwalk.

He quickly realised his mistake, and couldn't remember the last time he'd referred to himself using his former persona. He wondered if it was spending too much time with Tommy that caused his slip-up, because there was something infectious about Tommy's wide-eyed vulnerability that reminded him of himself before he'd allowed fame to corrupt him. And Tommy also had a quality about him that made Jake want to be completely honest about who he was and who he used to be.

Up until moments earlier when Tommy brushed him off, he'd even considered broaching the truth with him. But today's meeting was a reality check, because Jake understood Tommy was never going to want anything but friendship from him, and he hated his clichéd behaviour in falling for a straight man he could never have.

No, he thought, and decided against placing his deepest, darkest secrets upon Tommy's shoulders. Tommy was probably moving on from their friendship anyway, because friendships made in hostels were transient. And in his experience, that was the case with all his relationships.

TWO YEARS EARLIER – NOTTING HILL, LONDON

'What do you mean you and Katie did me a favour?' Stuart repeated slowly.

Geri stared at her fallen protégé, briefly wondering if it would be better to backtrack rather than admit the truth. She decided against it.

'What do you think it means?' she snapped. 'Pretty self-explanatory, sweetheart.'

'You set me up? You got Katie to put those drugs on my lap just as we arrived at the hotel?'

'That's pretty much the bare bones of it. Let's not forget tipping off the paps on your arrival. But I didn't expect her to shove so much of that shit up her nose that it'd kill her. Typical of Katie though, wasn't it? She took dying for fame too literally.'

'But why?' a stunned Stuart replied, 'I didn't do anything to you!'

Geri laughed. 'Why? Why not? Because I bloody can! And you're right, you didn't do anything to me but you were quite happy to do a lot to Zak Stanley.'

Stuart glared at Geri, unsure of how to respond. Nobody, bar Zak's sister, was supposed to know of their relationship.

'Don't think there's a single aspect of your life I don't know about, Stuey,' Geri continued smugly. 'I know about your little liaisons with the Hollywood hunk, I know you're not pure as the driven snow when it comes to using illegal substances in the bedroom; in fact, I even have video footage of you two indulging in your sordid sex and coke romps. Which is why you're going to keep your mouth shut about everything that's been said in this room, because if I hear one word publicly from you, my footage is going to "mysteriously" leak online . . . and how much more humiliation can you take in twenty-four hours?'

'If you . . . if you do that,' Stuart stuttered, 'then I'll tell the press about the miming, your secret tax shelters, how you and Katie set me up, how you're really to blame for her death. You'll be ruined.'

'And then I'm going to vehemently deny it before suing the arse off you as you signed a non-disclosure agreement when I let you into my band. And it's valid for five years after you leave – or are thrown out. I've got you over a barrel, sweetheart, a position, if I recall correctly, that you're quite fond of.'

Stuart stepped backwards, reeling from the storm of threats and revelations Geri was raining down upon him.

'You did all of this because I wasn't interested in you?' he asked hesitantly.

'Like I said, it's simply because I can.'

'No, there's more to it than that.'

'Well I guess you can throw ratings into it too. The new series starts in a month, and everyone's gonna be watching to see who'll be the next wannabe to fuck up.'

'You bitch.'

'I'll give you that, you're perceptive. Now, if you don't mind, it's been lovely catching up, but I have a meeting with a young lad who'll do anything, or more precisely, do me, to replace you.'

Suddenly anger, frustration, adrenaline and the drugs powering through Stuart's nervous system connected in an angry alliance Stuart had never experienced before.

Without thinking, he sprinted towards Geri, dragging her to the ground and clasping his hands around her neck. Twice he smacked her head against her parquet flooring before her security staff heard the commotion, dashed in and pulled him off her. One held Stuart's arms behind his back as the other punched him twice in the stomach and once in the face.

A stunned Geri struggled to her feet and steadied herself with a trembling arm on the drinks cabinet. She coughed and spluttered and her throat hurt but she was still able to find her voice.

'I rescued you from Holiday Inn hell, I made you a star and even after I ruined you, I still own you, you little prick,' she bellowed. 'And I will destroy you unless you get the fuck out of my house!'

Stuart struggled in vain as he was hauled out of Geri's drawing room and into the hallway.

'You can't get away with this,' he hollered.

'Already have, sweetheart, already have,' replied Geri, before pouring herself another glass of Scotch.

Geri's security men were too preoccupied with ejecting him from the hallway to notice what he'd swiped from a sideboard.

CHAPTER 59

TODAY

There were many things that terrified Nicole about Eric in a short space of time, none more so than the look of greed and victory spreading across his face as he held the pouch of diamonds in the palm of his hand.

Eric had killed once to get what he wanted, and she was convinced he would kill again. Her entire body trembled as she looked around for an escape route.

'I presume you've had them valued?' he asked.

'How could I? You never let me out of your sight,' Nicole lied.

'Your boyfriend could have done it for you. Remind me to pay little Tommy a visit before I leave.'

Eric poured the contents of the pouch into his hand, but before he could stop her, Nicole leaped into action. She lurched towards him and slapped the underside of his hand, spraying the gems across the car park floor. Then, gambling on Eric choosing greed over revenge, she ran as fast as her legs could carry her towards the exit. Nicole's hunch proved correct, as behind her, Eric hesitated, at first unsure of which way to turn before dropping to his hands and knees, frantically grabbing all the glistening jewels he could see.

He scooped them into his pocket and stood up, but as his right foot moved forward, he felt a crunching under his sole. He looked down to see a tiny fragment of shattered glass and suddenly, reality began to dawn upon him. He took out one of the diamonds from the pouch, placed it on the floor and trod on it. It too left a powdery residue.

'Costume jewellery,' he snarled, and pulled the syringe out of his pocket. 'You're dead, Nicole!' he yelled at her fading, running footsteps and turned around to pursue her.

'Put the syringe down, sir,' came a stern, female voice from nowhere. Eric quickly turned his head to see two uniformed police officers, their pedal bikes by their side. Eric's mind raced, as this had not been part of his plan, albeit a plan that had been altered the moment Nicole cleared out her belongings from their room. However, it had clearly been part of Nicole and Tommy's.

'This isn't anything,' he began, and walked towards them smiling.

The officers quickly reached for their guns and pointed them at him.

'Put the weapon down, sir!' shouted the officer.

'Guys, guys,' said Eric, panicking. 'This isn't a weapon – I'm diabetic, this is insulin.'

Eric dropped the needle, and while one officer covered her partner, the other pushed Eric against the side of the car, patted him down and handcuffed him.

'It says morphine here,' the first officer began, reading the label on the bottle he plucked from Eric's pocket, 'it doesn't say anything about insulin.'

'I can explain that,' stuttered Eric.

'I'm going to look in the vehicle,' the second officer added, and radioed for assistance.

'You need a warrant,' said Eric nervously, 'everything in there is rightfully mine.'

'Everything in this car is rightfully yours, you say?' asked the second officer, removing tarpaulin from the flatbed of the truck and looking underneath.

'Um, yes,' replied Eric nervously.

In the back of the truck was Nicole's suitcase, but as the officer unstrapped the buckles and opened it, its only contents were five brick-sized packages of shrink-wrapped cannabis resin. Eric looked aghast as a patrol car made its way up a ramp and onto their level.

'That's got nothing to do with me,' he protested, but his words fell on deaf ears as he was read his rights and bundled into the back of the police car.

CHAPTER 60

Nicole sprinted down three fire exits and two ramps, out of the car park and across the road to the safety of a bustling sidewalk.

She ran past the hostel and towards the beach, passing a parade of shops before she stopped behind a van parked outside a restaurant. She crouched down, struggling to catch her breath. Her head, stomach and nose ached, and her mouth felt dry before she was struck by an overwhelming urge to vomit. Last night's Chinese food hit the ground before she heard a disgusted muttering and turned around to discover she was being watched by diners eating on a restaurant patio just metres away from her.

However, disapproving stares from strangers were the least of her worries. Nicole waited nervously until she saw headlights appear from the car park exit and a police vehicle leave.

She stood up and squinted at the rear of the vehicle, and briefly made eye contact with Eric before he was driven out of sight.

CHAPTER 61

'He could have killed you!' began Tommy, as Savannah wiped away grit and dried blood from Nicole's forehead and nostrils.

Nicole lifted up her T-shirt and tentatively felt her ribs; none were broken, but she was quite sure they were bruised. Her nose was, however, broken, and she realigned it herself with a crack and a yelp before it had time to heal crookedly. Savannah had been keen to help when Tommy and Nicole turned up at her door looking for somewhere quiet to clean up and regroup, and she used cotton wool buds from Jane's first aid kit to clean a wound on Nicole's chin and cheek.

'Why didn't you let me come with you if you thought he might be that dangerous?' continued Tommy.

'He wouldn't have followed both of us, so I had to go on my own. And if you'd been with me, who'd have approached the police on the beach? What did you tell them?'

'That someone had been selling drugs to hostellers from a pick-up truck, and that I'd just seen him in the car park. What's Eric been charged with?'

'I didn't understand all the technicalities, but when I called pretending to be his sister Bridget to ask about bail, they said something about an intent to supply drugs, and possession of a potentially lethal weapon. The truck's been impounded, and because it was shipped over here and registered in his name, there's no link to me. And I can't drive, so I'm not even named on the insurance.'

'Why didn't you tell the police what he did to his mom?' asked Savannah.

'Because it's Eric's word against mine. Mrs Baker was cremated, so they can't do any toxicology tests on her body, and there's no way Bridget will ever admit to being party to her mother's murder.'

Nicole sighed and rubbed the tears pooling in the corner of her eyes. 'If what he was saying about Mrs Baker not believing he was being abused is true, then I feel terrible for him. But I did the right thing, didn't I?'

'I don't think you had much of a choice,' Tommy replied softly, 'And don't forget, you're a wealthy woman now. What are you going do with the money?'

'I've not really had time to think about it,' sniffed Nicole. 'I might stay in LA for a while and get my head together.'

Nicole held her hand out and placed it on Tommy's. 'Thank you, by the way. It's good to know who your friends are.'

Only Savannah noticed how tense Tommy's hand became in response, before he removed it and began picking up bloody cotton wool buds from the floor, dropping them into a bin.

Just two weeks ago, Tommy could only have hoped for a moment of closeness like that, but a lot had happened in that short space of time. Yet he wasn't ready to admit to himself that there was someone else he was developing much stronger feelings for.

'Oh yeah,' added Savannah, 'where did you come up with $20,000 worth of pot so quickly?'

*

Ron admitted he wasn't a man to express his emotions freely.

He couldn't recall the last time he'd cried; he'd fallen in love just once in his sixty-eight years, and the only thing that made him laugh were video clips of dogs doing silly things on YouTube. He couldn't remember the last time something, or someone, had left him speechless.

So when Tommy walked into his office, placing $19,000 in $100 bills on his desk, his mouth dropped before he'd even realised.

'Tell Peyk he needs to speed up production,' was all Tommy said before leaving him to count the cash. And as he made his way up the stairs, Tommy decided neither Ron nor Nicole needed to know about the $1,000 he'd anonymously pushed under Matty and Declan's door that afternoon.

CHAPTER 62

'Man, I really need this,' said Tommy, taking a long drag from a joint.

'I didn't think you approved of my relaxation methods?' asked Peyk.

'I need to start lightening up a bit.'

'No shit.'

Peyk was a little surprised when Tommy turned up at the door of room 23 asking for something to help him chill out after a stressful day. He rolled Tommy a spliff with just a little cannabis to get him used to the taste, and they sat on either side of the windowsill looking out of the only pane of glass not covered by a blind or cardboard. The condensation from the heat lamps meant the windows' coverings needed replacing every couple of days or they'd turn to papier mâché.

Tommy's head was already feeling like candy floss when he pointed towards Joe sleeping on a discarded mattress in an alley dumpster below.

'I wonder how it all went wrong for him,' Tommy asked.

'Have you ever taken the trouble to ask him?'

'I guess not. I just wondered why he started making such bad choices.'

'Are any of the choices we make the right ones?'

'Man, can we have just one conversation without this weird, cryptic shit?'

'Nope,' smiled Peyk.

'You're never curious why Joe's life is such a waste?'

'Who are you to judge him? Just because he hasn't got what you have doesn't mean he's wasted it.'

'Come on, nobody knows who he is. He's got no money, no home, no family . . . not even a roof over his head. Nobody deserves that.'

'But a man can live without all those things. And you have more in common with him than you think.'

'Please enlighten me, oh wise oracle.'

'Neither of you has any freedom.'

Tommy frowned. 'Well that's bollocks, because I'm not the one scratching around for money, my whole life dedicated to scoring my next fix.'

'That's true, but while he has no freedom from his addiction, you're not free from the limits you set yourself. You're one of the most uptight, frightened little shits I've ever met. You've come travelling to escape something – that's pretty clear to anyone – then you separate from your friend, you end up here and you don't have the balls to go anywhere else on your own. You hide, safely entrenched in the margins, never in the middle of the page. You're too scared to embrace freedom . . . you're like a fish in a bowl in the ocean looking out towards the big picture but always too gutless to make the jump.'

'Fuck you and your dumb-ass similes,' snapped Tommy, taken aback by Peyk's character assassination. 'Where's all this coming from? You don't know the first thing about me.'

'Tommy-boy!' continued Peyk, exasperated. 'I've met people like you countless times, and you're all the same. You're tourists, not travellers. You design your own problems then you bitch when no one gives you the solution.'

'No I don't!'

'Be honest with yourself, if not me. You have remained here in this hostel because it's the safest, most convenient option. You're scared of going home, scared of what to do with your life, scared of what you're feeling for Jake—'

'Jake's a mate,' interrupted Tommy, sounding less than convincing.

'He's more to you than that and you know it. You think he's found what you've been looking for; you think he's at peace with himself. You think he's everything you want to be but are too scared to find by yourself so you live vicariously through his anecdotes, hanging on his every word. But he's not any of those things, Tommy. He's a man, and men are flawed, some more than others. You can't live your life through someone like that, you owe yourself more.'

Tommy folded his arms defiantly, his partially stoned mind racing, desperately trying to justify his choices and devising a counter argument, all the time quietly aware Peyk's words were ringing true.

'Right here, right now, you can start your life all over again,' Peyk continued. 'You can do anything you want to . . . if you want to see the whole of the world, not just this little microcosmos, then go see it for yourself; if you want to experience a relationship with someone of the same sex, then just do it. In the great scheme of things, it doesn't matter. In the great scheme of things, nothing matters – but you. And the only people who will judge you are the people you shouldn't give two shits about. I know that people think I'm a joke – the stoner who walks around the hostel falling through ceilings. And you know what? I'm cool with that, I don't care. I know who I am and I know what makes me, "me". You don't – you are made up of everyone you know, those living and those dead. Now you need to find your own path and be someone, not everyone else. Just don't stand here casting judgment on Joe's decisions when you are too gutless to make your own.'

Peyk passed Tommy his joint. 'Finish this off,' he offered, and left Tommy alone, utterly bewildered.

CHAPTER 63

No matter how many sunsets he'd seen all over the world, the sixty minutes between the day ending and night beginning offered Jake more clarity than a sunrise did.

It was the time when he could reflect on his day and contemplate what the night might bring.

'Oi!' shouted a voice in his ear, and Jake's stomach lurched like he was driving too fast over a hump-backed bridge.

'Jesus,' he yelled, and swiftly turned his head to find Tommy chuckling.

'I'm not Jesus, but you're close,' began Tommy. 'I thought I'd find you on the roof. I just wanted to say I was sorry about earlier when you saw me at the beach. I was caught up in the middle of something . . . It's been an . . . eventful day.'

'No, I owe you an apology for the other day in the pub. I wasn't having the best of times—'

'Honestly mate, it doesn't matter. Let's just start again. I've brought you a peace offering.'

From the pockets of his cargo shorts, he pulled out four miniature bottles of vodka, a can of Coke, a small bag of pot and some rolling papers.

*

'I've not done this in years,' said Jake, taking another drag from the joint Tommy had rolled. The filter was moist and tasted like Tommy's kiss.

'I smoked a few joints with Sean at this backpacking place in the woods once, but that's about it. Were you a bit of a stoner in your day, then?'

Jake paused, knowing that with the booze and dope relaxing him, he couldn't allow himself to become too loose of lip. 'No more than anyone else,' he conceded.

They sat with their backs to the low wall from where the railings had fallen days earlier. Darkness was moving in, and the streetlights below reflected off the sidewalk, giving them a blue and grey tint.

'A toast,' Tommy suggested, holding up his glass and spilling some of his drink on his leg.

It made him giggle, and he wasn't sure why.

'What are we celebrating?'

'I've freed my inner sausage and given up the job on the hotdog stand,' continued Tommy, but decided against telling him of the $5,000 Nicole had given him for his help and in what circumstances. 'And you know what, for the first time in ages, I can honestly say I'm a happy man.'

'Why now?'

Tommy paused. 'I lost people close to me not so long ago. It's taken me a while to get my head around it.'

'Oh, I'm sorry, I didn't know.'

'Why do people always apologise, like it's their fault?'

'I don't know, it just seems like the right thing to say. Do you want to tell me about it?'

'Actually, yes, I'd like to, but not right now. There's something else I'd rather do.' Tommy stared at Jake and smiled, and Jake wasn't sure if it was the lighting or the weed that was making him misjudge the moment. Tommy took another swig from his vodka bottle for Dutch courage and with Peyk's words still ringing in his ears, took a deep breath.

'Do I have to stop you falling from the roof again before you kiss me?' asked Tommy.

'But you're not—'

Before he could even finish his sentence, Tommy had taken matters into his own hands and pressed his lips against Jake's.

CHAPTER 64

DAY FOURTEEN

Nicole spent much of the night awake and unable to sleep.

Above her bunk, Eric's bed lay empty, stripped of its sheets, and with his belongings donated to a confused Joe. Each time she moved she felt her bruised ribs, sore head and broken nose, but they didn't hurt as much as Eric's betrayal. There were too many thoughts swimming around her head to allow her to drop into an REM sleep, and each time she closed her eyes, she saw the venomous face of Eric glaring back at her, ready to end her life, and all for the sake of money.

Nicole was reluctant to leave the building's boundaries or to venture into the courtyard to clear her head, even though she knew she was being irrational, as Eric was elsewhere in the city and behind bars. He wasn't the only person she knew who'd been arrested recently, of course.

In the rare moments when she wasn't reliving her ordeal in the car park with Eric, Nicole worried about what had become of Ruth. Her best guess was that she'd been taken to some type of psychiatric unit to examine her mental state. When it transpired that Ruth had also killed her mother and brother back in Australia, she knew her shy, unassuming roommate suffered problems much deeper rooted than Nicole could have ever imagined or handled. Maybe Eric was right to tell her not to approach Ruth the day they followed her to Zak Stanley's home. Or maybe they could have saved his life. It was also possible Eric had seen more of himself in Ruth than he'd wanted to admit.

Nicole gave up on rest long before her fellow hostellers awoke, and quietly slipped out of her room to eat breakfast alone in the kitchen and ponder what to do with her new-found wealth. She was as certain as she could be that Tommy would keep her money safe until she made a carefully considered decision, but after barely three days in her possession, all that cash had brought her was misery and bruising. She was beginning to regret having ever met her benefactor.

After rinsing her dishes she went by the hotel reception and noticed Peyk taping posters to the wall. 'Free beach party, tomorrow night, Santa Monica. 8 p.m. till sunrise.'

'You got some time later to help me organise food and stuff?' Peyk asked.

'Sure,' replied Nicole, grateful for the opportunity to think about something other than her own troubles. Then, with the sudden urge for some familiar company, she was on her way towards Tommy's dormitory when the door to another room opened.

Tommy didn't see Nicole, but she was aware of him slipping out of Jake's room in just his boxer shorts.

CHAPTER 65

Four French girls Tommy had checked into the hostel days earlier stood in a line, stared at the television in the lounge and waited as a timer counted them down.

As soon as Pharrell Williams' 'Happy' began playing, the girls followed the on-screen instructions and copied each of the dance moves they were told to follow by an animated character.

'Where did that come from?' Tommy asked Peyk, pointing to a brand new 72-inch television on the wall.

'Ron bought it earlier and rigged it up.'

'Nice to know he's putting my earnings to good use,' Tommy replied curtly. 'Meanwhile the water pressure's still non-existent and there's next to no Wi-Fi signal.'

'Yet you're still smiling. What have you been up to, Tommy-boy?'

'Nothing,' he replied, blushing.

Tommy briefly reflected over the last week of his life and realised that if anyone had told him he'd finish the month selling drugs, framing a murderer or spending the night with another guy, he'd not have believed them.

'Let's just say I followed your advice,' Tommy continued. 'I jumped out of the bowl and I'm swimming in the ocean.'

'Good man. Just make sure you're swimming with the current and not against it. Don't let the wrong people drag you down.'

Tommy rolled his eyes, preparing himself for more vague life lessons. 'Like who?'

'He's not your brother or your father or your friend Sean or whoever else you want him to be. Don't mistake love for longing.'

'Peyk, you're next!' interrupted Elize in her heavy French accent, grabbing his arm and pushing him towards the game before Tommy could ask him to expand. Clearly drunk, she took Peyk's place next to Tommy.

'For an English guy, you're cute,' she slurred.

'What's wrong with English guys?'

'They're too pale and only want to drink beer all the time. If you like, we go to my room and know each other better.'

'I don't think that's a good idea,' Tommy replied, then gently placed his hands around her cheeks and moved her head backwards when her lips began to approach his.

From across the room, Jake watched, amused, as Tommy awkwardly rebuffed the inebriated girl's clumsy advances. What had happened on the roof and later in his bedroom had taken Jake by surprise, albeit a wonderfully unexpected surprise. But he worried Tommy's curiosity wouldn't extend past an experimental fling.

'Hi,' smiled Nicole benignly, distracting Jake from his concerns.

'Hello,' Jake replied, and then frowned at the bruising and swelling around her eyes.

'Didn't Tommy tell you?' she asked, pre-empting his question. 'I thought you two were quite close.'

'No, he didn't say anything.'

'It's a long story,' Nicole replied, reluctant to go into any further detail with someone she only vaguely knew.

As Elize continued to paw at Tommy, she noticed his attention was directed towards Jake and Nicole.

'I think you like that girl in the corner better than me. You look at each other lots. She can come with us if you want.'

'Nicole's my friend,' replied Tommy stiffly.

'And the boy?'

'Jake's my friend too.'

'You have a lot of friends. Jake is nice. He looks like that singer man. What his name . . . like you, English boy. Killed himself.'

'Stuart Reynolds?' replied Tommy slowly, and scowled at Elize.

'Shave away his beard, cut his brown hair and make it blonde, he could be a brother.'

Tommy took a moment to closely examine Jake, who smiled back at him.

And as Elize continued to talk, all Tommy heard was the sound of his heart racing.

CHAPTER 66

Matty lay on his bed watching Declan tidy their room.

Matty knew he left a lot to be desired when it came to tidiness, and no matter where in the world they travelled, Declan made order from the chaos that surrounded them.

'Why won't you talk about it?' began Matty, breaking a comfortable silence.

'Talk about what?' replied Declan, sniffing the inside of a pair of trainers and grimacing at their pungent scent.

'Me, dying. It's like having an elephant in the room and you keep ignoring it.'

'Not now, Matty,' Declan replied, refusing to make eye contact but feeling Matty's gaze upon him.

'Then when?'

'I dunno, just not now.'

'It's going to happen, Dec, and the sooner you face it, the easier it's going to be.'

'What's going to be easy about you not being here, you dope?' Declan snapped.

'Look, Dec, we've been through everything together. If you could've given me your own heart, I know you would've. But you need to let go of the hope that all this is going to continue indefinitely. I'm already past my expiry date.'

'I don't want to think about you . . . you—'

'Dying? It's just a word, you can say it.'

Declan folded a pair of jeans and placed them over the back of a chair.

'That's the problem though, isn't it? It's not just a word,' he said quietly but firmly. 'It's something so fucking monumental that nothing will ever be the same again and you won't be here to help shoulder the burden because you will *be* the burden. It'll be all your fault and I'll hate you for it, and I don't want to do that, so until I'm ready to get my head around it, it's something I don't want to discuss.'

'You have to!' said Matty, sitting up. 'Whenever it happens, I want to be ready for it but I can't unless I know you're ready too.'

'How? Tell me, how?'

'By acknowledging it. The biggest thing you can do for me is that.'

'I can't.'

'*I* have. I've had plenty of moments when I've hated God for putting me through this and thought, "Why me?" But *why not* me? Why does it have to be someone else, why shouldn't it be me? I've stopped being angry at the world, I've had the time of my life over the last year and I've made my peace with The Man Upstairs. You have to do the same.'

Matty recognised the look Declan gave him – the last time he'd seen it, they were little boys and Declan's mother had walked out on her family and wasn't returning. Back then, Matty had gripped his pal's hand tightly and promised Declan he'd never leave him. But it was a promise he was reluctantly going to break.

'I'm sorry,' mumbled Declan and left the room.

CHAPTER 67

A flustered Tommy took advantage of Jake being engrossed in conversation with Nicole and hurried out of the hostel lounge and towards his dormitory.

He took his iPhone from his locker and cursed at the empty battery symbol, before heading towards an internet café two blocks away. As he took long strides up the sidewalk, Tommy kept repeating to himself that Jake couldn't possibly be the same man as Stuart Reynolds. Stuart was dead, as far as the world knew. His belongings had been discovered by an elderly couple walking their dogs at Beachy Head. Tommy had even made a trip there once to see for himself Stuart's final resting place.

Tommy entered the café, paid the cashier $5 for thirty minutes' surfing time and plugged his phone into the wall. He began to scour Google images of Stuart Reynolds on the computer, blowing them up as large as the screen would allow and closely examining every inch of Stuart's face, comparing them to photos he'd taken of Jake.

The online pictures were at least three years old, and both men had the same shaped eyes, only Stuart's were a sparkling blue and Jake's brown. Stuart's eyebrows had been shaped while Jake's were more untamed, and two of Stuart's front teeth had chips in them whereas Jake's were nearly too perfectly aligned. The two years Jake had spent travelling gave him faint lines drawn across his forehead, framing the corners of his eyes.

Tommy scrolled through a dozen more pictures, and while there were similarities, it wasn't even close to being conclusive proof. Tommy played YouTube video clips of Lightning Strikes interviews and tried to compare Jake and Stuart's voices – their tones were similar but their accents completely different. Stuart's nose was straight while Jake's was slightly crooked and their bodies were also differently shaped – shirtless pictures of Stuart showed an athletic build, pale colouring and no body hair; however Jake had a moderately hairy chest that was much broader, his biceps and abs were larger and he was decorated with tattoos across both arms and down his side.

However, both shared the same tattoo, a number 23 between their left thumb and forefinger. When questioned about it, Jake had suggested Tommy Google the significance, so he did just that and found a Wikipedia page dedicated to the "23 enigma."

"The 23 enigma refers to the belief that most incidents and events are directly connected to the number 23. The number is considered unlucky, sinister, strange or sacred depending on the person drawn to it."

Tommy wondered why Jake would be drawn to a number with such a dark reputation.

He pushed back on his chair and let go of a big breath he wasn't aware he'd been holding. He questioned whether this need to find the bad in a person so good was some delayed, irrational reaction to being intimate with another man, like his subconscious was looking for an excuse to nip things in the bud despite the fun night they'd shared.

He expanded the picture on his phone's screen to examine the 23 rows of tattoos along Jake's ribcage again. Then, using the computer keyboard, he typed in two rows of numbers he saw etched on Jake's body – 34.0219N and 118.4814W.

'Santa Monica latitude and longitude coordinates' read the Google search page. The numbers 43.71964561 and 170.09146595 threw up White Horse Hill in New Zealand, where Jake had said he'd worked. Tommy continued, working from bottom to top, tracing every step of Jake's journey that had taken in India, Thailand, Japan, Italy, Iceland and a dozen other countries.

The last numbers he typed in were 52.2189N and 0.9202W, but before he could learn where Jake's journey began, a voice suddenly came from behind Tommy's monitor.

'You know you're not supposed to surf porn in public,' began Jake, and Tommy's whole body recoiled, much to Jake's amusement.

'You aren't the only person who can creep up on someone,' he joked.

'What are you doing here?' asked Tommy briskly.

'I'm stalking you. Well, I saw you leave and wondered where you were going. Why aren't you using the internet at the hostel?'

'The broadband is down,' lied Tommy. 'I just wanted to see what was going on back home.'

He moved the mouse slowly and clicked Jake's image off the screen.

'Come and get a coffee with me,' continued Jake. 'You look like you've seen a ghost.'

299

CHAPTER 68

'I wouldn't have had you down as a basketball fan,' Jane began as she arrived at Venice Beach Recreation Center's open-air court.

Savannah and Nicole sat on steps close to the bike path and under the shade of a giant palm tree canopy watching a game in progress. Savannah cheered on the team in white vests for no other reason than they reminded her of colours Michael wore when she'd watched him play for his college team.

'I've seen a few games over the years,' Savannah smiled, remembering happier times. 'How's your day been?'

Jane grinned and said hello to Nicole but didn't comment on the bruising on her face. She unclasped her handbag and rummaged around inside, finally pulling out a green folder stuffed with papers.

'I've been to four estate agents, or what do you call them over here? Real estate agents, that's right, and I've been to see five houses already. Do you like the look of this one?' She pulled out a brochure and passed it to Savannah. 'It's in West Hollywood, it has three bedrooms with a nice-sized garden in a quiet street.'

Savannah flicked through the pages of photographs of a modest but pleasant home.

'That looks gorgeous,' said Nicole.

'You don't waste any time, do you?' added Savannah. 'Can we afford this?'

'Don't worry about that, I've wangled a deal for the first six months and we'll see how we get on from there. That's only if you like it, of course.'

'I do, but I have to pay my way, Jane.'

'And you will, my girl, but not until you've had that baby and you're back on your feet. So what do you think?'

Savannah nodded her head. It might not be as grand as the house she'd grown up in and later escaped from, but it was a million times better than the four walls of the hostel she currently called home.

'Let's go for it,' Savannah agreed, and Jane swept down to give her a tight hug.

'That's a relief – I signed the contract an hour ago and we can move in tomorrow! Right, I'm off to call some furniture rental places – you're not opposed to wicker, are you? I have a thing for wicker.'

'No, you knock yourself out, girl.'

'Marvellous, see you later, roomie!'

As Jane walked with purpose out of sight, Nicole leaned over and patted Savannah's belly. 'Looks like you and your mummy have got yourselves a new granny and a new home,' she said, her happiness for Savannah tainted with envy.

'I'd better go and tell Peyk,' said Savannah.

'I didn't know you were friends?'

'He's a good guy, I owe him a lot.'

A sudden noise alerted them to Peyk's presence behind Nicole, listening to their conversation. He offered a half-hearted smile before walking away.

'Damn it,' muttered Savannah, and stood up to follow him. 'Peyk! Hey, wait up!'

CHAPTER 69

Until he could know for sure whether his eyes and his mind weren't playing tricks on him, Tommy needed space to think.

And he wasn't going to find that in Starbucks with Jake sitting opposite him.

'I think that French girl fancies you,' began Jake, oblivious to Tommy's inner turmoil.

'Is that a problem?'

'No, I was just saying, she was all over you earlier. It was funny. I think Nicole kind of likes you too.'

Tommy sipped his frappé and didn't reply, leaving an awkward silence between them.

'Okay, I'm putting my cards on the table here, mate. I did feel a bit . . . you know . . . jealous when I saw you with her. And I know it's daft because you're a free agent and we've only spent one night together, and I know I'm being irrational but I feel like we have some sort of . . . connection. Do you know what I mean?'

Tommy glanced down towards the table and stirred his drink with a straw, refusing to make eye contact with Jake. He was desperate to leave without Jake being suspicious as to why.

'Or not,' Jake continued, a little crestfallen. 'You're not making this easy for me, are you?'

'When did you say you started travelling?' blurted out Tommy, throwing Jake with the swift change of conversational direction.

'What? Um . . . about two years ago or so.'

'When, exactly?' Tommy persisted.

'October or November, I think, I can't remember. Why?'

'No reason. Look, I've got to go as I have a shift on reception in a few minutes. I'll catch you later, okay?'

Tommy dropped a $10 bill on the table, forced a smile in Jake's direction and left, his legs shaking beneath him.

CHAPTER 70

'I'm really sorry you heard it that way,' began Savannah, catching up with Peyk further down the boardwalk. 'I don't want you to think I'm ungrateful.'

When Peyk's eyes made contact with Savannah's, she knew she had inadvertently hurt him.

'No, I don't think that,' he said quietly, stopping to watch boarders grip the bottom of skateboards, soar off jumps and fly through the air above the concrete bowl of the skate park.

'What you did for me . . . that night and ever since . . . it was so sweet and helped me get my head together and save money, but this is such a great opportunity for me and the baby.'

Peyk nodded.

'You know I can't raise a child at the hostel and Jane, well, she has experience and knows what she's doing. I'm going to need all the help I can get over the next few months, and don't you worry, I'll come back and see you soon. I promise.'

'I hope so,' Peyk replied, but quietly believed that moment would be the last they ever shared.

Savannah rubbed Peyk's arm reassuringly and, as she turned around to head back to the hostel, she felt a slight thump in her stomach. 'It just kicked! My baby just kicked!' she giggled and grabbed Peyk's hand to place on her belly. 'Did you feel it?'

'I did,' said Peyk, and offered a genuine grin.

'He must like you and he wants to say goodbye.'

As she walked away, Peyk thought he caught a glimpse of a man carefully watching Savannah from a distance.

CHAPTER 71

By the time the two girls Matty and Declan met over lunch had left their room, Matty's chest felt heavier than ever.

Once the girl whose name he couldn't remember had climaxed, he'd faked his orgasm to bring the lovemaking to a halt and tucked the empty condom under his mattress without her noticing.

Of all the increasing aches and twinges he'd suffered silently from over the last few weeks, these were pains he was unfamiliar with. At first he'd put them down to sexual overexertion, but when they failed to taper off with medication, he gradually accepted it was more serious than that. Matty felt his body was slowing down; the clockwork inside him readying itself to grind to a halt, too rusty to be wound up again by chemicals.

'Those birds were fecking incredible!' said a still breathless Declan, opening the window to let the sex out and the fresh air in. 'Did you see where she had her fingers? Dirty birdie.'

Matty faked a laugh and quietly regulated his breathing. He knew telling Declan he was unwell would only worry his friend, and the afternoon they were enjoying would finish with him in a bed at the public Los Angeles County and USC Medical Centre undergoing more tests that'd only tell him what he already knew.

'You know, I hope you find someone,' Matty said eventually.

'Who d'you think that was bouncing up and down my wee fella? Casper the over-friendly ghost?'

'I mean I hope you find someone to settle down with – do the whole marriage, house, 2.4 kids, a dog and a Volvo thing. I like to think you'll be happy.'

'Please don't start this again,' replied Declan, knowing full well the conversation was heading down a road he'd no wish to travel.

'I'm not, I'm just thinking out loud.'
'You'll probably do all that before me.'

Matty gave Declan a knowing smile and then closed his eyes, counting the beats his useless heart was trying to hit.

CHAPTER 72

DAY FIFTEEN

Peyk smiled proudly as his eyes surveyed the crop of plants in his cannabis farm in room 23.

After gathering enough leaves, he placed them in the drying room in the corner of the converted dormitory and hung them upside down. From experience he knew that drying them too quickly meant they'd lose their taste, and if stored somewhere damp, mildew and mould would ruin them.

He hadn't questioned Tommy when he'd taken five bricks worth and returned with $19,000 in cash, and Tommy didn't tell him he'd got the money from Nicole or that she had so much more hidden above the ceiling tiles. The sale had rapidly depleted Peyk's stock and would take time to replace, and time wasn't on Peyk's side. Like his product, he too had a shelf life.

He'd grown accustomed to the room's stifling humidity and lack of ventilation, and was taking a break to rehydrate himself and mop the sweat from his brow when the familiar knock came at the door. As he opened it, Tommy pushed his way inside.

'Hey, I told you to come in sideways so you let minimal light out and nobody sees—' Peyk began, but Tommy was in no mood to listen.

'I don't care if the whole of Los Angeles knows what you're doing,' replied Tommy, 'why didn't you tell me that you knew who Jake really was?'

'Ahh,' replied Peyk and nodded, then returned to the plant he was pruning.

'Earlier, when you said, "Don't let the wrong people drag you down", you were warning me to be careful of Jake, weren't you?'

Peyk shrugged and passed Tommy a spare pair of sunglasses to protect his eyes from the powerful glare of the lamps surrounding them. Tommy hurled them across the room.

'I don't get it – we're supposed to be mates, then you find out who he is and you don't tell me?'

'It wasn't my place to, Tommy-boy. You had to find out for yourself.'

'How did you know? Did he tell you?'

'It's not important.'

'It is to me.'

'Maybe you needed to get to know Jake before you met Stuart or you'd always be that goldfish in a bowl in the ocean.'

Tommy wanted to grab Peyk's metaphorical bowl and smash it over his head, but he knew his anger was misplaced. What he wanted, above all else, was to go back to when it was just Tommy and Sean on their travels and everything was innocent and uncomplicated.

THREE MONTHS EARLIER – HOSTEL IN THE WOODS

The night air surrounding the Hostel in the Woods was cool, and the smell from Pauly's joint overpowering.

The young American with the shoulder-length hair and a handlebar moustache hadn't stopped talking at Tommy for forty minutes about why he'd never kill a cockroach. The essence of his theory, as Tommy understood it, was that the cockroaches you could see were the stupid ones who'd taken a foolhardy risk and been caught out in the open. By killing them, you'd be left with a race of hidden intelligent ones. And, according to Pauly, that had the potential to bring catastrophe to the world, although quite why, Tommy didn't have the energy to ask.

He was weary after a day spent chopping firewood and was quietly resentful of Sean for enjoying the fire Tommy had built. Sean was becoming steadily more drunk, and sang along as Stefan played Avicii's travellers' anthem, 'Wake Me Up', on his guitar. Tommy also felt a pang of envy when he saw Sean holding hands with a red-headed Australian woman he'd been chatting to earlier that day.

He was acutely aware of the widening gap between them since they'd arrived in the woods, a location that had brought out a side to Sean Tommy hadn't seen before. Going back to nature appeared to suit him more than the large cities Tommy enjoyed exploring – and that worried him.

*

'There's nothing here to remind you of the outside world, is there?' said a smiling Sean, swiping at the forest undergrowth with a discarded branch as they explored.

'You're saying that like it's a good thing,' muttered Tommy, following a few paces behind him on the woodchip path, trying to avoid nettle stings.

'And it's not?'

'Actually no, Sean, it's not.' Tommy stopped in his tracks. 'I've had enough of hearing people wanking on about the beauty of trees, shitting in a hole for a toilet, being bitten by mosquitoes and eating tofu with every meal. I want a warm shower, an HD TV screen and a Nando's.'

'Do you want to go home?'

'No, I just want out of here. We've been here a week now and I'm bored off my tits. There's nothing to do. We need to leave.'

'When?'

'Now? Well, not right now, but tonight when the minibus leaves for the station?'

'Okay,' Sean replied quietly, and continued to walk.

*

The rest of their day was spent in silence as an awkward atmosphere hung over them.

Tommy packed his rucksack and planned their next journey – to Memphis – while Sean hung out with the redhead whose name Tommy deliberately hadn't asked. And as evening approached and the minibus spluttered to life, Tommy strapped his rucksack to the roof rack while Sean took a lingering look around him.

'Pass me your bag,' Tommy asked, but Sean didn't move.

'I don't want to go,' he replied.

'What? We said—'

'No, *you* said. This is my beach, Tommy.'

'What do you mean?'

'That book you keep banging on about . . . the reason we both came travelling, to find our beach . . . Well I've found mine and I really like it here, and I'm not ready to leave. You and I want to see different things, so I'm going to stay for a while.'

'But I thought we were going to do this trip together?' Tommy replied, and tried to suppress the fear bubbling in his gut.

'We are, we have, but it shouldn't stop us doing stuff on our own, should it? We don't need to be with each other all the time. We've spent two months tanking around at a million miles an hour, never stopping anywhere or getting to know a place for more than a few days at a time. I want to start being a part of somewhere, and this is a good place to begin. But you're too busy running to really enjoy this. You're taking travelling too literally for me.'

'Okay, we'll stay here then if that's what you want.'

'No, mate, *I* want to stay here but I don't want *you* to because it's going to make you miserable, and I know better than most people how much sadness you've already had in your life. This trip is the chance of a lifetime, and I'm not going to be responsible for you not grabbing every opportunity you can. You can do this on your own, trust me.'

Tommy looked at his feet and said nothing because he knew Sean was right.

'Let's meet up two months from now in that Los Angeles hostel you liked the sound of,' continued Sean. 'The one in Venice Beach?'

'Okay, if that's what you want.'

'Yes, mate, it is what I want, and it's what you need. And Tommy – I hope you find your beach there.'

Tommy nodded, hoping for the same thing.

CHAPTER 73

TODAY

Like an army of worker ants, a dozen hostellers carried kegs of beer and trays of food in plastic wrappers from the kitchen, down the corridor and to the hired van Peyk had left parked outside.

Eager to take her mind off reflecting on her ghastly last few days, Nicole appointed herself as coordinator, and rallied the troops to help prepare the food for the beach party in Santa Monica later that night. Jake was the last in line, and picked up a 24-pack of Budweiser.

'Thanks,' said Nicole, taking a sneaky glance at his muscular arms protruding from his grey vest. If Tommy did swing both ways, then Nicole conceded he had an impeccable taste in men.

Jake reciprocated with a smile, but neither was completely relaxed around the other. Both were certain they had feelings for Tommy, and both suspected Jake had won in a battle that had never been declared. But as he hadn't seen Tommy since their awkward coffee together a day earlier, Jake was no longer so confident of his victory.

The speed at which Tommy had abandoned Jake's company and rushed away both disappointed and saddened Jake. His only explanation for it was that Tommy regretted what had happened between them, regarded it as a one-off and was now too embarrassed to admit it or spend any more time with him.

Already that morning, Jake had paid a visit to Tommy's dormitory and found his bed unmade and empty, before glimpsing the edge of a photograph peeking out from under Tommy's pillow. Curious, he edged it out and saw two almost identical faces – young men who must be twins, he assumed.

'You haven't seen Tommy around, have you?' Jake asked Nicole.

'No, I've not seen him much in the last couple of days. I presumed he was with you.'

'He's probably got a hangover,' Jake lied. 'He'll be keeping a low profile until it wears off.'

Nicole paused, and chose her words carefully before speaking. 'Jake, will you promise me you'll look out for Tommy? I know it's not my place to say, but he's had a lot to deal with in the last few years, so please don't let him down, okay?'

'I won't,' Jake replied, curious as to why Tommy had confided in Nicole and not him. 'You can trust me. You can both trust me.'

And for the briefest of moments, even Jake believed the words coming from his mouth.

*

'Penny for them?' asked Savannah when she wandered into the kitchen to find Nicole sitting alone in silence and staring blankly at the wall. Empty food wrappers surrounded her.

'Oh, you don't want to know,' Nicole replied. 'How was your last night at work? Jane said it was your final shift.'

'Yeah, and it was way better knowing my bikini line won't be chaffed by dollar bills ever again.'

'When are you moving out to suburbia?'

'As soon as I pack my stuff I'll catch a cab to West Hollywood with Jane.'

'Do you need a hand packing? As you can see, I haven't got much else on until tonight.'

'Sure, that'd be great.'

As they walked arm in arm towards her room, Savannah caught Nicole glancing at her stomach but apparently thinking twice about asking a question. However, Savannah guessed what was on her mind.

'Kind of messed up, isn't it? Not knowing who the father of your baby is, even if he walked past you in the street,' she began, and then explained the circumstances surrounding the night she became pregnant.

'I don't know what to say,' said Nicole. 'I can't even begin to imagine what you've been through.'

'That's why this new start is so important to me,' Savannah replied firmly, 'I'm done with being the victim.'

'I know that feeling,' thought Nicole.

The first thing Savannah noticed when she unlocked the door to her room was Jane's empty bed, stripped of its sheets and pillowcases. Her suitcase was no longer under her bed and the bathroom was cleared of her toiletries.

'Wow, she's so organised,' said Savannah. 'She must have got the keys early and moved her stuff already.'

'Didn't she tell you she was going?'

'No, we arranged to meet here later and then head up to the new place. She probably left me a message at reception.'

The last two days had been a harsh and steep learning curve for Nicole, and her natural instinct to trust people had eroded and been replaced with suspicion. She was glancing around the room when something in the dustbin caught her eye.

'Whose are these kids?' she asked, picking out a photo frame with two smiling faces inside.

'They're Jane's,' replied Savannah, puzzled.

'Why's she thrown them away?'

'I don't know.'

'Savannah, I don't want to worry you, but I don't have a good feeling about this.'

Neither did Savannah, and she marched over to where her locker stood and moved it to one side to reveal the space behind the wall where she hid her earnings. It was empty.

'What's wrong?' asked Nicole.

'All the money I've saved, I keep it here. It's gone!'

CHAPTER 74

Matty glanced around the walls of the pawnshop while an assistant found the corresponding pink ticket to the one Matty presented him with.

All around him, acoustic and electric guitars sat on plinths. Three separate drum kits were arranged to fill corners, and a variety of brass instruments balanced on shelves. The shop was a graveyard of abandoned ambitions, and he wondered how many dreams had died in that one shop.

'This the one?' the shopkeeper asked briskly, and passed Matty a silver chain and crucifix.

The necklace was the last gift Matty's parents had given to him before they waved their emotional goodbyes at Dublin airport a year earlier. He hadn't told Declan he'd pawned it the previous week so they could afford to eat, even though it had upset Matty greatly. But thanks to the ten $100 bills someone anonymously shoved under their door, he could now buy it back. Both suspected Tommy had something to do with their cash donation, as he was the only one aware of their situation, but they respected his desire to keep it quiet so they resisted mentioning it.

Matty paid the shopkeeper and gripped the necklace tightly in the palm of his hand, confident its next owner would treasure it as much as he had.

CHAPTER 75

Nicole ran with Savannah from her room to the hostel reception desk where Sadie sat with her feet up, engrossed in her Kindle.

'Sadie, is Jane still checked in?' Nicole asked, her bruised ribs aching from moving so quickly.

'Surname?' she replied, irritated by the disturbance. Nicole looked towards Savannah.

'Um, I'm not sure,' Savannah replied, embarrassed at not knowing the answer to such a simple question.

'There's a Jane who checked out at 9.45 this morning,' continued Sadie, scanning the guest register. 'Jane Doherty. Is that her?'

'Jane Doherty?' repeated Nicole, and closed her eyes. 'Jane Doe.'

'Tell me this isn't happening,' Savannah replied, her voice beginning to crack. 'That was all the money I had in the world.'

'Have you got an address for the new place?'

'The brochure's in my handbag upstairs.'

'Good, you go and get it and I'll find us a taxi.'

Nicole dashed outside and scanned the passing traffic. She didn't notice the brown station wagon parked on the opposite side of the road or the driver sitting behind the wheel.

*

Nicole and Savannah didn't say a word to each other as their cab drove along Wilshire Boulevard in the direction of West Hollywood.

Nicole was accustomed to consoling hospital patients when they'd received bad news, but today she had nothing up her sleeve that might ease Savannah's concerns. Meanwhile Savannah, spine rigid and fists clenched tightly into balls, remained silent. She was desperate to be wrong about Jane; hoping against all hope that there'd been some mix-up and the woman who was about to help turn her life around was not actually a scam artist.

After a frustratingly long forty-five minute journey in heavy traffic, the taxi reached its destination in a leafy West Hollywood suburb. Nicole paid the driver, giving him extra to remain by the kerb until they knew one way or another whether this was a terrible misunderstanding or deliberate deceit.

Savannah's legs felt heavy and clumsy as she stepped out, steadying herself against the car's door frame.

'Deep breaths,' advised Nicole, taking Savannah's arm as a brown station wagon drove slowly past them and parked further up the street. 'If you get stressed, the baby will feel stressed too.'

Slowly, they walked up the crazy paving that separated the lawn and towards the house Savannah had only seen in a brochure. The upstairs curtains were closed and the blinds in the downstairs windows pulled shut.

'Good luck,' added Nicole, as they reached the porch.

Savannah rang the doorbell, but was greeted by silence. After a few moments, she pressed the button again, but still there was no response. Finally she knocked, and then again, more loudly. And when she pulled the door handle and discovered it was locked, she couldn't hold back her tears any longer.

Nicole walked towards the window and peered inside, but it was too dark to make out anything but an empty, furniture-less room. She turned to Savannah and offered her a sympathetic smile, but Savannah had already accepted the inevitable.

CHAPTER 76

With no credit left on his mobile phone, Declan used the pay phone in reception to call home to Ireland and check up on his younger brothers.

Meanwhile Matty made the most of his time alone to take a look at photographs of their travels he'd had printed on his way back from the pawn shop. He temporarily forgot the aches in his chest and smiled at a picture of himself wrapped in warm winter ski wear in Grenoble, France, drinking a yard of ale at a bar, and laughed at a passed-out Declan lying on a Moroccan street. He removed a selfie of the two of them inside Rome's Coliseum, folded it in half and placed it in his shirt pocket. Then he put the envelope of photographs under Declan's pillow, along with their Travel America guide with his crucifix placed inside.

All at once, Matty felt light-headed and sensed his pulse racing, so he sat on his mattress, closed his eyes, put his head in his hands and composed himself. Although they had stayed at more desirable places, it was the only hostel that Matty had felt truly comfortable in and he was sure that when the time came to leave Declan alone, he would get the support he needed from the people around him.

Matty reflected on his time in Los Angeles and was confident he and Declan had gone out of their way to endear themselves to their fellow hostellers. They'd never lied about their intentions in their pursuit of the opposite sex, and as both had been upfront about what they were looking for, their consciences were clear.

The only thing troubling Matty about his forthcoming journey into the great unknown was the death of the postmaster and the role he and Declan had unwittingly played in it. He hoped that with just one transgression to his name – albeit a large one – he'd be allowed through the pearly gates.

'You ready for some scran before the party?' began Declan, bursting into the room, ''cos if I don't eat soon, Sir Bob's gonna organise a feckin' benefit concert for me.'

'Only if you're buying,' Matty replied, trying his best to put a brave face on the chest pains that refused to go away.

CHAPTER 77

'How could I have been so dumb?' sobbed Savannah, 'I thought Jane was my friend.'

'Sweetheart, I'm so sorry,' replied Nicole, trying to console her. She knew all too well how easy it was to be duped by someone you'd placed your trust in.

'It's not your fault, honestly. Sometimes we put our faith in people and they end up hurting us more than we can ever believe. We'll find a way of sorting this out, I promise you.'

'How? She has all my money. If I can't trust Jane, I have no one.'

Nicole pulled a packet of paper tissues from her pocket and handed one to Savannah as they began to make their way back towards the waiting taxi.

'Oh, you're here already!' a voice behind them suddenly chirped. Both Savannah and Nicole turned their heads quickly to find the front door open and Jane standing there, a bin bag in one hand and an empty cardboard box in the other.

'What's wrong? Is it the baby?' Jane asked, suddenly noticing Savannah's tears.

'You're here! But we knocked on the door . . .' cried Savannah.

'Sorry, I was out the back scrubbing the bins. The last tenants left the place looking like a pigsty.'

'I thought you'd left me.'

'Don't be silly! Why would I do that? I wanted to make the place shipshape before you and the furniture arrived. Oh, and I brought that money you hide so badly behind your locker just in case you forgot it.'

'But your kids' pictures were in the trash?'

'They've been in my luggage so long they've become dog-eared, so I got some reprints done and bought a nicer frame. Have I done something wrong?'

'Sorry, Jane, we were worried – you disappeared so quickly,' replied Nicole. 'And Savannah's money had gone.'

'Oh honey, I'm sorry, I just got ahead of myself without thinking. I'm your friend – I'm not going anywhere, alright?'

'Okay.'

'Now get your bum inside and I'll put a brew on. Will you join us, Nicole?'

'Thanks, but I'm going to head back and help with tonight's party. Do you want me to pack your things up for you, Savannah?'

'Do you mind?'

'Not at all. Come by and pick them up when you're ready.'

Nicole smiled as Jane put her arm around Savannah and the two headed into their new home and new life. And it restored a tiny, tiny piece of her faith in people that she thought she'd lost.

As her taxi pulled away, the brown station wagon parked further up the street remained.

CHAPTER 78

Nicole borrowed a key from an uninterested Sadie and let herself into Savannah and Jane's room.

Her ribs still ached so she moved slowly as she folded up T-shirts and towels and packed them into Savannah's suitcase. She wondered how she'd fill in the rest of the day until the party began in Santa Monica. With Tommy flying below the radar and Eric awaiting a court hearing, she had never felt so lonely in a building full of people.

Recent events had exhausted Nicole physically and emotionally, and she had no energy or desire to keep travelling alone, but she also had little reason to return to England. However, she did have two holdalls hidden in the hostel containing more money than she knew what to do with. How she would use it to her advantage she had yet to decide.

Nicole scooped up half a dozen bottles of shampoo, conditioners, fake tan and body glitter, then tested out Savannah's perfumes by spraying them on her wrists. She gave both sides of her neck a spritz with a large bottle of Beyonce's Heat Wild Orchid, but as she went to place it inside a bag, she tripped over the bathroom mat.

There was nothing she could do to prevent the heavy mauve-coloured bottle from leaving her hands, flying through the air and colliding with the full-length wall mirror, shattering it into pieces across the bathroom floor. And she screamed when she saw the face of a terrified man in a room behind where the mirror had been.

'Ron!'

CHAPTER 79

The photographs in the brochure Jane had shown Savannah didn't do their new home justice.

Savannah entered under the tiled pitched porch roof and into a light and airy reception room. Through the kitchen window ahead, she saw into the colourful planted garden where a sprinkler threw water into an arc above the lawn. Inside and to the left, behind glass doors, was a dining room with an eight-seat table and wicker chairs still packed in cardboard and bubble wrap, and to the right was an empty lounge.

'The beds are already here, but the rest of the furniture won't arrive till tomorrow afternoon,' advised Jane.

But Savannah didn't care; she was already in love with her new house.

'You don't know where to look first, do you?' smiled Jane. 'I was the same.'

'It's beautiful, thank you so much for finding it,' Savannah replied, and embraced her friend.

Jane led Savannah into the kitchen, and poured hot water from the kettle to make two mugs of herbal tea. 'Go and have a look around while I pop to the loo.'

Savannah picked up her mug and wandered from room to room, wondering if Jane had been economical with the truth about the rental price. But even if she couldn't afford to pay her way at the moment, she vowed to eventually.

'We're home,' she whispered to her stomach and smiled. 'We're home.'

*

'She's here,' Jane said curtly.

Inside the locked bathroom she whispered into a mobile phone. 'I'll give her a stronger sedative before she goes to bed, but wait until I call you before you send the car.'

Back in Montgomery, Alabama, Reverend Devereaux hung up the phone and gave a victorious smile.

CHAPTER 80

Ron and Nicole stared at each other, both equally frightened and uneasy.

Nicole took a step backwards, having learned from her showdown with Eric that when backed into a corner, human behaviour could return to its most basic, animalistic form at the drop of a hat. But the anger she felt towards Ron was stronger than her fear of how he might retaliate.

Confrontation did not sit well with Ron, but, try as he might, he couldn't find a way out of the situation. And in his sixty-eight years on the planet, he had placed himself in many an unusual situation.

*

Ronald Arthur Hancock had never come across anyone he could call a friend.

Home schooled on a remote corn farm in Oklahoma, and with no brothers, sisters or neighbourhood kids to play with, Ron was accustomed to his own company.

He was a shy, scrawny seventeen-year-old on a drive into town for farm supplies when the tornado struck. Ron and the general store's customers took cover in the storm shelter until the violent, rotating column of air passed. By the time Ron reached his home later that afternoon, it was scattered in pieces across the great plains, along with his parents' bodies. He was left with nothing but a generous insurance policy payout.

Being alone was made harder by Ron's lack of skills that others took for granted – the ability to empathise, relate to or identify with other people. He'd been told by his father these were necessary smarts to get by in life, but the developmental disability in his brain caused him to freeze when anyone, even a familiar face, tried to engage him in polite chit-chat. As a result, much of his time was spent alone in his motel room, passing the time practising conversations with his reflection in the bathroom mirror.

Ron took a rare excursion one Presidents' Day when Uncle Sam's Great American Circus rolled into town. As the townsfolk enjoyed the rides, stalls, animals and performers, it was the hall of mirrors that transfixed him. He was fascinated by how flexible glass contorted his face and body into mutated shapes. By simply standing and doing nothing, he could become something or someone unrecognisable from himself. It was, ironically, a moment of clarity.

Ron's first job after his parents' farm was flattened was working for a mirror manufacturer in Tulsa. Despite his lack of experience, he was employed as an apprentice and learned how to mix the reflective coating, apply it to suitable substrates and construct frames from various woods, metals and plastics. He adored his new career, and each time he completed a commission, he saw something different about himself in his reflection.

A decade had passed when Ron was tasked with manufacturing a 5-feet-square, two-way mirror for the Texas State Penitentiary at Huntsville. As he hung it in the warehouse for a final check and polish before transportation, he was delighted by how he could observe his workmates from one side and not be seen from the other. A two-way mirror allowed him to be a part of the world without ever having to interact with it.

Ron joined his foreman Hank on the truck ride to Huntsville to fit the mirror in a small, green-bricked, brightly lit room. On one side where the mirror was to be pitted was a row of wooden chairs, and on the other, a stainless steel table with five leather straps and two wrist restraints.

'It's where the death row boys get the needle,' Hank explained. 'The witnesses can watch him die, but he ain't gonna see them. All he can see is his own reflection and the light going out of his own eyes.'

Butterflies circled Ron's stomach, and for the next fortnight, all he could think about were what stories the mirror he created would be able to tell. When child-murderer Bobby Dalgleish's execution date was set for a month's time, Ron invented an excuse to contact the prison and lied, suggesting the mirror might have a near-invisible hairline crack in need of urgent repair.

After giving it a detailed once over in a convincing performance, Ron asked if he could remain there to witness the execution. The suspicious chief eyed him up and down – it wasn't a request he received often – but concluding Ron was innocuous, consent forms were signed and countersigned, and Dalgleish's execution was the first of sixty-two Ron observed over the next two and a half decades. Ron gained no pleasure or thrill from watching a state-sanctioned murder; it was the ability to covertly watch someone at their most vulnerable that enticed him.

Executions weren't a weekly or even monthly occurrence in

Texas, meaning Ron travelled the country seeking them out. Sometimes he'd pose as a long-lost member of a victim or perpetrator's family needing closure or to offer support; on other occasions, he pretended to be working as a reporter for an obscure small-town publication with a make-believe vested interest in the execution.

Not every appointment went the way Ron intended. When in Alabama he discovered the observation room contained a window and not a mirror, he immediately walked out. In Arizona, he felt short-changed when a curtain was drawn as soon as the lethal injection was administered. But over time, the criteria for witnessing an execution became tougher, the identity checks more rigorous and Ron more frequently refused entry.

When his employers shut up shop in the recession, Ron's savings and farm insurance payout funded his travels across America, and eventually he found himself as the oldest guest at a decrepit backpacking hostel in Los Angeles. The owner had made it known she'd happily sell for a bargain price, so Ron used the last of his savings to purchase his first home since the farm.

Although Ron didn't need to interact with people, he learned to appreciate being surrounded by them, and sometimes he'd sit in his office with the door ajar, going about his hostel business as the voices on the other side went about theirs.

Ron had yet to meet a woman who would make any impact on his life. That was until the night he sat inside a private peep show booth at a strip club and instantly fell for a beautiful dancer called Savannah, as she moved before him from behind a two-way mirror.

*

'You spied on Savannah while she was in her bathroom?' Nicole began. 'That's disgusting! Jesus, Ron, she trusted you.'

'I wasn't spying – someone had to look out for her,' Ron replied, his voice trembling. 'She was vulnerable and she needed me.'

'She was only vulnerable because of people like you taking advantage of her.'

'I didn't take advantage, I just needed to be close to her.'

'Yeah, I can see how close you've come,' Nicole replied, and gave a disgusted glance at the discarded tissues lying by Ron's feet. 'You're sick.'

'I'm sorry, please don't tell her,' replied Ron, and Nicole

recognised angst in his eyes. He moved towards her, but a wary Nicole temporarily forgot about her bruising and reached down to grab a piece of the broken perfume bottle and held it in front of her like a weapon.

'Why shouldn't I tell her? Because she'd see you for what you are? A dirty, grubby little pervert?'

'I'm not.'

'What you've done isn't normal, Ron! Surely you can see that? And Savannah needs to know.'

'But if you tell her she'll never come back, and I'll never see my . . .' Ron's brow wrinkled and he clasped his hand over his mouth.

'See your what?' asked Nicole.

When Ron didn't reply, the penny dropped for Nicole.

CHAPTER 81

The thumping beat of electronic dance music blared from six large speakers surrounding a DJ's booth as around 600 hostellers danced and drank across the floodlit Santa Monica beach.

Partygoers had walked or been bussed in from Los Angeles' six hostels in Venice, Santa Monica, Hollywood and Hermosa Beach to mark the end of the summer with an all-night celebration. As a rule, LA's vast beaches were legally out of bounds by 10 p.m., but tonight was an exception courtesy of a tourism initiative to promote the city hostels as places to stay rather than to use as stopovers between more traveller-friendly regions like San Francisco or San Diego.

The LA Tourism Board and hostel managers collaborated to fund two photographers and a film crew to take pictures and video footage for a print and online viral video promotional campaign. Marshalls handed guests wristbands, coloured to match their respective hostels, and keep unwelcome gatecrashers out.

A scout was sent to find the most attractive of the travellers to appear in the forthcoming promo material, but Matty and Declan politely refused the offer when approached, and relocated to a quieter section of the beach. Declan tucked into a second cheeseburger with all the trimmings while Matty lay on the sand, propped up by his elbows, staring into the distance. He kept his exhaustion to himself.

'D'you reckon we should start thinking about moving on?' asked Declan.

'Finish your food first.'

'I meant leaving LA.'

'Why? You love it here, we've made friends here.'

'I know, it's been a blast. I just thought you might want to try somewhere else.'

'Nah,' said Matty shaking his head. 'If you're happy, I'm happy, and this is a good place to be.'

Declan grabbed a plastic cup of beer and a bottle of water for Matty from an ice bucket behind him.

'Water, gee, thanks,' sniffed Matty, although even the thought of alcohol passing his lips made him nauseous.

'It's good for you – it flushes out your bad toxins.'

'It hasn't flushed you away.'

They paused to stare at two girls, dancing ahead of them.

'You're losing your touch,' smiled Matty. 'Look at the blonde one, she's been giving you the eye all night. Once upon a time you'd have been there like a rat up a drainpipe. Go over and talk to her.'

'You don't have to tell me twice. Are you coming?'

'No, I'm gonna get arseholed on Evian.'

'Stay out of trouble,' replied Declan, and wandered over towards the girls as Matty watched.

'I'll be with you in spirit,' he smiled.

CHAPTER 82

'Oh good God, tell me her baby isn't yours,' Nicole said to Ron as they stood amongst the shards of broken mirror and glass in Savannah's bathroom. The piece she'd use to fight off any potential attack remained in her grasp.

She genuinely hoped to hear a firm 'no', but Ron's shamed silence gave Nicole her answer.

'You drugged and raped her and made her pregnant, didn't you?' she asked quietly.

'I didn't drug her, I found her when she needed help,' replied Ron. 'And don't use that word – I didn't rape anyone. I love her.'

FOUR MONTHS EARLIER – SAVANNAH'S MOTEL

Ron sat in an armchair in the corner of Savannah's motel room, drumming his fingers across the arm, watching her as she slept under a tartan quilt.

Whatever drug had been slipped inside her water bottle in the strip club had had the desired effect, but not for the perpetrator. At first Ron wondered why anyone would want to do that to the girl he adored, but as he stared at her inert body, he began to understand.

From his usual seat in the shadows at the back of the club, Ron knew Savannah wasn't like the other girls she shared a stage with. Those girls' eyes betrayed the sexuality they were trying to promote; they were filled with either pretence or desperation. Savannah was different, and from the moment she'd sashayed past him in her black bra and panties and caught his eye, he knew they'd just shared something special.

However, his frustrating inability to engage with strangers meant he chose not to interact with her and, instead, he pulled his baseball cap down towards his thick eyebrows and sunk ever deeper into his chair.

During a fortnight of frequent return visits, Ron watched as Savannah contorted her supple limbs around a pole either on stage or in a back room, surrounded by peep show customers who sat in private booths masturbating behind two-way mirrors. He'd spent $3,000 getting to know her body better than she knew her own.

That night four months ago, the stars had aligned and their worlds collided. Ron could barely believe his eyes when Savannah stumbled in front of the car as Peyk picked him up from the club. Together, they lifted her into the vehicle and laid her out across the back seat, and when Peyk found her motel key inside her handbag, they drove her back to her room and put her to bed. Ron purposefully failed to mention he knew who the girl was, but offered to stay with her until morning to make sure she was okay.

Savannah had been unconscious for around an hour and half before Ron hesitantly plucked up the courage to approach her side of the room. He knelt by the bed and tentatively ran his rough fingertips through her soft hair. Gradually he moved his mouth closer to hers and gently kissed her lips. Then he slowly slipped into her bed, unbuckled his belt, slid down her shorts and guided himself inside her. In less than twenty seconds, he climaxed.

By the time Savannah awoke in the morning, Ron had left and Peyk had taken his place, fast asleep in the armchair. And in the back of the cab returning back to the hostel, Ron was immersed in the flavour of love for the first time in his life.

TODAY

Nicole shuffled uncomfortably from foot to foot, finding it difficult to comprehend that Ron couldn't see his actions had been despicable towards the woman he claimed to love.

'So what do you call it when a woman is unconscious and can't say no to sex?' she continued. 'Reluctance?'

'It wasn't like that. Savannah is so beautiful, and I'd sit at the back of the club watching her dance and she had this look in her eyes, like she was alone, like me. We understood each other.'

'Ron, this is all in your head, can't you see that? I knew you were a bit weird, but this . . . Christ.'

'I'm not weird!' exclaimed Ron. 'I told you, I love her.'

'"Love" isn't an excuse to rape someone.'

'She's been let down so many times before – if you tell her, you'll destroy her. Please let her think I'm her friend. For Savannah's sake.'

'That is the last thing you are.'

Nicole and Ron reached a stalemate, neither budging from their respective positions. But Nicole knew she held all the cards, only she was unsure how to play them.

'Tell me what you want me to do?' asked Ron out of desperation.

Nicole closed her eyes and shook her head. She knew the right thing to do would be to tell Savannah everything she'd learned at the earliest opportunity. She reasoned it must have been hard enough for Savannah to come to terms with her unborn child being the product of rape, but if she then discovered the rapist was a man she'd lived under the same roof with, how much tougher would that be to digest? From recent experience Nicole was aware how devastating it felt to be deceived by someone you know. And Savannah appeared so pragmatic over impending motherhood and her new life with Jane that Nicole made a snap decision – Savannah was better off being kept in the dark. For now, at least.

Meanwhile Ron felt close to tears, an alien emotion, as he awaited Nicole's response.

'I know what you can do,' she eventually replied. 'And you need to do it tonight.'

CHAPTER 83

'Guys, that's not a good idea. Guys! Guys!' shouted a marshal through a megaphone as a handful of young people ran towards the ocean at Santa Monica to go skinny-dipping.

Peyk watched as two lifeguards approached the water's edge and shone powerful torches on the naked figures larking around in the waves. He didn't bother to double check if they were watching when he sparked up a joint with his cigarette lighter.

'Got one spare?' asked Nicole.

'Sure,' replied Peyk, and handed Nicole a ready-rolled joint from his back pocket.

'It's a good turn out,' she continued, lighting it and taking a long drag.

'Sure is.'

'Want to join me in a toast?' she continued, and held up her beer cup to Peyk's. Peyk nodded.

'Aren't you going to ask me what we're toasting?'

'Let me see,' he replied, pretending to think. 'Ahh, to you buying the hostel from Ron.'

Nicole's eyes opened wide. 'How could you possibly know that?'

Just an hour earlier, she had taken Ron's bank details and promised to wire him a fair price for the hostel in due course on the proviso he left there and then. With his options limited, he had little choice but to agree. As Ron crammed his belongings into the back of his car, Nicole hailed a taxi and headed towards the beach party with a renewed sense of purpose.

'I may walk around stoned most of the time, but nothing escapes me,' Peyk replied.

'Apparently so.'

'And don't think too badly of Ron. He doesn't rationalise like us.'

Nicole paused to make sure Peyk had just said what she thought he'd said.

'What? You know what he did to Savannah and you didn't tell her?'

'"The supreme lesson of human consciousness is to learn how not to know. That is, how not to interfere." D.H. Lawrence.'

Nicole frowned.

'In other words,' Peyk continued, 'Ron will suffer for what he's done with or without my interference. He will never get to meet his child, watch him grow up, see his own eyes reflected in another's or be able to love or be loved unconditionally. And that's worth toasting.'

Peyk clipped Nicole's cup with his own and wandered away, leaving a coil of smoke unspooling behind him.

CHAPTER 84

Matty had never felt a tiredness like the one he felt that night.

He glanced wistfully across a beach illuminated by bonfires, lanterns, coloured lights, glow sticks and the red tips of cigarettes. Every so often, Declan turned away from the girl he was flirting with to check on his friend, and Matty would force his eyelids to remain open and offer a reassuring wave. But as soon as Declan's attention was diverted, they fluttered to a close. All he wanted was to fall asleep and wake up in the body of someone else.

'Everything alright, my friend?' asked Peyk, throwing himself onto the sand, cross-legged.

'Yeah, just watching my boy in action,' Matty whispered.

'So you've said your goodbyes, then?'

Matty looked quizzically at Peyk. 'Yeah, I have,' he eventually replied.

Peyk nodded and continued to stare ahead of them both. 'Does he know?'

'No . . . he's having a laugh and I'm reckoning it'll be the last time for a while. I don't want to take that away from him.'

'Would you like some company?'

Matty considered it for a moment, but decided he was happy being on his own. He began to understand why Levi, his mother's cat, had taken herself away to die alone in a neighbour's garage; there was something quite empowering about doing it on your own terms and leaving the world in the same manner in which you arrived.

'I appreciate the offer, but I'm good.'

'It's been a pleasure,' said Peyk, rising to his feet and shaking Matty's limp hand.

'Likewise. Explain to Declan for me, tell him . . .'

'He knows, Matthew. Don't worry about that.'

Matty and Peyk smiled at each other, and by the time Peyk was out of sight, Matty's eyes were already closed.

CHAPTER 85

As pop music made way for classic rap and old-skool hip hop, Nicole left the group of French students she'd been dancing with, and was making her way towards the shore when she spotted Tommy.

She'd only had three cups of beer, but combined with her first joint since her college student nursing days, she felt giddy. It was medicinal, she told herself, and it had certainly stopped her feeling the bruising on her ribs when she moved. But the expression on Tommy's face soon sobered her up.

'You look like you're carrying the weight of the world on your shoulders,' she began. Tommy didn't reply.

'Savannah's moved out of the hostel,' Nicole persevered. 'I think she's going to be really happy at Jane's place. Did you know she was pregnant?'

Tommy shook his head but said nothing.

'Have I upset you, Tommy?'

'No,' he replied. 'Not everything is about you.'

'That's unfair,' Nicole replied, offended by his offhand attitude. 'Is it Jake? I know you two are—'

'Jake and I are nothing,' Tommy interrupted.

'Oh, right. I saw him heading towards the beer tent a few minutes ago, if you're interested.'

When Tommy offered no reply, Nicole decided against telling him about her hostel acquisition and began to walk away, before halting.

'Tommy, please talk to me, you're worrying me.'

'If you see Jake, tell him to meet me on the pier. He'll know where.'

But before Nicole could respond, Tommy had the bright lights of the fairground in his sights.

CHAPTER 86

The Ferris wheel offered panoramic views across Santa Monica's coastline, way beyond the commercial shopping area, and up and along Route 66.

Mechanical failure had temporarily shut the rollercoaster, so all four corners of the nine-acre pier were eerily quiet long before its midnight curfew. From its furthest end, Tommy heard the grinding mechanism slowly moving the giant wheel as the tide below crashed against the pier's wooden stilts. He stood with his back to the rides, staring at the blinking orange lights on buoys bobbing against the ocean's current.

'You're a hard man to track down,' began Jake, approaching Tommy from behind. He placed his hand on Tommy's shoulder, then let it fall towards the arch of his back and held it there. 'Why are you up here on your own when the party's down there?'

'I used to love fairgrounds,' began Tommy, staring straight ahead of him. 'My parents would take me and my brothers when it came to Abington Park every summer. Lee won me a goldfish at one of those hoop stalls; eleven years later and it's still alive. Unbelievable, isn't it? For eleven years it's been swimming around in circles, day in, day out, all on its own.'

'I didn't think goldfish lived that long.'

'It's outlived Lee. And Dan.'

Jake paused. 'Is that who you meant when you said you'd lost people close to you?'

Tommy fell silent.

'Do you want to tell me about them? It might help.'

'I think you've done enough already.'

'What's that supposed to mean?' asked Jake, but didn't get his answer. They remained in a stilted silence, before frustration got the better of him.

'Why are you pushing me away, Tommy?' he snapped. 'You're acting like a kid. I'm old enough to accept rejection, so just be honest with me.'

'Be honest? Ha!' Tommy laughed. 'Do you remember when you said there was a connection between us? Well you're right, there is.'

'Okay but that doesn't explain why you're—'

'Not a connection in the way you think,' Tommy interrupted.

'I don't understand.'

'You talk about honesty, Jake, but just how honest are we with each other? The night you arrived and we went out for coffee, we agreed one of the best things about travelling is that you get to hear a complete stranger's life story. Well we're long past being strangers but we don't know the first thing about each other, do we? So do you want me to start?'

Jake nodded, puzzled by the ire slowly warping Tommy's face.

'I came travelling when my family fell apart after my brothers were killed in a car accident.'

Jake paused and squinted at Tommy, unsure of how his story related to him. Suddenly Tommy turned and looked Jake straight in the eye.

'Are you sure you don't know where this is going, *Stuart*?'

The look of alarm hastily spreading across his face told them both Jake knew exactly where this was going.

TWO YEARS EARLIER – LONDON

As Stuart left Geri Garland's house, the only thing he had any control over was her car, courtesy of the keys he'd grabbed when her security men were more concerned with bundling him out of her house. Stealing her Range Rover was a tiny victory against the woman who'd systematically built him up then torn him down.

As he fought his way through the congested London traffic and towards the M1, Stuart was acutely aware he could never take back the events of the last eighteen hours but he was struggling to come to terms with them. Zak was refusing to answer his phone calls, his Lightning Strikes bandmates had turned their backs on him and the woman he loathed had hung him out to dry. Try as he might, he could feel only limited sympathy towards Katie, who'd thrown her hat in the ring with the devil and paid the ultimate price.

As much as he hated it, there was only one place where he could retreat and regroup: his former shared house in Bolton. But there was a three-hour drive ahead of him and he struggled to focus on the road, so each time the cocaine's effects began wearing off, he took another hit.

When the overhead gantry signs warned the motorway ahead was closed at junction 15, he followed the diversion signs and drove towards an estate called Hunsbury.

Then, without warning, Stuart's heart felt like it was beating its way out of his chest. He struggled for breath, his temperature soared and his vision blurred as he frantically searched for the button to put the window down. He stretched his arms out against the steering wheel and tried to regain control of his body.

He failed to notice the first red light he passed through, but by the time he'd driven through the second, it was too late to hit the brakes.

After being pushed 50 metres along the road, the vehicle Stuart ploughed into finally came to a rest on its side, almost broken in two by an equally broken man.

Stuart felt a shooting pain tear up his nostrils and spread across his temples when the airbag deployed and caught his face full on.

But Geri's bulky 4x4 offered him much more protection than the vehicle he'd collided with, which lay in the road like a crumpled concertina. He blindly fumbled around to unclip his seat belt, and struggled to find the handle to open his door. He staggered outside, his legs almost buckling beneath him.

Stuart stared in horror at the carnage before him, struck by the gravity of his actions. He remained motionless until he heard voices and turned his head to see figures hurrying towards the scene. It was only then that his survival instinct kicked in and he knew what he had to do.

He pulled his hood up over his head and limped past what was once a Mini, glancing through the broken windscreen. He clamped his hand over his mouth when he saw two mangled bodies lying in the front seats and he could just about make out a third figure in the back of the car, lying motionless but for his blinking eyes.

Stuart dry heaved as the voices behind him became louder; then with all the strength he could muster, he ran. And he didn't stop running for another three years.

CHAPTER 87

TODAY

What had begun as Declan striving to chat up a girl he didn't know had turned into something quite unexpected with a familiar face.

As he took a break from flirting with the girl Matty had pointed out, Declan trudged across the sand to check on his friend and bumped into a fellow hosteller. They'd seen each other around the building many times and had enjoyed brief conversations, but the beach was the first place either of them had taken any time to do more than exchange pleasantries.

The conversation flowed naturally without Declan relying on his tried and tested lines, jokes and flattery, and he became slowly aware that he was winning her over simply by being himself. For the first time in a long time, if ever, Declan found himself making plans to meet a girl the next morning for breakfast, rather than waking up with her.

Nicole was feeling the same way. Butterflies only circled her stomach when something awful loomed, but now, chatting to Declan, their wings felt lighter. Their easy-going repartee came as a welcome distraction from Eric's betrayal, Ruth's breakdown and Tommy's mood swings. Declan made her laugh at a time when she'd have been well within her rights to cry until Christmas.

With plans made, Declan traipsed towards Matty with a spring in his step.

'Lazy bollocks, you'll never guess who I've been gassing with,' he began, and sat down beside his friend. Declan couldn't take his eyes off Nicole as she chatted to another hosteller, occasionally looking over to him but pretending she wasn't. 'That Nicole girl, Tommy's mate. She's a bit special that one, d'you hear me?'

When Matty didn't acknowledge him, Declan turned to see him lying on his back, his head resting on a folded blanket and his eyes snapped tightly shut. Declan turned his head again to stare at the party in front of them.

'Hey, sleepy head, come on there fella. Let's get you home.'

Even as the words tripped from his mouth, Declan knew Matty had left him. For a full minute, he remained as lifeless as his friend, processing the fact that the inevitable had arrived.

Then, gently, he placed Matty's hand into the palm of his own and stared up into the night sky as a fireworks display illuminated them in whites, greens and oranges.

'I'm not ready,' Declan whispered. 'I'm still not ready.'

CHAPTER 88

'*Stuart.*'

Tommy pronounced such a simple word with such venomous precision, there was no doubt in Jake's mind his cover was blown. But he didn't want to admit it.

'No, that's not possible,' Jake muttered, his muscular shoulders dropping by the weight of his shame.

'It is, Stuart, believe me. I am walking, talking, proof that it is possible.'

Jake took two steps back, and with wide-open eyes, he glared at Tommy, hoping to find something in his friend's expression that revealed this was some kind of sick prank. But there was nothing but abhorrence etched deeply into Tommy's face.

'How did you find out?'

ONE DAY EARLIER – VENICE BEACH

In desperate need of solitude in a city of noise, Tommy slipped José a bag of weed and locked himself in the store cupboard of the hotdog trailer.

The 10 foot by 10 foot room was windowless and reeked of cheap frankfurters, but it was air conditioned, and most importantly, quiet. Tommy felt like someone had used his head as a football, leaving his thoughts jumbled and nonsensical. The dark clouds were rolling in as everything he thought he knew about Jake was in flux.

He removed his iPhone from his pocket and waited for a signal to appear, then he skipped through his photos until he found the one with Jake's torso tattoos on display. Then, making a mental note of the final coordinates, he typed 52.2189N and 0.9202W into the search engine.

He watched carefully as they threw up the location of where Jake's journey had begun – Hunsbury, Northampton; the place where Tommy's life changed with the speed of the car that smashed into him; the Tarmac graveyard where his brothers were killed and he was left to die; where Stuart Reynolds ceased to exist and the journey of Jake Bellamy began.

A strangely calm Tommy took the memory card he had, until now, refused to view and placed it inside his camcorder.

His finger hovered above a button, then he closed his eyes and braced himself before he pressed play.

First came what he'd recorded as their car drove through the streets of Northampton, and goosebumps bubbled across his arms upon hearing the voices of his brothers teasing him about porn websites they knew he secretly surfed. Then came their words of encouragement about finding a job, and Tommy knew what was coming next.

The footage was shaky as his camera had flown around the car upon impact, and then the screen turned black. Tommy sat in silence recalling the smells of broken fluid pipes, the sharpness of glass crunching beneath his legs and the sounds of panicked onlookers outside. He remembered the confusion over what had just happened before he realised Lee and Daniel's fate.

He hadn't noticed he'd closed his eyes until a noise brought him back to his senses. He thought someone else was in the room, before noticing the camcorder hadn't stopped recording that day. It must have landed somewhere near to him on the back seat, he thought, and when he'd moved, it had sprung back to life, the autofocus settling on the shattered windscreen.

At first he heard the concerned voices of witnesses in the distance, then slowly, he watched as a figure – a face mainly shadowed by a hoodie – slowly limped past the car.

Tommy rewound the footage and watched it again, and then pressed pause. When he zoomed in, Stuart and Jake's bloody face filled the screen.

*

TODAY

'We looked at each other, do you remember?' continued Tommy. 'You were running away from the Mini when suddenly you turned around . . . and just for a split second we made eye contact. Then puff, you disappeared, just like that.'

In rare moments when Jake's subconscious caught him off guard, he recalled the moment that altered the course of his life with such clarity, it was like yesterday. Then in the days that followed as he plotted starting his life anew in a succession of cheap hotel rooms, he'd turn the television off and avoid newspaper pages when confronted by the names and faces of those he killed so as not to risk humanising them.

'Tommy . . .' Jake began, his eyes having conceded defeat. But Tommy wasn't prepared to listen.

'It was a journalist who tipped us off that the police were looking at you in connection with the crash, but the police refused to confirm it, even after you supposedly died. And I remembered seeing you on TV the morning of the accident; they said you had something to do with the death of that soap star. I mean, I knew who you and your shitty band were anyway, but I'd never really taken much notice of you. Then, as hard as they tried, the police couldn't find any concrete proof it was your fault. Your fingerprints were all over that car so it should have been a no-brainer, but there was never any evidence you were behind the wheel that day. Your manager refused to confirm you'd stolen it; there was no footage of you on CCTV, no blood or DNA on the airbag, and no you. They couldn't even question you because you'd vanished. And then when they told us it looked like you'd killed yourself, everyone thought it was something to do with that girl dying. The police never named you as a suspect in our crash so you got away with it. But I knew who you were and what you did, and even hearing one of your songs, like the one the girls were dancing to on the Xbox game, made me so angry.'

Jake brushed his hand through his hair and rubbed his cheeks. He'd spent the last few years learning how to organise his thoughts and place those that frightened him to the back of his mind.

He'd explored a multitude of religions and belief systems; he'd learned from teachers and seers and read books and pamphlets, all to help him understand how to move forward and turn his back on the reckless stupidity of his actions. His ribs were inked with the coordinates of every location he'd seen, to remind him of how far he had travelled both physically and spiritually. And just when he'd forgiven himself for his actions and found the peace he craved, his past and his present were colliding with the speed of a runaway freight train.

'I was obsessed with you at first,' Tommy continued. 'I must have surfed a thousand pictures of your face to try and work out if it was you I saw while I was trapped in the back of the car and I could never be 100 per cent sure. But my gut instinct was that it *was* you. I hated you . . . in fact hated is probably too much of an understatement. But your suicide, well, that made the pain ease a little – not much, mind – but eventually it was just about enough to help me crawl out of my hole and start trying to live my life again. Only now I find out you're not just alive but that you and I have . . . that we've . . . shit, I can't even say it . . . now you've made me hate both of us, not just you.'

Jake swallowed hard, his arms and legs trembling with Tommy's every word. Eventually, when he thought Tommy was ready to listen, he spoke.

'I'm sorry, Tommy, I'm so, so sorry,' he began. 'I need you to understand, I was a different person then; I was so fucked up – I'd lost everything I'd ever worked for. I was at such a low point and I wasn't thinking straight, and when that accident happened, I panicked and I didn't know what to do.'

'So what you chose to do was to run away. You killed my brothers and then you ran away.'

'People on the street were coming to help you, I saw them, that's why I left. There was nothing I could do.'

'But you didn't know that for certain, did you, Stuart?'

Jake's lips parted and he wanted to defend his actions but he knew he couldn't.

'That's what I thought,' continued Tommy, before raising his fist and catching Jake clean on the jaw.

CHAPTER 89

Savannah dreamed she was floating somewhere between the bed in her new home and the ceiling above her.

She felt her body drift through the door, turn mid-air above the landing and gradually descend the stairs. But when she felt two arms supporting her back and legs, she understood she wasn't floating, she was being carried.

She opened her eyes but the walls surrounding her swirled like water slipping down a plughole. Her lips and throat felt parched and when she tried to speak, she could only hear herself mumble. Instantly she likened the feeling to when she stumbled out of the club and into the path of Peyk's car and a new terror began to rip through her. But her body was too sedated to spring back into life.

Savannah was lugged across the hallway but there was a pause when she reached the lounge. Through her misty eyes, she thought she saw Jane, sitting on a wooden chair with something covering the smile Savannah had found so kindly. Something wasn't right, and when her eyes slowly began to focus, she quickly realised Jane's mouth had been gagged and her arms and feet bound to the wicker chair legs.

Scared, Savannah desperately wanted to kick and punch the person carrying her, but her limbs barely twitched. However, it was enough to make the person whose arms held her notice the dead weight he was lifting was reviving.

'It's okay, Savvy, I'm gonna get you out of here,' a male voice whispered. Savannah's tired eyes slowly widened. She looked down at his strong, bare, brown arms and then up towards his face.

'Michael?' she mouthed, and felt the familiar warmth of his breath as he carried her out of the front door, down the path and towards a brown station wagon that had been parked out of view for much of the day.

CHAPTER 90

Jake staggered backwards and clutched the jaw Tommy had just whacked.

Tommy clasped his fist with his other hand, in obvious pain but trying hard to disguise it. Jake began to pace up and down, hoping the movement would jolt his thoughts back into a normal running order.

'What happened, happened, and there hasn't been a day that's gone by where I haven't prayed to God it hadn't,' Jake offered, his palm still clenched to his face. 'You don't know how bad I feel.'

Tommy narrowed his eyes and laughed. 'How bad *you* feel, Stuart? Really? So this is about how *you* feel, is it?'

'No, no, that's not what I meant,' continued Jake, closing his eyes and growing frustrated with himself. 'Tommy, Stuart Reynolds died as well that day. I don't want to be the person I was then, and I'm not, I swear to you, I'm not. You know me, the real me.'

'The real you is a coward who thinks a couple of months in a Buddhist temple means he's absolved of all his sins. Well, newsflash, Stuart, you're not. It's nowhere near enough.'

Suddenly Jake's emotions got the better of him and his eyes became watery. 'Tommy, please . . .' he begged and put his hand on Tommy's arm.

'Take that off me or so help me God, I will kill you.'

'I understand why you're upset.'

'You have no idea what I am!'

When Tommy felt Jake's fingers grip him tighter, Tommy pushed him hard in the shoulder. Desperate to prove to Tommy his sincerity, Jake tried to hold Tommy's arm again, but Tommy punched him hard on the side of his face. Jake lost his balance and fell to the ground as Tommy winced at the pain in his knuckles and fingers.

'Why did you run away?' yelled Tommy. 'Why did you just leave us?'

'I wasn't thinking straight,' continued Jake, pulling himself up to his feet. 'I didn't think there was anything I could do to help.'

'You couldn't know that because you didn't stay to find out.'

'I know! I know! But Tommy, we can work our way through this, I know it won't be easy, but I really believe we can if you just try. You have to give me a chance.'

'You know what the most pathetic thing about all of this is, Stuart?' Tommy wiped his eyes and sniffed up the mucus dripping from his nostrils. 'Me. I'm the most pathetic thing because I thought if I couldn't "be" you then maybe I could be "with" you. How fucking stupid is that? That I wanted to be with the person who destroyed my family.'

'It's not too late, I promise you.'

Tommy shook his head and glared at Jake. He had said everything he needed to say but he felt no better. Jake's explanation hadn't made a blind bit of difference and Tommy knew he must walk away now or risk his anger getting the better of him.

As he began to leave, Jake grabbed hold of his arm one last time. And it was all that was needed to tip Tommy over the edge. Tommy hit Jake again, missing his face and catching his neck. Jake staggered backwards and Tommy's second blow caught him on the bridge of his nose. Both of them heard the bone pop.

Neither the noise nor the pain in Tommy's fist stopped him from raining more blows on Jake's head as his adversary attempted to shield himself with his forearms. Jake refused to retaliate and staggered backwards into the railings while Tommy continued on autopilot, unleashing every drop of wrath and ferocity his body possessed until he was close to empty.

There they remained, rooted to the floorboards of the pier, exhausted, battered, bruised and breathing heavily before Jake finally spoke.

'I love you, Tommy,' he pleaded.

One final blow to the side of Jake's head was all it took for him to topple backwards off the pier and into the choppy waters below.

CHAPTER 91

'He's dead,' came a voice in a measured tone.

Tommy stopped in his tracks, and turned around slowly to see Declan staring at the words *Welcome to Wherever You Are* on the poster in the hostel reception before him. Tommy's mind raced ten to the dozen, trying to figure out how Declan could have known what had happened between him and Jake on the pier.

'He's dead,' repeated Declan.

'It wasn't what it looked like,' Tommy replied carefully. 'It was an accident.'

'He was my best mate.'

Tommy paused. 'I don't understand.'

'Matty's . . . gone. He's . . . dead.'

'Oh, Christ, I'm sorry.' Tommy felt a combination of relief that his secret was safe and sympathy for Declan's loss.

The diversity of Venice Beach's occupants and visitors made the unusual, usual. So nobody who passed Declan carrying Matty's body over his shoulder along the boardwalk gave the friends a second glance.

Once Declan had returned Matty to the security of the hostel and carefully laid him on his bed, he was at a loss as what to do next, so he ventured through the silent corridors and back towards reception. There, he slumped to the floor and leant against a wall, entwining the fingers of both his hands together like he was in prayer. He fixated on the poster's words and knew that without Matty by his side, Declan had no idea where he was.

Meanwhile Tommy was short of breath, having run the mile and a half from Santa Monica back to Venice, only stopping midway to prop himself up against a parking meter and to vomit into the road.

Repeatedly, he replayed the two seconds it took for Jake to disappear over the pier's railings and the heavy sound the water made when his body plunged into it. Tommy squinted into the dark waves below him, horrified by what he'd done, calling Jake's name, not Stuart's, but receiving no response. He sprinted the length of the pier and then back on himself across the beach, rushing waist high into the water shouting for Jake over and again. In desperation, he used the flashlight app on his phone, but it wasn't powerful enough to illuminate more than a couple of metres ahead. And after a frantic fifteen minutes or so, he knew it was too late.

Tommy hurried back towards the beach party and his head swept from side to side, hoping against all hope to catch sight of a soaking wet Jake amongst the revellers, but he wasn't anywhere to be seen. Suddenly feeling exposed and vulnerable, Tommy made the decision to return to the hostel.

It was only while he ran that Tommy noted the irony of his actions. He had followed the same path as Stuart Reynolds; rather than face up to a terrible mistake, contact the authorities and suffer the consequences, he'd taken the easy way out and simply run away. Nevertheless, by the time he reached the hostel entrance, he knew he was in too deep and had to clean up the mess he'd created.

'Where is Matty now?' Tommy asked Declan softly.

'I put him in our room.'

'Okay, well you come with me to the lounge and I'll be back in a minute.'

After leading Declan to the sofa, Tommy made his way up the corridor to remove any trace of Jake from the hostel. He opened a cupboard door and grabbed a roll of plastic bin liners, deciding to hide Jake's belongings in the alley dumpster for the following day's collection. Then he would change the booking register so it looked like Jake had checked out midway through the beach party and continued with his travels.

But as he approached Jake's room, the normally locked door was ajar.

CHAPTER 92

Michael drove the first leg of his journey with Savannah for six hours straight, while she slept by his side in the passenger seat.

She used the handbag Michael had taken from her room as a pillow, and every so often, he placed two fingers on her wrist to check her pulse or turned the radio off just to hear her breathe – a sound he wasn't sure he'd ever hear again after she vanished from his life.

When he'd bundled Savannah into his car, he'd briefly but gently informed her that Jane was a private investigator employed by Savannah's father to track her down, befriend her and bring her home. Savannah was unsure whether it was that awful information or the sedatives in her bloodstream making her feel queasy. Most people have never been drugged once in their lifetime, she thought, and here she was with two incidents under her belt, each with differing end results.

A purple and orange patchwork of light began to illuminate the sky as the sun appeared from behind the hills ahead. Michael stretched out his fingers as straight as he could manage. They were healing nicely, he thought, although his orthopaedic hand specialist warned him they might never function as fully as they once did. Michael was grateful his university tutors had shown understanding about the 'car accident' that had rendered him useless as a potential surgeon, and for them permitting him to change courses when the following semester began.

The rush of fresh air coming in through the window finally woke Savannah. She stared at Michael, still in disbelief, like a child meeting Father Christmas.

'It's really you,' she croaked. 'I thought I was dreaming.'
'Drink some water,' he smiled, and passed her a bottle.
'Where are we going?'
'Well, I figured we could start in Arizona and we can decide from there.'

Savannah had so many questions, she wasn't sure where to begin. 'How did you know where to find me?'
'Girl, you hid yourself well.'

CHAPTER 93

Tommy held his breath and nervously opened the door to Jake's room.

Inside it was empty of Jake's belongings, leaving just a stripped bed. Tommy realised Jake must have survived his fall, returned to the hostel before him and cleared out.

'You're alive,' thought Tommy, and let out a long sigh of relief. He covered his face with his hands, rubbed his sore eyes and let out a deep breath.

Tommy had teased Jake for being a neatness freak and always keeping his belongings packed away in his rucksack, but now he understood Jake was preparing for a moment just like this; for when his past and his present collided and he needed to escape them both.

Tommy's eyes looked around the room for any trace of Jake and focused on an open locker. From inside, he removed a silver bracelet and a scrap of paper.

'*What we are never changes, Tommy,*' it read, '*but who we are never stops changing. Remember me better than I am. Jake.*'

As much as he hated Stuart Reynolds, a significant part of Tommy was already missing Jake. Now he understood that Stuart's death wouldn't have brought him any closer to closure, but Jake Bellamy's purpose in Tommy's life was to help set Tommy free. But in doing so, it meant Jake had chosen to keep running, forever trapped in a moment of madness from his past.

Tommy turned the bracelet over and read the engraving, '*Don't look back.*' He wouldn't, he promised himself. Then he slipped the bracelet onto his wrist to remind himself how one reckless moment can change everything you thought you knew about yourself.

*

Twenty minutes after Tommy dialled 911, an ambulance arrived outside the hostel's entrance to take Matty's body away to Santa Monica's UCLA Medical Center.

Declan followed the stretcher on which his friend's body lay from their room, along the corridor, down the stairs and into the back of the vehicle.

Many of the other guests who'd returned from the beach party quickly sobered up at the sight, and stood in a silent line of respect as one of their own embarked on his final journey.

CHAPTER 94

Savannah couldn't take her eyes off Michael as he drove.

The only thing that looked different about him was a concave scar in the centre of his forehead, and she shuddered when she recalled the sound her father's mallet had made when it collided with Michael's skull.

She listened intently as Michael explained how he'd searched for her everywhere he could think of back in Montgomery, Alabama, but to no avail. Then, just when he was about to reluctantly give up, he received an unexpected email from Savannah's sister Roseanna.

He agreed to meet the desperate-sounding girl in a busy shopping centre where she tearfully revealed everything she knew about the whereabouts of her sister in Los Angeles, gleaned from flirting with one of her father's young assistants. The boy explained that Reverend Devereaux had put up a $250,000 reward to find his daughter, and several private detective agencies were fighting to be the first to bring her home. They'd all begun at the Montgomery Greyhound station where she'd purchased a bus ticket to LA using his credit card.

There were more than 400 hotels of varying size in the city, and with her father freezing her bank accounts, her hunters assumed all Savannah had in her possession was the money she'd stolen from his wallet. And as that wouldn't stretch far, she'd need a place to stay that was basic and affordable.

That narrowed the field down to around 120 motels. One agency's team was deployed to the city to visit all the cheap dives and boltholes armed with photographs of the missing Savannah, but with no success. Another hired a personality profiler who normally tracked down serial killers to build up a picture of her likely pattern of behaviour. Based on her hobbies, talents, skills and qualifications and a need to keep a low profile, they narrowed her potential line of work down to three cash-in-hand jobs where few questions were asked – waitress, prostitute or exotic dancer. And at the Flesh For Fantasy strip club, they'd found their target.

The Reverend showed no loyalty to any of those hunting his kin, and was happy to pass on updates from one detective agency to another. One tried the softly, softly approach and paid one of Savannah's colleagues a $1,000 tip to drug her water bottle with

Rohypnol. But when Savannah realised something didn't feel right, she hurriedly left the changing room and then fell into the path of a stranger's car. The next morning Savannah had disappeared, quitting her job.

It took four more weeks before another detective located her, dancing at the Pink Pussycat Club and residing in a backpacking hostel. Savannah constantly surrounded herself with people either at work or in the hostel, making her a hard target to pick off. But Reverend Devereaux was an impatient man and sent his own team, all guns blazing, to swipe his daughter from the street. No one involved anticipated that Savannah might be armed and just how ready she was to fight back.

So when that plan backfired, a persuasive British private detective heard on the grapevine about the bounty and asked the Reverend to give her a chance. And when he agreed, Janet Davies became Jane Doherty. She wormed her way into Savannah's life with a fabricated backstory and a plan to befriend the girl, win her trust and lure her out of her comfort zone.

'Your dad got wind that Roseanna was seeing his employee and fired him,' continued Michael, 'so hearing Jane had that day just moved into your room in the hostel was the last piece of information your sister could get, and I never heard from her again.'

Savannah shook her head, worried about her sister and feeling foolish and gullible for desperately wanting to trust Jane.

'It's okay,' Michael reassured her, sensing Savannah's sadness. 'You weren't to know.'

Michael explained he'd arrived in Los Angeles six days earlier and begun following Savannah and Jane from a safe distance, waiting for the moment when he could approach his girlfriend on her own and lead her to safety. On several occasions he considered just bursting his way into the hostel and finding Savannah, but he couldn't be sure if Jane was working alone.

When Michael followed Jane to the house in West Hollywood, he contacted the real estate agent from the number on the board outside and was told the house was being rented on a three-month short-term contract. So Michael knew he must act quickly. And although he abhorred violence towards women, Jane would be the exception to the rule. The moment she'd opened the front door thinking it was the Reverend's team, he'd knocked her out cold.

Savannah was scared that if she took her eyes off Michael even for a moment, he might disappear and she'd wake up to find herself caught in another of a series of nightmares that seemed to

plague her life. He kept glancing to his side to return her gaze.
'It's all going to be okay, you know,' he smiled. 'You, me and the baby, we're going to be just fine.'
Savannah smiled at Michael and moved her bag from beneath her neck, placed it in her lap and stretched her arms and legs out and yawned.
Then she slowly slipped her hand inside the bag, and before Michael could stop her, she pointed a gun at his temple.

CHAPTER 95

It had been a long night for Jane, gagged and tied to the chair in her lounge.
    She ran through the range of escape methods that her military training had taught her, but the stranger who'd burst though her front door that night and taken her by surprise with a right hook had made an impressive job of securing her. She cursed herself for resting on her laurels once she'd had Savannah sedated.
    The cuckoo clock above the fireplace revealed it had been almost six hours since she'd watched helplessly as a man she assumed was the one her employer had referred to as 'black Satan' carried Savannah out of the house. The two dozen times she'd heard her mobile phone ring also told her the Reverend would be furious at not receiving his promised update.
    Suddenly the front door handle turned and Jane watched as three men entered, each as broad shouldered and burly as the next. They glanced around the hallway and up the staircase before they spotted Jane. The tallest of the trio approached her and ripped the gag from her mouth. She drew in a long, deep breath.
    'Where is she?' the man asked gruffly.
    'Someone came and took her. Now untie me, we need to move fast.'
    Instead, the man cocked his head and stared at Jane, then took a mobile phone from his pocket and dialled.
    Jane couldn't hear what he said to the person on the other end of the phone but she guessed who he was reporting to. And when he drew a gun from the back of his trousers and screwed a silencer to the end of the barrel, Jane knew what he'd just been ordered to do.

CHAPTER 96

Declan stood with his back to the window, staring at Matty's empty bed.

Matty's unzipped sleeping bag still bore the impression of his lifeless frame, and he could smell his friend's knock-off Tommy Hilfiger aftershave lingering in the bathroom. Declan turned around, lowered himself onto his bed and lay back. His pillow felt lumpy, so he put his hand underneath and removed the well-fingered Travel America guidebook that had inspired many of their excursions. He opened it up to a folded page and out fell Matty's silver crucifix. He smiled, kissed it and placed it over his head and around his neck and tucked it inside his T-shirt. He noticed a packet of photographs had been left too, but he couldn't bring himself to open them just yet.

'Declan, are you in there?' came Tommy's voice from the other side of the door.

Tommy tentatively entered and saw a Declan he hadn't met before – a man with the demeanour of a beaten dog.

'I think this is for you to watch.' Tommy smiled awkwardly and handed Declan his digital camcorder before giving him privacy. Declan pressed play and Matty's face appeared across the tiny screen.

'Hey, eejit. Well if you're watching this then you know where I am. I'm sorry I didn't say goodbye. I tried, but as you said, you weren't ready to hear it. You know, I don't think I've ever thanked you for being my best friend. I wouldn't have lasted as long as I did if you weren't there to kick me up the arse and force me to live whatever time I had left. So, thank you. Be happy, Declan, enjoy your life, and don't waste time thinking about me, okay? I've had the best time I could have possibly had, and that's down to you. You're my man.'

With a smile and a final wink, the screen turned to black.

For the first time since he'd discovered Matty's body, Declan curled himself up into a tight ball and allowed himself to cry like he'd never cried before.

CHAPTER 97

'Oh my God,' gasped Nicole, gobsmacked by the events of the night Tommy had just relayed.

She sat in the hostel courtyard listening as Tommy spoke from the heart for nearly two hours. She wrapped his hand in bandages to protect his broken knuckles as he left nothing out, from the aftermath of the accident that killed his brothers; his family's treatment and blame of him; his failed attempt at university; his brief stint in the army; his separation from Sean; how he developed feelings for Jake before realising who he really was; and their final confrontation.

She understood why Tommy hadn't raised the alarm when Jake toppled over the railings at Santa Monica pier. Although if it had have been Eric who had fallen, she wouldn't have tried to find him.

Then for a moment Nicole allowed herself to think about Eric languishing behind bars and how she would probably spend the rest of her life living in fear that he might return. She shook her head to shake the bad thoughts out.

'Just how bad a judge of character are we?' she asked. 'Me with Eric, you with Jake.'

'We make quite a pair.'

'So what are you going to do now?'

'Well, I've put it off for long enough, so I'm going to call my parents later, and then I'm going to start making plans to continue my travels properly. I've been here for too long, it's time to stand on my own two feet and really see the world before I return home. Jake's still running, but I feel like a free man now.'

Nicole nodded. She understood the desire to travel, but now she wanted to plant some roots, and Mrs Baker's money would allow her to do just that with the hostel.

'Do you mind if I tag along?' a voice behind Tommy began. He frowned, then turned his head, and a huge smile spread across his face when he recognised who was speaking.

'Alright mate,' continued Sean, as Tommy leapt to his feet and the two friends hugged. 'Mum said you called, and I was just up the coast so I thought I'd drop in and say hello.'

'You couldn't have picked a better time,' replied Tommy.

'Have you found your beach then?'

'No, I found something better than that, but it's a long story.'

'So what's new?'

Tommy glanced at Nicole and the two began to laugh at the absurdity of their week.

'Oh, not much,' grinned Tommy, 'just the usual.'

CHAPTER 98

'What the hell, Savvy?' began a panicked Michael. 'Why are you pointing a gun at me?'

'Pull over to the side of the road,' Savannah replied coldly.

'What are you doing?'

Savannah cocked the trigger. 'Don't make me ask you again.'

Michael did as he was ordered and directed the car towards a dirt verge.

'Now give me the keys and get out,' Savannah demanded. Michael obeyed and she followed him out of the car. She stood two metres opposite him with the gun pointed directly at his head.

'Savvy, what's going on?' Michael pleaded.

'How did you know I was pregnant?' Savannah asked slowly.

Michael hesitated. 'Your sister said you told her.'

'No, she didn't. Now I'll ask you again. How did you know I'm pregnant?'

'Roseanna told me the last time we spoke – really, she did,' continued Michael, swallowing hard.

'When I called Rosie, I didn't say anything about the baby. You said the last she heard about me was just as Jane moved into my room. At that point Jane didn't know about the baby either. So if you haven't spoke to Rosie since, then the only way you could know is either through Jane or the mighty Reverend himself. So which one are you working for?'

Michael's mouth moved but his throat suddenly felt dry.

'Which one?' Savannah repeated, more firmly.

'Your father,' Michael eventually replied.

'Why would you do that to me?'

Michael looked at his feet, unable to meet Savannah's gaze. 'The $250,000 reward . . . that's a hell of a lot of money, Savannah. I told him I could bring you home for less, so he told me everything Jane and the other PIs had found out.'

'And did Jane know my father had pitted you all against each other?'

'I don't think so. He doesn't care how you come home, whether it's me or her – it doesn't matter, just as long as one of us managed it—'

'So you sold me out.' Savannah interrupted.

'Yeah, I did,' Michael replied, his tone becoming angrier. 'But then you were the one who ran away and didn't tell me where you were going. All I knew was that my fingers were busted, I have a fucking dent in my head and my girl didn't want anything to do with me.'

'You didn't even give me the benefit of the doubt!'

'When you left, I had nothing. Loving you robbed me of my career, so what else was I supposed to do? That money was going to pay for the rest of my education and my rent.'

Savannah shook her head, disgusted by his excuses. Yet she wasn't entirely surprised to learn Michael had switched allegiances; she was learning quickly that she couldn't trust anyone but herself.

'Look,' Michael continued, regaining his composure. 'It's not too late for us, we can just drive away and start again, forget about the money. A clean slate, just you and me and the baby.'

'You think I'd want you anywhere near my child? You're a fool, Michael. And I'm a fool for trusting you. Now start walking or I'll start shooting.'

'What?'

'Start walking, over there,' Savannah replied, and pointed her gun towards a fence and a field full of corn, 'and don't stop until I'm gone.'

'Savvy,' pleaded Michael, 'let's talk about—'

The sound of the gunshot and the bullet landing inches away from Michael's feet made him quickly realise there was no talking her round. He looked at her one last time, turned his back and began to walk.

Wiping a tear from her cheek, Savannah climbed into the driver's side of the car, started the engine, locked the doors and slowly pulled away.

She didn't look back at Michael in the rear-view mirror; instead, she rubbed her stomach and understood she didn't need anyone to rescue her from her old life, only the baby growing inside her.

EPILOGUE

ONE YEAR LATER – VENICE BEACH INTERNATIONAL HOSTEL

Nicole sat behind the hostel's smart new reception desk, clicked away from the spreadsheet of finances on her laptop screen and then scrolled through the favourites section in her toolbar.

She revisited the Daily Mail online page she'd read many times in the last few days. *'British Drug Dealer Killed During Prison Riot'* read the headline, followed by a mugshot of Eric taken a year ago in his orange, prison-issue uniform. The story revealed that while awaiting trial for the cannabis discovered in the boot of her pick-up truck, he had become embroiled in a behind-bars fracas in which a solitary stab wound pierced his heart. She felt nothing for either Eric, the friend she thought she knew, or the monster he actually was.

Nicole closed the lid of her computer and turned her thoughts to more positive things. She looked around the recently redecorated hostel reception with pride. Half of the rooms had been furnished with new bunk beds, the plumbing was in full working order, new carpets had replaced the threadbare ones and a bank of computers were hooked up to Wi-Fi.

She estimated she had spent around a quarter of the money from Mrs Baker's gift on getting the building up to code, but there was much more work to be done. Other money had been swallowed up by lawyers to ensure the property was legally in her name, along with a work permit and a visa to stay in the country. As the hostel's standards improved, she could afford to charge higher rates, and a viral marketing campaign on Twitter, Snapchat and YouTube assisted in its promotion and popularity.

Eric wasn't the only person she'd thought about that day. She'd wondered how Savannah was coping with her new baby at Jane's house, but was puzzled as to why she'd never come back for the rest of her belongings. She hoped mother and child might one day stop by the hostel to say hello.

Tommy had remained in touch by email as he and Sean made their way around the rest of America, alternating big cities with the wilderness to suit each other's wishes and taking cash-in-hand work where they could to fund the extension of their trip.

A few months after leaving, Tommy emailed Nicole a photograph of him with his parents, who'd flown out to meet them in Seattle. Sean had persuaded him to reach out to his folks, and in his absence, they had finally understood he had not been to blame for the deaths of his brothers. About time too, Nicole thought. Their reconciliation made her smile, but at the same time, she was sad that she had no one from her past to reconnect with.

The last thing Peyk had mentioned about Ruth was that she had been sent to Twin Towers, Los Angeles' largest mental institution. After being diagnosed unfit to stand trial or to be repatriated back to Australia, there was little choice but for her to join more than 1,400 other mentally ill patients in the institution. Nicole worried whether Ruth had been swallowed up in the system or was actually getting the help she so desperately needed.

The subject of Ruth was also one of the last conversations she and Peyk ever had, because the following day he'd disappeared from the hostel. Nobody saw him leave, and when Nicole checked the register of visitors back three years, he had never actually officially been a guest or assigned a room.

Even his cannabis farm that Tommy warned her about the day he left had gone back to being two empty disused dorms before Peyk vanished.

'Do you want to come to the beach for a couple of hours?' interrupted Declan, appearing from the stairs with white paint flecks stuck to his face and dungarees.

'Sounds perfect,' Nicole replied, and Declan planted a kiss on her lips. She smiled and rubbed his arm affectionately.

'There's just one thing I want to do first.'

She took the paintbrush and pot from Declan's hand and approached the poster on the wall that read *Welcome to Wherever You Are*, one of the only items of decoration to remain from Ron's days.

Then with several simple brush strokes, she painted across four of the words so it simply read *Welcome*.

***

ACKNOWLEDGMENTS

When I wrote my debut novel *The Wronged Sons*, I had no idea if it would find an audience. Eighteen months later and with thousands of downloads worldwide, I think it's safe to say it found one! Its success gave me the confidence to write *Welcome to Wherever You Are*, and in doing so, I'd like to offer heartfelt thankyou's to the following people.

To my mum, Pamela Marrs, for being my biggest fan and for encouraging me as a child to embrace books. And now, to write them.

Thank you John Russell for your faith, your optimism and your confidence – and for helping to make poor Ruth just that little bit darker. You also have my gratitude for putting up with me constantly hunched over my phone tracking download data and mumbling random figures towards you.

A huge thank you to my Facebook Fairy Godmother, Tracy Fenton, for your continued, unwavering support and friendship. You've been on this journey with me for almost as long as I've been promoting my books and it's been great having you on board - long may your guppies thrive, my dear! And of course I'm in debt to you for helping to expose my first book to an army of readers who go by the name of Facebook's THE Book Club. My gratitude is offered to the now thousands of members and book lovers for being so enthusiastic, witty and passionate. I love our online conversations, banter, and, of course, your support.

To Sean Costello for making my first experience of working with a book editor an absolute delight.

To my old Herald & Post colleague - and LA Woman - Nicola Pittam. Thanks for your assistance with Los Angeles' geographical locations. Likewise, to John Wallace for help with Ireland's locations and language.

Thank you Kath Middleton, Katie Elizabeth, Samantha Helen Clarke and Anne Lynes for your invaluable proof-reading skills, it's very much appreciated.

To Tim Bradley for our many conversations about writing that helped spur me on when I needed that extra little push. And similarly, to Eleanor Prescott for your advice, encouragement and friendship.

And to Sean Mabbutt, my old travelling buddy. 1992 was a heck of a year that neither of us will ever forget. I couldn't have done it without you! Thanks for allowing me to borrow some of our shared memories for this story.

Finally, to every reader and book lover out there who takes a risk on an unknown author and downloads their book … you have no idea what that one small decision means to each and every one of us. THANK YOU.

ABOUT THE AUTHOR

John Marrs is a freelance journalist based in Northampton and London, England. He writes for publications including Total Film, Guardian's The Guide, Classic Pop, Q, OK! Magazine, The Independent and GT. This is his second novel, following his 2013 debut The Wronged Sons. Follow him on Twitter @johnmarrs1

ALSO BY JOHN MARRS

The Wronged Sons

What would you do if the person you loved suddenly vanished into thin air?

Catherine's cosy life as a housewife and mum-of-three is quickly thrown into disarray when husband Simon disappears without explanation. She is convinced he hasn't left by choice as confusion and spiraling debts threaten to tear her family apart.

Meanwhile Simon has begun a carefree new life travelling the world. And he's determined not to disclose his past to all he meets, even if it means resorting to extreme and violent measures. But why did he leave? Catherine only gets her answer 25 years later when Simon suddenly reappears on her doorstep.

During their furious final confrontation, they discover the secrets, lies and misunderstandings that tore them apart, then brought them face-to-face one last time.

PRAISE FOR THE WRONGED SONS

"A compelling, dark read that gets you thinking." **** - *The Sun*

"It's crammed with twists and turns that'll keep you guessing right until the very end." - *OK! Magazine.*

"Looking for a thrilling read? Then look no further." - *TV Extra Magazine, Sunday Star Newspaper*

"A magnificent story, one that truly captivated from the start with its style and grace and ever so subtle disclosure of the ultimate history." - *littleebookreviews.com*

"A story that left me on the edge of my seat. I couldn't put it down. You simply must read this book for yourself." - *Book Lover's Attic*

"The story is masterfully told ... the book is one that will stay with the reader for a long time. It is an extremely impressive first novel." - *Online Book Club*